CW00903474

GREEN HILLS OF SOMERSET

Muriel Walker

MINERVA PRESS
MONTREUX LONDON WASHINGTON

GREEN HILLS OF SOMERSET

ISBN 1 85863 688 4

First published 1995 by
MINERVA PRESS
1 Cromwell Place
London SW7 2JE

Printed in Great Britain by
Antony Rowe Ltd., Chippenham, Wiltshire.

GREEN HILLS OF SOMERSET

Author of:
Old Somerset Fairs
Old Somerset Customs (1980s)

CHAPTER I

"Here's a darl'd fool way to be settling t'question," said Luke, agitatedly. He was but nineteen, the youngest of the three Scott brothers and he had an instinctive fear the choice, as always, would go against him. He would turn out to be the one out of luck; just as he was the one to be given the filthiest jobs when the weather was at its very worst; the one for whom duties on the hill farm rarely seemed to go quite as hopefully planned, despite his skill with sheep. He had even, of late, begun to think of himself, in a vaguely, self-pitying way, as 'Unlucky Luke', rather pleased at the rhythmical sound of it. Unlucky Luke!

His thoughts were gloomy, for truth to tell, where could be the 'luck' in this, either way? Would it lie with the one so haphazardly selected to leave the farm and take up the burden of a new, strange life; or would it be more 'lucky' to stay behind on the farm to cope with even more work and worry?

The brothers were gathered in the large barn, well away from the main farm buildings, a building somewhat over-large now for their needs as sheep-farmers. But they did not want their mother, Hannah, to interfere, as interfere she most certainly would the moment she got to hear of the scheme.

It was but a few days past April 15th, the traditional cuckoo day in the south-west and, predictably, this precursor of spring had not disappointed, despite the wretched winter and the slow start to the spring. The lambing had largely been concluded, though there were other farmers in the district still lagging behind. If change was inevitable, then perhaps this was as good a time as any to follow it through.

Though they lived in Somerset and had been born there, as had their farming father, Joseph, they were originally of northern stock, indeed of ancient Viking strain, though none of them knew this fact. Their grandfather, William Scott, had come down south with his young bride, the daughter of a local squire, following a quarrel with his own family and his wife's in Northumberland. The pair had then slowly made their way to this part of Somerset, Whytbrook, in the Mendips. Here they bought a house, built for a former mine-owner towards the end of the eighteenth century, but long empty, since the mines closed. They had gradually acquired more land, apart from the few acres which went with the house and in this they were fortunate, for most of the land round about was entailed. It was poor land as far as agriculture was concerned, suitable only for growing oats, barley, buckwheat and potatoes, but it was excellent for sheep, and William had been a sheep-farmer in the north.

They had prospered, when, according to the best local knowledge, they certainly ought not to have done. For one thing, it did not seem right now, did it, for foreigners to come along when folks was leaving the land? It was *her* money, of course, and *her* grand ways trying to make 'scollards' of her children. Then again, William had done many things not in accordance with recognised custom. He had, for instance, planted a copse of 'elums' in a very awkward, windy spot, and hedges near the house, instead of making do with excellent dry-stone walls, merely for the appearance of the hedges. Everyone had waited with suppressed glee for inevitable failure; but the trees had taken and not failed, despite the powerful winds there about. William had been unusually fortunate. He was a jovial, God-fearing man and he gave needed employment to others, it was grudgingly acceded.

Joseph had married a local woman and since his sudden death from a ploughing accident some ten years hence, the local community had finally accepted the Scotts. There had been one disaster following on the heels of another and none of them had been spared. For the past few years the weather had been truly perverse. It was becoming ever more difficult to make a really satisfactory living in an area, warm enough most summers, but which could be bleak and dreary in these Mendip Hills in winter. It was not unknown for them to be snow-bound and, indeed, every five or six years the farmers here about were in deep dread for their sheep and lambs. Should the coming winter turn out to be like the last, God help us! There had been very heavy snow as late as March in 1878 followed by inevitable floods and though the hilly land had drained better than the levels, the following winter had been especially hard, reckoned to have been the worst for about one hundred years. Last winter had not been all that better either and the Scotts, like most of their neighbours, had lost several lambs.

To speak truly, the serious decline in farming was not entirely the result of the weather, though it had not helped. Agriculture everywhere was suffering from the increasing competition from America and from Australia and New Zealand. Wool prices had been falling ever since 1870 and at the previous autumn market no-one had been able to dispose of any but fat cattle, and these for low prices. And who could afford to keep and feed lean animals all through the winter in the hope things might improve? The Scotts were thankful they had never owned more than five cows and at the present time, only three.

Even so, they had not been spared. Apart from spasmodic outbreaks of foot and mouth disease, involving laborious washing of hooves with a solution of salicylic acid as a preventative, as well as a hopeful cure, there had been various worrying eruptions of swine fever in the locality and finally an outbreak of scab in the sheep on several farms, including Redesdale Farm, owned by the Scotts. This dreaded acarus, which burrowed in the skin, causing serious irritation and bad sores had been a very difficult time, and the animals had been wretched. All the Veterinary Officer, brought over from Kimsley Mendip, had been able to suggest was a wash with powdered tobacco and sulphur.

They had struggled through their problems and ignored Hannah's hints that it was high time one or other of them got himself married - and she could do with more help than she had, as well as a bit more female company. Then three things happened in quick succession. Less than two months ago, the finest of their milking cows had inexplicably sickened and died suddenly of anthrax, the splenic fever. This had been a frightening blow, for the body had had to be burnt and the ashes also later buried where the poor animal lay. The blood oozing from the open sores could be dangerous, even to themselves. They had heard tell that once an entire island in Scotland, or some such place, had had to be abandoned because of this terrible plague. And suppose it spread and reached their sheep? Thankfully, it had not done so, but the swiftness of the calamity had reminded them all of the precarious life farming could be.

Then a farmer they knew well, of the name of Burgess, had suddenly taken his own life in a most savage manner, committing suicide with a pruning knife. It was said that he had been depressed about his wife's death in childbirth. But was that the sole reason? Women often died in childbirth, but the grieving husbands did not take their lives! Usually a man found someone else to care for his 'childun' and his own needs. The suicide had seemed like a bad omen. Burgess had appeared such a sane and reasonable man.

Finally, a week ago, there had arrived a letter from David Jackson, who was married to a cousin of the Scotts. He lived in Glastonbury and worked for the Somerset and Dorset Railways. It was his whole life and he had frequently extolled the virtues of the railway and hinted that if ever one of the boys was so inclined, he was sure he could fix him up with work, profitable work. No trouble at all. He had not mentioned any employment possibilities in his last letter, but for the first time, a strong cord had been struck, initiated by Thomas, of course, the eldest brother. Why not? Here was their chance.

Thomas looked at young Luke calmly.

"'Tis the fairest way, we've agreed on that. If it were just 'tween you and Patrick, then it would seem as I'm aiming to grab Redesdale all for m'self. That's not so. I'm ready to take me chances, same as you."

He was but twenty-four, since his birthday in March, not quite as tall as Luke, but exceptionally well-built with good, strong shoulders to him and, without being handsome in any conventional fashion, he carried with him a strong male attractiveness, an air of authority that managed to appeal almost equally to men and women. His light brown hair was somewhat darker than his brothers, who were markedly fair, Luke's thick thatch showing gleams of red in bright light. Thomas's eyes were also a darker blue than his brothers. This eldest son was reckoned to be the reliable one, the natural head of the household - if one discounted Hannah, who kept a very tight grip on all spending. If Redesdale was to survive, Thomas must remain. Yet here he was, exercising his authority in a very strange manner.

"What've you done with the straws I prepared?" he asked Patrick with an unusual touch of impatience.

Patrick took them from the pocket of the ancient jacket he was wearing. Smocks they never wore, nor did scarcely anyone else in 1880, except at special times, such as fairs.

"'Tis not the end of the world," said Patrick, placatingly to Luke. "If you don't like it, Luke, 'ee can come right back home again, can't 'ee, now? But there's no harm in going and having a good look." His voice was the slowest and most markedly, with its heavy, creamy tones, of the locality. The middling one, fairest in colouring, his cheeks invariably rosy, his eyes a clear, almost innocent blue, Patrick seemed quite devoid of the northerner's fighting qualities. He had made up his mind that the choice must, in God's good wisdom, fall upon Luke, the youngest, and least useful member of the family. God played a large part in Patrick's life. Luke was getting above himself of late. A spell away from home might well do him some good maybe. He was equally sure that he did not want to leave the farm himself, not at any price, but if it did chance to be God's will.... well, then, he would have to bear it.

He sighed lightly and selected one of the straws from the three now held out to him.

"You next Luke." Thomas held forth his fist with the two remaining straws.

"Happen, you've another bit stuck up your sleeve," said Luke suspiciously. He flushed. Thomas said nothing and, reluctantly, Luke picked one of the straws.

"Now, let's compare them, shall us?"

It was immediately plain that Thomas held the shortest of the three straws. There was a moment's silence. Then Thomas burst out laughing.

"Well, then, that's how 'tis then! I'm seemingly the one to leave the nest and I'm, mebbe the best able to cope, at that." And he laughed again, wildly. The other two did not laugh. They looked at each other in dismay.

"Well, now, this doesn't have to be final," said Patrick. "Suppose we have a second try, just to be certain sure?"

"No," said Thomas, firmly. "Ma'll be coming to look for us, wondering why we've not come to supper. We don't want to upset her needless. The decision's made.

Luke felt outraged. How dare Thomas talk like this, bringing in their mother's name to make everything seem kind and considerate? How dare he, when she would certainly go up in the air when she heard?

"You'd best be the one to tell Ma," he said, virtuously. "I wouldn't want to be in your shoes." He nearly added, "And you her favourite son," but he restrained himself.

"I'll tell her straight after supper," said Thomas quietly.

Luke said no more, but his suspicions began to grow and he flushed again as though his brothers could read his thoughts. There had certainly been no chance for trickery. But Luke clenched his teeth. In his guts he knew quite definitely that Thomas had made up his mind from the beginning that he was going, though why Luke did not know, not yet. Chance had favoured Thomas, but if it had not done so, Thomas would, somehow or other, have got his way, without any hesitation.

'He's deserting us,' thought Luke, angrily. 'That's what he's doing. How did he think the two of them and an old shepherd would manage come shearing time in mid-June? If he felt he had to go, if he was sick and tired of being reigned over by their mother (though he had never raised a word of complaint about her) why could he not have waited till the autumn?' Thomas had always been Luke's hero, a substitute father since Joseph died, a dependable strength in times of trouble. Suddenly, Luke felt a sharp and bitter resentment towards Thomas.

He was convinced Thomas was about to do a terrible, unforgiveable thing. They had been cajoled into this foolishness and because Thomas was stubborn, he would not be diverted from his decision. He had made up his mind to go, and go he would. Luke had always felt he was more intelligent that either of his brothers, but he had never cared to acknowledge this, even to himself. It would have seemed like disloyalty. Now loyalty hardly seemed to matter.

'Very well,' he thought, the immature side of his nature returning in full force. Very well, much good may it do Thomas! Who would want to work on the railways, with all that clanging noise, all that rushing about, being at the beck and call of everyone? Here he had been his own master, if one discounted Hannah, their mother. And what could Thomas do that would be of any use? They were all right greenhorns about everything but the land and sheep. Mind you, all of them could read and write and well, if they put their minds to it, which was a great deal more than many folks about these parts, even a few prosperous folks. But of what use would that be? They'd be wanting someone to drive their trains for them, thought Luke in all innocence. Well, he'd never wanted to drive a train, though it would have been nice to have taken a journey on one, as both Thomas and Patrick had done many years ago with their father. There had never been the time nor the money for travel that was not essential. Luke envied Thomas that experience. He might well be living on the moon for all the difference the railways had made in his young life. But to work on them? Never! he told himself, disgustedly.

Thomas left Redesdale Farm towards the end of the month. It had needed those two weeks to settle various matters on the farm, including a long talk with Hawker, the shepherd. His small amount of packing in an old bag, once belonging to his father, took little time. Hannah was not to be reconciled. Thomas realised she never would be, so he made no attempt to argue with her into a kind of acceptance, but merely smiled, put his arms around her thin shoulders and said calmly, that the matter was settled.

"It's not settled!" stormed Hannah, angrily. "Don't 'ee go thinkin' that, me lad! You's not leaving here and that's that! I forbid it!" Exactly as though her eldest son was a lad of less than half his years.

Thomas, who could usually win round his mother when no-one else could, contented himself with a quick peck on her cheek - an intimacy she tolerated only from him - and his indulgent smile. She did not smile back. The situation, to her, was gravely serious. But in a day or so, Hannah became persuasive, though her tongue was still very sharp.

"Look 'ee," she said, "I know things haven't been so easy o' late. They've not been for any on us. That's the way farming goes, i'n'it, though? Always was, always will be. But 'ee, Thomas, be the one best suited to get things a-goin' agen. That's what your father'd want."

"I reckon," put in Patrick, "Thomas don't see any future in farming, not if we's all t'marry and have families."

It was badly put, for Patrick had no gift with words, but it echoed what Hannah had said many a time herself, that Redesdale would not be able to support three grown men and their wives and children. In a flash Hannah had answered this with a demand as to why either he or Luke would not go instead of their brother, if one of them must take it into his head to go. In fact, she felt terrified of losing any of her sons, as they were her strength, apart from the little she had laid by, but the thought of Thomas leaving was unbearable. What had got into him?

"Look 'ee," she said, when she had the opportunity to get Thomas on his own, "Mebbe we've not been over-fair to 'ee, Thomas. Tell 'ee what! You just come along with me to Lawyer Ridley's over Kimsley way and I'll see everything is drawn up proper and legal, so the farm's in your name. That's what your father always wanted. He said so. You's the eldest and that's as it should be. If he'd not got hisself killed with that silly ploughing competition, I know he'd have made a will leaving you Redesdale."

"Ma, Ma," Thomas said sadly.

So Hannah stormed again, threatened, predicted all manner of disasters, not only to her and the farm, but also to himself and feared, that for once in her life, she was not going to win.

"P'raps, I might find a little money for some of the things you say we're needing now, I don't know."

"Things is good 'nough as they be, Ma," said Thomas.

Luke joined in.

"Where d'you keep all that gold o' yours, Ma?" he asked, his face glowing and innocent-looking. He had teased her in this fashion ever since he was a young boy, and she had always smiled knowingly and said, "Never 'ee mind!" Now she merely tightened her mouth.

"'Tis not the end of the world," said Thomas, repeating his younger brother's words. "I'm only going to Glastonbury, just down the road, as it were. Why, before 'ee've had time to make another batch of butter, I'll doubtless be back on a visit."

Luke made things worse.

"I reckon as our Thomas is off to find himself a bride. Girls 'round here aren't good 'nough for our Thomas!"

Hannah was suddenly very still. One could feel this stillness, almost as though she had been struck senseless. This she dreaded. Locally, there was no-one she counted as being good enough for Thomas, or else the girls were far too young.

She certainly totally discounted Maisie Bevan, who had recently been pursuing her Thomas. The girl was no more than fifteen, she supposed, but she was also the daughter of a drunken labourer, that is when Bevan chose to work, rather than let his sons keep him. Maisie's mother was the daughter of a curate and was said to have been 'edicated', but she must have been a bit missing to have married a man like Bevan, and everyone knew she was growing sluttish. But a townie girl with no understanding of farm life would be an even worse disaster. She turned to Thomas a face of despair. He might have found it amusing on some other occasion.

Then another thought came swiftly to Hannah. You's not thinking of goin' off to sea, Thomas?" Her voice quavered a little.

"No, Ma. 'Tis too late for that now."

Luke watched all the interchanges that took place in his presence with astonishment. Never in his entire nineteen years had he seen his mother display so much and so many different kinds of emotion. It had hardly occurred to him that she had any emotion in her, not at her age. It was embarrassing, like seeing a stranger suddenly emerge. She had surely not gone on like this when their father died? Or, at least, never in front of the children.

The day of departure arrived. Not a Sunday, as Thomas would have preferred for the sake of the Jackson family. Whilst he could easily have caught a very early milk train on the Great Western, known locally as the Cheddar Valley Line, this train only went as far as Wells, and on Sundays there was no connection to continue the journey as the Somerset and Dorset Railway no longer operated on Sundays, except for a few very special excursions. It was not the sanctimonious who had forced the railway to cease running on Sundays; it was hard financial truths. It simply did not pay. So it would have to be a Saturday and the late afternoon seemed most sensible. The Jackson family had written that Thomas would be very welcome to stay with them for as long as he required until he was settled elsewhere. Again, nothing was said about work, but Thomas kept this to himself. He also kept to himself a growing certainty that he was never coming back.

Patrick drove his brother in the smaller of the carts all the way down to Wells, as though reluctant to have him go, leaving Luke and the shepherd, Hawker, who was usually willing to turn his hand to anything needed, to attend to the animals.

Having left the cart temporarily in the yard of a reliable inn, Patrick and Thomas walked though the marketplace to the railway station. The market was crowded with people searching for Saturday bargains. The cross, standing at that time, in the very centre before the Bishop's palace took up a lot of valuable space. There was a huge black cannon, as well, but the gas lights had not yet been lighted.

The train was very crowded, most people in cheerful mood. Where had all these folks come from and where were they going, wondered Thomas. The journey itself took a mere thirteen minutes, a ludicrously brief time, almost an anti-climax after all the fuss.

There appeared to be no-one to meet Thomas at Glastonbury and, on enquiry, he learned that the Station Master was not presently on duty. Feeling a bit disappointed, Thomas handed over his ticket to a smartly dressed platform attendant and turned out of the station, looking about him. He knew the Jacksons lived quite nearby. Now where.... ?

A group of noisy, loudly chattering children, headed by a boy of about ten years, suddenly rushed across the street towards him. He appeared to be asking Thomas if his name was Scott. His accent was vile: lilting tones, roughly harshened by town dwelling and gang rivalry.

"That's right. I'm Mr. Scott. Who're you?"

"Mr. Thomas Scott?" insisted the youngster, determined to get it accurate and when Thomas nodded, he announced that he was Mr. David Jackson's son and he was to take him home. "Oi'm Albert."

"And are all these children your brothers and sisters?"

"Naw!" Albert's face showed both scorn and amusement. "Only her." He pointed to a small girl of about seven years. "Her's Lily and us've three more sisters back home."

Lily was desperately shy, too shy even to smile. The others had nothing to say, either, but Albert made up for them all, keeping up constant chatter till they reached the door of the terraced house where the Jacksons lived.

"You's to sleep in me room," he announced as he marched Thomas into the house, via the back-door, leaving all the rest of the small children, apart from Lily, who followed meekly, standing in the street, unsure what to do.

Mary Jackson, Thomas's cousin, hastened from the kitchen, where she had been preparing pies for the next day's mid-day dinner. She bent a little to wipe her hands on her white apron, embarrassed at being caught thus. Albert ought to have brought Thomas to the scarcely-used front-door. Then she kissed him, while three freckle-faced girls came to stand beside her and be introduced to their 'uncle'.

"Welcome to Glassen, then, Thomas! It's good to see 'ee!"

"And you, too, Mary. Where's David? They said at t'station he was not on duty today."

She frowned a little in puzzlement.

"David is Glastonbury Station Master?"

"Oh, no, not yet, though he's as good as. It'll be his turn when t'Station Master retires next year." David, she explained had had to call on Mr. Curry, but she did not think he would be very long. She seemed to take it for granted that Thomas ought to know who Mr. Curry was and, truth to tell, Mary could never quite remember his designation and grand title of Chief Engineer. She was full of bustling joviality. Her father had been Hannah's brother, now dead, but there was very little family likeness between Hannah and Mary that Thomas could see. She showed Thomas into a tiny back kitchen, where she told him he could have a good wash to get rid of the soot from the journey. An enamel bowl of hot water was brought, a new cake of scented soap and a spotless towel laid beside the bowl.

"Us calls the Somerset and Dorset the Slow and Dirty," she laughed, indulgently, "but David 'e doan't like that!"

Thomas grinned, then saw in a small mirror, that as a result of hanging his head out of the window for most of the short journey, his face was soot-speckled.

Presently, David appeared. There followed a great deal of talk about the family. How was Aunt Hannah? And Luke? And Patrick? They also recalled the names of people they had heard about or met many years previous, proud of their recollections. But neither Mary, nor even David, enquired as to the state of Redesdale Farm itself and when Thomas attempted to impart various snippets of information, they stayed silent, asking no questions. They lived in a small market town with farms all around, but they knew next to nothing about farming; it was not their world. Equally, Thomas realised it had never occurred to him to wonder how his cousin had come to meet and marry David Jackson.

They all squeezed round the kitchen table somehow, the girls remaining silent, but all the children were well-behaved, not cowed but very obedient to their father's word.

As soon as he was able, David changed the conversation to talk about railways. It was his pet subject, his whole life's topic.

"Railways is t'biggest change ever to come to this country," he pronounced, emphatically. "Never forget that, Thomas. Us was a bit late off the ground in these parts, but we're catching up."

In fact, the railways had only arrived in the south-west a comparatively short while before, much later than the industrialised north and midlands, and there had only been a station at Glastonbury itself since 1862. Even in the short time it had been running, the line had encountered many problems, names had changed, amalgamations had taken place and it had all but failed at times.

"We've had some worries about finance," said David, grandly, ponderously, exactly as though he was one of the major investors, "not that us weren't making money, mind you, and paying our way; but 'tis the cost of modernisation, that's t'trouble, me lad. Gettin' old broad gauge to narrow, so us can cope with t'other trains, if 'ee sees me meaning."

Thomas nodded.

"British trains is a shining example to the world, Thomas. We've sent quite a lot of engines abroad y'know, and it's not only the engines, but our methods o' doin' things, me lad!" he added proudly.

"'Ee's right wound up," laughed Mary kindly, and she shooed her children away from the table and sent Albert a little further down the terrace, where he was to sleep, while Thomas remained with them.

Thomas began to wonder when the subject of work for him would be discussed. Surely, they had not forgotten the reason for his coming?

"It was a rare feat of engineering gettin' lines up hills as far as Bath a few years back, I can tell 'ee," continued David, as though he had been personally involved in this stupendous achievement of the time. "'Course, nowhere exactly near you folks in Mendip," he added, as though that would have been the equivalent of laying a line in an African jungle.

Several times Thomas tried to bring in something about employment, for he was beginning to get a little worried. Each time, David avoided a direct reply, or appeared not to have heard the younger man's tentative enquiry. Suddenly he stood up. It was time he took Thomas for a drink, or maybe even a couple! They could talk over the situation then. They went to a nearby hostelry and several of David's colleagues were quietly drinking, mainly cider or beer, in the bars. The only women were a few crones in the Ladies' Bar, known as the Saloon. David called for drinks, then said, "'Tis a bit awkward presently. I've talked to Mr. Curry and he's willing to give you a trial, but you's to see him tomorrow evening at his home. It's a bit urgent, as a job needs filling." He sighed. He had had a hard task trying to prove to Mr. Curry, the District

Engineer, that his wife's farming cousin would not be a complete waste of time. "Happen there'll be somethin' else later on, I don't know."

He had kept his voice low, but someone standing near had over-heard.

"Be that Fireman Wither's job?" he asked loudly.

"What of it?" David was annoyed.

"He'd a nasty accident had Withers. Broke 'is leg. Lucky it weren't 'is neck some say!" put in another voice, cheerfully.

No introductions were made, it being naturally assumed that everyone ought to know everyone else.

"How did the Fireman break his leg?" asked Thomas, not greatly interested.

"Driver 'e pushed him out o' t'train, o'course!" laughed someone else.

David scowled.

"No, it were 'is own fault," said someone else with no sense of humour, very eager to put the record straight.

"Mind the time when Driver Philips got hisself kill'ded, nigh on three years ago now?"

They did indeed. Who could forget? The signals had got mixed up and this terrible accident, not at all uncommon, had resulted. They were silent for a moment as though giving the tragedy the respect it deserved, puffing quietly at their pipes. Then they were off, recalling all manner of happenings in recent years. Some had been stressful, some almost droll. Glancing at them out of the corner of an eye, Thomas well knew they were testing him, trying to discover his merit, as though he were about to join an exclusive club, or be initiated into a secret society.

"An' d'ee mind the time when hosses and wagon got stuck on level-crossing? Train driver 'ee shut off steam fast and blew hard on 'is whistle. But this 'ere wagonner he just kept on, not looking to left nor right, not takin' a darl'd bit o'notice!" One man guffawed.

"What happened?" Thomas enquired, obligingly.

"What happened? Why, train it got itself caught in rear of wagon, hosses they some'ow got loose and goes off a'screaming to t'fields, and the waggoner he jest stands there and looks about 'im all 'mazed, not knowing what fuss is 'bout!"

Thomas reacted in exactly the right manner. He looked suitably impressed, but not cowed. Then he put his hand into his pocket and fingering some of his small amount of cash, he offered them drinks. He did so politely, as though it would do him a favour if they accepted. And accept they did, toasting him to his new work (the temporary job, hastily vacated by Fireman Withers) as though the matter was fully settled.

Next morning there was church-going. Thomas was not an eager church attendant and if he could find some task on the farm to do that would keep him from making the effort of going, without annoying Patrick, he frequently contrived this. But he had no strong feelings about the matter and no wish to offend, so he went along with David and Albert, while Mary (in traditional fashion) prepared the best meal of the week, with the help of two of her girls.

"I like Evensong the best," she said, just in case Thomas might think her ungodly.

There was virtually no traffic, but the streets were quite packed with people hurrying to church. The bells from the various churches tolled loudly. Afterwards, there was a certain amount of parading and greeting of friends, especially by gay young girls, who could spare the time, Sunday being their only day of freedom. They were more concerned to ensure that everyone had noted and admired their fairly recently acquired Easter bonnets.

The midday meal was a very hearty affair with a roast, followed by the fruit pies Mary had prepared the previous day and lots of custard. Thomas acknowledged to himself that the pastry was a good deal lighter than Hannah's, but then Mary had a small, but quite modern cooker.

Afterwards, David insisted that he and Thomas should take a walk, leaving the dish-washing to his uncomplaining wife. He led Thomas to the top of the tor. There were quite at number of people on Glastonbury Tor, the ladies modestly holding down their skirts, their bonnets mostly tied down with scarves against the strong wind.

It was here that, centuries ago, a group of monks had established St. Michael's Monastery, choosing, in time-honoured custom, the most elevated situation they could find. All that remained were ruins, for the monastery had been devastated at the time of the Reformation; it had also suffered through neglect and several small earth-tremors. Indeed, there were those who still believed firmly that a great barn, part of the possessions of the Abbey and which had not belonged to the monastery at all, had nevertheless once stood on top of the tor and had been thrown down the hill (to arrive upright) during an earthquake. David was uninterested in ancient legends, accepted by gullible people. That he chanced to be standing almost on the exact spot where the last abbott had been hanged aroused in him no feelings of sympathy, nor terror for the murdered man's shade. He drew closer to the ruined tower to light his pipe, watching Thomas stride about and breath in the deep, fresh air. He was a countryman all right.

Would he serve? Never for a moment had he considered that one of the Scott brothers would actually take it into his head to come down to Glassen for work. Emigrate, yes, he could just about understand that, but this move made no great sense. What future was there for him? A man of four-and-twenty, he was too old to start a new way of earning a living. Why, at his age, he had been married with two young children. And the money he could earn whilst he learned to be of use would barely keep him, unless he had money of his own. He seemed a bright enough, likeable, young man. But why on earth had they sent the eldest? Had he quarrelled with Hannah? Was something seriously wrong at Redesdale? He could make neither head nor tail of it, that was a truth.

He looked about him at the various small groups of people, almost all of them young. Then he looked at the cattle, rough-grazing on the lower slopes. Perhaps he ought to suggest Thomas find work on a large farm hereabouts? He would be more use there, no doubt. He hoped, he sincerely hoped, Thomas wouldn't let him down with Mr. Curry, whom David revered. He also hoped Thomas would find himself somewhere else to live before long. They could not be inhospitable, of course, but Mary did like to have the parlour to herself now and then, a change of scene. It was her one luxury.

CHAPTER II

At that time, the District Engineer resided in an extraordinary building, near the station yard. It had long, narrow Victorian Gothic windows, which contrasted badly with the bright red brickwork. It was double-storied with a basement and part of it still served its original purpose as the Abbey Arms and Railway Hotel before the later Railway Arms was opened. Thomas thought it impressive. The part where Mr. Curry lived had formally been railway offices, and he still conducted a fair amount of his business from his home.

The room into which Thomas and David were shown was crowded and very uncomfortable, being furnished partly as a sitting-room and partly as an office. Mr. Curry rose from where he had been seated at a mahogany desk, immediately his housekeeper showed in the two men. He solemnly shook hands with them, David first, then Thomas.

He was a small man, wearing silver-framed glasses, his grey hair unusually short, at variance with the fashion of the time. Nor did he sport a moustache, even though he quite liked to see this badge of seniority and responsibility on those directly under his control. He spoke for a few minutes to David alone, making Thomas feel like a child being presented for his first day at school.

Thomas studied the room, quietly observing the portrait of the widowed Queen, dressed in black and with a white lace cap on her head, which hung directly above the desk. He also noted, without being aware of their significance, two other pictures. One was a photograph, sepia coloured, of the present chairman of the railway line and the second was a framed crude reproduction of the Somerset and Dorset seal. On its right-hand side was a depiction, supposedly of Dorchester, and on the left of the picture a toy train wended its way past the parish church towards Glastonbury Tor.

"Well, now, Mr. Scott," said Mr. Curry at last, "so you'd like to work for us, would you?"

David nodded and went from the room to wait in the hall.

"I heard there might be something, sir," Thomas said, belatedly remembering that he must not forget the formalities. Mr. Curry studied Thomas over the top of his glasses, his face unsmiling. He liked what he saw. An honest face, a reliable-looking man, but not right for this job.

"So you want to be an engineer, do you?"

"Engineer?" Thomas was startled.

"Oh, yes." This time Mr. Curry did manage to smile slightly. "Our train drivers and even our firemen think of themselves as engineers. What d'you know about mechanics? Not a lot, I imagine?"

Thomas told the other he knew a certain amount about farming equipment, indeed had some flair with machines.

"H'mm," said Mr. Curry. "When I take on a youngster I like him to be no more than fifteen or sixteen years old, if he's to shape up as an engineer at our Highbridge Works. Then he's given a first-class training; and he has to study in his spare time. Repairing trains is a vitally important work. These engineers are the elite, you understand."

The two men surveyed each other.

''There must be other work beside engineering," suggested Thomas, gently.

"Not as far as I'm concerned." There was a moment's silence. "Oh, I suppose you have it in mind to take on Fireman's Wither's job? But that's only for a few weeks. He's very upset about it and in some places he'd be sacked at once, but we're humans and we've promised to keep his job for him. We look after all our men, you see, and no doubt his own Friendly Society will help him out, but Fireman Withers doesn't want to be off work a day longer than he must."

It was on the tip of Thomas's tongue to ask why there was no-one else Mr. Curry could use to replace the injured fireman. The District Engineer guessed at this thought, but considered it wiser not to mention that there was a certain amount of superstition. Men simply did not care to stand in for another, when he had met with a serious accident, if they could possibly avoid it, especially as this was the second or third time a fireman on Driver Bryden's train had been hurt.

"Well, let's see what you can do." He then proceeded to test Thomas with various mathematical problems, as though he was an inspector at school. Thomas did not show his irritation, and quite unlike his brother Luke, nervous excitement did not nullify his ability. Calmly, but rapidly, he answered, always correct in his replies.

"H'mm," said the District Engineer, "not bad. Now read me a page of this."

Thomas saw he had been handed a copy of the Fireman's Rule Book. He looked up in surprise. For the first time, Mr. Curry smiled broadly.

"That was a trick, I'm afraid. Take it home and study it. Meanwhile, we'd best have your signature to this agreement. You can take time off during the week and go down to Highbridge and see Mr. Philips. He may be able to use you in his store, but it'll be up to him, of course."

Thomas felt confused, "The agreement?"

"Sign here." Thomas did so. He saw he had been appointed, on a temporary basis, as a Fireman, and only then did the District Engineer mention what he would be paid in wages. "You'd best sign this also." He turned to a page in the Fireman's Rule Book, which read,

"I hereby declare that I have carefully read them over (or) that they have been carefully read over to me, and that I clearly understand them.... "

"Those are the rules, Mr. Scott, and make sure you've read them all by tomorrow morning."

"Tomorrow morning?"

"Of course," said Mr. Curry, sounding suddenly annoyed. "What d'you think I gave you a book of Fireman's Rules for on a Sunday evening if the matter wasn't urgent? You'll have a full day with Driver Bryden's son, Horace. How you'll all squeeze in, the Lord knows and that's against the rules, too. That young lad knows more about trains than he ought to, but he'll help you out. And don't forget, you'll be under the control of the driver. Driver Bryden's word is law, Mr. Scott. Don't you forget it."

Driver Bryden was a squat little man, briskly efficient, very much over-weight and with a very fine opinion of his own worth. His son was a hulking lad, as conceited as his father, to whom Thomas took an instant dislike. He was glad this youthful instructor was only going to be with them for the one day.

The branch line Thomas was to work on ran all the way from Highbridge to Evercreech, but Thomas joined the train on the Monday morning at Glastonbury. He was allowed to do this, but after his first day of initiation, he was compelled to catch a very early workmen's train to Highbridge to start his day's work. At the end of the day, he had to make his way back to Glastonbury, as had Driver Bryden and others living in the town. This journey was either made by train, if there chanced to be a suitable train, or if there was not they went by means of a local carrier. Thomas wondered why the driver did not live at the start of the line, and so save himself all this extra travelling, but the driver did not seem to appreciate this point. He had lived all his life in "Glassen", all his family and friends were there. Why should he move? His son, however, was soon going to Highbridge, but only for a time. He was going to learn how to make trains, he said proudly.

"Every lad wants to be a driver," he said. "Horace is different."

The train was an 0 - 6 - 0, and this Thomas was informed by Horace referred to the number of wheels on the train. It had a tank engine, which meant, in effect, that it bore along its own water, fire-box, grates and boiler, low-slung between the wheels. It was freight-carrying and painted in the rich blue of all the Somerset and Dorset trains at that time; it was not dissimilar to a train of a few years back, which had then been affectionately dubbed, 'The Bluebottle'.

On that first hellish day while Thomas sweated and struggled and shovelled in coal, shouted at by the driver and sneered at by Horace, it required all his equanimity not to lose his temper, but this, he knew, would be fatal and even dangerous. So he continued cheerful in manner, soot-blackened and more exhausted than he had been in many a hard day's farming. It appeared he was expected to leap up and down the metal steps, perilous in the extreme, whenever the train stopped.

Conversation once they were moving rapidly was virtually an impossibility. And unnecessary. It needed every bit of their concentration. As the train climbed up the steep track to Evercreech (except that in the quaint language of the railways, this was termed going 'down' the line) Thomas felt himself shaken in every bone. A sudden stop, a sudden jerk and one could very easily be flung off the train in a flash. Small wonder Fireman Withers had fallen and broken a leg. Several times, it seemed to Thomas, Driver Bryden took reckless chances, either because he was not as skillful as he made out, or was deliberately seeking to alarm Thomas. The driver was endangering his own life as well, for there were no windows nor doors to his cab.

Despite the rules, despite the fact that no train, not even an express, was supposed to travel at more than an absolute maximum speed of forty miles an hour, Thomas had a horrid conviction on that first awful day, that Driver Bryden was somehow or other pushing the vehicle to its very limits. When they stopped at a station, Driver Bryden stretched himself by standing upright on the narrow top step outside his cab for a moment or two.

"It takes years an' years to be a driver," he said, complacently.

Thomas was unused to protection from the elements, but he could not but wonder what it would be like in mid-winter in the driver's cab. At least on the farm one had good clean air and could move about to get the circulation going. Thomas had already learned from his talks with David and his reading of the Rule Book, that there were very strict rules concerning the sharp curve close to Glastonbury station, especially on the return journey from Evercreech. The speed must not exceed eight miles an hour as it approached the station and again left it. Thomas, being too preoccupied with his tasks, had not noticed anything unusual on the first journey, but it did seem to him that the speed definitely increased with the later runs. Imagination? He could not be sure. He felt it wiser not to comment, nor react in any way that might annoy Driver Bryden. There were four complete runs each day. Tired, but not dispirited, he was quite astounded when the driver turned to him, smiled and suggested they meet later for a drink. So he had passed Driver Bryden's criterion? He grinned back and agreed.

It had been quite a day! Thomas really needed the good swill down in the back kitchen that evening. As he removed the old jacket David had loaned him till something else could be provided for him, he saw it was singed in several placed by flying sparks, and even his good heavy cords which he had brought with him had not been spared. They had suffered badly with a multitude of tiny burns. Clothes would not last long in such a job. But he had no regrets whatsoever and remained cheerful. It was, after all, but a step along the road.

It was not until much later as he prepared for bed, that he noticed, as he had not so far done, that the room he occupied, was the best front parlour, not young Albert's room at all; in fact, the lad had no room of his own, only sleeping at nights in a bed, which was folded back into a cupboard during the daytime. So Thomas was depriving the Jacksons of their parlour. The room was over-crowded, with heavy furniture and the mantle-shelf cluttered with glass and china ornaments, as well as some pieces of brass. Yet the Jackson family was prosperous, by comparison with many families living in towns.

Indeed, around Whytbrook way were those who would consider the Jacksons to be rich. He had never given such matter much thought. He must try to find somewhere else to live, perhaps with a widow, living nearby.

There were six bedrooms at Redesdale, as well as several attics. Some of the rooms stood empty, as Luke and Patrick had long since shared a bedroom from the time Luke had suffered as a child from nightmares, even though these horrid dreams had ceased. But Thomas had had a bedroom of his own. It had been taken for granted. It was where he would eventually bring his young bride.

It now occurred to him that it might well be many years before he was able to enjoy the luxury of such space, a place he could call his own. He realised he did not care a toss. Where he slept was totally irrelevant, as he felt Freedom had to have its price.

Of two things only was he certain. The first was that he had been totally right to leave the farm as he had done. The great pity was that he had been compelled to wait so long, but that could not be helped. He had not the faintest regret about his action, come what may. His mother had laid a heavy burden on him after his father died. There had been neither rows nor recriminations, and he had never spoken out loud to anyone of his growing discontent with farm life. In fact, he had hardly been aware of it himself until chance played into his hands. He told himself that he had waited till both Luke and Patrick could be regarded as responsible adults.

Sometimes as he scythed long grass at Redesdale; though he was not a poetic man, it seemed to him like gentle waves rippling the sea and something had moved in him. He had been reminded of his very first glimpse of the sea as a small child. How he had been stirred with strange longings! Then ten years ago, he had thought to run away to sea, simply because he had happened to meet someone who was a sailor, on a visit to Whytbrook. He had talked about it for days and his mother had come upon him as he debated in his room what he would take with him. His father's sudden death had thrust all such embryo notions from his head. The time was not ripe. He knew now that when a man was set to do something, he did not argue with himself about it. He simply did it.

Yesterday afternoon, as he walked on top of the Glastonbury Tor, he had had a sight of Bridgwater Bay and the very distant Bristol Channel. Beyond that again, lay the great Atlantic Ocean. He had, without warning, been assailed with an almost unbearable excitement. Something in his blood, that he could not begin to understand, responded to the sight and the imaginings. He had wanted to shout out loud! He had wanted to laugh madly! He had known then that this was why had had left the farm.

He had no lucid plans of any kind. He was in many ways without ambition. But the sea was for him, sooner or later. Highbridge was that much closer to the coast and there must be encounters which would help him. Going to work for the railways might seem a strange way of achieving his ultimate goal, but it did not seem so to Thomas. He had little money and must earn a living of some kind. All that his mother had given him before he left home had been a watch, cuff-links and an old diamond tie-pin, belonging to his father. These were sacred treasures and the thought had immediately flashed through his mind that they might come in useful one day if he had to 'pop' them for some ready cash.

Meanwhile, he was perfectly content to take whatever life offered, going with the stream until the important moment of decision.

CHAPTER III

Luke grew ever more restless, 'twily', as Somerset folk might well have said, as the slow, cool spring advanced into a very grudging summer. Since early childhood, his tense, somewhat over-sensitive nature had suffered a certain amount of teasing from his more equable brother Thomas for over-reacting to minute matters; and he had been chided by Hannah because he ate much too quickly or seemingly not sufficient. Even at sixteen he had been taller than the other two brothers. At nineteen, a little over six feet tall, he appeared to have ceased sprouting, but he was just as thin as ever. He was prone to worrying and sometimes, thoughtless, well-meaning men would make remarks about his appearance, to which Luke took undue offence. He would even sulk for a while, no-one being aware that he was in a sulk, but himself.

In fact, he was not at all bad-looking when he chose to smile and showed his boyish sense of fun. His hair, whose colour he did not at all appreciate himself, was exceptionally abundant, as though nature was trying to protect the frail creature beneath. This was deceptive. Luke was anything but frail. He was also, according to his mother, "As sharp as a needle."

He was now seated on a gentle slope in a patch of warm sun on the outskirts of Whytbrook. It was a Sunday afternoon, and he was taking a short rest after calling on friends of his mother's, before returning to the farm. Behind him was a hedge of blackthorn and hazel, and for some reason of its own, a blackbird was singing alone not far away. At the bottom of the slope ran the brook which had given the village its name many centuries ago. For it was here, on Whitsunday, or White Sunday as it was called, that the early Christians, had been baptised, according to tradition. The brook gradually wended its way towards the enlarged, man-made pond in the middle of the village. Luke had fished in the brook as a child and wild birds came from time to time, including swans, to rest a while on its waters or even to take up a habitat. There were two swans there now and knowing the pen had recently made a nest, Luke had made a special visit to look for the results. All he had found was one sickly pale egg, as large as his hand, lying in the grass. Even before he picked it up and held it to his ear to listen, he knew the egg was addled, but he still laid it back in the grass gently, almost reverently, for he had a strong feeling for birds and animals, which did not always extend to humans. The pen herself had doubtless discarded the egg for some reason. This was far from being the first time this had happened. He felt briefly distressed; and angry. Why did such beautiful creatures have to be such fools?

Enjoying the sun, Luke wondered not for the first time, why his grandfather, William, had chosen such a place as he had, surely the bleakest in all the Mendips? Then he had deliberately renamed the place, giving it a style that belonged to the far north. That must have annoyed the local people, who had always referred to Redesdale simply as 'Scotts' Farm'. Having come so far, why could they not have journeyed further south? He did not at that moment ponder the question of availability of land and at a price that was affordable. Had he been his grandfather, he thought, he would have pulled down the farm-house, which had never been intended to be a farm-house, and built lower down in a sheltered place. The architectural merits of the house he did not value at all. It also seemed to Luke that much of the area where they lived was barren. Luke did not mind the emptiness; indeed he loved the feeling of space and he rather liked sheep, stupid though they were, especially the young lambs. They were at least fairly controllable, if one had good dogs.

It was the warmth of the sun he lacked. He could never get enough of it. His body seemed to demand sun. He supposed he ought to emigrate somewhere or other, but he had not the faintest hope of being able to do that, nor any idea of how to go about it.

His other love was money. Not out of pure greediness, but because money was power. He could see that. Apart from personal expenses, his mother Hannah took charge of all expenditure on the farm. No-one went to a market carrying money in his pocket, beyond his small needs. What was ordered would be delivered and Hannah would pay for it later and so there was no opportunity for any of them to make a little for himself, not that Patrick would have done so, given the chance. She was really tight about money was Hannah and Luke sometimes wondered if she did not argue with the farmers or carriers and gain for herself an even better price. He flushed. It was awful to be having such thoughts about his own mother, but it was puzzling. Times were hard, but he could not think they were as desperately poor as she made out. It did not make any sense. Sometimes he dreamed of going away and making a fortune and coming back and being very generous with everyone. Small chance of that. They had all of them been no more than farm labourers, unpaid. No wonder Thomas had taken it into his head to escape.

He mused, remembering a time when he was no more than seven or eight years of age and Farmer Ridley, one of a few prosperous farmers, had asked Luke to keep an eye on his horse while he called in at The Wool Pack. Gypsies had been seen in the locality and it was a simple matter to untether a horse and ride away swiftly. The farmer was related to Sir Montague Ridley the local Member of Parliament (and the closest Whytbrook came to having any gentry) and also, conveniently, to Lawyer Ridley in Kimsley, so he was an important man. When he returned to the street, Farmer Ridley in amiable mood, had given the child a whole shilling for himself. Luke had treasured the bright coin, loving its colour and had played with it, without fully knowing its value. Then Hannah had come upon him. She had immediately assumed the boy had somehow stolen the money from her purse and, without waiting for any explanations, she had thrashed him severely.

Later she had discovered she was wrong, but she had made matters worse by saying the child ought not to have taken the money for a small favour. In this way, she tried to hide her feelings of guilt. Not for a moment did it enter her head to apologise to Luke. An adult did not apologise to a mere child. Luke had borne the incident as a grievance against his mother ever since.

"You looks nice and comferbul!" said a cheerful voice. "Takin' yer ease, eh?"

Luke scowled, liking neither the interruption to his thoughts nor the implication that he was shirking. Sunday or no, he had been up early as usual to milk the cows and see to various matters, while Patrick cleaned out the sty, before either of them could put on his best suit for church. It was a pretty, lilting voice, almost as pretty as its owner, a young girl in her mid-teens, with brilliant red hair, a delicately tinted complexion and startlingly deep grey eyes. Luke was aware that he had never really noticed her eyes before now. It must be some trick of the bright light, but they looked almost like wet pebbles, or, he thought, half-ashamed at his own fanciful notions, not unlike his mother's opals. He looked away quickly. Then, very reluctantly, he began to rise, since he had been taught to believe no young man stayed lying down while a young woman was standing.

But the next moment she had dropped on the grass beside him. Luke decided to ignore Maisie Bevan. It was his brother she had set her cap at in any case, not him.

"How's your brother?"

"Which brother?" said Luke.

She giggled. "You know who I mean. Thomas, of course!"

"All right, so far as I know," said Luke indifferently. "Hasn't he bothered to write you himself?" he added nastily.

Maisie did not appear to be upset by this at all.

"I 'spect he's busy," she said.

She was dressed in a blue and white floral print, with a white lace collar and sleeves, also lace-trimmed, which only reached to the elbows. On her head and tilted towards the back, was a flower-trimmed straw bonnet, with blue ribbons, which fell down the back and mingled with her long red hair, for she had not yet put up her hair. There was a feathering of little curls, carefully achieved with rags, peeping from the bonnet and framing her forehead. She removed the head-wear and dropped it on the grass beside her. The bonnet, fashionable to Whytbrook, was a year or two out of date. Luke noticed that neither was she wearing gloves. The priggish side of his nature, encouraged by Patrick, thought her appearance unseemly for a young lady on a Sunday. Not, he reminded himself firmly, that Maisie Bevan was in any way a lady, whatever airs she might give herself.

"He's that a'right," said Luke, referring to his brother Thomas, belatedly. "Busy, I mean."

"What's 'he doing, now? I know as he's with the Somerset and Dorset," she added, swiftly.

Luke sighed heavily, as though bored with the conversation.

"He's a fireman." He was fairly sure the naive Maisie Bevan would have little idea what that meant. It had not sounded all that marvellous to him, either, come to that. Shovelling in coal, so the boiler could keep the train going. A right dirty job, that! He said, "He helps to drive the trains."

"Oh, does he?" She frowned a little in puzzlement. She was nobody's fool, for all her ignorance and there were questions she wanted to ask, but thought better of it. She had been taught by her great friend, Mrs. Squires, that a girl must never be too persistent; or at least, not show that she was. "It's nice here, isn't it?" she said, changing the subject. "I like this spot."

"Aren't you scared of catching cold?" remarked Luke, pointedly. "I mean - I mean after all the rain - grass must be damp."

Maisie patted the ground with one hand.

"Seems dry 'nough to me," she remarked. "Anyhow, I never catch cold. I'm always as warm as toast. See!" And she laid the back of the hand nearest to him on his forehead, as though taking his temperature. Luke jerked away as though she had seared him with an iron. Indeed, for a moment, he felt sure she had burnt him. It was incredible! "You're quite warm yourself," she said, unperturbed and pleasantly satisfied at this state of affairs. She smiled gently. At the moment the world was a delightful place. She felt at peace.

Luke was very far from being at peace. Ye, gods, what was the matter with the girl? There must be something wrong with her. He stole a swift glance at her, noticing the tiny gap between two of the upper teeth, giving her a charming, childlike appearance of incompletion. For the first time in his life Luke found himself pondering what his brother Thomas had done when it became too much to bear, as it must have done sometimes. He was a virile man and far too old at twenty-four to be indulging in - well, self-abuse, which was a sin, wasn't it? No! There must have been some woman in the village who had obliged him from time to time. Not this silly chick, who was only after finding herself a husband and plain for all to see. But Thomas must have had some woman he could call upon. Luke wished he knew who this was; then, he immediately wondered how on earth Thomas had managed to pay her.

He had certainly been very cautious. There had never been a hint of any gossip to reach Hannah's sharp ears.

"Must seem funny working on t'railways with trains, after being a farmer all your life," said Maisie. She giggled again, happily. "It wouldn't suit I!"

"No-one's asking you, Maisie Bevan," replied Luke.

She refused to take offence. She was incorrigible. She jumped up. "Must be off now, but 'spect I'll see you at Farmers' Ball come July after sheep shearing, if not afore?"

"P'raps," he answered, without enthusiasm. Was she hinting he should accompany her? He was darl'd if he'd let himself get caught on that.

"Now don't forget to give Thomas my love when you next write him." This time she did colour a little. "And my love to your mother, of course," she added. "And you can tell her from me, not to worry about her Thomas, as he'll be back home 'gain in no time!"

She was about to turn away, but Luke had leaped to his feet and gripped her arm, restraining her.

"How d'ee know that? Has Thomas written to someone in Whytbrook, then?"

"I dunno, but I do know as he's not staying with railways. 'Cause he told me so afore he left. He tol' me so hisself," she said, lapsing into the local tones and speaking quite emphatically. "He's only goin' to Glassen for a little while."

He let her go, pondering what she had just said. A short while at Glastonbury, perhaps, but that did not mean Thomas would be returning to Whytbrook and Luke felt sure he would not do so.

It seemed to Luke at the supper-table that evening, that his brother Patrick was certainly taking his time over saying grace. No longer was this the perfunctory mumble when Thomas had assumed this duty, but it was as though Patrick was revelling in spinning out the agony of waiting for food, as though his words were, for him, food enough, a deep spiritual sustenance. What had got into Patrick of late? Twice he stretched forth a hand for a 'hunch' of bread, only to find the rhetoric still continued. But at last the torment ended.

Luke let out a loud, exaggerated breath of weariness.

"Reading Lessons this morning's not good 'nough for'ee, eh? Aiming to be a preacher, as well, Patrick?"

Patrick looked at his younger brother, thoughtfully.

"If God had meant us to rushing to our food, he'd have given us engines 'stead o' stomachs," he pronounced.

"Leastways, I don't suppose the trains are prayed over every time their tanks are filled!" declared Luke. This humorous picture suddenly took this fancy and he began to splutter with mirth. Neither his mother nor Patrick took any notice, but after a moment of quiet eating, Hannah said, "You's far too long, just the same, Patrick."

It seemed to Hannah that her middle son was taking his duties as a substitute for Thomas over-seriously. She looked at the two sons remaining with her. They were so different! Indeed, all of them were very different, apart from a vague similarity of feature. It had frightened her sometimes. A woman ought to know her own children, understand why they were as they were, why they behaved as they did. In some ways, she could see that Luke was a bit like herself, except he was thinner, taller, his brown hair even thicker than hers had been at his age, and she had never had any red in it to unsettle her. But what were they thinking, she sometimes wondered? It was better not to know. A woman of her age, which was forty-seven, needed a daughter, Hannah decided. She had borne two and much good they had proved. One died in infancy and the other had married when but sixteen years old, twelve years hence. This eldest child, Jane, had moved right out of the locality, then emigrated to America. Hannah thought she would never be able to find it in her heart to forgive such desertion.

The meal over, Luke hinted to Patrick that a walk down to The Bell for a pint of cider might not be a bad idea. They could see some of their friends.

"That's if you've any money, or can get some out o' Ma. I've nowt, as usual."

Hannah, busily clearing the table, ignored this. Patrick looked up from reading his Bible and, for a moment, Luke half-expected him to say something about Sunday being the day for the Lord, not revelry, though Sunday was always a quiet time at The Bell, which Saturday night most certainly was not. Luke curved this mouth into a smile, ready with a quick witticism, but Patrick merely put down The Book, and quietly stood up, enquiring if their mother would be right enough left on her own.

Redesdale Farm was a good two miles from the village, going by means of the dirt roads, but it was barely a mile and-a-quarter, going by the fields, crossing a few stiles; and this was the route the brothers took, for they knew the terrain well and the rough ground did not cause them to stumble. It was hardly a comfortable walk, though.

There were a few hovels hereabouts, lived in by desperately poor families, who scraped a living from the infertile ground, but who were unable to attempt to recover the land from the immense damage done to it by mine workings in the past, either because of economic reasons or ignorance. Most of them kept pigs. Many in the past had kept goats, which had made the land even worse. Nowadays the pigs grazed in a small copse of beech trees. There was one family, named the Coxons, whom the Scotts had employed from time to time. All of these few families were, in fact, squatters, belligerently declaring that the land, all of it, was common land, though this had not been the case for many a long year. Patrick gave a long, clear whistle and the youngest of the dogs, whose mother had been a firm favourite, came reluctantly to heel. Jessie was a cross-labrador and an amiable animal. She was a good gun-dog, but seldom used with the sheep, unless there were special reasons for needing another animal, as she was not so disciplined. She thought every walk was a hunting expedition. Patrick loved her dearly and even Hannah, who did not like dogs in the house at all, tolerated Jessie, as she was docile and attractive in appearance.

At some distance there stretched the eroded remains of the barrows; the long barrows of the Stone Age, the rounder barrows of the later Bronze Age. In silence they walked over bits of ground the locals called 'gruffy', referring to the deep grooves caused by the old mine workings in the past. Close by on their left, they passed the grisly remains of an old lead mine, whose chimney, erected for smelting, was already showing signs of crumbling. It was more than fifty years now since there had been any mining at all in this area. There were signs, too, for those able to detect them, of far more ancient surface workings. Tradition averred that there had been mining in Roman days, and even long before that, on the Mendips.

The Bell, the nearest of the two public houses, had originally been no more than a room in a farm-house, where the farmer had sold his own home-brewed cider and, it was hinted, sometimes other illegal brews, as well. It was conveniently almost opposite the parish church, as well as the village green and the large duck pond. It was here that most of the local farming community gathered to gossip and exchange news. The Wool Pack, on the other side of the village on the road leading to Kimsley, was a hostelry and it was here that visitors to Whytbrook, usually on farming business, would stay. The Wool Pack charged a half-penny a pint more for its cider and, quite outrageously in the opinion of the villagers, a whole penny a pint more for its ale.

Luke immediately noticed that two brothers, much older than Maisie Bevan, were in the public bar, sitting quietly in one corner, playing at dominoes. The rarely sober father, ever on the look-out for a hopeful free pint, was not there this evening. No doubt he was recovering from the Saturday night's indulgence. The sexton was there, though. This man had once been to America himself in his youth, but having returned and declared that Whytbrook could beat any place he, Harry Barton, could mention, he considered himself not only an authority on America, but on all else. Luke had once remarked that it seemed no-one had any right to do anything, even die, without consulting Harry.

This evening he did not disappoint. As soon as Luke and Patrick reached the counter, they were appraised and questioned about Thomas. Sometimes strangers to Whytbrook were startled when Harry chose to speak what he considered was good Amer-i-can; seeking to impress them. This evening he was playing a different role. He typified the Somerset countryman. Secretly, he was annoyed that Thomas had not sought his advice before leaving the village.

"Ee's a fool that'un," he declared. "Land mayn't be much these'n days, but 'tiz there. 'Appen Great Western takes o'er the S and D? Then what? Oi could've warn'd Thomas, but Oi reckon as 'ee'll 'av t' larn for hisself. 'Ee'll soon be back and us'll have the laugh on 'im! 'Ee's too old t'be breakin' new ground."

"Mebbee, Thomas'll emigrate to America, where 'is sister Jane his," someone suggested tentatively.

That was dirty and there was a moment's silence, though not out of any sensitivity. Simply it was that no-one knew what to say. But it started off old Harry Barton on his reminiscences, years and years out-of-date as regards facts, but few knew that. Luke looked supercilious.

At length even old Barton grew tired of the sound of his own uninterrupted voice. The conversation turned to matters concerning the land. Someone had been to Kimsley market the day before and had various things to tell, such as that a group of young people had been fined for playing pitch and toss on the green near the parish church one Sunday.

The sole reaction to this news was to enquire the size of the fine. Then they relapsed into silence. The informant had also heard the time had arrived for the stallions to go travelling and were on their way to these parts.

"Us knows that!" Harry Barton declared. "Hosses been visitin' a week o' more." He turned to Patrick. "'Ee'd better book 'un for that frisky young mare o' you's, Patrick."

Patrick nodded and avoided his brother's eye. It was a sore point. They both knew their mother had flatly refused to allow their far from robust mare to be mated. Hannah had insisted that the animal needed another year to get her full strength, unwilling to admit the animal had been a poor buy and she was not prepared to pay out stud money for doubtful results. She declared the owners pushed the stallions much too hard, all for greediness, and by the time a suitable horse reached Whytbrook it was fair worn out with no lustiness to him.

Luke had tittered.

"But, Ma, that mayn't to say foal'd be no good!"

"If there *was* any foal," said Hannah, darkly.

Someone else now came up with the news that the gypsies had been seen in the neighbourhood, though they had not camped anywhere close by. They were a cunning lot, who moved by night, stealing as they felt inclined. Several farmers had lost milk. All the men nodded their heads over this. They knew all right! Some thought the laws of the land should be changed. There were those who would even like to see all the gypsies hanged, and good riddance to them!

The eldest Bevan young man lifted his head from the board where he had played dominoes with the concentration of a world chess champion.

"Some say 'tizn't diddikies a'all," he remarked very slowly. "Farmer us knows 'ee be certain-sure as 'tiz 'edgehogs as his up to they's old tricks, a'stealin' o' t'milk."

"Hedgehogs?" Luke could not contain his mirth. "No-one believes that old wives' tale! Can 'ee see a good milking cow lying quiet in a field while - while a hedgehog...." He spluttered with merriment.

"Oi believes it," insisted James Bevan. "Farmer 'ee believe it also. Ee' say as 'ee caught a gurt 'edgehog nearbe, an' 'ee kills 'er and skins 'er an' 'ee's a-goin' to tie this 'ere prickly skin round cow's dugs."

The men laughed aloud.

"That'll larn 'edgehog a lesson," James Bevan said, joining in the laughter.

Luke smiled disdainfully.

"What an idiot! That won't stop the gypsies!"

Harry Barton stopped laughing and turned to stare at Luke.

"You's far to critical by 'alves Young Luke," he said severely. "Too clever also, but 'ee wait, me lad, 'ee wait" There's a-plenty things 'ee doan't knows. Plenty!"

Patrick caught his brother's eye. He saw no point in deliberately setting people by the ears without whom they would be lost. They were good folks at heart. It was time to go. Jessie had lain quietly at Patrick's feet during all the time the young men had been in The Bell. Luke bent to stroke her. "Come along, Jess, old girl, this talk's not for 'ee."

The animal wagged its tail as she liked Luke, but Patrick was her master and, thought Luke to himself, a bitch was a lot more faithful than any girl or woman.

The two brothers walked in silence for a short time.

"D'you think Thomas'll be back soon?" asked Luke suddenly. He was thinking as much of Maisie Bevan's words as those of the sexton.

"I dunno. I doubt it sometimes. He's off to Highbridge now, it seems."

To his annoyance, Luke found himself thinking about Maisie. Patrick had quite different thoughts. How he missed Thomas! He was the only person to whom he could talk about important things, such as the deeper meaning of a sermon, or the rights and wrongs of something that troubled him. Thomas never said much and Patrick did not deceive himself that his elder brother cared as he did about religion, but he had always listened, with apparent kindly concern. He could no more have talked to Luke about things of the spirit than he could speak to a musician about his music. It was not that he doubted that Luke had a divine side to his nature, even though he kept it well hidden, but he was far too impatient. He would interrupt or laugh aloud at Patrick's fumbling thoughts, for he knew he did not possess great gifts of rhetoric. He said, "When you's out this afternoon, I'd a visit from young Coxon."

"Lammie Coxon," said Luke, using the cruel nick-name by which the village had long called this unfortunate. Jimmy Coxon was slightly hunch-backed and had a strange walk, so to the villagers he was a lamager, a cripple. He was also mentally retarded with, at eighteen years, an age of barely twelve, so he had never minded what people called him, or appeared not to do so. "What does he want?" Already Luke thought he knew the answer to that one!

"He lost his job with cooper in spring 'cause of his bad cough and he's not worked since then."

"So we're to be a charity now? 'Spect you offered him Thomas's work, didn't you?"

"I was thinking more about Ma. She ain't so fit. Haven't 'ee noticed?"

"Ma's all right," said Luke, suddenly, frightened. "She's a-grieving 'bout Thomas, that's all! She's not ill - is she?"

"I don't like her looks and you know what she is. Won' t see no doctor, till she's kept to her bed. I was thinking Jimmy could give her a hand with t'digging in her vegetable plot and carrying things us don't have the time to do nowadays. I was thinking that store opening to barton us don't use much now, could make Jimmy a nice little room. Nice and dry and no stairs to climb. He'd like that."

Luke stood still.

"What's wrong with his own home?"

Patrick sighed, softly.

"You know what 'tis like there. It weren't so bad when Old Mother Coxon was alive. She was kind in her rough way and she kept that brute from hitting Jimmy over much, so folks say. But nowadays with this woman he has living with him, 'tis different, Luke."

"Well, I don't know, but if you's decided that's that."

"No, I said as how I'd have a word with you. Only fair. Jimmy doesn't want much money, but he needs a bit of a home and he'll earn his keep right 'nough.

"He's fond of you," said Luke. "Follows you like Jessie, here. Have 'ee spoken to Ma 'bout this?"

"Not yet."

"But listen! Rose's back now in village. Wouldn't she be a lot better?"

Rose was one of those put-upon females of her age, who travelled from distant relation to needy friend, helping where required and somehow remaining cheerful and good-natured as though she had no further wish than to serve others. She was in her mid-to-late twenties, a plain and wholesome young woman, tending a little to plumpness, as was Patrick himself of recent months. It occurred to Luke that Rose and Patrick could make an ideal match, a couple of dumplings, in time producing further small dumplings.

"Rose would be best."

"I've already suggested Rose. Ma won't hear o' it What's the joke? You're always laughing to yourself about nothing, Luke," Patrick reprimanded.

"All right," said Luke. "If Ma'll agree, let's have Lammie Coxon, but he's your problem, Patrick."

Once a job was explained to him carefully and demonstrated, Jimmy Coxon had shown himself a good worker; indeed, better than many with more brains, for he did not allow himself to be distracted by anything. Realising he could do but one thing at a time, he had given that one thing all his attention. He had been an excellent cooper's assistant. He was also stronger than he looked. Luke found himself wondering why the old man, his grandfather, so ill-treated the boy. Was it simply his foul-temper or did the awful appearance of the lamager annoy him in some way. Of course, it was a bit hard on old Coxon, in a way. His daughter had got herself in the family way, no-one knowing who the man responsible might be. It was whispered, or had been around the time of the birth, that it was entirely due to unsuccessful attempts at aborting the unwanted child, that had caused Jimmy to be born as he had been. One could not be sure, of course, and no-one had had the slightest sympathy for young Hetty, though they had always been kind to the lad, apart from calling him 'Lammie'. Three month's after the boy's birth, Hetty Coxon had vanished from the village, run right away, leaving her poor parents to cope.

The brothers walked on in silence for a while, not unfriendly, but unable to find anything to say of interest to the other, now the matter of Jimmy Coxon had been settled.

Luke's thoughts returned to The Bell and the people they had recently left. Then, by a curious swing of fancy, he started thinking again of Maisie Bevan. He supposed her colourings had come to her from her mother, though Mrs. Bevan's hair was now quite white. Bevan, too, though it was hard for Luke to imagine this, was said to have been a fine-looking Welshman when his future wife had first set eyes on him. But it was difficult to realise Matthew and James Bevan were her brothers. They seemed like a different breed. No, one couldn't call Maisie a lady, but she had a certain air to her, a refinement that was quite lacking in her brothers and her father, very puzzling.

CHAPTER IV

Thomas was surprised at the number of invitations he received during the first few weeks of his stay in Glastonbury. Usually on a Sunday, of course, for afternoon tea or supper. In the country, whilst they tried to entertain lavishly for special occasions, such as Harvest Home, and even the poorest usually managed to scrape by a little extra for Christmas or Easter, only those with ample means and plenty of leisure entertained at other times, such as the hunt balls. There was not even the excuse of a birthday or an anniversary. It seemed astonishing. Thomas had a fine baritone voice and had sometimes sung at the piano in The Bell, but only a modest number of these people owned the luxury of a piano. Then it dawned on him. The womenfolk were interested in him as a possible suitor for their daughters. The men were largely indifferent.

Apart from a natural dislike of strangers - it was not so very long since young men had been chased from villages with stones when they came courting a favoured girl - Thomas did not see himself as a good proposition and would not have been regarded as such, in his present circumstances, in Whytbrook. They were judging him solely on his appearance and some vague future possibilities. So, the town was more sentimental than the countryside, it seemed. But, in any event, everyone knew by now that he was soon going to Highbridge. The railway was like a bush telegraph, news travelling so fast, that there was not much those connected with the line did not know in a very short while.

Thomas took the opportunity to call upon Mr. Philips at Highbridge Works, delaying the train some twenty minutes. Driver Bryden did not seem to mind. It was not a passenger train. The driver simply took his ease.

The Works were situated incongruously in the midst of fields. There were several horses grazing, most of them used for transporting purposes after the train had delivered its loads. Strict rules had to be observed about the blowing of train whistles in this area, in case the horses became alarmed and stampeded into grave danger. The Works were expanding all the time. Even so, Philips had no need to hunt about for a suitable applicant for the new store, let alone agree to use a man with virtually no experience. But Mr. Philips had liked Thomas at that first meeting, and admired his demeanour. He was polite without being servile and had a goodly bit of education, from all accounts. Most of all, he was impressed by what the District Engineer in Glastonbury had written on Thomas's behalf. Presently, he sent Thomas a formal letter of appointment, minutely detailing the terms of his engagement. Thomas learned that he could be discharged, without notice or a reference, for certain breaches of trust.

Mr. Curry was pleased to release Thomas. He had already re-arranged his personnel, as he had fully planned to do had not David Jackson talked him into employing his relation. Another fireman would stand-in for Withers and, as it was now mid-June, the District Engineer did not doubt but that the regular man would soon be back at his work.

He called Thomas to his office and made quite an occasion of wishing the younger man a good future at Highbridge. It was early days, of course, but he had no doubts about Thomas. Indeed, he had high hopes of this young man. So far, he had not in any way confounded his good opinions of him. Indeed, he had proved to be rather better a fireman than Curry would have credited. He got along well with others also. It was all a matter of being a sound judge of character, the District Engineer told himself.

Thomas went on a special Sunday outing to Burnham-on-Sea in early July. Ostensibly, this had largely been arranged to facilitate the Annual Day's Outing for several local firms' employees, as they were so termed. The Somerset and Dorset Railway very enterprisingly, in the view of all those concerned, not only provided the special train, but also arranged for a steamer to carry those interested along the coast to Ilfracombe, Lynmouth and Clovelly in Devon and Cornwall. There were quite a number of people, in holiday mood, taking advantage of this outing and Thomas noticed that most of the men wore bowler hats and the women were very smartly turned out in their Sunday-best dresses and capes. A special occasion demanded proper, reverential attire.

It was clear Burnham railway station was fast becoming of some importance. At each side of the central booking office, white enamel signs jutted out, proclaiming the use of the room below. Apart from the usual indicators for Telegraph, Cloakroom, and Parcels Office, the social ranks had been carefully segregated, with accommodation provided for First Class and Second Class lady passengers (with an appropriate general waiting-room) on one side and on the other side accommodation for those women (still termed 'ladies', however) who travelled in Third Class carriages.

Much as he would have enjoyed it, Thomas did not join the steamer. He made his way to Highbridge, walking the nearly two miles (a mile and fifty chains, according to the precise railwaymen). After arranging suitable lodgings for himself at a small, recommended boarding-house, he returned to Burnham, taking a two-horse omnibus part of the way.

Ah, but it was good to smell the sea! There was a tiny pier and a boat that had just pulled in and was on its way to Cardiff in Wales. In fact, there was a surprising number of small craft, mainly at anchor, tugs, cutters, even a collier and two more steam-boats, as well as plenty of very small rowing boats, these beached high up on the sands. Except for the passenger steamers, whose crew wore smart navy suits with huge white collars, hanging down the back and small round caps with the name of their boat printed on the band, none of the men Thomas noticed were in uniform of any kind. Thomas ate his packet meal in a sheltered place down on the beach, which was becoming crowded. Several of the women, he saw, had now donned sunbonnets. As for the bathing machines, those for the use of the men were well apart from those intended for the use of the ladies. There was to be no spying. Once the horses had drawn the machines into the sea, it seemed to Thomas watching carefully, that very few ventured into the water for more than ten minutes at a time. Not all of the men could swim and very few of the women. The rest merely bobbed up and down as though in a vast tub.

Thomas smiled to himself. It seemed very different to the times back in Whytbrook as a child when he and his brothers had gone bathing in the nude (unknown to Hannah) in a quiet stretch of the brook. Other youngsters had done the same. Here it was all very civilized, all very proper.

But it was the sea! And once well away from the stifling, confining proprieties of the shore.... that would be a very different world.

Only a week or so before he left for Highbridge, Thomas met by chance at one of the social gatherings a man who was to have a profound influence on him.

"Well, if it isn't Patrick O'Neil," someone had cried, and then proceeded to give a terrible imitation of an Irish brogue. Everyone had laughed and Thomas had turned round, simply because of the name 'Patrick'. The man he saw, and who liked to be called Paddy, could hardly have been less like his own brother. He was somewhat below average height, thin with a sharp weasel-type face and a spreading nose, which looked as though it might have been broken at some time in the past, which it had. His tongue was rough, though he had no Irish accent at all, having been born in Bristol. It later transpired that he was married with two children, though living apart from his family for some time. He was about thirty-five, but looked much older. On the face of it, the two men had nothing whatsoever in common, but in the strange way of such things, they took to each other at once.

The day after they met, Paddy took his new friend on a round of visits to generous friends - and goodness knows how they managed it in a small town like Glastonbury and at a late hour - but they both got very drunk indeed.

Thomas somehow saw his new friend to the place where he was presently staying with elderly relations, then made his own way back to his lodgings.

"Tut, tut, Mr. Scott," said his widowed landlady. "This is no state t'be comin' 'ome, now is it?"

He grinned at her amiably. She was helpful, though next morning she spoke to him with a certain severity, as though he had been a child.

"I thought better on 'ee, Mr. Scott. That's what comes o' mixin' with rubbish." She had heard of Paddy O'Neil.

"Sorry, doubt if it'll happen again."

"I should think not, indeed," she replied, but she smiled, indulgently, amazed that he was able to eat quite a good breakfast. Indeed, despite a raging headache, Thomas did not feel too badly. He even experienced a certain triumph, for he had not totally disgraced himself. He could hold his drink, which was more than could be said for Paddy. It was all a matter of learning where lay the magical demarcation line, seemingly.

The next evening, Paddy called round, bleary-eyed, half-apologetic and very good-naturedly anxious to make amends. Would Thomas care to go mud-horse fishing on the flats at Bridgwater Bay Sunday next? Thomas would indeed. He had not the least idea what mud-horse fishing entailed and was well aware that as Sunday was his very last day in Glastonbury he ought, by rights, to be spending this in saying farewell to his many new friends and preparing for his early start next morning.

Thomas already knew that Paddy would soon be returning to his usual work on boats. This time he would be employed on a trow, skippered by the young son of his former employer, whom he knew well, and who owned several such barge-type boats, usually plying along the Bristol Channel to North Devon or to Wales. This was the lad's first charge, and Paddy almost made it seem as though he was going along mainly to see the boy did not fall into difficulties nor drown!

"There's just the three o' us," said Paddy. "It'll be a rare squeeze, as usual, as we'll be carrying stone and sand all the way down the Severn this time. It's rough, hard work, but there's a grand fellowship. 'Ee can't beat it. Anyway, it's all I know 'bout. Boats. Been my whole life since I were twelve years and even afore that, Thomas." He fell silent, giving his attention to the small horse-drawn gig he had managed to borrow. Even had it been a week-day and Thomas had been free, they could not have journeyed to Bridgwater at that time by train. Although trains ran from this busy inland port, all the way to London, there was no connection from Glastonbury, on account of the Polden Hills lying between. Time and time again, David Jackson had told Thomas, the idea of a line had come up, but the railwaymen had been defeated. They left very early in the morning, when the dawn was barely breaking, passing by the turnstile, and so out of the town. Then there were the rhines, often willow-fringed, with bigger streams in some places slicing across the straight, narrow ditches. They were quite full after the long spring rains. They went by flat-lying eerie places, where ancient battles had been fought out - and lost; and they passed by a strangely-shaped windmill, that was hardly a windmill at all by Mendip reckoning, being quite low, with straight sides and a thatched roof.

At Bridgwater, they left the gig at an inn, saw to the horse and walked the considerable distance to the edge of the flats, where a man was waiting for them with two wooden 'horses'. These turned out to be crude-looking box shapes, attached to a curved board, higher in front than the rear, not unlike a child's idea of a sleigh. There were willow baskets for the fish, and presently, nets were draped about the front. The two men removed their socks and boots and rolled up their trousers to as far above their knees as they were able. There were few people about, as it was still very early and a Sunday; they thought it brought bad luck and there were those who refused to buy fish caught on the Lord's Day. But on any other day, Paddy and Thomas would have been deeply resented by those who either earned a small living by this means, or eked our their meagre wages.

Thomas soon found it was more difficult than it had at first appeared to push his mud-horse into the muddy waters, far more tricky than ploughing a straight furrow at home. Once in a suitable position, the unsightly contraption had to be weighed down with stones to prevent the tide from washing it out to sea. Both men were splashed from their heads to their very dirty feet and realised oilskins would have been helpful. They cleaned off the worst of the dirty, wet sand and ate their packed breakfasts. It was all a matter of waiting for the tides to do the work for themand of knowing about those tides.

Thomas learned that Paddy's grandfather, like his own, was not a native of the place where he worked. It was he who had come from Ireland long ago.

"And what did he do?"

"My folks was hobblers. They'd their own boat, worked for themselves. They helped the big ships move into harbour, y'know, and what I don't know about ropes, 'tis'n't worth t'knowing!"

"So I imagine."

"Not their reg'lar names y'know. We've had our own way of calling 'em, but it's the results that count. It's not just the boat, your life can depend on a properly tied knot, Thomas."

Thomas nodded, thoughtfully.

"Then again, my folks looked after some of the stores when the ships were at anchor, acted as buyers and agents, getting the best price for the ships with the crafty chandlers! It was all drawn up and done properly, all above board. Tidesman saw to that all right. Christ, those men! 'Cause they was checking the cargoes and the papers, looking out for contraband. And for all their care, there was those as managed a bit of smuggling on the quiet."

In due course, when the incoming tide had done its work, the two men went out to the mud-horses to see the results. One net was badly torn by an unwanted eel, which had coiled itself into the net and become badly tangled. Disgustedly, Paddy released it, tearing the net even further and threw the eel back into the water. There was a large number of squirming, unattractive grey shrimps, caught in the small special nets, which had been devised for the purpose. These they could take back with them, and after rinsing them, they were set to boil at once in a large tub, which the man who had provided the mud-horses had set up as far from the incoming tide as possible. Raised on stones, and with a good fire going, the shrimps were soon a more appetising pink colour. There were also some flounders, all of them very small, so Paddy gave these to his helper, declaring he could catch far better any day in the old Brue.

At midday, Paddy and Thomas made their way back to the inn, attended to the filly, which they saw, either out of hunger or simple boredom, had already devoured three-quarters of the contents of her nose-bag. They swilled themselves at the pump in the yard, then ordered hunks of bread, Cheddar cheese and pickles, washed down with cider, the latter not a patch, thought Thomas, on the good 'scrumpie' they served at The Bell in Whytbrook.

Paddy had suggested setting the mud-horses for a later time in the day, but Thomas had had enough. He could not help thinking that, all in all, the outing must have cost his friend quite a fair amount, but Paddy refused to allow him to contribute to its costs in any way, and said he had been able to borrow the gig for nothing.

"Have y'ever been to the place your folks come from?"

"Ireland?" Paddy shook his head. For- a short while, he was lyrical about a place he said he would dearly love to see one day. There was a strong sentimental streak in him, but Thomas suspected his friend feared reality might shatter his dream. I'm the same, he thought. I'd never go to

Northumberland, but there's not any other place on this earth I wouldn't go to, if I'd the chance.

"Have y'ever been to the capital, Paddy?" he asked, hardly aware of the slight note of wistfulness in his voice.

"Several times," said Paddy, almost with indifference. "All the way round the coast into the Atlantic and right up the Channel one time. That was a hell of an experience, Thomas! It was winter and it took a fair bit o' navigating, I can tell 'ee."

"Not in a trow, surely?"

"In a trow! Mind 'ee, there's good boats and bad boats, same as everything else."

"Why didn't you stay with y'family, Paddy?"

"Wanted a change. To be honest, we was getting too much competition and not enough work." He was silent a moment. "Y'see, Bristol's not what it was. It was a great port, but while they hummed and hawed and talked o' making the harbour better, all the good trading went off to Liverpool, even as far away as London, now there's good railways in b'tween. They was too slow, Thomas!"

Again he was silent. They were on their way back to Glastonbury and Paddy gave his attention to the gig; the filly, out of sheer female 'cussedness', it seemed to Paddy, was going too quickly at times. Wanting to get back home.

"The way you swallowed the drink and kept it all down t'other evening! Better than me. I saw that much. I've never had much of a head, never will have, always lacked ballast. Don't learn other things, neither," he added, sadly. Y'know, I bet if I was to take you to a whorehouse in Bristol and you slept with everyone on 'em harlots.... "

"God forbid!" Thomas was laughing.

"No, but I'm joking, 'course, but you see my meaning? Me, I've had the clap twice, but you'd be coming out still smelling like a violet. You've more sense'n me."

"I don't know that!" Thomas was still laughing.

"No, I mean it, like the man in The Good Book who walks in the Dark Valley or somethin' and still fears nothing."

Thomas wondered what his brother Patrick would have made of this misquotation from the Twenty-third Psalm.

"We should've met up a long, long time ago, Thomas. You've the luck and the cleverness, but me, I've the cunning *and* good sea legs. That counts for somethin' too."

"O' course."

"We could've been privateers, in the long-ago days when Bristol was a famous port. Did y'know they was on the pay of the Admiralty? Respected, honoured, a cut above the common pirates."

"Really.... ?"

"Oh, it all stopped about forty years agone. Officially, that is," and Paddy turned his head quickly to wink at Thomas. "A hundred years ago and we could've been making our fortunes shipping out niggers to the sugar plantations! A lot of Bristol wealth is based on that."

"You wouldn't mind about.... ?"

"Slavery? I've no special feelings one way or the t'other. There was good masters and bad, no doubt. .... Anyway, it's all talk, isn't it! Belongs to the past. We've just got to knuckle under and make the best o' things as they is."

"I've enjoyed today, Paddy. I'm hoping Mary Jackson likes shrimps, though."

Paddy grinned.

"Take some more for your train-driver as a farewell gift. They won't keep after today, and I'm not that keen."

"We must meet again sometime, but I honestly don't know how we can do it with me in Highbridge and you on the water."

"But I'm coming 'long your bit o' coast, don't forget not that far from where you're working and I've your address. Don't expect any letters. I'm no good at it and I won't have the time, anyways, but I'll get a message to you one o' these days. When you're least expecting it and wondering, now who the hell was Paddy O'Neil, that's when I'll surprise you! And that's a promise!"

Round about the time when Thomas was preparing to move to Highbridge, the farmers of Whytbrook and most of the surrounding villages, were thinking about their sheep. Farmer Ridley was the first to come to a sudden decision, prompted by a few days of fine weather. Word soon went around, and all those with the necessary skill and the time to spare, were presently engaged for the sheep-shearing period by the head shepherd. The Scotts loaned their own excellent man, Hawker, for the two exhausting days, but neither Luke nor Patrick took part themselves, as they had done when younger. They were much too busy.

There were those, always looking for grim motives, who shook their heads. Ridley was altogether too sharp! He wanted to grab the labour while it was readily available, but he might yet learn his lesson. The nights were still chilly and newly shorn sheep, especially little 'uns', could easily come to harm.

In fact, the farmer wanted to get the whole business out of the way, trusting to his man to complete the negotiating of the fair price for the fleeces, he had been promised, as he planned to make one of his periodic visits to his ailing wife. Mrs. Ridley was consumptive and presently staying in a sanatorium. After that wearisome, but necessary visit, he planned to spend some time in London, both business and pleasure, with his cousin, Sir Montague Ridley. The two men hoped to return to Whytbrook at the end of July. He himself might not return till mid-August. Farmer Ridley felt he thoroughly deserved the break. He let it be known that he would not, therefore, be giving any party for the men until late August. There were those who read into this something sinister, not to say niggardly. His head shepherd, who was a lot more than that, being a kind of manager, could have seen to the celebrations. August was a busy time, what with the harvest, hay-making to complete and the annual sheep fair. And what about Midsummer's Eve? What about Harvest Home?

Ridley had never provided a Harvest Supper, as he had virtually no agricultural land, certainly none under grain. As for the Mid-summer Balls, his wife had given these years before, but since she became sickly, he had not bothered, and even so, the farm labourers had certainly never been invited.

The Bell advertised a Mid-summer Revelry, mainly to attract flagging custom. All through the village the sound of stamping feet, punctuated by wild laughter, could be heard. Luke went to the inn, then made his way to the old barn, merely to watch, with a glass of cider in his hands, and a slightly supercilious look on his face. The elder of the Bevan brothers was there, prancing about in the country dances, with more energy than skill, but Luke could not see Maisie.

Then it was time for the Scotts to carry out their own shearing and dipping. They were fortunately able to do so in the open. Hurdles having been set up, the sheep were brought down, being placed first of all in a small section, tightly packed, before being released, one by one to their waiting shearers. It had been a lengthy process getting them settled, but once a few of the older sheep had submitted, the rest calmed down as they came into the spacious shearing area. The flock was far larger than could be comfortably contained at one time in the hurdles, though smaller than that of big farmers like Ridley; so it had needed all the skill of the two collie dogs, assisted by Jessie, to ensure the animals were brought down the hills as required, without any waiting. A steady, remarkably rhythmical flow. It seemed to Luke there was something almost poetic about the feat. He wished, at that moment, he could see sheep as far as his eye could reach. He sighed. Perhaps, one day!

Both he and Patrick were excellent at the work, swift and competent, Luke rather swifter, as he could not resist competing with others, as he watched the splendid yellow fleeces pile up beyond them. Once, years ago, he had had a bitter experience. Showing off a little in front of some of the older hands at Farmer Ridley's shearing, Luke had out-stripped them, then suddenly nicked one of the sheep, a difficult wether. Apart from marking the fleece and risking infection to the animal, at that time this carelessness was regarded as quite unpardonable. Ridley's shepherd had rounded on Luke, chastising him to the point of humiliation, refusing to allow him to continue. Flushed and angry, Luke left, unwilling to return later when he was needed. The older men had merely looked up briefly, smiled slightly and got on with work, which called for all their concentration. The humiliation had gone deep with the youngster, but it had never happened again.

The ludicrous thing was that at this very same time, Ridley, who knew far less about sheep than any of his men, had insisted upon an alteration in the usual pattern. He had made a real fool of himself. Instead of all the sheep going to lower ground, he had decided to reverse this process, and had had the great dip set up, not without considerable difficulty, on a hill. This was a more convenient, spacious place, he declared. Unfortunately, the sheep had not been co-operative at all, loathing the change in their routine. They became quite terrified, and after a great deal of rushing and chasing about, of loudly barking dogs and frantic men, several of the sheep had actually had to be physically lifted, squirming madly, and taken to the dip. It was pandemonium! Luke had enjoyed that. The men had had a hard job to contain their titters. But at least it went smoothly enough this year at Redesdale Farm.

Hannah, who had Rose and young Jimmy Coxon to help her for this special occasion, had seen to it that large flagons of cider were sent out to the men. However tight-fisted she might seem, she had the good sense to see that it was important to keep the men happy. Somewhat reluctantly, it seemed to Luke, she also gave her usual supper when the shearing was over, providing a good, homely spread at the large kitchen table. Though plentiful, the food was very plain and the only extra was a large dish of Hannah's furmity, made to her own recipe. By tradition this belonged more to Good Friday, but it was a tasty enough dish with its dried fruits, spices (and in Hannah's case, nuts also); and with its base of wheat, milk and sugar, very filling.

Then it was time for the annual Farmers' Ball. Though primarily attended by young people, a good sprinkling of older people always went along to watch (and criticise) and Hannah had always been amongst them. This year she declared she was not going. She did not feel like it and she had nothing suitable to wear.

"But, Ma," Luke protested, "why not? You always enjoy it, you know you do!"

Patrick joined in, agreeing with this.

"'Ee do so like to watch dancin', Ma, now doan't 'ee? Get you'self somethin' purty to wear, Ma."

"Go to Wells," put in Luke, greatly daring.

Hannah turned on him.

"And how much would that cost? I've no money to spare for silliness."

"Then get Rose to run you up somethin'," suggested Luke. I've heard tell she's clever with her needle."

Hannah sniffed.

"How long d'you fools think it takes to make a decent-looking dress, eh? Five minutes? And where would I get the stuff round here? There's nothin' in village I'd care to be seen dead wearing! I'd have to waste time goin' to Kimsley." The two young men looked at each other and sighed. It was clearly going to be no use. Their mother had made up her mind. "'Sides," she added for good measure, "I think naught o' Rose Ford's sewing, neither!"

"Not feeling too well, Ma?" Patrick hinted, kindly.

"I'm right enough most days!" Hannah retorted. "Good days and bad, same as most women m'age."

So, in the end, Patrick decided not to go at all; he would remain at home and spend a bit more time with his mother and Jimmy. Thankfully, Hannah had taken a liking to the misshapen creature and though she bullied him at times, he seemed not to mind this and appeared happy enough. Luke then made a slight fuss, saying he would probably not bother about going himself, being highly critical of the Farmers' Balls, saying he had no-one to go along with; then at length allowing himself to be persuaded into joining a party of the more prosperous tradespeople and craftsmen, including the blacksmith, who were going from the village.

There was always plenty to eat and that was no small consideration. Luke dressed himself in the good suit he kept for such occasions, glad that it still fitted him as regards his girth, though it was a trifle short in the legs. He changed into his old dancing pumps in the village, after walking there in his good, strong 'best' boots. He refused to take the trap. It seemed silly for one, he said, and someone might well give him a drive back home. He would enjoy the fresh air after the stuffy ballroom, if he had to walk back. There was another reason he kept to himself. If by any possible chance he was very late in returning, his mother would not hear him.

The large room at The Wool Pack, kept for such grand occasions, had been cleared for the dancers and a small three-piece band of flute, fiddle and harp, occupied one end of the room. Luke soon left his companions and wandered along with the others from room to room: down stone corridors, into private rooms, into the bars, and into the room set aside as a cloakroom for the men and, most of all, in which to stare at the food being laid out for the coming feast. Already the tables groaned. Few rooms were on the same level, as the inn had been added to in very hap-hazard fashion over the centuries. When it was time to eat, the gentlemen (as they had suddenly become for the evening) were required by the excellent master of ceremonies, to assist the ladies.

There was a great deal of giggling and suppressed excitement. Eating was a pleasure in their lives and, though most of them lived well and very differently from the mere labourers, the sight of so much splendidly arranged food was a joy in itself.

Luke suddenly became aware of Maisie Bevan. Not with her brothers, oh, no, but an older couple, the husband wearing a clerical collar and a young man, hardly much older than Maisie herself. A badge of respectability! Luke felt both satirical and jealous. He was not for long allowed to sit and watch by himself, however. This master of ceremonies took his duties seriously and he soon had even Luke joining in some of the familiar dances, such as Sir Roger de Coverley. On the whole, Luke did not mind overmuch, as the long lines, facing each other, participated in the dancing with more humour than skill, prancing about and laughing a good deal, changing partners frequently. Maisie came near him, passed him, smiled at him, lightly touched his hand, and then was off again. It was very energetic and it made Luke feel extremely hot. But it was not until the square dance, the Lancers, with only eight people to each set, that Luke found himself in the same group as young Maisie, facing her several times as his partner. Yet each encounter seemed but a tantalizing moment. When it all ended, he sought out the girl and, amidst much laughter on all sides and smiles from her, he escorted her back to where she had been sitting.

She walked carefully, as she had tried to dance with care. She must not, she simply must not, spoil what her friend had called 'a beautiful creation', meaning the dress Maisie had made herself. It was of a gauzy material in mauve, lined with a deeper mauve silk taffeta. There was a frill with gold stripes in it, round the hem and more such frills around the sleeves, which reached to just below the elbows. Though the bustle was now well out-of-date, Maisie had contrived a kind of bustle of blue material, which matched the wide blue sash and the blue ribbons in her red hair. There were those who thought the dress totally unsuited to a young girl and there were those who thought the neck a little too low, though the girl wore only a string of seed pearls borrowed from Mrs. Squires, her friend. All the materials had come from one of Mrs. Squires's trunks. Luke had no understanding of women's clothes and he failed to take in any of the details, but he thought the picture Maisie made was exotic.

The man and his son had disappeared and only the woman was sitting alone. Shyly, awkwardly, Maisie made the introduction. It seemed this woman was the niece of Mrs. Squires and was staying with her at present. This accounted for Luke not having seen her previously in Whytbrook. Thank goodness, Maisie was thinking there were only the two to be introduced, for she was finding it hard to recall whether it must be lady who was introduced to the gentleman, or the other way round. And what was it about respective ages? She wished Mrs. Squires could have been with her.

A waltz was announced.

"Oh! I can't waltz at all, I'm sorry," said Luke hesitantly.

"Never mind. Let's watch t'others for a bit. 'Tis ever so easy, Luke. You might pick it up, if you watch. Really, Luke."

Her self-confidence seemed to have returned, but he fidgetted and tried to make polite conversation to which he was unaccustomed and which he had usually scorned. Then the older woman wisely suggested he take Maisie and try to find her something cooling to drink, since they were so warm.

"And look for my husband at the same time," she smiled at them.

They found their lemonade drinks, then wandered about, as others seemed to be doing, partly out of curiosity, partly to stay together a little longer. The night was warm, unusually so. Several couples strolled outside and they did the same. He led her towards the stables at the back, not knowing for what he was searching. A stable-door was ajar and the stable seemed to be empty. He drew her into the shadow.

"Where're we goin', Luke?"

A man suddenly appeared to stare at them and a horse whinnied, so they made a fuss of pretending to be looking at the horses and of trying to recognise some of them. A cuckoo abruptly called out loudly, hopefully.

Maisie laughed.

"Ooh, listen to 'im!" She laughed happily. "I heard 'un five o'clock this mornin'. Honest! Time they left off and flew back to Africa, i'n't, Luke?"

"They're making the most of their chances while the weather's warm!"

"D'you suppose that man'd think we was after stealing his horses? We'd best not stay here."

But they did not return to the inn. Almost by agreement, they began walking as if going into the village, then they took the path that led towards the bank where they had met all those weeks ago. She made no protest when he put his arm about her, telling her she ought to have brought a cloak with her.

"Oh, I never feel the cold. Remember?"

He remembered all right and the sudden recollection stirred his blood.

"You'll spoil your shoes, though." He was not really interested whether she did or not, and it was such a warm night.

"That won't matter."

It did, of course, but not too much at that moment. But when he made to pull her down onto the bank, she protested. Not entirely out of coyness. She was concerned about her dress.

"Oh, come on, the grass is quite dry this time!"

"We shouldn't, though," she said, giggling a little.

He took off his jacket, a gesture of courtesy he had never before made in his life, and spread it for her on the bank. So she allowed herself to be brought to the ground. She arranged her skirts with much care and he glimpsed, in the graceful movements, white petticoats, which momentarily reminded him of the washing-lines at Redesdale; for a brief space his ardour was quelled. They talked. But presently, he told himself that if he didn't make a move to kiss her now while it was quiet with no-one about, it would be too late. Almost fearfully, he debated this problem for several very long seconds. Then the moon suddenly went behind a cloud. She kissed him back. Not expertly, but then neither was he all that proficient, he supposed. She kept her mouth tight shut, but she put her hands into his hair and that, to him quite extraordinary show of feeling, was enough. Nothing could nor would stop him; nor did the girl complain when he raised her skirts, as though taken too much by surprise. She even helped him, as if the spoiling of her dress was her only worry. But suddenly, it was no longer a teasing game. He was on to her, tearing at her undergarments, seeking a very determined entrance, pressing her hard into the ground and himself into her loins. Even then, though she did not respond, neither did she make too much protest. Partly, this was because she had no breath left with which to call out. Mainly, it was an overwhelming shock that this was happening to her. It was as though the whole clamorous struggle was beyond her comprehension, bearing no relationship to what she had dreamed, or thought she knew. She was simply stunned.

Only at the very end, when the final unbearable thrust (bringing more torment) stirred latent memories, did she feebly flutter her pinioned arms and begin to whimper. But it was then far too late. When the warm, sticky fluid began to ooze out of him, Luke eased off his violence as swiftly as it had begun and the girl did a strange thing. She raised her arms as though trying to hold him, as though seeking to rescue something of beauty out of this untenderness, but he angrily jerked away. Then he lay on his back panting.

"Sorry," he murmured, his tone perfunctory, as though he had merely trod on her dress while dancing. He could hear her weeping now, wildly, unhappily. He was suddenly scared. "Look, I didn't mean it to happen! Honest, not like that. I just couldn't help it Maisie! For God's sake, pull yourself together. Best to forget all about it."

"I'll never forget!"

"Yes, well, there's naught we can do now, is there? Get yourself tidied up a bit and when we get back, you'd best go in on your own."

"I can't go back in there!"

"You must! Tell the people you're with you've a headache or something and you want to go home. Maisie?" He turned to look at her in the dark and a feeling of pity overcame him. He was not a brute. "I'm sorry, really I am. But you're none the worse now, are you, Maisie?" Suddenly, he bent his head to kiss her gently on the lips, the very first genuine compassion she had aroused in him.

CHAPTER V

Patrick was deeply troubled in his spirit With the easy complacency of the devout, he had long accepted that there must be many things on this earth a man could not hope to fully understand, terrible-seeming injustices. But as the Lord was never unjust, it remained the old story, that he, and others like him, lacked that profound faith, to accept unquestioningly what appeared unfathomable. This half-explanation had sustained him reasonably well - until recently.

Even in the matter of young Jimmy Coxon, Patrick had thought and prayed his way to a kind of groping comprehension, or so he believed. This misshapen creature was in no way the fault of a careless 'Potter'. Oh, no, God had nothing to do with this creation, which must be the plain result of Sin and the working out of the Law of Cause and Effect. It was hard on young Jimmy, but was it not plain in the Bible, that there was always redemption for those forced to bear the sins of their fathers, when they themselves dearly loved the Lord? Lammie Coxon, with his sweet and gentle disposition, seemed to Patrick especially 'blessed'. He appeared not to mind his inadequacies, asking so little from life. He grinned a good deal, admittedly at almost nothing, and had surely been compensated by the clever hands he had been given.

Poor Jimmy Coxon! With the terrible irony of it, though he had little brain he could use efficiently, his forehead bulged, his head being quite out of proportion to the rest of him, like a baby's head, without the charm. His back curved badly, though he was not really humped, and his belly, as though attempting to balance this deficiency, protruded - and Jimmy was very fond of his food, which did not assist. His short legs, one a little longer than the other, carried him along at a fair speed, but he soon became tired with inclines or stairs and only in his huge shoulders, arms and hands had he developed to the normal size and power of his age. Everyone said it was a mercy his being clever with his hands and so able to earn a bit of living for himself. He had been a remarkable useful helper to the cooper, till his bad chest claimed him, yet again. Every now and then, when the weather was bad, his cough grew worse and the chest became quite painful.

Patrick treated the boy better than anyone had so far done, tending him when necessary and very determined not to send him away, if he was unable to work for some weeks at a stretch. It was the least he could do, as he had been given so much. He could see his brother, Luke, could hardly bear to be in the same room with Jimmy.

Never did he look at him directly and he usually contrived at meal-times, to keep his eyes on his plate, which was far from difficult for Luke. On the other hand, he was never in any way unkind to Jimmy and had stopped referring to him as 'Lammie' when the lad was around. Patrick had little patience with such sensitivity and he was thankful that their mother, Hannah, seemed to have taken a liking to Jimmy. Of course, he was costing her little, but she bullied and directed him and rewarded him on occasions and he seemed content.

So, whilst Patrick could not but feel that the Great Laws had been over-scrupulous in this case, he did not worry himself unduly. If ever there was a young soul destined for heaven, this was he. Poor innocent, simple-natured Jimmy Coxon! Then one day he received a terrible shock. Jimmy had a habit of going to his room not long after the evening meal, the supper, usually termed 'tea'. He whittled away happily at scraps of wood, played with various pictures he had collected together, or been given, then like a child went to bed and slept soundly. He needed a lot of sleep did Jimmy.

Luke had come home with a very young vixen he had rescued from a forgotten and broken old trap. The animal was scared, but unharmed, and Patrick felt annoyance that he had brought it home at all, instead of chasing it away, as far as possible. It would have to be shot, whatever Luke said, unless he had a mind to take a walk over the fields to release it, and goodness knows what could happen to it then, for it was hardly more than a cub.

"I wish I could keep it," said Luke, wistfully.

This from a sheep-farmer! Sensibly, Patrick did not trouble to answer him, but watched as Luke stroked the bright fur, which the frightened young fox did not altogether appreciate. The vixen made a futile attempt to snap at Luke's fingers. He held her tightly, but gently.

"Go and get Jimmy," he said, suddenly. "I'm sure he'd love to see this 'un." As though none of them had ever seen a vixen in their lives before! But Patrick quietly went, pondering why it was that his brother seemed to have so much more regard for even wild animals than he did for human beings.

Patrick found Jimmy weeping loudly to himself. For an incredible instant, it had seemed as though Jimmy already knew about the young vixen and had guessed at its sad, inevitable fate; that the boy held an unearthly affinity with the animal. Quickly, Patrick recognised the absurdity of this notion. Jimmy was crying for some other reason.

"What's amiss, Jimmy?" he asked.

It was quite some time before the little fellow was able to bring out enough words to make Patrick appreciate what was wrong. He gulped and rubbed his red eyes, which got even redder; a horrible mess.

"Did - did Luke... ? Has some on us upset 'ee, Jimmy?"

The cripple shook his huge head, then went on shaking it, as though he would like to shake it off, as though its weight and size troubled him. Patrick managed to calm him, then finally began to piece together the cause of the distress, though Jimmy still rambled on, disjointedly. No, he didn't mind being called Lammie, it was friendly. What then? Almost incoherently, Jimmy sobbed out odd words, of meaning only to himself. Slowly, revelation came to Patrick. He put his arm around the boy, unable to say anything. How could he? He felt utterly helpless. This particular trouble had begun with his grinning at a girl in the village and she had taken it badly, taken it quite the wrong way, hurting him unnecessarily. He knew he was not the same as others, he sobbed, and he hadn't minded, but.... He rambled on and on....

Suddenly it seemed to Patrick monstrous, beyond all mercy. He was shaken as he had not been before in his life. There was no comfort he could give, that was not false. He prayed the boy would soon forget his upset.

Lammie showed very little interest in the vixen, but he brightened up later when Hannah gave him a slice of cake and Patrick took it upon himself to entertain him with some simple string games.

Clearly loathing having to do it, Luke set off with the vixen in a bag, warned by Patrick to put a very good distance between the animal and Redesdale. She was capable of attracting a whole pack of foxes, and at this thought he smiled slightly. She was a pretty thing!

The next pricking of his rotund and comfortable spirit was far worse, much closer to his heart, for it concerned Hannah, their mother.

Being, as he thought himself, largely without material ambitions and, he also supposed, a trifle indolent about what did not directly concern him, he had accepted the odd state of affairs at Redesdale, as being part of his mother's 'funny little ways'. She liked to have full control of the purse-strings and had always done, since their father died. And why shouldn't she, indeed?

She did a most excellent job in her way. She had seen that they never lacked for food and the essentials, though it was very hard to get money from her for improvements, as he well knew. Between them, Thomas and his mother had coped very well with trying times, and they had been trying. Since Thomas's departure, however, there had grown an anxiety that made him feel ashamed to dwell upon. She refused to find the money when he was convinced they not only ought to do so, but that it should be available. At first, he told himself she did not trust his judgement, as she had trusted Thomas's opinions. Luke had constantly dropped hints, which Patrick found distasteful. Of course, their mother was not hoarding! This was a disgraceful idea!

"Ee'd best not let Ma hear 'ee talk like this," he said, with some indignation. "Her knows full well what her's a-doing."

"Well, I'm darl'd if I'm a-putting up with 'un much longer!" Luke, too, in his agitation, had fallen back on the rich Somerset dialect of their childhood, and which their grandmother had tried determinedly to curb. "Small wonder Thomas ran off," he continued, more quietly, knowing full well, his boast was recklessly impossible to fulfill. He turned away.

But these final words had taken root in Patrick's mind, unwillingly at first. And the day came, not so long after, that he began to realise something was wrong, very wrong indeed. They had sold a second milker, leaving only the one cow, as Hannah said she could not cope with the cheese and butter-making. There was no dairy, as on a large mixed farm, and the work was carried out in the kitchen. It was absolutely true that one milking cow supplied more than sufficient for their needs - and left some butter to dispose of now and then. So two days after the sale, Patrick broached his mother. It was high time they did something about the re-roofing of the great barn, which was not only in a deplorable state, it must also be a superb nesting place for rodents, as well as birds. It could also be very dangerous if there was a bit of a fire any time.

Hannah sniffed. The roof was good enough for its purpose. They hardly used the barn these days. It would be a waste of good money.

"It'll have to done sometime, Ma. It'll only get worse."

She was sullenly silent, then she conceded, "Later on, perhaps then, though I don't see why you and Luke can't do something between you."

He sighed.

"If we had to, Ma, but we've little time to spare and 'er ought to be done a-for winter, I reckon." Then he asked, quietly, firmly, "What happened to the money for the cow, Ma?"

She did not answer for a while and when she looked at him, there was a strange and stubborn expression on her face, he did not care for one little bit.

"Don't keep on at me, Patrick," she pleaded. "That money's gone."

So he had gone away, saying no more, but very worried. Small fires were a fairly common occurrence in Whytbrook, but Redesdale was a good distance from the village itself, too far for sparks to fly on the wind and they ought to be thankful, he supposed, that the house itself had good Welsh tiles to its roof. He was being unnecessarily pessimistic, always looking these days for the very worst to happen. But the very next day he seized the opportunity when Hannah was out to do something he would have considered outrageous not so long ago.

Under the large, old-fashioned four-poster bed Hannah had shared with Joseph, and where she still slept, lay a deed-box. Inside were kept the deeds of the house and various other papers. He had long known, as they all had, as Hannah made no secret of it, that this was where she kept household cash. The key was in the pocket of an apron, hanging behind a door, near the dresser in the kitchen. He went through the contents of the box twice, unable to believe his eyes. There was no copy of a will, he noticed, and in a small draw-string cloth bag, lay exactly three sovereigns. Mentally, he began to calculate all the various money paid in and spent during the past few weeks. It did not make any kind of sense. There had to be far more than this. What had she done with it?

Being Patrick, he immediately sought out his mother on her return, watching for an occasion when neither Luke nor Jimmy was around. He told her what he had done. He asked her outright to account for the curious discrepancy.

She was silent for a moment, and when she spoke she did not sound angry, nor did she raise her voice. She merely smiled and said, "So now 'ee knows, don't 'ee?"

For a long moment, he stood there stunned. Then he went to her and put his arm around her, unaware that she flinched at this. She had only wanted Thomas to show her real affection, as he had done, she was sure.

"Ma," he said, gently, "we want to help 'ee. We want to take these worries off your shoulders, Luke and me. I'm not wanting to go on at 'ee, but truly 'ee have got us fair meaz'd. Now, where's rest o' the cash, Ma?"

"You're a good son," she said, almost reluctantly, "but I must do things me own way."

"But, where, Ma? Is it invested?"

She was silent again for a moment, then she smiled and said, "Yes, invested.

"Where?"

"It's invested, " she repeated, stubbornly.

He looked at her with a mixture of exasperation and alarm, still not wanting to face the truth. It was on the tip of his tongue to try to reason with her, to point out that they were not young children and ought to know how matters stood. He was even about to issue a small sermon and she his own mother! - about the hateful love of money. He stopped himself. Hannah had unexpectedly retreated to what, in any other woman, he would have judged to be feminine wiles. Tears sprang to her eyes. She began to tremble.

"Oh, Patrick," she wailed, "why can't 'ee let me be! 'Ee can see I'm not well these days. Why d'ee not leave me alone? Can't 'ee see? Why can't I do as I feel best for the little time that's left to me?"

Now he was truly alarmed.

"Ma, Ma," he cried, "don't 'ee talk like this! 'T'won't do. Why, 'ee'll live years and years yet, out-live all on us, I don't doubt!"

She shook her head, dolefully.

"I think not." Patrick saw she was in real distress. "Leave me be, Patrick, there's a good lad. You an' Luke'll get everything I've got one o' these days, when I'm gone. Every penny." Then she added, and it was a half-moan to herself, "I'm feared Thomas's never comin' back to us."

He patted her arm and left her alone, as she wished. If only Thomas was around, a man he could talk this over with. Had Thomas known their mother had this - this curious fancy, this strange habit. Patrick could not bring himself to use a stronger word, but he did a lot of serious thinking and much praying as well. Luke was hopeless these days, he told himself. What had got into the boy of late he did not know. He had believed his young brother was maturing after the departure of Thomas, accepting responsibility, without arguments, but just recently he had been so high-pitched, he seemed to be living on his nerves and he was certainly getting on everyone else's nerves.

He wrote a carefully worded letter to Thomas. As this could not be done in the house where the ink and pens were, he wrote it in pencil in the barn, licking the tip of the pencil, absently, thoughtfully, as he had done when a small child to give it a sharper tone, and all the time pondering his words, for he did not write with much skill.

When the reply arrived, a week later, there was nothing in it that Hannah could not read, without puzzlement. There was also not a word about returning to Redesdale. Hannah was now trying to convince herself and everyone else that Thomas planned a surprise visit. Patrick was doubtful, but he kept his thoughts to himself. For a day or so, he trifled with the idea of going to Highbridge and seeking out Thomas and demanding that he return. He thought better of it and went off to Lawyer Ridley in Kimsley Mendip instead, following this interview with a visit to the bank in Wells; for what he had learned was shattering - had he been a man easily shattered.

He spoke to Luke in their room. He had thought it out clearly now. They simply had to take charge of all money affairs, making sure that, in future, they dealt with as much as possible away from the farm. Luke reacted angrily at once. Firstly he was peeved that dull, unworldly Patrick should have thought up all this himself. It was ironic! He spoke emotionally, "Ma won't like it! 'Tis a terrible way to treat our Ma!"

Patrick reasoned quietly and with surprising firmness. It was their fault things had become as bad as they had. They ought to have seen. She had behaved towards them as though they were still small children, and they had allowed her to do so. She should have been checked long ago.

Luke still argued, out of habit.

Patrick moistened his lips.

"Luke," he said at last, "it 'tis far wors'n 'ee realise. I'd a long talk with Mr. Ridley, t'lawyer up Kimsley way. Seems Ma had two or three legacies some years back, soon after Pa died."

"What of it?"

"She wouldn't let him put it in t'bank or invest it, whatever she do say now. She insisted t'money be brought in cash to t'house, against his advice. So, it were not his place to argue and he's not spoken o' it to anyone."

They looked at each other in silence.

"How much?" asked Luke, suddenly.

Patrick frowned slightly.

"I don't know and it don't matter now. It were her money, but for the future - it were quite a lot, actually."

"I suppose it could've been spent," said Luke. "Times've not been good since Pa went."

"True, but not as bad as made out to us. I've done a lot of calculations of what we've spent in past weeks, and it's just gone, 'tis not in the house at all."

"Perhaps she's hid it all in her cabbage patch," said Luke with a hint of flippancy, which jarred on Patrick.

"Ee've got to see, Luke. 'Tis not the money I'm worried 'bout at all, though we must pay our way on t'farm."

Luke looked sardonic, but said nothing.

"'Tis this - this hoarding that frightens me, Luke."

"You're saying Ma's mad?"

"No, no," said Patrick, unhappily, "she be sane 'nough in most ways, only this unfortunate.... "

Luke was serious now.

"What d'ee suggest? 'E seem to have worked it all out."

His brother explained. There would be notes given, promises to pay, and then either Luke or he would meet the creditor at Kimsley market when the agent from a bank in Wells came once a week. Again, he would see that money was paid into their own hands when it was only small amouts; or into the bank otherwise.

"It'll waste a lot of time," said Luke. "And folks round here won't take bits of paper. They'll want gold."

"They'll get it. It'll be just a bit of arranging." Patrick tried not to sound worried. Luke grasped, not for the first time, that whilst Patrick could work steadily with his hands, he had very little skill when it came to planning for wider issues and the future of the farm. He relied, perhaps too much, upon the seasons and his faith. "Luke, it'll only be three or four times o' year there'll be big sums to handle."

"We'll still have to keep some money in t'house. Everyone does. And what about Ma's spending?"

"I've thought o' that. She'll be given what she needs and a bit over, o' course. If she saves it, that's her affair. Then, she'll have a bit put by for when it's needed. There's a place in Jimmy's room'll do nicely. Ma never goes in there and 'tis nice and handy for the barton."

Luke shrugged. There was still that slightly sardonic expression about his mouth. The 'Holy-One' was not so holy after all. He was capable of some cunning.

"I still don't like it."

"Can 'ee think o' anything better?" asked Patrick, almost desperately hoping that this none too reliable younger brother would unexpectantly display the strength he needed so badly at present. He felt wretched. He even felt soiled. In order to safe-guard their mother, must he be forced to play this role of duplicity? The whole thing was distasteful to him. How could

God ask him to play this sly game? And yet, he reasoned to himself, had they not all allowed Hannah to continue their childhood far too long because that seemed easiest, turning a blind eye to what they did not want to see? The feeling of guilt was too much to bear. For the first time since Thomas's departure, Patrick felt indignant. A fine mess he'd left them to deal with.

Despite the fuss she had made over the Farmers' Ball, Hannah made it plain she had every intention of going to Farmer Ridley's delayed supper party for the sheep-shearers. He always issued invitations to other farmers and friends - and Hannah was an old friend - at the same time. She did not go so far as to indulge in a new dress, but she brought out a plum velvet, some few years old, which she had worn but once before. This she hung up to get rid of as many of the creases as possible, as well as the smell from the camphor balls. Then she busily trimmed it with cream lace, good lace she had saved for some special occasion. She was not much of a needlewoman, but Patrick, for one, was impressed. He said a short prayer of thanks. Perhaps his worries about his mother had been excessive? He had told her, without going into any details, that in future he intended to manage the money affairs of the farm. After a moment of studied silence, when she had turned on him a glower of indignation, she had turned away and merely murmured, "Please yourself."

Farmer Ridley's house, Whytbrook House, as though there were no other house of importance in the village, fronted onto the main street. He had a smallish stretch of land lying behind the house and its quite large garden, but most of his land was well away from the village, having been acquired at different times. This gave him a good excuse to do a lot of riding. It was a classic Georgian house, built about 1760, the six rectangle windows of the second floor, perfectly aligned with those of the ground floor, and with two dormer windows peeping from the roof. The only ornamentation was in the shape of a large scallop shell, appearing in the triangular arch above the elegant front door with its two slender squared pillars. There were three steps leading to the door and a curved, not unattractive, iron railing of a later period.

The three from Redesdale ate in the dining-room, along with the farmer and Sir Montague Ridley, who had joined his cousin for a short stay, mainly for shooting, since the birds were strong on the wing, but also to keep a watchful eye on his property and eventual votes. There were a few others in the dining-room, making a dozen in all. Soon the farmer would have to steal himself to make another troublesome and lengthy journey to Switzerland to see his wife, if his conscience was not to be bothered later, for he had been warned in a letter that her health had seriously declined. For all the good the expensive stay at a sanitarium had done, she might just as well have remained in Whytbrook. But it was expected, he supposed. He had numerous other problems, not money thankfully, but all needing handling with care. He was glad his own staff were loyal and still fairly dependable, but this could not be said of all casual workers and there were those he well wished he could do without. They could be dangerous elements. These men, together with some of his own men and their wives, were presently all crowded into the vast kitchen. It was a rotten arrangement, for when the doors were open, one could not but hear them, though they seemed to be quiet enough at the moment, perhaps bemused by the spread laid before them. No doubt they would all take themselves to the field behind the house for the entertainments to be later provided. May the warm, dry weather continue! There had been several bad storms this summer.

He looked across at Hannah Scott, Hannah Jenkins as he remembered her from his youth, and smiled faintly, as though she could guess his thoughts. He paid no attention to what she was wearing, nor thought it rather inappropriate to be attired in such a warm velvet dress in August. Nothing could make

Hannah beautiful and had he met her for the first time that evening, he would have been unimpressed; but at that moment she seemed like an ally. He had totally forgotten that he had once asked her to marry him long ago, but Hannah had not.

Luke glanced, not too overtly, at the spread of beef, capons and game being carved and served from the large sideboards, then handed around together with a plentiful supply of salads and good bread. He wondered if they were eating the same supper in the kitchen and thought it likely. Then he wondered if, by chance, Maisie Bevan was amongst those eating there. This was not so likely and Luke knew he had no intention of going to look. He was always thankful when the door leading to the passage and kitchen was tightly closed, and any sound quite shut out. He drank a little too much, telling himself that each day that passed since the Farmers' Ball was like a reprieve. He had gone into the village as seldom as possible, and never alone. Not once had he encountered Maisie Bevan. She could have been avoiding him, but it was far more likely she had gone to visit relations, or had even been packed off to service. He dared not make any outright enquiry about her. There must be more to life than getting married and having children and he wouldn't be ready for such a step, not for years yet. To throw away his hopes, his dream of one day emigrating to Australia would be tragic. Oh, no, he wasn't going to be caught as easily as that! To see everything on which he based some kind of promising future fade away utterly!

There were more pressing worries, more immediate, even if he did not let the girl lead him into marriage. His nerves had grown taut with fear. He was truly scared of what the Bevan brothers might do to him once they heard about the little episode with their young sister. He had not gone to The Bell once of late without taking a very quick look around to see if either of those hulks were there, and ready to depart again if he did glimpse a young Bevan in the corner of the bar. So far, he had been lucky, but they could be waiting their chance. He knew they would not demand any words from him; indeed, he would be given no opportunity to explain anything at all. He would be felled to the ground, without a word spoken, and when he least expected it. He would have no chance to defend himself and at the end, he would be very lucky if he escaped only with broken bones and was not maimed for life or even murdered. There would be no half-measures about their actions.

Luke also knew the violence would have scant relationship to morality, or even to brotherly affection. In the end, it would come down to the primitive urges of ownership, and to the more recent malcontent and envy, springing from the fact that the Scott family owned good Somerset land (and hadn't William Scott, their grandfather, come here as a stranger, an interloper?)

He began testing Sir Montague, who chanced to sit opposite. The baronet was, at first, highly amused, then irritated, but he kept that well hidden. He had encountered young men like Luke often enough before; it was all part of this new Age of Reason, lately spawned, he supposed, by Darwinism, a very inelegant Age of Reason, when compared with the last century. His appearance was in complete contrast to that of his cousin, his face being criss-crossed with deep lines, as though he had spent his early years in a hot climate, and most of the time out-of-doors, which had been the case until some fifteen years ago. He had served in India and he still sported a large, well-trimmed, but incongruous moustache. Farmer Ridley had the smooth, puffed-up countenance, intelligent, but non-intellectual, usually expected, but seldom met, in the successful farmer, though he lacked the healthy ruddiness and his hands were very well-tended.

Politely, Mr. Ridley enquired about Thomas. He had a fondness for the young man and as he had considerable investments in railways, he was not as critical of his action in leaving Redesdale, as many people in the village. Hannah brightened. She told what she knew, embroidering it a little,

Patrick noticed. The farmer merely nodded, but his cousin looked interested.

"You probably don't know this, but the famous George Stephenson - you'll have heard of him, of course? -"

"Who hasn't?" put in Luke.

"At any rate," continued Sir Montague, unperturbed, "he was a pioneer of trains. He won the trials on the Liverpool and Manchester line with the Rocket, as you may know."

"Eighteen-Twenty-nine," said Luke, promptly, like the annoyingly bright child in class.

"Yes, it must've been about then. Well, he was later invited to design a train for the Somerset and Dorset Line."

"Is that so?" said Hannah, managing to look more interested than she felt and smiling at James Ridley.

"D'you know what he said, though Mrs. Scott?" The baronet leaned towards her, amusement in the deep ruts of his face.

"We've no idea, have we?" said Hannah, smiling again at James.

"Why, he didn't even bother to reply!"

Everyone but Luke managed to laugh.

Though he was close to hysteria inside Luke contrived to remain unsmiling.

After a little while the conversation turned to education, a topic of which Sir Montague was very fond indeed. It had given him many of his best electioneering speeches in the past. For several long moments he was fully launched. He looked briefly at Luke, but turning to Mrs. Scott, said, "Its very different today to what it was, thank goodness. You may have heard of a woman called Hannah More, Mrs. Scott?"

"Hannah," mused Hannah, "that's my name, you know. Yes, yes, I'm sure I've heard the name, Sir Montague.

"Well, this good lady started educating the miners' children in the Mendips - not round these parts, of course but she made a good beginning. Years and years ago this was. They were a real ignorant lot of children at the time, I'm afraid. They swore most of the time. They stole, they were filthy dirty, lived like animals, poor things. Appalling it must have been, if you'll forgive me for speaking of this at a supper table to a lady."

"How awful," said Hannah, flatly.

"The parents were the same, naturally. And this gently-bred lady started her Sunday schools for them."

"How splendid of her," said someone vaguely.

"I've seen young'uns like those these days," Luke murmured, his face growing flushed. "Live like pigs, some o' them. Worse'n pigs, really."

"Oh, surely not?" Sir Montague hid his annoyance. "You must be mistaken, I think."

"Not in Whytbrook," said the farmer, suddenly taking a keen interest. He owned a good many of the farm cottages in the village and elsewhere and was immensely proud of them. "Not in Whytbrook," he replied, firmly.

"Yes, in Whytbrook," said Luke, "on the outskirts, anyway. Patrick and me know some families not so far from us." He looked hopefully towards his brother, but either Patrick had not heard, or he was determined to stay clear of any dispute.

"Oh, gypsies," said James Ridley with some relief in his voice. "Waste of time bothering about them."

"Not gypsies," said Luke, stubbornly, his face a furious red.

His mother looked at him.

"Luke, " she said mildly, "I think you've had a little too much to drink." Then she smiled, glancing at the farmer.

Patrick was truly amazed. Between the two of them, what was he to make of this? Luke was right, but there was a proper time and place, as the Good Book made very plain; and as for his mother, who was speaking in her most refined tones, reserved for genteel company, what had got into her this evening? A more different woman than the one she had appeared so recently to be, could hardly be found. The way she kept looking towards Farmer Ridley.... It was disturbing. Surely, to goodness....? At her age? For a moment, Lucifer popped into his mind to whisper a terrible, cruel reminder, *James Ridley is a very rich man, Patrick.*

The furrows on the face of Sir Montague remodelled themselves into a semblance of a gracious man. He ignored Luke, but he continued talking about education in general and finally, in particular, Hannah More again.

"She lived not far from here at Redhill."

"She lived in a cottage, called Cowslip Green," said Luke. He added that he had seen it years ago on a Sunday School outing. This time when he turned to his elder brother, Patrick nodded, but he was feeling weary. He took the chance to mutter, "For God's sake, Luke, don't be so hare-brained!"

"It's not too far from Cheddar," said Luke, not to be silenced.

"I must get you to take me there one day to have a look at it, when I've the time to spare, that is," said the baronet, pleasantly. "And come to think of it," he added, wasn't it around there that the hymn, 'Rock of Ages', was inspired? I believe the Reverend Toplady was sheltering from a storm. In the seventeen-Sixties."

For a fleeting moment, Luke was non-plussed. Then he looked triumphant.

"Oh, but it wasn't Cheddar Gorge, exactly!" he declared, delighted. "I remember now. The Reverend must've had a lot of imagination! He was only in a crevice down in Burrington Combe!"

Hannah appeared torn between admiring the cleverness of her son (where had he got his knowledge?) and due embarrassment. But Sir Montague was fully equal to the challenge. He said, "Where on earth's this Burrington Combe? Can anyone tell me? I've never heard of it." Then without waiting for a reply, he smiled at Luke. "No doubt, young man you're right, but you must admit Cheddar sounds so much better!"

Mr. Ridley suggested that the ladies get their wraps and that they all take themselves to the field behind the house where a simple display of pyrotechnics, as he called them, was to be given. This was a rare treat for Whytbrook. They might also like to watch the dancing. It was essential, however boring, that he make an appearance amongst his workers, sometime during the evening. It was when the display of fireworks had almost ended, that Sir Montague came over to Luke. He had been considering this young man and had made a few brief enquiries about him of his cousin. He now spoke to Luke at some length, mainly asking questions about farming. Luke answered quietly, sensibly enough, though puzzled. Sir Montague then suddenly asked, "Ever thought of emigrating, Luke?"

Luke's heart gave a sharp lurch, of shock, of excitement; but he was suspicious.

"Not 'specially," he said, trying to keep all emotion from his voice.

"We're not trying to get rid of you, young man!" Sir Montague laughed, his most convincing laugh, but a moment later he said, more soberly, "I fancy you're the type that might do well in the colonies."

"Do - d'you think so - sir?" said Luke, thawing a little. "I've sometimes thought of Australia or New Zealand, but - well - it's difficult."

The other studied him carefully. The young man's intelligence, his 'cleverness', as the baronet preferred to term it, would not necessarily be an asset; it could well be a hindrance, in fact. But it was clear he learned quickly, had a good memory and, most important of all, had tenacity. He was very young, obviously healthy, despite his thinness and his lack of tact would not count against him if he chose the right place, as it might do in England. He was clearly wasted, stuck in this village. He said, "If ever you seriously consider moving abroad to work, you might like to get in touch with me. It so happens, I've quite an interest in promoting emigration one way and another."

"Why, thank you," said Luke and his thanks were not tinged with doubt. He really meant it.

Sir Montague Ridley beamed at the young man before him, almost, but not quite, liking him, for nothing raises a man in his own opinion more than to be able to forgive pettiness and lend a helping hand. Especially when it will not cost him a penny of his own money....

For the rest of the evening and during all the return journey home in the trap, Luke was enveloped in a haze of wonder. Who knew what - who could say.... ? Perhaps, his awful luck was about to change at last? It all went to show one! Though exactly what it went to show, he was not at all clear about.

Well before the annual sheep fair, held that year on August 21st, there were discussions, involving Hawker, about the number of sheep to be sold and any purchases to be made. The ancient fair, which had continued for hundreds of years was termed 'The First Day of Winter Fair', which seemed ludicrous to everyone when the weather was suddenly warmer than it had been all summer. But the fair's name related to the coming winter, since farmers must always be thinking well ahead. Patrick seemed calm enough, but he was clearly worried and missing Thomas's guidance. They were the more disturbed, both of them, when Hawker made it plain he would prefer not to go to the fair.

He had jobs he wished to attend to and he did not think the brothers would need him. Added to which, his legs were hurting him badly of late. The long walk would be too much.

"You could come along in the trap," said Luke, swiftly, instinctively knowing that all this preamble was leading up to something far more important than Hawker's absence from the great annual fair. He was right. The shepherd took his time about it, but at length made it plain he thought it high time he retired, as he was near-enough seventy and he had a sister, living in Dorset, and he thought he would probably go to stay with her. Immediately, he hastened to make it plain, he would not desert them until they had found someone else to replace him, but he did not feel he ought to go without a good deal of warning.... and so on.... and so on.

Here was another problem and a big one at that. There were plenty of shepherds, but a replacement for Hawker would take some finding. Another man would not match his devotion and he would be most unlikely to be prepared to walk up from the village and to spend night after night on the cold hills in the lambing season in a very rudimentary shelter. The two cottages the farm possessed were in a deplorable state and would need much attention to bring them to a habitable condition; and Patrick was well aware that no shepherd these days would be willing to live-in, not if he had a family. (He preferred not to think of his exacting mother as being a hindrance.)

But the day of the fair arrived and an exceedingly early start was made, the sheep to be sold having already been moved the previous day to a convenient field near the road. Though barely light, it was a clear morning with not a hint of mist. Patrick hoped it would stay fine, as August could be variable. Luke hoped it would be nice and hot and very soon it was warm enough, even for him. He was in high spirits. The world at that moment seemed a very good place. One day, one day, perhaps; but meanwhile, it was not so bad, really. He viewed the small flock with affection and in the narrow road, there seemed to be more sheep than there actually were. As the road twisted and turned, he not infrequently made swift diversions climbing up the banks to arrive back on the road, ahead of the sheep, laughing. Patrick also smiled, though he did not emulate his brother's action. With his dear bitch, Jessie, by his side, he felt free, as he knew he never did feel free these days at Redesdale. The two collies (and they had brought them both along with them) kept happily to their droving work, for nothing pleases an animal more than to be earning its living in the fresh open air. Luke took off his jacket and slung it over one shoulder.

Patrick was still a bit puzzled in his mind as to the number of ewes to buy. It would depend on the price, but they had lost too many lambs last winter. And would the price of more good pure-bred Jacob rams be justified?

The sheep to be sold were carefully checked in and penned with wooden hurdles, then the two brothers went off to a local inn for a quick drink and some light refreshment. The greetings, the jokes, the exchanging of news all took a long time. The buying and selling, which could never be hurried, also was laborious, but they did better than they had expected. Then a quick visit to some of the stalls, the purchase of a cheap fairing of sweets, dressed up with ribbons, for Hannah, and Patrick indicated that he would like to make a start home. He was keen to get the few animals they had purchased on the road before the crowds made progress difficult; if he could keep them moving without too many stops for nibbling, then he would have them settled in their new field long before dark. There were also the dogs to feed and he must make sure young Jimmy, with Hannah's supervision, had managed to milk the cow. He saw the look of disappointment on his younger brother's face.

"Now, why don't 'ee stop awhile, Luke?" he suggested. "I can manage this little lot with no trouble a' all. Dogs'll see 'em back for me!" He grinned. "Happen 'ee'll be able to beg a ride with some folks goin' back to Whytbrook." He felt more amiably disposed towards Luke than he had done for days past. He was very young, he told himself, and he had few pleasures; overlooking the fact that he was but three years older than Luke and did not have many pleasures himself.

So it was agreed. Patrick set off. A short way along the road, he paused to light his pipe, then he was off again, walking quietly, steadily. He had purchased a shepherd's crook at the fair, which he not only thought might be useful now and again on the journey, but would make a nice present for Hawker to replace the old one he owned. Without being consciously aware of it, or examining his thoughts, Patrick was blissfully, wholly, content.

As for Luke, he went around the stalls several times and made a few more purchases, since he had a little money. Patrick had shown himself more generous than Hannah, but not all that. There was still need for caution, for Luke saw that Patrick was as wary of handling finances as of explosives. Poor Patrick, he thought, momentarily drawn in affection towards his brother, all this is Thomas's fault. He forgot about Thomas. There were no travelling entertainments, for there was not the space for them, but when he looked about, he found more than he had at first noticed. A fortune-teller!

The booth was a little apart from the rest and Luke debated whether to risk entering, even though he knew it was a lot of foolish nonsense, wasn't it? Someone passing himself off as a genuine Romany! He'd need to watch nothing was stolen in that half-light of the tent. He'd need to be very careful indeed. But it would be curious if he chanced to be told he was soon going overseas; a mere coincidence, of course, but....

He became aware of someone standing immediately behind him, breathing heavily and he smelt the fumes of alcohol, oppressively close.

"Oi thought it might jest be 'ee," said the familiar voice of Matthew Bevan. Luke's heart gave a gigantic lurch, then hammered at his chest, like an angry prisoner, hating to be contained, but unable to escape....

He turned nervously.

"Been 'iding 'eeself o' late, eh? Eh, Master Luke?" said the other in a voice of boozy fraternity.

CHAPTER VI

"Wh - what 'ee doin' here?"

The other looked surprised.

"Why, same as 'ee Master Luke. "'Aving a look 'round, enjoyin' mezel'." He grinned, a little self-consciously.

Why was Matthew suddenly calling him 'Master Luke'? He had never done so before. Luke was not his master; he did not employ him, nor did the Scotts own any land used by the Bevans. He swallowed, painfully, and tried to stare back at Matthew steadily. Some six or more inches shorter than himself and, at less than twenty-one years, only a little more than a year older, Matthew was of utterly different build, muscularly solid. This was especially noticeable this afternoon as his shirt sleeves were rolled up to the elbows, the neck button unfastened. He wore no collar, but he had jauntily tied a red neckcloth about his massive bovine neck.

He had been drinking right enough. Like father, like son! Then Luke realised Matthew Bevan was very far from being drunk, despite his foul breath. The youngest Scott brother glanced about him nervously, convinced Matthew Bevan was quite capable of delivering a felling hammer blow. Here, a little apart from the self-absorbed crowds, would be as excellent an opportunity as any. No-one would even notice!

He murmured something hastily about the sheep to be got home and made a slight move to get away, as quickly as he possibly could. He must find some friend, perhaps in one of the inns and stay close to him. Of one thing he was certain; he could not make the long, lonely walk back to Redesdale alone, not in the dark.

"I seen Patrick leave some time away back. I'as only wantin' a fren'ly word, Luke." He sounded puzzled. "Us 'as not seen 'ee for many a day, 'ee know!" He grinned, hopefully. "Now, I'm on me own. You's alone. Why doan't us go and 'ave a li'le drink, Luke, eh?"

"If you like." He forced himself to look into the other's eyes. They were innocent of any ill-intent. But not entirely innocent, for it very soon transpired that Matthew had been most unlucky. Someone had managed to relieve him of his purse while he was taking a drink. Now he had no money at all on him. Not a penny. His arm fell about Luke's arm, like a vice. Slowly it dawned on Luke, as he listened to the other's unfortunate little tale, that not only was he seeking sympathy, he was trusting that Luke would be able to stand him one more drink or even a couple before he went home.

A drink? Luke could have burst out laughing. This, then was the reason for the strange, obsequious greeting! Of course, he would buy him a drink. It would be a kind of celebration, though Matthew would not appreciate it; a freedom from weeks and weeks of stress and worry. And all for nothing! What a fool he had been! How he wished he could tell someone all about it, but that person could only have been Thomas and certainly not Matthew Bevan.

Young Maisie Bevan had thankfully kept her mouth tight shut about their little escapade; and no-one had succeeded in forcing the girl to speak out against him. Oh, the blessed relief! He felt a rush of near-affection towards the young girl.

Now, at long last, he could breath freely. What, after all, had been no more than a trifling indiscretion, could be totally wiped from his mind.

In September Mrs. Ridley died. The end came swiftly and Ridley was compelled to make yet another journey to the continent to bring back his wife's embalmed remains. He went alone, since, apparently, no-one could spare the time to accompany him. At the end of the long travelling when he reached Whytbrook, he felt utterly drained, as he had been forced to spend part of the time shut into the luggage compartments of trains, along with the corpse.

Two days later, the funeral took place at Whytbrook, and now there was a satin-lined coffin with splendid brass handles. The hearse had thick glass panels, so the villagers, who had taken time off work and lined the main street, were able to have a clear sight of the magnificence. Traditionally, the hearse was drawn by two black horses, and the way in which the villagers gaped as the small cortege wended its way to the parish church, it could have been a grand cavalry parade. Some of the watchers wore black armbands, as a mark of respect; a few solemnly crossed themselves as the procession made its sombre way, accompanied by the heavy intoning of a single bell, and one or two women even wept. Goodness only knows why they did so, as the farmer's wife had had almost no contact with anyone for many years. Most likely they were reminded of their own sad losses.

Only employees of the Ridleys attended the funeral service and not many more than them and the friends and relatives of the family stood at the grave-side. There were a great many flowers, brought from sheltered gardens, conservatories and even, it was said, by a florist, all the way from Wells. They contrasted with the wild flowers, some of them drooping, which adorned most of the graves. A handful of people returned to Whytbrook house for sherry and light refreshments. Hannah was amongst them, though her sons both left immediately after the funeral to change into working clothes and get back to work. Whatever the circumstances, the farm still had to be attended to. Hannah recalled hearing her mother-in-law speak of the great funeral teas of the north-country, but she sipped sherry politely.

Barton, the sexton, was the most important person in Whytbrook at this time, at least in his own view, far more important than either the widower or the vicar. Though not one of those who joined the family after the funeral, he might well have been with them. Later in The Bell, that same evening, he regaled everyone with an informed description of the gathering, down to the very last biscuit. He had also acquired - and goodness knows from where - the most meticulous details about the long, stressful journey made from Switzerland to Whytbrook by the farmer with his late wife.

"Poor man," said the inn-keeper's wife, who had just come into the bar and listened for a moment or two intently. "What a sad experience! But, of course, he wouldn't want to leave her in a foreign country, that wouldn't be right at all. But fancy shutting him up in a carriage with the corpse! It fair gives me the creeps, does that! Who'd want to go stealing a coffin, I wonder?"

Barton looked at her severely.

"Some folks'd steal anythin', ma'am," he said. "Sides, 'tiz the law on t'contee-nent."

Suddenly the woman gave a small gasp, as she prepared to pull a pint. She had remembered something; the delayed sheep-shearing festivities, to which she had not been invited. She reminded the customers of this occasion.

"Fancy him giving parties and his poor wife lying dying. Now, that don't seem right, do it?"

No-one passed any comment.

But Matthew Bevan, not usually noted for his wit, looked up from his eternal domino-playing and said, "Leastways, 'er was a true-born lady was Mrs. Ridley, goin' when weather's nice and fine and ground's comferbul. Not like some, waitin' till mid-winter when ground's hard as iron!" He looked across at Luke and the other smiled back at him. A few of the others chuckled, but Sexton Barton looked offended.

Ever since the sheep fair when the two men had walked back home the long miles to Whytbrook, loudly singing old Somerset ballads (though neither had much in the way of a voice) Luke had felt a decided fondness for Matthew, as though the other had done him an unanswerable benefaction. Matthew might well be as thick in his head as his brawny arms, but Luke was main sure the young man was the best-natured oaf he had ever encountered.

A fortnight after the funeral, James Ridley called at Redesdale Farm. Intuitively, Hannah had known that her old friend would call, sooner or later, though she had not known precisely when this would be. As he had ridden up from the village, along the rough lane from the road, she did not see him until he was in sight of the house. Quickly, she took off her apron, tidied her thick, bright brown hair, which she wore, as usual in a coil on top of her head for convenience, then turned to young Jimmy Coxon, who was with her. She reminded him how he was to do the filling and trimming of the lamps, then she went to the front-door and waited patiently under the gabled porch, while the farmer carefully tethered his horse and walked up the pathway to the farmhouse. The front door was but rarely used, but it was convenient for the parlour, into which she now led her visitor. Aside from Patrick going into the room now and then on a Sunday, when he wished to read his Bible in peace, the parlour was only used on Christmas Day. It was tidy, having recently been dusted, but it was about as inviting as a doctor's waiting-room of the period. As if to emphasise the remoteness of the room from the family's daily lives, a monumentally large Bible lay in the centre of a mahogany table, covered with a red plush cloth. It was precisely placed and it was open. No-one ever used it, even Patrick, as it was much too cumbersome. Hannah's action was quite deliberate, and it had little to do with social custom. Not only did she prefer to keep the repulsive-looking Jimmy well out-of-sight at this time, but the formality of the room raised a curtain between them, old friends though they were, that was seemly and proper.

James scarcely noticed the room at all, but sat down, without waiting to be invited, in the nearest upholstered chair. He was full of himself. The truth is that James wanted what he could not have and did not even realise he desired, this hard-headed, unemotional, middle-aged farmer. He wanted a little, gentle mothering, the assurance that the pain would be made better in due course. Instinctively, he had sought out Hannah, not an especially maternal sort of woman, though she *was* a mother and a woman he had known for most of his life. Furthermore, Hannah was herself widowed, and for the first time in more than ten years, James found himself thinking of her with admiration, even awe.

"I've been thinking, Hannah, it can't have been easy for you all these years, since Joseph went. You've coped very well, really." He sighed. "Of course, you had the boys to help you," he added and sighed again.

Even at fourteen years of age, Thomas had shown enormous good sense. He envied her the boys. What had he got, for all his work and striving? His wife hadn't even managed to produce one healthy child, that lived, not one. Even the girl had died when only a few days old.

Hannah fetched parsnip wine, very good wine, made by Patrick the winter before. She began talking quietly about this and that, but James was not really listening.

He had expected to feel sad; that would only be natural, since they had been married twenty-two years, even if she'd been no sort of wife to him for some five or six years. But he had not expected to feel much more distressed than if he had had to have a favourite bullock put down; and rather less than when he had been compelled to shoot a dearly loved horse. Yet, here, a fortnight had passed and he was still depressed and he deeply resented it. It seemed excessive, even unreasonable. He had had a most tiring time of it, of course, goodness knows. Perhaps that was the main cause for his gloom.

Every time he went away, something went amiss. They were like children! However excellent the men one put in charge of them, they seized upon those periods of absence to get into difficulties. Back in August, a young fool, set to scare away birds from the fruit trees, had gone and shot himself badly through his own hand! Even worse, had been the dreadful accident that had happened to a really good hay-tosser driver, when one of the bars to which the spikes were attached had broken, without the man noticing. The machine had continued to revolve and some of the broken bits had flown out into the driver's body. He was still in Kimsley Mendip Cottage Hospital and very lucky not to have been killed, poor fellow. Still, he would not need to be away from his farming interests in future at these busy times, though he would have to go away sometimes.... That thought brought him immediately to the little lady, a milliner in London, whom he had been in the habit of visiting from time to time.

This was what he found most intolerable, his sense of guilt. His little lady friend may have had several admirers, for all he knew - he had wisely not enquired - but that was a great deal better than a dozen men in a night, which could have been the case had he chosen to call on whores. He had not regarded Amy as his mistress (a word he detested) as she earned her living and was not solely his responsibility. She did, however, according to the girl, have a very large family living in Kent, so James had seen himself as a kind benefactor, in a manner of speaking. There had never been even a hint of a scandal and Mrs. Ridley, being totally unaware of his little lady's existence, had not been harmed in any way. He had never, for a moment, felt the least pang of guilt. So, why now was his too-tender conscience chiding him? It was absurd.

He could not talk of such matters to Hannah, but her company was a curious kind of comfort. He did, however, begin talking of the time when they were both young, for it took his mind from the present. Suddenly, he remembered something.

"Tell me, Hannah, didn't I once ask you to marry me? Can't quite recall when, after some ball, I think."

"That's right," she laughed gently. "It were after t'Farmer's Ball. Fancy you remembering!"

"Oh, we were a couple of young idiots. Couldn't been more'n eighteen at the time."

"I'us just seventeen," said Hannah.

"We boys made a habit of proposing after every ball or grand occasion to someone or other." He smiled slightly. Then he thought that if, by chance, she had accepted him and he had married her (which was most unlikely at that time) she would not have been allowed to wear the breeches. Oh, dear me, no!

They fell silent for a brief while.

Then he asked her, "How many cows've you got now, Hannah?"

She looked startled for a moment, then she said, slowly, "Only the one shorthorn." She noticed his expression and hastened to explain that she could not cope with the butter and cheese-making. Since Thomas left home there had been more work for her in the garden and so on. "Patrick does his best.... " She left it unfinished.

He nodded. But he was not Thomas and never could replace Thomas, who was his own preferred member of the Scott family - after Hannah. It was ill-judged, nevertheless, getting rid of cattle. Redesdale ought to have at least five cows if the land was to be kept sweet and in good heart for the sheep to follow. Even a small herd of heifers, if Hannah did not want the bother of the butter and cheese, would be a lot better than this retrenching.

This was unsound policy, no good at all, in the long run. One had to be far-seeing and prepared to take risks. Willing to spend a bit and lose from time to time, he thought, tranquilly. If the land was his, now....

Even as he continued to talk to Hannah about trivialities (she doing most of the talking in her most leisurely Somerset tones) his mind was busy elsewhere.

Only recently in London and even more recently in Switzerland he had come to realise more and more that land was always an asset, in the long run, even poor agricultural land. If one could afford to spend a little on it - and wait in patience. It was truly amazing the places up which they could take railway tracks these days and more land might one day be wanted for that. Many had fought against progress, but not himself, thank goodness. Then, after its set-backs and the competition from the railways, the motorcar was coming along nicely on the continent, though it still had a very long way to go in England. It was a rich man's toy and frankly, he could not ever see it taking the place of the railways - that was absurd - but if motorcars ever did manage to take off in this country, then much better roads would be needed than muddy lanes.

"Hang on to your land, Hannah," he said, unexpectedly. "It's not worth much now, but one never knows." He knew, as did everyone else, that William Scott had started off with no more than nine acres, a mere small holding, but when the huge emigrations started, many landowners had thought it better to sell land and get something for it (and so see it used properly) rather than risk a series of doubtful tenants. His own family had acquired more land that way. He had early on also seen the good sense of not having all one's irons in one fire. If his farming interests didn't make him a penny for several years, he could happily continue. Still, Hannah hadn't done too badly, he supposed, for a woman. Damn it, he thought, if she could survive all she had done reasonably well, then he could certainly get back his zest for life, before long.

He smiled at her and made to go. She held out to him a hand, a hard, care-worn hand, but far more comforting to him at that moment than the touch of any pampered beauty would have been.

Hannah smiled back at him. She knew he would be calling again in a very little while.

CHAPTER VII

It was just three-thirty on a warm mid-October afternoon; the eighteenth of October, to be precise and, as it was St. Luke's Day and looked like being yet another warm sunny day, Luke had made a little joke at breakfast-time about it being a St. Luke's Summer. And, he had added, before going back to his work, quite cheerfully, that if the Lord was really on the side of the farmers, then he ought to make sure the hot weather came at the proper time, when it could do the most good. He noticed his solid, dull brother had not even smiled.

Hannah went to feed her hens and to collect the eggs, going, as usual, through an open-fronted building on the left of the farm-yard and so, by means of a strong wooden door, which gave direct access to the chicken field. The only other approach was to take the completely open right-hand side of the barton, a very wide gap intended for the animals, and go round the farmhouse. Long ago, there had been a narrow passageway immediately next to the house and dividing the farm-buildings, on the left. This had been blocked off by Hannah's mother-in-law with a good stone wall on the outside and a stout wooden structure facing the yard. Hannah could not recall the reason for this, whether it was to reduce an excessive draught or, more likely, on account of straying hens, and piglets. All Hannah knew was that she had no intention of asking for the passageway to be reopened, even if it did save a little time and was rather more convenient. Oh, dear me no!

There were only the six eggs this time. Fortunately, she had long finished putting down eggs for the winter months. She duly noted the number of eggs on the slate, provided by Patrick. Some people, nowadays, insisted upon keeping the most strict records of everything, in notebooks, but Hannah thought this a lot of foolishness. One couldn't be - well - so *scientific* - not about hens. Some of them were no longer laying, and as they were over two years old, she would soon have to get either Patrick or Luke to wring their necks. They would be fit only as boilers, and not much at that, but good enough for soups, she supposed. That would mean more chickens to purchase in the spring.

She thought of the pig. The prosperous butcher and farmer who lived in Kimsley Mendip and happened to be a relative of the Bevan family, would soon be making his rounds with an assistant to butcher and neatly joint the pigs in the neighbourhood, and then take away with him all that was not required for salting-down by the farmers and farm-workers. Some people slaughtered their own and three years ago Hannah had told Thomas to kill their sow with Patrick's help. It had been a quite horrifying experience, as well as ruining good working clothes. Patrick looked stricken and protested, "I don't think 'ee should ask our Thomas to do this, Ma!" Though Thomas said not a word himself, he had looked grim.

Hannah had never asked him to slaughter another pig.

But, she had assured herself frequently, this had not been mere economy. She wanted all her sons to be proper farmers, real men, not mollycoddles.

The pig, too, would want replacing.

Finally, apart from the annoying prospect of losing Hawker, there was the young mare, which still continued to be fractious. Something would have to be done about that also.

Yet these routine farm worries, which had formerly fretted Hannah out of all proportion, hardly touched her at this time. She viewed everything with an almost unnatural detachment and calmness. For one thing it was out of her hands, wasn't it? Patrick had seen to that. So, let him have the worry! The reality of Redesdale seemed more like a dream, neither pleasant nor unpleasant. She had trained Jimmy to bring in the cow and milk it to the very last drop, though he took about as long to do this, as she had taken at one time to milk three or four cows. She thought of this also with near-indifference.

She was probably saner than she had been in some little time. For nearly four weeks she had not put aside any more cash in what she thought of as her 'nest-box' - not that she was given much chance to do so! But she had not even troubled for over a week to go and see if everything was as it should be and she had not been robbed.

The unseasonable hot weather, bringing about a physical relaxing, had also slowed her emotions. There was even a flush to her normally pale cheeks and small tendrils had loosened themselves from the severe coiling of her hair. But there were other reasons for this mood of gentle hopefulness, almost like the middle stages of pregnancy.

James Ridley called on her almost every day now, though he did not stay long. She looked forward to his visits.

Nothing whatsoever - had been said about a closer relationship, but from time to time, Hannah had thought vaguely that it might be nice to have someone take charge of all the farming worries. She had also thought that, if for any reason, she was to leave Redesdale, this would make all the world of difference to the way Thomas felt about returning home. She was certain now it was just a question of time before Thomas did come back. James was inclined to agree with her, for she had shown him the last few letters from Thomas, which had hinted at a dissatisfaction with his life; indeed, though Thomas was not normally given to grumbling about anything, his final letter had sounded positively disgruntled! What did he expect? He was a farmer, an out-of-doors man.

Yet, now that she was certain of the outcome, Hannah was prepared to be generous. As numerous mothers before her and since, might declare, she said, "Oh, let him have his taste o' freedom, James. I realise now I was a bit hard on him, forgetting he was a full-grown man. But I wouldn't make that mistake again, I think."

And James had voiced aloud what he had only previously thought to himself, "You know, Hannah, you wouldn't have been allowed to wear the breeches, not if I'd had anything to do with things!"

Hannah laughed quietly, but just a little.

"Let our Thomas sow his wild oats, if that's what he's a-doing of! He'll settle down all the better for it, later."

Though the kitchen was large and had a flagged floor, it was still very close in the room, almost airless. A low fire burned in the grate and a kettle stood at the side on a trivet, gently simmering. It would never have occurred to Hannah to take a chair and go and sit outside, so she opened the side window on the left, well away from the fireplace, towards the front of the house. Then she sat down on the seat below the window, next to the red geraniums. She had picked up the local paper, but she was not much interested in Gladstone and his speeches, whatever Patrick might have to say in his favour. Not a soul she knew well had either died or had a golden wedding celebration of late. It seemed odd and a short while ago, this would have made her feel uneasy; now she barely noticed. Idly she stared out of the window. The single-storey buildings which had been added to the farmhouse, blocked out the view towards the barton. There was mending of socks that ought to be done, but she could not be troubled in this heat.

Outside was the sound of loud voices. Hannah's tranquillity was suddenly shattered. Luke! And wasn't that Patrick's voice, more subdued?

"Just leave me alone!" screamed Luke, angrily.

A girl's voice seemed to be mingled with the others, though Hannah could not make out what was being said. Surely, they must be quarrelling! She looked out of the window quickly, but could see nothing. They had moved. They must have passed beyond the low buildings and be making their way to the house through the barton!

Then Luke burst into the kitchen and flung himself into a chair, legs outstretched, a look of exasperation on his face. Patrick followed him, more slowly, and Hannah saw he was leading a reluctant Maisie Bevan by the arm.

Oh, my goodness. Now, what? She arose. Luke noticed her then, but he only continued to glare beyond her at the window, unseeingly.

"What is it, then? What's all t'noise about? What were you fighting about out there!" Not this girl, surely? she thought.

"I thought it best to come inside and talk things over calmly," said Patrick. He had brought forward a chair for Maisie to sit down on, but she seated herself very upright, very rigid in the large Windsor chair.

Hannah looked across at her youngest son, but his lips were stubbornly drawn together.

"I'm expecting," said Maisie, suddenly and her face flushed. She lowered her eyes, but not her head. "I told Luke he'll have to marry me and he says he won't!" Her lip quivered.

Hannah sat down again on the window seat, very abruptly. It was not so much a shock - certainly there was at that moment no sense of moral indignation - but rather a feeling of unreality, even of the absurd. A faint smile curved her lips. Her youngest? Her baby? She had not thought of Luke in that way for a long time.

"You must be mistaken, me girl. At your age - how old are you, anyway?"

"I'll be sixteen next March."

"Well, then, it can happen like that - a bit irregular sometimes. You'll have been told that, surely?" Then she added, for good measure, to make everything nice and simple, "It takes more'n a bit o'kissing, Maisie."

She could sense the girl's shrinking from her words, but Maisie spoke quite firmly.

"I'm sure 'nough. I'm over three months gone now." Again her lips trembled.

Three months? Then, by no stretch of imagination, could this have been some indiscretion on the part of Thomas.

"I'll make us all a cup of tea," she said briskly, as though this was going to solve the problem.

It gave her something to do while she tried to grasp how this was going to change their lives. She noticed the girl was very smartly dressed, as though making a social call, and she was wearing the little flower-trimmed straw bonnet or hat she had worn to church during the summer. No-one spoke while Hannah set about her small task. She moved the trivet into place nearer the fire and gave that a quick poke to hurry up the heating. By the time she had brought cups and saucers, warmed the large brown tea-pot and spooned into it leaves from the cannister, conveniently placed on the mantle shelf, the kettle was boiling.

Hannah took her time. She poured out the tea with slow, careful movements, that had once been judged graceful by Joseph.

"And you think Luke t'father?" she asked, as she handed a cup to Maisie. She looked across at Luke.

"Yes," said Maisie, sipping the hot tea, she did not want. "The Farmers' Ball," she added.

"Ah," said Hannah. She looked again at her youngest son and then at Patrick. "I don't know how you come to be into this, Patrick?"

He looked a little embarrassed, but he offered no explanation and the girl would not say that she had tried to speak quietly to Luke on his own and when he seemed disinclined to listen, she had made the mistake of calling out to Patrick. That had really angered Luke.

"Well, leastways, I think you'd best go and see what Jimmy' s up to. Us don't want him wandering in here right now," said Hannah, suddenly a little agitated.

"If 'ee like, Ma," said Patrick. He quickly gulped down the remains of his tea and went outside.

"Luke'll have to marry me," said Maisie, with childish stubbornness, "whatever he says. He's got to."

"Do your fam'ly know?" asked Hannah, more quietly.

"Not yet."

"Your Pa's not going to like this, is he?"

"Oh him! But that James! He's a rare temper to him. He'd kill me if he knew! Kill Luke too, like as not. So I want it settled."

Hannah looked from one to the other.

"Well," she said, at last, addressing her son, "*you've* not said much, have 'ee? What 'ee got to say for yourself, eh?"

Luke, who had hardly touched the scalding tea, gave a great sigh of weariness.

"As I told her, I don't see why I've got to marry her. Why me? It could've been someone else, couldn't it?" He flustered, his face growing pink with shame. "I mean.... " he said, but said no more. It was a monstrous implication and Maisie did not even trouble to contradict him, as though his words were beyond her contempt.

"Well, anyway," he said, pulling himself together, "I mean - only the one time - and hardly that... "

"Look," he said, as though trying to make out a solid case for his defence, "it's absurd!" He grew angry. "Why, I know folks 've been trying for children years and years! Why, a couple I know.... just the once!" He sounded disgusted.

"Once can be quite enough," said Hannah, dryly.

Luke could not bring himself to look in Maisie's direction. He only knew that he felt trapped. This was going to be the end of all his dreams, his hopes of a better life. He would never be able to persuade this girl to emigrate anywhere, nor would he want her with him. Oh, he was trapped right enough! It was typical of his rotten luck, and just when he thought.... If he'd been a rich man's son, no doubt they would have paid the girl to go away and later she would have married someone else. If he'd been desperately poor.... but, there it was, he was trapped in the middle with the respectable farming community. If only Thomas hadn't gone away....

"Well," said Hannah, after the long silence, which had seemed even longer, and with a renewal of her old firmness, "if you're quite sure, Maisie, then that's it. Luke'll just have to marry you and make the best on it, and the sooner the better. Us don't want folks talking."

She collected together the cups and saucers, and announced that she intended to get Patrick to harness the trap to take Maisie back home. They could both accompany the girl, in case of any difficulties. She swept from the kitchen, and not a single word did the two of them say to each other during her absence.

Taking the trap was unnecessary in Patrick's view, but he saw his mother's mood and he did not argue. Pride, of course. Mind, if there was any trouble, it might be as well to have the trap so they could get away, he thought grimly, seeing no humour in this at all. It entailed a deal of bother, since Jenny, the older mare and thoroughly reliable, who normally pulled the trap (amongst her other duties) had slightly damaged one of her front hooves, and Patrick would not risk letting her walk on the rough road, till it had had his attention. As for the young mare, whom they refused to call by her name, she was still being too untrustworthy. That left Sammy, the cart-horse. His proper name was Worthy Samuel, a splendid black gelding, bred on the Somerset Levels. Sammy was docile and dependable, as are most of his breed, but he had worked hard that day and deserved his meal and a rest. Harnessing the great horse to the small trap was no easy task and Patrick had to find a length of rope to make everything secure. It was a somewhat incongruous picture; Patrick only saw it as an insult to Sammy.

Nor did he let himself dwell on the work he would have to do on his return, but wiped down the old leather seat and even found a cushion to place behind Maisie's back. She sat upright in the middle, between them and Patrick was the only one who spoke on the journey. He mentioned the unseasonable weather, various small items of local news, and from time to time, the girl would murmur an agreement, or, "I suppose so." Patrick was valiantly trying to put the girl at her ease. Luke spoke not a word.

Maisie sat quite rigidly, as though trying to avoid contact with the men on either side of her. She removed the little straw hat and let the breeze blow through her red curls. The tea had made her warm. Also, holding the hat and playing with the little daisies, gave her nervous fingers something to do.

She was utterly devastated. Shattered. All her bright self-confidence had been swept away.

Like not a few young girls of that age, Maisie was a curious mixture of knowing and total innocence. But what she knew was submerged, hardly recognised as knowledge, for it had failed to penetrate the misty veils of romance, which largely occupied her conscious thoughts. She could not have lived in the environment in which she did live, so close to the earth, without hearing snatches of crude conversation now and again and of seeing things better not seen, but none of it had smeared her clear, untroubled spirit. She had no sisters. From her childhood, Maisie's mother had suffered from spells of deep depression, with which no-one (not understanding) had ever sympathised. Early on, the child had been taken under the wing of Mrs. Squires, the former lady's maid, who had travelled and thought she knew the world. Mrs. Squires did a great deal to help Maisie, encouraging her in her fine sewing, her reading, and a variety of little accomplishments. The substance of her faith evolved upon the strong Victorian principles of her day.

"Maisie, dear, you can't help the circumstances of your birth. None of us can. But we can all of us do something to *improve* ourselves." She had added that Maisie's mother had come from a good family. The implication was plain. Mrs. Bevan had allowed herself to be dragged down to her husband's level, rather than helping him. Mrs. Squires loaned Maisie books and some of her genteel magazines. She did an immense amount of good for the child - and not a little harm. For Maisie grew up believing herself to be superior to the other village maidens, never haughtily - she was always cheerful - but quite convinced she was destined for a very different future to the common run.

Thomas Scott was not exactly Maisie's idea of a Prince Charming, but he came closer than any man she had met so far and he would, in due course, Maisie was sure, inherit the farm. Her approach had never been calculated - it was too innocent for that - but she had dreamed in vague terms of a perfect wedding, as though the wedding itself would be a sure guarantee of being 'happy ever after'. She imagined the lovely dress she would wear, even if she had to make it herself. It would be magic. There would be bridesmaids. Flowers. Music. Oh, everything!

And now this!

There was far worse. She now had an awareness she had not recognised and had failed to appreciate beyond a kind of disturbed dream. For years the girl had shared a large double bed, which almost filled the smaller of the bedrooms, with her mother. Whether this was a belated and futile attempt at contraception, who can say, but Maisie had always accepted the situation on account of her mother's indifferent health. Her father slept in the slightly larger bedroom along with his two sons. They were better off than many. From time to time Hugh Bevan had returned home from his drinking bouts and, if not too drunk, he had hammered on the bedroom-door where his wife slept demanding his marital rights. Half-asleep, the little girl had been lifted out and placed in a nearby cot, or laid at the bottom of the bed. More often, they had not troubled to do more than push her aside.

So now, poor Maisie felt soiled in her understanding, all her lovely fantasies destroyed. Not once had her mother, living mostly in a trance herself, noticed anything amiss and Maisie rose early and contrived to be sick in the privy before anyone was up or the neighbours came spying. Mrs. Squires was rather more perceptive and by dint of gentle questioning she came to the conclusion, without distressing the girl too much, which made her give advice.

In order to be 'regular' again the girl was to obtain from the apothecary in the village certain items and make a brew according to her instructions. The apothecary (who sold a great many other things, including pills and ointments for horses) sold Maisie the pennyroyal, poppy seeds and snuff, without hesitation. But after she had taken the vile compound, the only result was to be a little more sick. Terrified that she might produce a creature resembling poor Jimmy Coxon (for Maisie had heard garbled tales) she did not dare to repeat the experiment.

Mrs. Squires had also told her something which she had long treasured. It appeared that some wealthy relations of her mother's, a brewing family living in Bristol, had once approached the Bevans, offering to take young Maisie and bring her up as their own child, having no children themselves. They had offered a considerable sum, but Bevan had been angry and flatly refused.

"Don't tell your mother. It might upset her. But, you see, you might have gone to a Young Ladies' Academy, instead of the village school."

Maisie had never spoken of this to anyone, but she had hugged it to her. Not only because of the future she might have had, but also that anyone should have wanted her sufficiently to be prepared to pay a lot of money for her. It would have been sad to leave her mother, of whom she was fond, but she would have visited her regularly and brought small gifts.

But it was her father's refusal of the offer which had most warmed the child's heart. Her father had always seemed quite indifferent to her (though she had to be thankful he had never been actually violent) but, deep down, he must have loved the little girl greatly. Now, it seemed as though her eyes had been forced open. She saw the truth. Her father had refused to let her go merely out of pride. Love? He had probably never loved anyone in his whole life, beyond himself.

So, now, there was no prospect except to marry Luke, though she did not love him, not one little bit. And, she was sure, he did not love her either. She felt despairingly unhappy and utterly crushed.

CHAPTER VIII

It was a Wednesday in early December and Hannah's frame of mind had drastically altered. In just three days, on Saturday, the wedding would take place in Kimsley Mendip church, Maisie having gone to stay again with the Bailiff family. Hannah only knew she would be immensely relieved when it was all over and they could settle down again. The past few weeks had been trying in the extreme.

Despite the inevitable shouting and threats from the father and his elder son, despite the weak tears shed by Maisie's mother, and despite the assertion, at one stage, by Maisie, that nothing on earth would ever make her marry Luke Scott, everything had finally been arranged. In time, that is, but not that swiftly; certainly not on the occasion when the two brothers accompanied Maisie in the trap back to her home. Several meetings had had to follow, with Matthew putting in the occasional favourable word for his friend, Luke, and poor Patrick finding himself in the unwanted role of mediator, for (to Hannah's chagrin) the three men had stormed up to Redesdale Farm the very next evening following upon Maisie's visit.

Seemingly nothing - even this most urgent of affairs must be settled in haste and without excessive pondering, even though they all of them knew the outcome. The young people, despite Maisie's outburst, were never consulted at all.

All Hannah now knew was that once the wedding was over, she wanted nothing further to do with any of the Bevan family, apart from Maisie herself, to whom (much to her surprise) she had rather taken a liking. But it was upon her coming grandchild that Hannah fixed all her expectations. She knew, instinctively, that the child would be a boy. The thought of him was her link to sanity. Hannah thought about the child far more than either if its parents. She knew she was a little jittery, 'twily', as she termed it, but she failed entirely to realise that she was slipping back towards unreasoning. Twice that day, both before and after she had been to Whytbrook in the trap, she had gone to the place where she had hidden her treasure to make sure it had not been moved, even though she well knew she could not reach it, any more than anyone else. Knowing it was there was her secret strength, and long ago, she had rationalised her curious foible by telling herself, over and over, that whatever happened to her or the farm, she need never end up in the Workhouse. Not she!

There had always been in Hannah an obsessive streak, not helped by her being the youngest member of a too large and busy farming family, and in an age when young children were not encouraged to seek attention and spent far too much time in the company of nursery-maids, rather than their own parents. There had been well over three thousand acres of good pasture land, but when Hannah's father died, she had gone to live with a brother and his wife in the Mendip area on a much smaller mixed farm of less than nine hundred acres. This had not affected the child, but the break with familiarity had done so. She began to hoard small, worthless items, a broken comb or mirror, a few beads, a piece of bright ribbon too small to be of use. They gave her a mysterious feeling of having something that was wholly hers, not to be shared with anyone.

Perhaps it was inevitable that when she married Joseph, Hannah should dote upon him, but this could not be spoken of to anyone, nor did she wish to do so. Joseph knew her feelings and knew why she kept part of an inheritance in the deed-box under the great bed. Joseph laughed over it, indulgently.

"Look after your bit o'gold, Hannah, jest in case I've a mind to take it into me head to run off with a milkmaid or some such little baggage."

"Never you dare!"

Joseph would chuckle. It was a good joke.

But after the good years, there followed the disasters; the sudden death of a little daughter, who was going to grow up to look after them when they were old; the marriage and unexpected departure to America of the eldest girl, Jane, and most stressful of all, Joseph's untimely and quite unnecessary death.

The bad times on the farm had seemed especially bad. Worry after worry. Somehow Hannah had coped with each fresh difficulty, not seeking advice from anyone, but it had taken its toll, far more than even she herself realised. That was the beginning of the really compulsive hoarding; not trusting banks, not trusting a soul really, even her own children, unless she had full control of them. And all of it she justified to herself most sensibly, most soberly.

She could not help her possessiveness over Thomas, merely hide it at times with criticisms or sharpness of tongue, even when he clearly chafed. She had frequently wished she could feel towards Luke and especially Patrick, who was such a good man, as she did towards Thomas, but she could not do so. She had asked far too much of Thomas and now.... Since October there had been no letters from Thomas at all, merely a few post-cards, without any message, since messages were not permitted by the Post Office. One card had been from Cardiff and another of a boat with a large white wheel, like that of a water-mill, taken at Burnham-on-Sea. It had reminded Patrick of a picture of a paddle-steamer he had once seen, somewhere on the Mississippi River. Even Jane, the self-appointed relater of tidings, both good and bad, had nothing to contribute. She had heard, she wrote, that Thomas had left his job in Highbridge, so where was he now? Where, indeed?

James Ridley had called on Hannah once, when she had told him about the intended marriage. He had not been since. He was away from home at present, she knew, but it seemed strange that he had not even written a few lines, when they had grown so close during the past weeks. It was nothing of any importance, of course, and James was a very busy man. Still, it hurt a little.

Lastly, her thoughts turned to Luke. Since her visit to Whytbrook this morning, she had been fighting a presentiment, a terrible feeling that something quite fatal was about to happen to him. That the marriage could not be expected to be a happy one, she well knew and accepted. How many marriages were that happy, come to that? She had been exceptionally fortunate with Joseph, even though he had had a reckless streak in him.

No, this fear was more concerned with the immediate present. The roads were icy, as she had seen for herself, and she had prayed there would be an improvement by Saturday. Luke had rode off to Kimsley Mendip and possibly, he hinted, to a nearby small town, which was holding an early Christmas market. There were pieces of clothing he wanted to purchase for the wedding. He had certainly left it late enough. And how Hannah wished he had not gone off on that ridiculous mare, but nothing she said would alter his mind!

"'Ee can come with me in t'trap," said Hannah, "then try and get a ride from Whytbrook when 'ee sees how t'roads are. No point bein' silly."

Luke merely replied that if he could not make it back home, he would stay overnight somewhere with a friend. He would be calling on the minister in Kimsley to ensure that all was well for the wedding. They had been most fortunate in getting a minister to readily agree to marry them, out of their own parish and under the circumstances. Some priests were very awkward about anything they regarded as irregular.

These heavy frosts were unseasonable for the time of year. They normally did not arrive till January. But then, hadn't the entire year been strange? Disturbing, really. And Luke so impatient. She hoped he would ride with some care. Perhaps she was worrying for nothing. It would be alright. After all, Luke was the only one who could even ride the mare, the only rider she would tolerate. It would be alright. Only.... this awful feeling.... a feeling of helplessness.... This premonition of coming disaster.... and the roads so perilous.

Luke tethered the young mare, made one or two useful purchases, which he stuffed into the large pockets of his coat, then quickly made his way to Kimsley Mendip church, almost as though he was constrained to visit the place.

The church was a sturdy Norman building, standing on a slightly elevated piece of ground with several steps leading up to the porch. It had an unusually large square tower, though no steeple, since Somersetshire had never gone in much for steeples, but the tower gave the church a solid, dependable, braced-against-the-wind appearance. It was empty and Luke stood just inside the nave, beyond the heavy door, which had, as usual, been left unlocked. Apart from a rather fine barrel-vaulted roof and some stained-glass windows, which had miraculously survived both the ravages of time and the Cromwellians, it was a simple little church. A few wall plaques commemorated the lives of various departed members of a local family, the de Kemsleighs, now long extinct.

It was an exceedingly pleasant setting for a country wedding.

For a moment or two, Luke lingered in the shadows, perversely enjoying an imaginary picture, a malicious scene, even though he knew it could hardly be so; the two families would be fore-gathered, though no other guests, since the minister had insisted that it must be a quiet, seemly wedding. The bride would be waiting in the vestry, waiting to be told the groom had arrived and she could now proceed into the church through the main doors. Waiting ever more anxiously, for a groom who had no intention of appearing!

He turned aside and made for his horse. It would not happen like that. It could not do so. When he failed to return home this evening, it would be assumed that he had stayed overnight with a friend, as he had hinted, the roads being difficult. But by tomorrow afternoon it would be a very different matter. There would be a search for him, at first apprehensively, then angrily. But by that time, Luke trusted that he would be well away from the area.

He went on his way, quietly, glad not to have encountered anyone who knew him well; though he did not doubt that in two days' time any number of people would claim to have seen him in Kimsley Mendip. He was highly relieved that the going had vastly improved. Indeed, once he rode out of Whytbrook, the roads were nothing like so slippery. The height dropped. There was more shelter and with every mile there was a difference, a world of difference. He began to feel more hopeful. Perhaps, for once, luck was going to be on his side.

He located the half-gypsy to whom he sold the mare, after a certain amount of argument about the price, but he knew he could not waste too much time over this and that he had no papers to prove that he owned the animal. The half-gypsy shrewdly guessed this. However, the saddle was a good one and Luke managed to sell this for a reasonable price to another cheap-jack. Now he must walk until he was able to beg lifts from any carrier or farm-cart going in his direction.

A faint smile came to his lips and he had a half-hysterical desire to laugh outright, for his nerves were taut. Only in early November when his brother Patrick had decided to plough a small vegetable field, so the frosts could break up the ground nicely, ready for the spring planting, he had set the mare to work. So far she had refused to let herself be harnessed to any plough or anything else, but had simply sat down and refused to budge, no matter how they coaxed her. Patrick said he was really determined this time to make the creature work, for a change. On this occasion, she had not remained firmly planted into the ground, but had actually backed away, then sat herself down, plump down on plough. Not for long, though. The dowel-pin biting into her backside, caused the mare to rise in great haste and go careering away, with Patrick giving chase! In a way, Luke reflected, he was doing everyone an immense favour in ridding Redesdale of this darl'd nuisance, this most 'pestacious' of beasts.

He was still in an excitable state of mind when he reached Glastonbury, though he had been fortunate in obtaining several lifts. He knew by now he had made a mistake. Somehow or other, he should have made his way to Castle Cary and then tried to catch a train going from there direct to London.

The thought of London petrified Luke; but he knew it was his only hope of vanishing completely.

It was growing dark now. A bed for the night would not come amiss. And a hot meal. It was as though he had, unknowingly, been following in Thomas's steps. Indeed, from time to time, for the past hour or so, he had visualised a meeting with Thomas, though he well knew it was most unlikely he would encounter his elder brother. He had imagined telling Thomas the whole story of his hasty departure from Whytbrook. And Thomas, listening, had been most understanding, even sympathetic. Luke could hear his words in his head.

"Not a 'tidy way t'do things Luke, maybe, but in t'long run, far'n way the best 'n wisest. Those Bevans, why they'd never let you go, Luke!"

"That's how I reckoned, Thomas."

"And the two o' you, why you'd only have been mis'rable for the rest of your lives. All your born days! Maisie as well!"

"I know."

"She'll meet someone else, Luke, don't you fret."

But there was no Thomas, no-one to offer any kind of comfort at all, no-one to salve his conscience. It occurred to Luke, however, that as he had come so far it might be an excellent idea to call on the Jackson family, saying he was seeking urgent information about Thomas's whereabouts. Saying he was needed at home on the farm. Then, if he had any good fortune, David and his wife might ask him to stay overnight. It would save his own money, which was vitally important till he found work. He could also make some quiet enquiries about the best way of getting to London (and the cheapest) without arousing any suspicions that he was headed for the capital himself.

So he want to the Station Master's office, politely introduced himself and began his tentative enquiries as to where the Jacksons lived. Almost immediately, David appeared. He looked none too pleased at first. So here was another of these Scott brothers! What did this one want? he wondered. But he listened quietly to Luke.

The young man sounded plausible, because he found he did not even have to lie. Thomas was wanted back at Redesdale, desperately wanted, by their mother, at least. Nor was it necessary for him to play any kind of role. He looked anxious. He looked even pathetic, chilled and with his shoulders slightly hunched. He looked, exactly how he felt, as though a good, hearty meal would not come amiss. Despite his doubts, David softened. The boy looked utterly miserable. He would take him back home with him and see what his good missus could do. He spoke a few words to the Station Master, arranged his work and then hurried Luke from the station towards his home and the generous welcome he was certain Mary would somehow provide.

"So, you want to find Thomas and talk some sense into him?" David asked again, after supper. He nodded to himself. As Luke put it, it sounded reasonable. It did not occur to him to ponder (at least not until very much later, long after Luke had departed) why the younger brother should have chosen to come down to Glastonbury, rather than going to Highbridge where Thomas had last been working. He shook his head, in quite a kindly manner.

"I'm sorry, me boy, but I can tell you nothing! Your brother, Thomas, was a big disappointment to us on t'railway. 'Course, I well knew he'd not settle for being Fireman, though that's a very responsible job, Luke. Very responsible. Could have become Driver one day, perhaps, if he showed real interest. Anyway, our Mr. Curry went to a lot of bother getting your brother fixed up at Highbridge. He must've thought him quite exceptional or something 'cause Thomas was really too old to be starting a new career.

"What happened?"

"What happened? He stayed for a few weeks, and then seems he suddenly made up his mind to discharge hisself! No notice, just went the same day, even lost his wages."

"But, why?"

David shrugged.

"Oh, seems he went off with some friend of his, as worked on a tug, if you please. A gurt, dirty boat, going nowhere in particular!"

"Why?"

"You ask *me* why? I've no idea what madness got into him. He threw up all his chances at Highbridge. Could've had a job for t'rest of his life. Us don't like folks doing things like that on t'railway! When us takes a man on, us likes him to stick, through thick and thin! A big disappointment your brother, Thomas."

He insisted upon taking Luke to the local hostelry. He thought it would brighten the boy and there might just be someone who had heard a word or two about Thomas. This was something Luke would have preferred to avoid, but he went along with David, having no other choice. In the bar that evening there happened to be, by chance, both Driver Bryden, with whom Thomas had worked for a short while and Mr. Curry, the District Engineer. Introduced to Luke, the driver looked him over and remarked, "Well, you don't look too much like your brother, do you?" He then proceeded to speak back-bitingly of Thomas and several of those present agreed. Perhaps, this was for Mr. Curry's benefit, for he turned round for a moment, gave a somewhat curt greeting to the newcomer, then again turned to his own friends. It was as though Thomas having been admitted to an exclusive club, after due consideration, had turned out to be a cheat, a bounder and worse.

Even David had to protest. "Hold on, hold on! The boy's not to blame, is he?"

After that they were all far more amiable, even condoling. All except Mr. Curry. He had been distressed out of all proportion to Thomas's failure. It was not merely that he saw the desertion as both recklessly foolish and disgraceful towards the railways, almost a crime; the District Engineer had also humbled his own judgement, for he had believed himself to be a sound judge of humanity. But, clearly, here his confidence had been misplaced. It made him very uneasy.

When David took his young cousin back to his home, he was given a comfortable bed for the night and a hot drink, but the bed was merely the sofa in the kitchen, not the front parlour, which Thomas had occupied. Luke was comfortable enough and warm, but he could not sleep. Restlessly, he tossed, telling himself he would find work, any kind of work in London, so he had a bit more money before he thought of emigrating. Then, he thought (and his temerity alarmed him), he would seek out Sir Montague Ridley at the House of Commons and ask for his help in going to Australia, or wherever the baronet thought would be best. It had been one thing to argue childishly at a supper-party in Mr. Ridley's home. It was going to be quite another thing to go and request needed help.

But he would do it! He'd be darl'd if he'd go running after Thomas any longer. He was on his own feet now, sink or swim! Briefly, he thought of Maisie Bevan. Now that his decision was made and he felt a reasonable certitude of being able to see it through, he could feel a near goodwill towards the girl; he could recognise that she had not actually harmed him at all. On the contrary. In all honesty, would he have had the courage to leave Redesdale, if this had not happened to force him to take action? He rather doubted it. And the girl would be all right. She'd marry some-one else. Concerning the coming child he did not think at all. He was not really callous. It was that fatherhood had for him no reality whatsoever. He could not relate to any baby.

His conscience pricked him a good deal more about Redesdale. He worried whether Patrick would be able to cope, but surely Hawker would stay on for as long as he was needed and Patrick would find someone else, if necessary. He worried about the young lambs. Suppose some of them arrived sooner than expected? Suppose the winter turned out to be a really bad one, the frosts being so severe lately? He'd miss the lambs right enough. But it would only be for a little while, not for ever. There'd be other young'uns for him to tend.

Then he told himself proudly, that once he had made his way, he would have the money he had got for the mare sent back to Redesdale Farm. That he would! He meant to prosper, but no-one was going to point the finger at him and whisper that he'd made his fortune by being crooked. He had his pride too. People always said things about wealthy men, out of jealousy. And he intended to be wealthy, one day. Then he would come back to England on a long visit just to show them all - and - and - imagination failed. He fell asleep.

CHAPTER IX

It was in early August that Paddy O'Neil suddenly appeared at Thomas's workplace with his proposition, having persuaded his very youthful employer that he was sure he knew just the very man to replace the third member of the crew, who had become seriously ill. Thomas guessed his friend had gone to considerable trouble before he came down to Highbridge and located him.

But even had it not been so, and fully realising he would exchange the modest comforts he had achieved for the utmost discomfort, Thomas did not hesitate for a moment.

The boat, called the William II, was a sturdily-built square-rigged trow, converted a year or so back with an ancillary engine, housed near the small wheel-house, so sails were rarely, if ever used. Indeed, in narrow places, as when the boat passed into the Gloucestershire countryside, it became necessary to unship the main boom. So the trow was really quite different from barges which slowly plied the waterways, more often than not hauled along by horses walking on the nearby banks. In 1880, however, there were still plenty of owners who did not fully trust any kind of boat unless it carried along with it sails just in case!

There was no cabin, nor indeed, any space for one, the only shelter from the elements being the simple wooden structure containing the tiller, and the few other items of importance to the journey, including the log-book. There was an ample supply of tarpaulins, though, and the men merely slung their hammocks anywhere convenient. Life was rough in the extreme with very little space in which to move around for the snaking ropes and the cargo itself; but whenever possible they stayed overnight at some village with friends of the youth, so they could have a hot meal and a good wash. That is, two of them might go ashore, but one always had to remain on deck as a kind of watchman. As the cargo was building stone and sand, this did not add to the general tidiness. They started at Portishead, going all the way up the Severn into Gloucestershire, and then making the return journey, usually carrying timbers of various kinds. They were able to make several trips, though the water level had seriously dropped by the autumn with the drought, and finally, they could no longer continue. They had been reasonably lucky, Paddy declared. He had known some years where it had only been possible in many places to reach inland during two or three months.

Despite the grinding hardship and the dirt, Thomas loved it on all counts. He had been cooped up indoors a good deal of his time at Highbridge, and the natural beauty of the countryside had been destroyed at the site with its functional wharfs, sidings, its own small railway station and vessels. There was also a vast amount of noise. Now, Thomas was in the open air again with constantly changing scenes and plenty of movement. Even when he was soaked to the skin (as did happen on two occasions, despite the mild weather) he felt he was achieving something again, being directly involved and using his capable hands.

All the time he was learning. Paddy, he soon discovered, was a very different person, even on board this meanest of boats, to the comrade at leisure. He never shirked work and he adopted a cheerful paternalism towards the somewhat arrogant and insecure nineteen-year old, Mark. Then he generously set about steadily teaching Thomas, at any spare moments of the day, everything he knew about ropes and their functions - and it was a very great deal.

"Firstly, though," he explained, "though we're going up t'Severn, if you looks at your atlas, to the boating folk, 'tis 'sailing down."

Thomas grinned.

"It was similar with the railwaymen."

"Then, whenever we takes off, 'tis always 'letting went' - don't ask my why! - not 'letting go."

Thomas nodded, smiling.

"And there's many and many more things like that you'll learn in good time."

He set about showing Thomas a multitude of rope skills, demonstrating with the limited sorts of ropes they had to hand and improvising in some cases to make his point. So Thomas found out how ropes were best fastened to each other under different circumstances, to a variety of objects and to the bollards on the wharf, and how to make safe the cargo and the different uses of cord, marlins, ropes, hawsers and cables, though they had, of course, none of the latter on board. He showed his friend how to cope with rotten rope, how to splice neatly, how important it was to get the twisting right, so it did not uncoil, how to cope with extra strain, and with ropes that had become excessively wet. As he talked, Thomas almost felt Paddy had his favourites, as though he had known their families from a long way back, immediately recognising the natural fibres of which they were made, as well as how well. Ropes, said Paddy, with philosophy, could be like people at times: some tending to stretch, some to shrink, and not a few (when they got soaked) a darned nuisance! Thomas learned about serving, parcelling and working ropes; and he was filled with knowledge about hitches, half-hitches, running knots, thumb knots and the good old fisherman's knot.

"You may think you knows about ropes, Thomas, working on a farm, but never forget it can be a matter of life'n death on board a boat."

Above all, there was the fraternity; not only the companionship which grew between these three utterly different men working on the William II, but amongst all users of the waterways and even extending to those living close to the wharfs, whose lives were touched by the boatmen. It was rare indeed not to be greeted by a friendly smile, not to be given any help or direction required, without the least hesitation. There was little of the suspicion of strangers to be encountered in Whytbrook; and if their horizons were far from limitless, neither were they restricted by the gauge of the Somerset and Dorset railway lines.

When the work ended on the William II, both Paddy and Thomas made their way to Bristol, Paddy firstly to see his children and his old father, before rejoining his friend. Thomas was much impressed with Bristol, more than he cared to admit, this being his first visit to the great city. So many tall buildings! Paddy, when he turned up, had much to say about the city. He, who had decried it for being out-of-date with its harbours, became almost lyrical in his reverent admiration before his friend. He had a knowledge (not always historically accurate) of many of the great ships, which had sailed from Bristol in the past. He told Thomas that quite early on ships had sailed from Bristol as far as Iceland and America.

"Well, you'll have heard of Cabot, maybe? 'Tis not so unlikely as some of me own kith and kin set sail with Cabot when he was seeking a new route to the Far East."

Thomas burst out laughing.

"Now, here's a rare cock'n bull yarn, if ever I heard one! Didn't you tell me plain it was your grandad first came to Bristol from Ireland, trading with corn and fish and hides, eh? Cabot, if I'm not mistaken sailed long afore that, in the sixteen hundreds, I fancy."

Paddy was quite unabashed.

"That was me father's side. But what of me mother's? I'm not saying it was so, mind. I've no idea where they came from, to tell the truth, but it could've been like I said."

Thomas was still laughing, and presently Paddy joined in, good-naturedly. Bristol still seemed to him overwhelmingly large, so what must London seem like?

Soon he was able to find out for himself, for the two men got themselves engaged on a much larger boat, sailing from Bristol to London. Paddy happened to be well acquainted with the skipper, Captain Matheson.

The Welsh Princess was fully sea-worthy, but from her appearance, not a great deal more than that, being shabby of sail and well past her prime, but her owner-skipper could not afford to do more than the minimum to keep her going. Even so, when she was fully rigged, from her main sail through to the little moonraker she was a splendid sight. She had not the graceful elegance and flighty speed of any clipper-type ship, being a little top-heavy, as becomes a dowager, but she could still lift the heart on occasion. She carried a figure-head of a flimsily-clad maiden with flowing mellowed gilt hair, a diadem on her head, which symbolised the boat's name.

Built in 1859 in Cardiff, the Welsh Princess was a three-masted wooden barquentine, some one hundred and twelve feet long and weighing over 200 tons, and she would have been quite capable of deep-sea sailing in any reasonable conditions. She had, in fact, been intended originally for that purpose, though her design was not quite right for maximum speed and already steam was increasingly threatening sails, even at the date when she left her dock. Mr. Matheson now kept solely to coastal trips to London and back again. Even at that, competition from the railways had been fierce and the skipper realised, being almost seventy years of age, that when the Welsh Princess could no longer safely continue, he would also fade out of the picture. Nevertheless, though it took them a full eight days to get to London, such boats as the Welsh Princess could often accomplish the journey cheaper than the railways. They had none of the delays, inevitable when different railway companies, not always cooperative, were involved; they paid their men less and they did not have the very high costs of engine maintenance to consider. They were also willing to carry goods, either cumbersome or dangerous, at which the railway companies balked. The patched canvas sails were of hemp and not cheap, and both the captain and his bo'sun would have preferred fine cotton, as this was much less porous, and no more weighty, but they knew this would have been a mere luxury. The men were engaged, initially, for a single trip, their wages to be paid at the end of it.

Now there were sails about which to learn, though Thomas soon realised it would be some time before he was allowed to do anything other than the most menial tasks, chiefly helping Paddy. But learning all the time.

"And for God's sake," said Paddy, "you'd best learn fast this time, man, or you'll be left stranded in London!"

Despite this grim warning, the skipper took quite a liking to Thomas and spoke to him on several occasions, questioning him about himself. He had his story ready. He had left the farm as times were bad, and as his younger brothers were now perfectly capable of managing without him, Thomas said, and he meant it, that he had always wanted to go to sea. Not a word did he say about the crazy way in which his fate had been settled and he thought it wisest not to mention the railway experience at this time.

The skipper nodded.

"I think you must be mad, Scott, preferring the sea to the dependability of the land!" He was smiling, but there was a hint of envy in his voice. "Why, if I'd known any other sort of life.... And I'll tell you what, Scott, when I do pack it in, I'm going to find myself a cottage with a good bit of land and sit quietly and watch the roses and the cabbages grow!"

The old sailor's dream, thought Thomas. And they all think that's all you have to do - sit back and watch nature do everything for them. For a moment or two, he paused to cast a thought towards Redesdale, wondering how his brothers were coping and telling himself probably a lot better without him. Patrick had relied upon him too much to do his thinking for him. He thought then briefly of his mother, Hannah. Once he was properly settled he would write her a long letter, he told himself, but he would not want to worry her at present.

Apart from a man falling overboard during a heavy lurch and very swiftly brought out, fortunately, for the sea was icy cold, it was a quiet enough voyage. The bo'sun did not fail to address the poor fellow very sharply, not only for scaring them all, but because the accident had been largely his own fault as he had not taken adequate care. The men fished from time to time when the current ran to their liking, using any kind of makeshift tackle they could find, and not much caring whether they caught anything or not; it was simply something to do to fill in the odd half-an-hour. Once the boat was preparing to round the difficult waters near Land's End, there was no time for fishing nor anything else. There were certainly no attempts by 'wreckers' to misdirect the boat by deliberately placing lights so that, in poor weather conditions, the sailors thought they had sighted a lighthouse. That all belonged to the more romantic past.

Thomas noticed that the sextant more usually than not rested on the skipper's bunk, when not in use. It seemed an odd spot for it to be, but handy. There was clearly going to be no time for this vital piece of equipment to be explained to him, though he watched closely whenever he had the chance to do so. It seemed there was a special way of even lifting the instrument out of its case.

None of them, including the skipper, wore any kind of uniform, which they would have regarded as an affectation when there were no passengers nor tourists to delight. When he went ashore, the skipper put on a smart, hard hat.

The weather suddenly worsened in mid-December and the skipper let it be known they would be making but one more trip, then waiting till the spring. He was hardly considering the comforts of his crew. The barquentine needed some repairs and it would be altogether too foolhardy to risk seriously damaging her or worse, let alone ruining the cargo they carried, a variety of grains, as well as sugar, which had been transhipped in Bristol, from much larger vessels. Not only did the insurers take their time about settling claims, such disasters gave a very bad name to the boat and her skipper.

Paddy O'Neil decided as it was so close to Christmas and he was feeling sentimental, that he would sign off in Bristol. His old father was now very frail and his estranged wife had apparently written him a pathetic letter saying his children wanted to see him. Thomas had come to realise that his friend did not care for boats like the Welsh Princess; he much preferred canal and river work, or possibly even hobbling. For himself, he was longing to get really 'to sea'. In Bristol he made a few tentative enquiries and finding nothing, decided to continue to London and seek work there. Skipper Matheson was agreeable and wished him the best of luck. With all the boats and ships about, he reasoned to himself that he ought to find something, however humble. He started off very hopefully, going the rounds of the docks, but it seemed no-one wanted to sail at that particular time and they certainly did not want to take along with them a mere 'greenhorn'. Skipper Matheson had actually written him a recommendation, without giving too great details about the length of time he had worked on the Welsh Princess, describing Thomas as 'a young man of promise'. It was not enough and Thomas soon began to realise he might have done better to continue on the Welsh Princess back to Bristol and try again with the smaller boats. Did nobody want to sail in winter? After tramping the docks for two days he was dismayed.

He had wisely found himself lodgings at a Seamen's Mission, partly to conserve his very slender purse, but also in the hope that he might meet up with a sailor who could point him in the direction of a likely boat. As no-one was allowed into the dormitories till the evening to safe-guard the bags and meagre property of the men, Thomas was forced to seek shelter wherever he could during the daytime. He spent more time in various churches than he had done in his life. He even visited a large art gallery, though he cared little about any kind of art and knew even less. He pawned his father's hunter-watch and bought cheaply several books, though he had never taken kindly to book learning. These three were different, though, and anything he could glean would be helpful. One was a well-worn copy of the classic, 'A Universal Dictionary of the Marine', first printed in 1781; then there was another about the

arise on a ship due to sail within hours. This would be his chance. They would not be over-fussy about whom they engaged.

It was a remarkable experience. The den, which was housed close to the docks, had been divided into minute rooms, all having low ceilings; and the entire place reeked with the odour of the fatal poppy and heavy smoke fumes. There was a kind of shop at the front and a cheap cafe, serving grills. Behind were a number of small rooms, containing a divan, but no occupants. Upstairs, all the tiny rooms had mattresses laid closely together on the floor, then on berths around the rooms in three layers. It seemed obvious that even a room of no more than 12' x 8' could contain at least ten to fifteen people, all tightly squeezed together. No-one took the very smallest notice of Thomas as he moved from one room to another, stepping over prone bodies and, in fact, most of these upstairs rooms were also empty. It seemed a disappointment. Where had all the smokers gone this evening?

He found them on the third floor. They had piled up mattresses and laid on top a soiled cover, so forming a makeshift table. A large group of men was excitedly gathered around. They were gambling!

It was a game of Chinese origin, which Thomas did not comprehend, but for several minutes he watched with interest. Few of the sailors could speak much English he found, but there were one or two capable of talking to him in stilted terms. So it was, as luck would have it, that he was told, casually, of a Dutch ship, which had been hoping to sail that very evening. His informant was unable to explain any details, but Thomas concluded there had been some transgression and a sailor had been sent packing, as a result of which his fellow-seamen had, in their own worst interests, staged a petty mutiny.

Thomas did not scruple. He sped to the Mission, flung the few items he had troubled to unpack into his bag, and hurried off to the Van Dyck.

He was almost turned down. His appearance, despite weeks of hard living, was very different, suspiciously different, to that of the average pitiful deck-hand; yet, upon the other hand, he could offer no certificates to qualify him for much else. Had this one arrived to stir up more trouble? However, time was pressing. The Van Dyck was still very short of crew and as she carried a few passengers as well as cargo, the ship's captain was anxious not to delay further. Once again, Thomas's good manners, his obvious healthy looks, tipped the balance in his favour. He was polite, without being servile.

The Van Dyck was an iron-clad steam-boat, very efficiently run, cleaner than any boat Thomas had so far visited - though it seemed to him later that he spent a vast amount of his time keeping the decks in such a pristine condition - and the food the crew ate was decidedly better than any he had come to expect. The pay was also marginally better. But, withall, he could not be sorry he had been taken on for only the single trip, lasting approximately one month. He felt he learned little and did not belong anywhere. The Dutch officers ignored him, except to give orders; to the rest of the crew he meant nothing at all. They could not relate to him, a strange experience for Thomas.

The Van Dyck had started from Holland before coming to London, and it now made its way to Denmark and the Baltic, before returning to Rotterdam. This was Thomas's first taste of foreign travel and sometimes a considerable time was spent in ports, but the weather was bitterly cold, and he did little exploring beyond the vicinity of the various docks. Yet, in this poor weather in a difficult part of Europe in winter, he was not seasick, even once, and he knew, moreover, that he loved the sea. This must be his life. If only he could find a ship like the Welsh Princess, perhaps a little larger, but sail, he felt he would be happy. He missed Paddy far more than he had done in London. He missed the comradeship on smaller boats. Everything on board the Van Dyck was meticulously ordered, though it always smelt unlovely to his senses.

When the ship finally docked at Rotterdam just before February ended, Thomas made his way back to Tilbury, lucky enough to be taken on as a deck-hand for the passage across. Then began another search for work.

Briefly, he considered the Navy, but dismissed the idea. It did not appeal; it would be the same story - he was too old to commence years of study and training, if he was to amount to anything. It was ironic, though, when fifty years ago and less men had been employed as press-gangs, supposedly seeking volunteers where they could, but quite prepared to use force, if need be. Conditions had been very bad then, and he still much preferred the freedom of the merchant service.

For the first time he questioned the sanity of what he was doing when there was a good life waiting for him back home, a life he thoroughly understood with people who valued him and cared deeply about him, even if he did detest sheep. Yet, he reasoned calmly, that was the coward's way; if he stayed quietly convinced that something would come his way, if he remained stubborn about his determination to get back to sea on a good ship, no matter what he did, then things must work out. The spring was on the way. That would make a big difference. After all, there had been plenty of ups and downs on the farm. He had found for himself some very cheap lodgings and again he pawned his watch.

It was at this stage that Thomas discovered those humble souls, far worse off than himself. Almost by chance, he stumbled upon various groups, living on a waste piece of ground, but a short distance from one of the docks. These were the raggle-taggle; a few half-gypsies, tramps, who still preferred the out-doors to any institution, and the seasonal workers. A few of the better-off had caravans, but mostly they had made for themselves pitiful, make-shift bivouacs out of whatever came to hand. Such dwellings looked hardly capable of withstanding the grim cold. Amongst this crowd were several Irish, who had flocked to London, for reasons best known to themselves, perhaps thinking it would offer the chance of some casual employment until they could leave to go hop-picking and so on. There were discontented rogues, without any kind of purpose and with hardly a scrap of intelligence to have earned them any kind of living. Such would have stolen from Thomas (little though he had) without compunction.

But amongst the groups were some genuinely decent, hard-working folk, if childlike in their expectations of life. They were simply following a way of life they had always followed and which they did not trouble to question. They were seasonal workers on farms, as well as hop-pickers and, like moles, they went to ground in winter. Thomas fell into conversation with a few of them.

A man told him he had slept rough for most of his life, usually under railway arches, but now that he was getting on a bit, he preferred more shelter and more companionship. Next year he was going to get himself a room in a lodging house. Another man, who had his family with him, told Thomas he had travelled the length and breadth of England, working wherever he was wanted, when he was single, but now he went each spring back to the same farm, where he was always expected and welcomed. His wife, meanwhile, earned a little by doing sewing of a rough nature. A sheep-farmer, this was an aspect of farming Thomas had never considered. Each group kept quite separate from the others, like minute villages.

It was almost a pleasure, as well as a great relief, to be taken on immediately when he enquired at the warehouse, for which he had previously worked. He made up his mind that when they did not want him any further in some week, he would not stay about in London, but make his way to Southampton, where he was sure there would be better opportunities.

Yet, it was at the warehouse that Thomas had a chance meeting, that was to drastically alter his whole life.

Captain Aldridge had a friend in the Far East and he had promised to despatch to the captain a few antique Ming vases, as well as a coffee service of eggshell porcelain, for the collecting of delicate oriental china still continued to be fashionable with the well-to-do. Copies of the relevant papers had been received and the crates ought to have been on a certain vessel. But they had not come to hand. Exasperated, the captain had gone personally to the warehouse handling the ship's cargoes.

He addressed Thomas, as he happened to be readily to hand and looked, in his view, 'as though he might have a bit of sense', as he put it later to his young daughter. Thomas left his work and busied himself, and after about ten minutes his sharp eyes discovered two small crates, which looked hopeful. The markings were nearly obliterated. Captain Aldridge was able to confirm that the crates belonged to him, and after completing the formalities, he had them put on one side ready for collection.

"I'm hoping you'll find everything in order, sir," remarked Thomas.

"So'm I. The Lord only knows what might have happened on the voyage, though they swear to pack everything so thoroughly, even this fragile stuff is considered virtually indestructible. Thanks for your help, young man. They've a lot of fools round here!" Then, he looked at Thomas again. "Haven't I seen you somewhere before? There's a look about you that's - well- almost familiar."

"I was here for a short time before Christmas, just before I managed to get taken on the 'Van Dyck'."

"Ah, that must've been it, then. He continued to stare at Thomas, quietly, reflectively, and in some puzzlement. In fact, he had not seen Thomas earlier, but he bore a passing resemblance (which the captain himself did not realise till much later) to a young nephew, killed in South Africa. The boy had been as a son to him, having no sons.

The captain continued to linger and talk to Thomas, questioning him about his experiences at sea and about his life before this. Some impulse compelled Thomas to be quite frank, without mentioning the crazy way in which his fate had been decided, so he spoke of working on the railway, both at Glastonbury and Highbridge.

"What I don't understand is why you didn't make your way direct to Bristol or London, if you wanted to go to sea."

"I had to take whatever work offered, sir," said Thomas. I'd family in Glassen to help. I suppose I was waiting for my chance." He smiled wryly. "I'd no idea it was going to be so hard - to find a berth, I mean."

Then some petty official called out sharply to Thomas, demanding that he get on with the work assigned to him. Thomas shrugged, smiled at the captain - for by this time he knew the other was a captain of a large ship - and made to leave. Captain Aldridge detained him with a hand on his arm.

"Just a minute, young man. What's your name?"

"Scott, Thomas Scott, sir."

"Well, Scott, this is my card. Try and see if you can come down to my ship this evening. I'll be on board then; and we're sailing in less than a week. Ask for Mr. Bates, my Chief Officer. I'll get him to come down to the ship as well. I'd like him to meet you. We might be able to fix you up. We'll see. The S.S. Great African, don't forget!"

A shortish man with a fresh complexion, white hair, glasses and the most innocent of blue eyes, which reminded Thomas briefly of his brother Patrick, the man did not look much like a sea captain.

Thomas answered gravely.

"Thank you very much, sir. I'm willing to do any mortal thing which lies in my power, if I can get taken on a good ship."

"Well, we'll see, we'll see. It'll be for others to decide, really. I can't interfere, but should I recommend you to my Third, he'd probably agree." Captain Aldridge looked for a moment mischievous. "See you tonight, then, about seven, with a bit of luck?"

Captain Aldridge bustled away.

Thomas was elated, not to say, overwhelmed, but also cautious. It was surely unusual for a captain to be bothering himself about someone as humble as he had become? Where was the catch? There must be one, surely! Then he brightened. Need there be one? And if so, what did it matter? He could cope with it, somehow.

Thomas left his cheap lodgings that evening, which were only a short walk from the Seamen's Mission, where he had previously stayed. But all about him was a strikingly different world from that orderly routine he had known. There were the saloons, which as the evening proceeded, would become increasingly rowdy. Every nationality under the sun, it sometimes seemed, congregated there, from light-haired Norwegians to negroes, consorting with tawdrily dressed 'hostesses'. Towards dusk, from many of the lodging-houses girls would emerge to stand in doorways, yelling out to any passing man. Sometimes they became demanding and tried to grab hold of a half-reluctant male. Apart from having no money to spare for these unappetizing creatures, Thomas was altogether too wary after all that Paddy had told him. Sometimes there were a few freaks, possibly male, but dressed up and painted. Even to walk in some of these dark streets at night was risky. Yet by day many of the buildings appeared as solidly-built brick erections, reassuringly respectable. Perhaps they had once been so, but sadly had degenerated and housed, often enough, a multitude of every kind of malefactor.

Ever since Brunel's Great Western had crossed the Atlantic, in 1838, taking fifteen days and five hours to reach New York, though beaten by four hours by the Sirius, sailing from Cork, a sense of pride and perhaps injury had encouraged some ship-builders to assume the name 'Great' for their steam ships. Yet the S.S. Great African fully deserved her name, in Thomas's view. He stood and looked at her, anchored some little distance from the quay, as a position had not yet been allocated to her. She was well over a thousand tons and capable of carrying some 360 passengers, as well as much cargo. She had chemical refrigeration for the storage of some goods, brought back from South Africa or India, for she did alternative trips. One time she went around the Cape via the West Coast and then up the east coast and through the Suez Canal, which had been opened to traffic in 1869. On her next sailing she went down the Suez, crossed to Bombay and Ceylon and then made her way to the Cape and so back to port in London. She had twin screws and electric light.

Thomas hired a boat to take him to the S.S. Great African. He could see this was a luxury ship and everything he was later told confirmed it; and yet there was a giant note of disappointment. What a pity she was not sail!

There were few people on board. He enquired for Mr. Bates and was presently greeted by the Chief Officer, who led him, without hesitation, to the captain, who was dressed in uniform this time. He was offered a drink, though Thomas, who had eaten little that day, would have preferred a good meal, but he surmised that this was the way with it of such people. The conversation was easy and he was treated without the least hint of condescension. The captain asked his officer to explain to Thomas something about the ship and its working, and from the way everything was expressed, Thomas knew he was being considered for a very sacred trust, in his opinion. For all its size and grandeur, here was another little world, self-contained in many ways, like the Somerset and Dorset Railway. Thomas could not quite make out whether the boilers had not been designed quite large enough or there was some trouble regarding the storage of coal (the officer was very explicit on this point) but expensive bunkering en route was always necessary. It seemed, too, that the ship was still using sea water, so the four boilers had to be regularly desalted. (Some instinct told him, 'This is going to be your job!')

"I see the ship has three masts, sir," remarked Thomas.

"Yes, and we once had six," the officer replied.

"So, the ship carries sails?"

Captain Aldridge smiled and spoke himself directly to Thomas.

"A certain amount and let's hope we never need them! But few passengers, even in this enlightened age, Mr. Scott, are prepared to trust themselves wholly to steam, not going all that way round the Cape, I'm afraid."

This gave Thomas his opportunity to tell of his brief experiences on the William II. There was a moment's silence. To Mr. Bates this young man's almost non-existent knowledge of ships was irrelevant. As far as he was concerned, Scott would have to learn from the beginning.... but if the captain had got some bee in his bonnet, well there it was.

Yet, in the end, Captain Aldridge had spoken calmly and quite sensibly.

"If you're looking for romance with the sea, you'd best forget about being a sailor, Mr. Scott and go back to your farm. Sails may look splendid, but they belong to the past. Everyone will have to face that fact sooner or later. It'll be a hard life, hard and dirty. But if you want to be a trainee engineer - well, I reckon from all you've told me you know enough about how engines work to be of some use. You say you've always been handy with machinery?"

"Yes, farming equipment, but the railway was my first taste of a steam engine, though neighbours owned one to power the harvester." He was thinking of Mr. Ridley.

The conversation continued and Thomas thought, 'It'll be back to shovelling coal, Thomas!' Curiously, he found he did not mind.

He left the ship a short while later, having been given directions to report in a day or two to someone else, another officer. Whatever Captain Aldridge said, sails took a lot of beating. The clippers were still carrying tea and often able to compete, not only on price, having no expensive coal to buy, but on time. They clipped off the days and the hours on journeys and had become a symbol of all that was finest with sailing boats. Why, Thomas thought, a clipper had been built only some five or six years ago. That was surely not to be the last of them? He sighed, just a little. One day, perhaps.... Meanwhile, he had to be thankful that fortune seemed to be smiling on him. He was very well aware that Captain Aldridge had taken a liking to him and he accepted this, without vanity, prosaically. He only hoped he would not disappoint him.

Two days later he went again to the ship, this time berthed at one of the quays. It meant taking time off from his work at the warehouse, for which he was paid daily. It was a fruitful visit, however, and the details of his engagement were quickly settled. What he did learn that day surprised him. It seemed the captain had it in mind to help Thomas obtain his 'tickets', the necessary certificates of qualification for promotion on the ship, provided he worked well during this first voyage. He would have to study, a prospect which did not appeal very much, and would then have to sit some kind of examination.

"How long will this have to last?"

"It's up to you, isn't it? Could be years."

"Then what?"

"Then what? You could end up as a proper officer, even a captain one day!" The third officer laughed, as though he thought that highly unlikely. "Think yourself very lucky indeed. Not many are given a chance on a ship like this one. It'll be up to you. I'm not letting you get away with anything, but if you shape up - well, then, you've a good future, a job for the rest of your working days."

Thomas grinned, but there was an echo in his mind. Where had he heard that phrase before, 'a job for the rest of your life?' It made him feel faintly uneasy, as though he was about to walk into a trap.

The third officer was speaking again.

"Captain Aldridge has no need to work at all," he announced, as though this was the height of human achievement. Apparently, the captain had financial interests in the small line - there were two sister ships, somewhat smaller.

"So, you're very lucky indeed he's taken an interest in you, Scott." The envy in the voice was plain to hear.

Next day Captain Aldridge surprised Thomas yet again by coming down to the warehouse to speak with him. He was still bemused and even more so when the captain said he wanted the younger man to meet a member of his family, who was anxious to meet him.

"Once you've joined the Great African on Tuesday, you and I'll have no more contact till the voyage is over. We'll live in different worlds. I'm sure you understand that, but I'll be receiving reports on your progress, from time to time. Nothing goes on that I don't learn about, sooner or later. He beamed and once again, Thomas had a feeling of unreality. So far there had been no hint of anything sinister, yet. "You've clearly had responsibility in your life and I think you're capable of accepting it again. I see you as a natural leader, Scott."

"Thank you," said Thomas, quietly. A natural leader. How often had this not been said to him at times in the past. But did he really want to lead?

"I'm inviting you to tea on Sunday to meet a member of my family, whose opinion I value. Spruce yourself up a bit."

It was an order, rather than an invitation, and not very convenient as Thomas was working till the last minute to earn every penny he could. Would he have time to redeem his father's watch from the pawnshop this evening? If not, they would just have to take him as he was, shabby suit and all.

He met the captain at the agreed place and was led to a waiting cab. The young lady inside, of perhaps nineteen or twenty, was introduced as, "My daughter, Olivia."

Afternoon tea, Thomas learned, was not to be taken at the Aldridge home, but at the Grosvenor Hotel, a most imposing building, some twenty years old. He recovered swiftly from his slight embarrassment. Good manners, he had already learned, could take a man anywhere; clothes not always. Olivia and her father were perfectly friendly, and not a word was said about the Great African. He was very much attracted to the girl. Small and pert and dark, she was well-educated by the standards of her day and not shy at all. Thomas took an instant liking to her, indeed more than a liking. Very clearly, unless the girl was a consummate actress, Olivia was equally attracted. Captain Aldridge beamed from one to the other; and all the while Thomas was deeply puzzled. It seemed a strange thing to be introducing him to his only daughter. He had learned that the captain was a widower. He realised that the man doted on the girl.

As the conversation rolled on about trivialities and occasionally about the farm Redesdale, Thomas questioned the reason for this meeting. A rich man's only daughter could do a lot better than himself, any day!

Was he being assessed to see whether he could make the almost miraculous transformation into an officer, worthy of the Great African? Was that it? They visualised him, after he had been carefully moulded into an image they could, perhaps, accept? Thomas grinned to himself, wryly. The truth was possibly no more than curiosity. The wish of Miss Aldridge to see a country yokel determined to be a sailor.

Just the same, she was a remarkably pretty girl.

The morning after he arrived in London, Luke immediately set about trying to find work that would tide him over till he could emigrate. He had been exceptionally fortunate with his last ride with a carrier to the outskirts of the great city. This man, not only refused to accept any payment (having completed his work for the day and being glad of some company) but he tore out of a notebook a lined page and pencilled down for Luke an address close to Euston Station, where he could find clean and reasonable lodgings.

"And safe, too," he added, in a voice so strongly cockney, Luke had some difficulty in understanding him. It appeared there were, "Some funny places in Lunnon."

"Thanks, I'm grateful to you."

"You'll be al'right there. Don't have much baggage with you, have you?" He laughed.

"I - I - my portmanteau got lost. I'll get some tomorrow."

"Get something tonight, if you can. Looks a bit queer arriving in Lunnon looking for work with no baggage." The carrier also advised Luke to make the remainder of the journey by omnibus and told him where to wait for this transport, outside a hostelry. Luke did as he suggested and the room he engaged, though he had to share it with a total stranger for two nights and was sparsely furnished in the extreme, was certainly clean. Indeed, it smelt heavily of carbolic, and the landlady was clearly a decent, if shrewd-eyed, woman.

Luke was impressed with the appearance of Euston Station with its mock Greek temple exterior, the enormous pillars deeply fluted. It suddenly flashed into his mind that as Christmas was approaching, there might just be work for himself as a porter, for a few weeks at any rate. He was in luck. Staff was needed and though Luke did not give an impression of great strength, he was tall (possibly wiry) and clearly very willing to do all he was told to do. He spoke of the Somerset and Dorset Railway, hinting he had worked for the Company, but no-one was interested. Until Christmas was over he would be paid daily; after that, his continuance would depend on several things.

To his disappointment, tips were very few and far between. He was allotted work moving various bulk consignments and spent much of his time pushing trolleys. Rarely was he allowed to carry the personal effects of individuals; in any event, these were often sent on in advance. He earned just enough to scrape a living, with care, but not a penny could he save for his future plans. He would have to do better than this. It occurred to him to try and find work as a porter in an hotel - there would be scant hope of his being taken on as a waiter - but, at least, if he lived in the hotel, he would have a roof over his head and food of some sort to eat, though, no doubt, very different to that provided for the guests. This idea met with success and he was able to leave the railway station immediately after Christmas.

Meanwhile, he made the best of things. The splendour of the station did not at all match up with its surroundings; there were dirty, cobbled streets all around the vicinity.

Invariably about the entrance there would collect all manner of petty traders, creeping back, no matter how often and angrily railway officials tried to move them from the entrance; the seller of matches, pins and needles and of the shoddiest of trinkets. Sometimes doubtful post-cards. Some of these hopefuls were mere children, raggedly dressed, even deliberately so, in order to gain sympathy from the travellers. The look of sadness in their eyes was enough to gain them deepest pity. There were usually an organ-grinder or two, working in competition with each other; perhaps some sandwich-board men, sheltering for a while near the vast portals for a little warmth before recommencing their dreary trudging. Several times Luke bought hot roast potatoes, as they were cheap and warming from a potato seller. Ingeniously, the vender had contrived to make an oven, mainly out of old tins and discarded containers, crudely welded together. A tired-looking donkey was tethered to the cart, and whenever an irate railway official shouted at the roast-potato seller for blocking the grand entrance, the donkey obediently and immediately moved away a few paces - but never very far and he soon inched back again.

Luke's work, as he pushed and shoved was exceedingly heavy, but it had its moment of quiet humour, for the porters were, in the main, an amiable lot. On Sundays, when he took a walk about the capital, rather liking the look of Bond Street with its discreet blinded windows and its plentiful show of royal appointment signs, he could see for himself that there was obviously plenty of money about in the city, even though little of it seemed to be coming his way.

Nevertheless, he disliked London intensely and what he did not dislike, petrified him with its strangeness. So much noise!

So much bustle! And everything costing so much! He begrudged having to pay even the modest sum he was forced to find for his lodgings. By Whytbrook standards, it would have been daylight robbery! When he had to work late, he was ever fearful of having to walk through dim streets back to his miserable lodgings.

So, it was with much relief that he took up his porter's work with living-in accommodation provided. He was not that much better off; he worked every bit as hard as at the Euston Station, and the food was very far removed from anything provided for patrons or guests. But he felt a greater content. For one thing, he had by this time plucked up the courage to go and see Sir Montague Ridley at the House of Commons, after first writing him a brief letter. The baronet spoke to him at considerable length, arranged a second interview with Luke and promised to do all he could to further his hopes to emigrate to Australia.

"I don't want to be tied up for years," explained Luke. "So long as there's work I can pay my own fare, then I won't be tied." He still had untouched the money he had brought with him, as well as for the sale of the young mare. Sir Montague asked no questions whatsoever about why Luke had left his village in the Mendips. It was not his concern and Luke knew, in his heart, he could be trusted not to mention his name when he returned to that area. It was not, however, a matter of discretion nor trust; the baronet was simply far too busy to bother himself about anything waiting beyond the essential moment.

It was now the third week in April and within the month, Luke would be sailing. He was both excited and terrified. He was sorry, too, to be leaving a young woman who had befriended him, a chambermaid in the same hotel. In a moment of ill-judged fearfulness, he had even made a half-hearted proposal. Why not join him in Australia? The young woman, a widow, some twelve years older than Luke, had shown herself to be far wiser than he. She mothered him. She had taught him a great deal, not merely about the trivialities of sportive sexual behaviour, but more importantly, a little of how a woman's mind works. Most of all, she had kept him from the agonising loneliness of living and working in the vast city. He was genuinely grateful to her; he felt that in these few months, he had matured. Now twenty years of age, he was able to convince himself that once he had left these shores behind him for ever, all his dreams would gradually materialise. Sheep, stretching as far as the eye could see; space, the heat of the sun, and one day, money - to spend and enjoy - perhaps even to send home to his mother. He had managed, without much difficulty, to almost completely forget about Maisie Bevan.

So it happened, that on a Sunday afternoon in the spring of 1881, Luke took his ease in a basement kitchen, always aware that he could be summoned at any time by a ringing bell, but for the moment he enjoyed his peace. The Grosvenor Hotel could be extremely busy, even on Sunday afternoons.

And around this time Thomas was, of course, being entertained and, no doubt, appraised, by Captain Aldridge and his charming daughter in another part of the same large hotel.

The two brothers did not meet.

CHAPTER X

It was a miserable Christmas at Redesdale. In the late afternoon, the four of them, Hannah, Patrick, Jimmy and Hawker sat down to a meal of roast goose, which Hannah had stuffed and partly cooked the previous day to enable her to attend morning service. Immediately after the meal, Jimmy went off to visit his grandfather and Hawker went back to the village ('to walk it off', as he said).

Hannah had not wanted to go to church at all. She had not been there since Luke's absconding, for she declared herself too deeply shamed to show her face in the church!

"Ma, who's to mind? The wedding was t'ave been in Kimsley, and I do hear as Maisie Bevan is still there, residing with the Bailiffs. Who's to know ought about it?"

Hannah had merely given her son a scathing glance and he well knew that he spoke foolishly. Of course, everyone would know what had happened! Didn't the villagers regard the most minute occurrence as being their legitimate responsibility? But at length, Hannah had been persuaded to go to church and Patrick drove them there in the trap, though he would himself have preferred to walk into the village, greeting any he chanced to see on his way. Perhaps the presence of young Jimmy, who had come along with them and even of Jenny and the trap, raised a small barrier of reticence, for no-one spoke a word out of place, though they stared a good deal with speculative eyes; and Hannah was too swiftly invited to the rectory for the following afternoon by the minister's wife, who also promised to arrange a brougham to fetch and return Hannah. This would leave the menfolk free for their sport, the minister's wife said, smiling.

Patrick was relieved. He had been asked to join a party on an estate, Boxing Day being a traditional shooting day in the area. There was no fox-hunting in the immediate vicinity, for the simple reason that the terrain did not encourage foxes, offering little cover in the way of spinneys, bracken and heather; though remembering Luke's arrival with a young vixen the previous summer, Hawker and he were always on the look-out and prepared to stop-up any likely fox-holes they chanced to see near Redesdale.

The icy frosts of early December had given way to milder, but very wet weather, and Patrick rode carefully, only too well aware how much damage could be done to banks if one slithered down them. They could be turned into a muddy quagmire and the grass sliced into spiralled ribbons.

Hares were also very scarce on all the estates at that time, and indeed, had all but died out till their reintroduction several years later. As for rabbits, large numbers of them had been wiped out during the past year, due to the presence of coathe, a terrible disease not dissimilar to that which attacked the sheep. A pheasant-shoot offered a good day's outing, but it could hardly compare with wildfowl, especially as these particular pheasants had been very carefully and expensively hand-reared. Patrick handed over his mare, Jenny, to a groom, then joined a group of men and two or three hearty-looking women, together with the beaters and dogs. The men were composed of a few landowners, publicans, three or four army officers on leave, and the minister of Kimsley Mendip parish church. The shoot was not that tame, however, as strict rules had to be obeyed. The beaters were helped by the small, lively beadles, those plebeian relatives of the aristocratic foxhound, who together drove the spectacular-looking birds out of the undergrowth coverts. The dogs were held back till the birds soared well above the tree-tops, some good forty feet in the air, and not until then was a shot fired. A cleft stick had been stuck into the ground as a kind of marking peg. Missed shots were frequent and though the men always blamed the chatter of the women or the poor light, no-one took the sport with desperate seriousness. There was a good deal of chaff. Not a few wild partridges appeared from among the pheasants.

Hot soup and a sumptuous picnic was brought out to them, when they took a break and some of them went back up to the house. Patrick knew he could not spare the time to continue, so he handed in his gun to be cleaned and locked away with the other shot-guns in the gun-room. In the past there had been many such outings and many social occasions afterwards; but since Thomas left there had not been the time, Patrick told himself. He also knew he would never be as popular as his brother, who had been welcomed everywhere.

He found the time to speak to Farmer Ridley, but only a few minutes. He brought up the topic of buying heifers in the spring, then selling them in the autumn.

"Yes," said Mr. Ridley, "not a bad idea." He had completely forgotten that he had suggested to Hannah that she might try this.

Patrick was still worried.

"Early on this year, us lost a milking cow, our best. You doubtless heard, Mr. Ridley? It was anthrax, Vet said."

"Hmm." Ridley looked at the younger man, hardly knowing what to say. He enjoyed giving advice of a general nature, but it irritated him if he was taken too seriously, knowing not much more about cattle than sheep. "If you take all precautions, it should be all right," he said, sharply. "You did all the veterinary officer told you? Well then. I'd take a chance," he said, comfortably. Then he asked after Patrick's mother, sent his regards and the promise that he would be along one day ere long to see her, though he was a bit tied up with several important matters at present. He changed the subject. He was eager to get back to the shoot. Patrick was given a couple of pheasants to take home with him. It was hardly a day of triumph and Patrick could not but think the very excited, tail-wagging, happy little dogs had scored best. He thought for a moment of his beloved Jessie. He must find some excuse to take her out with him on a short shoot. Patrick had enjoyed himself, for all that. It had been such a relief to escape into the company of ordinary people, with a mental age of a little above twelve years. He well knew he had allowed his head to be over-ruled in the matter of Jimmy Coxon, who was staying overnight with his family.

He wondered whether Jimmy had yet returned from the 'Barrow' as some of the locals referred to the area where the Coxons dwelt. He attended to Jenny, called out to Jessie, who came to him with almost ingratiating eagerness, as though she had not merely missed him, but had suffered deeply in his absence, then he went to Jimmy's room. He stood in the entrance, stunned. What in dear heaven's name had happened? The room was in disarray, the bed pulled out from the wall, the bedclothes tossed aside and the towel, which normally hung over a chair, was on the floor, together with most of the few possessions poor Jimmy owned. Patrick's heart lurched for a moment. Had the gentle, little simpleton suddenly gone berserk? No! He could not believe this. Another person had been in his room in his absence. It was a scene of petulant, childish chaos, as though someone having searched and failed to find what he sought, had taken his revenge. Nothing appeared, in fact, to have been taken for there was nothing of value in the room, but Patrick at once knew what lay behind this display. Inadvertently, Jimmy must at some time have let slip a few words about the box hidden in his room by Master Patrick. It was no longer there, since Patrick had had second thoughts and put the box with the spare cash in his bedroom.

"Jimmy?" There was no reply and for a frightful moment, Patrick feared something might have happened to the cripple. "Jimmy, where are you?" It was Jessie who located the boy in the hen-coop. He was patiently collecting the eggs and marking down each one with a single mark on the slate provided, as Hannah had taught him to do. From appearances, he had already fed the hens. There were very few eggs, hardly worth the trouble and expense of feeding the hens they had left; but since Jimmy could not be expected to do two things at once. Patrick took the egg-basket gently from his hands before questioning the boy. Had his grandfather come back with him to the farm.

Jimmy took his time, looking at Patrick. "'Ee mean t'day? 'Ee mean did Gran'fer came 'ome with Oi, Master Pat'ick?" He nodded, that this was so, then went on nodding for a second or two, as though he enjoyed making the movement. Then he stopped, suddenly. "But 'ee left agen, Master Pat'ick. Jimmy didn't want 'ee with 'im, honestly. Is 'ee cross then, Master Pat'ick?" He looked truly worried.

"No, no, that's all right, Jimmy. Get on with the hens, then go 'n see if 'ee can find Mr. Hawker 'round somewhere. He may be back."

Suddenly, without warning, a redness came to the boy's eyes and he looked as though about to cry. Now what was the matter? He tried not to look at him, but the noise of loud blubbering was not to be ignored.

"Now, what is it, Jimmy? No-one's cross. Did I say I was cross?"

Jimmy shook his head. Then Patrick heard the words, "Me Muvver shouldn't 'ave lef' Jimmy."

What had caused this? Patrick could guess. Some cruel remark of his grandfather or the slut he lived with since his wife died.

"It's a long time ago, Jimmy."

"But 'er shouldn't ought to, should 'er?"

"Well, perhaps not, but you've got us, Jimmy. Now stop bawling and get on with your work, there's a good boy."

He went back to Jimmy's room, straightened the place swiftly, determined not to have the boy more upset, but inwardly he sighed. One never escaped for long. Then a thought struck him. Suppose Mr. Coxon had not left? Suppose he was still looking for 'the box'? He went into the kitchen and then, on an impulse, he continued down the passage to the front parlour. There was still a residue of heat in the room from the fire which had been lit the previous day, but it was gloomy and for a moment Patrick did not see the figure stretched out on the large sofa. For a moment he thought the shabbily-dressed man, who smelled of human dirt and decay, might be some tramp, though they were very infrequent in winter. Then the other, who had been snoring a little, stirred and began to sit up.

"Well, Mr. Coxon, what 'ee doing here?" His mother would be furious, if she knew.

"Uh? Uh?" The other, taken at a disadvantage, grinned at Patrick and slowly got to his feet. "Must 'ave drop' off." He grinned again, showing an almost toothless mouth. At once Patrick felt a compassion, he did not want to feel.

"Best come to the kitchen," he said mildly. "'Tis warmer in there." Coxon ambled after Patrick and sat down as he was bidden. He waited while Patrick struck a vesta, removed the glass-globe from the lamp on the window-sill and having lighted and primed the lamp, brought it to the table the better to see the man's face. He had the good sense not to enquire whether the gifts sent by Hannah and himself had been to their liking. He knew he would not be thanked and they would be regarded as simply Coxon's due.

"What were 'ee looking for in Jimmy's room, Mr. Coxon?"

"Oi weren't lookin' for nothin', but oi do 'ave the h'right to see as 'ow me boy's gettin' h'on!" The old man had recovered.

"There's no money in the room y'know."

"That's as maybe. But oi do reckon as tiz time me and you 'az a little talk, Mr. Scott. Oi've zummat to zay to 'ee! Jimmy's been with 'ee many a month and not a h'penny 'az us 'ave out-o 'ee. Fair's fair, now i'n't?"

"Listen, Coxon," said Patrick, angrily, wishing with all his heart Thomas was here, "if Jimmy wants to give you anything, that's his business, but you must know he barely earns his keep. He's often unable to work." He came to an abrupt stop. In fact, Jimmy was more of a liability than an asset at times. Why didn't he tell the man to take his grandson and get out of his sight? He only said, more quietly, "Look, I've work to do. I can't waste time talking.... " He lowered his eyes and plunged his hand into his pocket to bring out the few coins he had on him. "If you're really in need, take this. It's all I've got with me. Won't the Parish help 'ee?" He raised his eyes and saw that the money he had placed on the table had not been picked up and that there was a look in the old man's eyes almost of hatred. "Go on, take it!" he said, sharply and very slowly the other put the money into his safe inner pocket, the movement deliberately insulting, but before he stowed away the last coin he bit on it, staring at Patrick all the while. "You'd best go a-for Mother comes back."

Coxon laughed as he ambled from the room, still looking aslant at Patrick. There was in the look a volume of meaning so that Patrick felt uneasy, for it seemed to him he hinted that here was the last of Hannah Scott's over-ruled sons. There was also a sly, unfathomable look to his face. Patrick could not prevent himself from adding that Coxon had better not come back and upset Jimmy!

The man turned just as he was about to leave the barton, for Patrick had gone with him that far, wanting to make sure Jimmy was not about at this moment.

"Upzet Jimmy?" Coxon turned away and Patrick thought he heard him mutter to himself something about, "That 'un shames uz all."

Hawker had, indeed, returned and he was never niggardly about defining the boundaries of his work. If a job had to be done, Hawker was willing to do it, provided the sheep had his first priority.

It was quite dark when Patrick heard the sound of the brougham and guessed his mother was returning to the farm. He had already lit two more lamps in the kitchen and now he took one of them to the front and placed it so it could assist his mother alight, for the brougham would not stop in the farm-yard at the back.

Hannah's face was flushed and animated. One might almost think she had been drinking, instead of sipping tea with the minister's wife and her genteel friends! She listened to

Patrick's account of his outing, then she said, "When I was a girl, we used to go fox-hunting. That was real sport!"

"Where was that, Ma?"

"Different places," she said airily. "We travelled, stayed overnight, sometimes several nights." She laughed and became excited and her normal lilting Somerset tones returned, having been submerged during the well-bred tea-party. "I remember once when I was seventeen or so, afore I married your father. What a time we had! 'Twas with the Taunton Vale if I do rightly remember!"

"But did 'ee ever go more'n three or four points, Ma?" her son enquired with interest.

Hannah shrugged. She did not know. She had been no skilled hunter, but she had enjoyed it.

"This time I'm telling you of, the wiley old fox ran right down the village street and hounds after him."

"Where was this, Ma?" Patrick repeated.

"Oh, I don't rightly 'member, round the Otter way. The fox ran straight into the churchyard and 'course hounds had to be called off. I swear he sat there on a grave with his tongue lolling and looking so pleased and laughing at us! Then rumours got about and bits were added to the story and 'twas made out the fox had picked one of the graves of the squire's ancesters deliberately!"

Patrick laughed with her. It was good to see his mother in this mood. It had happened so seldom of late. They had had a terrible time of it when it was finally realised Luke was not coming back. Patrick had had to go to the Bevans and try to pacify them and that had taken a lot of doing. The eldest son had but recently left Whytbrook to take up work in another area where he had a young lady, it was rumoured; or it could have been that he was growing tired of supporting his father. Matthew, the younger brother, who had become fond of Luke, said very little and the father, in a high mood of pride refused the financial help Patrick offered. (Perhaps he had by now changed his mind.) Be that as may, old man Bevan had made far less fuss about Luke's desertion than he had about learning of Maisie's pregnancy. He had blustered, of course, but Maisie was not living under his roof, so it was fairly easy for him to forget about her situation.

"You should go out more, Ma," said Patrick now. "It does you good. What's done, done and 'tis best to carry on as usual. No-one'll ever blame you." It was now after supper and he suggested a pot of tea to be shared between them. Jimmy had gone to bed and so had Hawker, who was presently sleeping in the house to save him the journey back to the village in winter; and also in case the weather suddenly worsened. There was a real feeling of communion between mother and son.

"You're a good son, Patrick," said Hannah, suddenly. "I do know you'll not be leaving me."

"No, that I won't," he replied, but his tone was heavy as though he felt burdened, not only with the past, but the future as well. He shook off the mood and, smiling a little to himself, made up his mind to tell Hannah about Coxon's visit. He would make a little story of it, though he well knew he had not much of a gift as a raconteur. So he began, telling of finding Jimmy's room disordered, though he played this bit down. He had thought some gypsy must have got into the farmhouse!

"Gypsy!" snorted Hannah. "'Twas that man, Coxon, wasn't it, eh? Did 'ee go anywhere else?"

"Well, as a matter of fact.... " he carried on with his tale, omitting that he had given Coxon any money. "He'd a nerve, hadn't he, Ma?" Patrick chuckled. "But I sent him packing." This more decisive picture of the events made him feel better. Truth, however, must always out with Patrick. "He got t'better o' us, though! When I went into t'parlour to put a lamp there so you could see your way up t'steps, what d'you think? He'd taken one o' your little blue glass bits from the whatnot!"

Hannah sat up and like a flash she went to look in the parlour, taking one of the lamps with her. She was back in a flash.

"A thief," she said indignantly. "Villagers have come begging, many and many a time, but stealing.... " Words clearly failed her for a moment. "That was one of my Bristol glasses, given us when we married!"

Patrick was puzzled.

"I know, Ma," he said, "but a finger-bowl! What earthly use'll that be?" He was still chuckling, unable to believe his mother could be angry about such a triviality. "Maybe he liked the colour."

Hannah did not smile, but she grew calmer.

"You must never leave this house unlocked again," she said, severely.

"Well," he said, awkwardly, "I don't reckon it'll happen again." He frowned. "Forget about it, Ma! There's no real harm done, is there?"

She slowly shook her head, as though in deep thought.

"I don't mind if he'd taken the lot, so long as.... " She stopped abruptly. "Have you checked to make sure the box with the spare cash is still under your bed?"

He entirely missed the significance of that statement.

"It's all right," he said, trying hard not to sound irritated. "A finger-bowl, for goodness' sake!"

He patted his mother's shoulder, bade her goodnight and made his way to his icy bedroom. He had only wanted to cheer her up a little, but it seemed he had failed for some reason. He sighed, thinking he would never come to understand his mother.

That he had, in all innocence, just committed a tragic error of judgement, did not for a single moment enter his head.

Early in January there was another outbreak of swine fever and Patrick was glad they had no pigs as yet. Then sheep rot was reported in the Mendips with seven dead sheep at one farm; but the disease was very wide-spread, if not yet severe, with no less than sixteen sheep dead near Bridgwater. Later they heard that a local farmer, who often called at The Wool Pack, had had a very bad set-back. He had sent off twenty sheep to London and on arrival, ten of them were discovered to be dead of the fluke. Not only had all the rest had to be slaughtered on account of this Contagious Animal Act they'd just made law, but the poor farmer was fined into the bargain. There were some who felt sorry for the farmer, but others (amongst them Barton the Sexton) saw in it a moral lesson, directly winged from the pulpit. Had this farmer not formerly traded with Bailiff, the Butcher? But no, he did not like the price he had been offered for his sheep, so he had thought to do business with London directly himself. So much for greed!

Towards mid-month the weather grew colder again. This would cleanse the ground of all disease, remarked the optimists. The pessimists shook their heads. They didn't like the look of those skies, not one little bit! A real dirty white, that. There was a 'gurt' lot of snow up there, they were sure, and it wouldn't be long before it came down.... And the pessimists were right. It snowed and snowed and by the eighteenth of the month, Redesdale and several other farms in the locality were snowed in, marooned. There was nothing they could do about it for the time being, but wait and pray. Patrick did a lot of praying, thankful they had plenty of stores, thankful he had Hawker still with him; and thankful he managed to get the sheep down to the two large fields nearer the house, as they usually did in winter. These were called Long Dale and West Dale, though they were hardly hills, but the ground did slope slightly and beyond was William's long-ago tree planting which, even in severe winters, provided a barrier against drifting snow.

Once the blizzard eased a little and they could assess from their knowledge of the land, how the drifts might lie, the men, together with Jimmy and the dogs, were out. They had to push hard at the back door, but the rear of the house was largely protected, not only by the lie of the land, but also the three sides of the barton. At the front, though, it was a very different matter. The snow had drifted down towards the farm and was piled high against the windows of the front parlour and other front-facing rooms. The porch was completely smothered. The sheep were on fields across the narrow road, facing the front, but there was no question of any direct approach. Reaching them from the back, testing each step, was hazardous and time-consuming and without the dogs would have been impossible. All the sheep were located in time, seemingly quite safe. They had huddled together, not only for warmth, but also for protection against the wind, and almost all of them had turned their backsides to the elements. For all their supposed lack of brain, Patrick could not but wonder how many humans would have shown as much sense. But that was later. The sheep were very hungry, so there was the laborious and time-consuming task of feeding them. Troughs were set up and weighted, so they would not blow over. The wind was more worrying than the snow. Bags and sacks and bales were dragged out, all by hand. It was as he cut the cord of a bundle of hay, that Patrick suddenly smelled on the cold winter air, a breath of last summer and, it seemed to him, of all the happier summers before that. The fresh-mown grass seemed to tingle his nostrils, lift his spirits.

The road to the village was completely blocked and no-one had any time to bother about that. The washerwoman could not visit, of course, and as soiled and damp clothes piled up, Patrick lit the fire of the copper in the wash-house, which also opened out to the farm-yard, and lent Hannah and Jimmy a hand with the enormous wash. It was just over a week before the snow began to clear, the thaw leaving a sodden, bloated, unlovely world, that seemed condemned to eternal hibernation.

Yet despite the punishing swings of mood, already well before February was out there were the most hopeful signs of a slowly evolving and graceful spring. Patrick felt his spirits revitalized. He even found a little time to read some of his few books, trying, yet again, to painfully absorb the great religious gift of noble minds, so often incomprehensible. He found time also to go down to The Bell once or twice. But usually he was too busy and much too tired. The rebuilding of one of the small cottages, which was to serve the new shepherd, was well underway. Sometimes Patrick even lent a hand, chiefly to demonstrate how things were to go and how he hoped to see the results. He dreaded Hawker's departure. The man had been a friend as well as an employee, almost one of the family.

When reading his Bible one evening, his eye fell upon chapter thirty of Proverbs with its passage about the three things 'too wonderful for me'. The final line, 'and the way of a man with a maid,' set Patrick thinking. He supposed he really ought to marry soon. He was now twenty-three and it was high time he did. It would also solve a lot of problems with his mother. Then the thought immediately crossed his mind that he could scarcely select a wife between the lambing, which was drawing very close, and the shearing, as he might well buy a young mare. A useless mare could be got rid of. Luke had stolen theirs and seen to that problem for them - but a wife? Besides, whom did he know? No girls at all of a likely age and disposition.

There was Rose. She was a few years older than he and did not appeal very much; but Patrick's main objection to her was that Rose, for all her sensible spinsterly, bustling, was at heart, a restless spirit. The circumstances of her life would not allow her to travel far, as she might have done in a different age; so she positively revelled in minor disasters, family dramas and household muddles. In her chosen sphere, Rose was superb, trying to bring perfect order and sweet content, crying out for her sacrificing goodness. Would Rose be content to stay in the dull confines of Redesdale for the rest of her life? Never, thought Patrick, honestly.

In late March, Patrick chanced upon a nest with thrush's eggs in it. He knew this was very early indeed and it cheered his heart. For a moment, he suddenly wished young Luke (who knew far more about wildlife than he would ever do) could have been around.

And now was the time of the lambing.

The winters of the south-west being generally short in duration, the rams, or tups, as they were more usually termed, had been turned into the fields with the ewes towards the end of October. Allowing a full gestation period of about five months (one hundred and forty-seven days, to be precise) the first lamb should not have made its appearance until about the 20th March. Unfortunately, this year, several ewes produced their lambs a week or more before this date and one sheep died. Patrick blamed himself for not being more watchful. He carried the small fluffy mites into the kitchen, cuddled in his coat, for the ewe had given birth to twins, which was not at all commonplace at that time.

Hannah, who was at her very best at that time, looked after the first two untimely arrivals, placing them, as she had done in the past, in the oven, damped down and with the door slightly ajar. The feeding was a tedious ritual, but once they had recovered, a ewe with only the one lamb of her own was soon very happily suckling an orphan and the other, not without some difficulty was adopted by a less co-operative ewe, who had lost her own lamb. Ewes, Patrick reflected, could well be like human mothers, incredibly sensible and kindly, but occasionally very stubborn and stupid.

The new man, Cursons, was able to join Patrick and Hawker a day or two after the unfortunate tragedy with the lost ewe and from then on there was constant vigilance.

Always one of them stayed all night in the hut, ever alert for signs of imminent lambing.

In 1881 there was little knowledge of animal vaccines, preventative measures, let alone the feeding of vitamins, so it would have been considered monstrously unnatural, as well as highly dangerous, to huddle together several hundred ewes, all penned up, till they had completed their birthing. The sheep took their chances with the weather and with having their lambs, and every year, however hard the men worked, there were always some losses to contend with. This spring there were no more than five difficult births, at which one or other of the men had to gently and skillfully assist as a midwife and there were no more losses beyond the initial ones.

"Reckon us 'as done very well, Mr. Patrick," said Hawker, one morning with some comfortable satisfaction. Better'n many 'un. Did 'ee see they paper? 'Tis all in as 'ow a farmer over 'yon Kimsley way 'ave lost two hundred lambs this season."

"What?" said Patrick, appalled.

"Seems 'is shepherd give all 'is ewes a big dose of medicine 'e says 'e bought at they fair last year. So 'e says, leastways."

"More likely, he made a mistake and got the containers mixed up," Patrick suggested.

"More'n likely." Hawker nodded. "Lookzo, doan't it? Anyway, all they lambs was 'borted. Two hundred. 'Tis in they paper, Mr. Patrick."

"D'you know t'shepherd, Hawker?"

"No, but I do 'ear on 'e. Seems as 'e was under notice to leave. So some do say as 'e did it all o' purpose!" He looked at Patrick slyly for a fleeting moment.

In early April, Jimmy who had survived the winter surprisingly well, suddenly fell ill with bronchitis and was in bed a full week, coughing for all his poor chest would allow. This added to the burdens, for there was still the rest of the farm work to be attended to, but coming upon the poor little soul weeping one day because he feared he might be discharged, Patrick had spent some time comforting him, and even contrived to do a little nursing to relieve Hannah. For several nights he had not more than four hours sleep, and Patrick needed his sleep.

Cursons, who had been living in the farm, moved into his cottage with a minimum of furniture from the loft spared to him by Patrick, though he still ate in the big farm kitchen. After thinking about it a great deal, Patrick had, in the end, discarded the idea of heifers. He was not going in for any different kind of farming. The young animals would be eating away for months on end and bringing no return whatsoever, he told Hawker. Hawker agreed with him, so Patrick bought three good milch cows, who still had their calves with them, which Patrick hoped to dispose of in due course. How he longed to have Thomas with whom he could discuss these matters! He knew he hated taking decisions, hated having to plan ahead in terms of finance. Yet this was how it must be. It was also apparent that even if he got in temporary labour for the shearing, he might well be compelled to get another man by next spring. Thomas had persuaded them there was insufficient of a living for four men - they would never have dreamed of getting rid of Hawker - but it was clear there was going to be far too much work for only Cursons and himself. Jimmy could largely be discounted. He was simply a small help to his mother.

Cursons did not like Jimmy and was truly amazed that Patrick kept him.

"I heard tell he was a cooper's help one time."

"Yes, from the time Jimmy was twelve or so. Then 'e fell ill.... "

"He's going to lose his bit o' skill and never be the least use to me as a shepherd."

"Jimmy's all right," said Patrick, stubbornly. "Mother likes him."

This new man, Patrick could well see, was never going to be so generous and accommodating as Hawker, who had been more like a family friend.

In March there had been the usual annual ploughing match, the very same event which had killed Joseph Scott all those years ago. Hannah had never failed to mention the fact each year, but this time she did not do so. Patrick was heartened. The match was held on the same large estate where Patrick had gone pheasant-shooting on Boxing Day. In some places the soil was just good enough for wheat, as well as the usual barley. Patrick wished he could have spared the time to go along. He noticed that the prize money of £2 for the first prize and £1 for the second, was precisely the same as it had been at the time when Joseph took part. It seemed to Patrick a remarkably small sum for which to risk a life. Then he immediately saw the absurdity of this thought. Ploughing accidents occurred, but not invariably, and Joseph had simply been extremely unlucky that his accident had proved fatal. Probably he was not nearly as skilled at ploughing as he imagined himself to be. Why had his father joined in, and at such a busy time of the year? They had more help then, but it still seemed to Patrick a curious, even childish exploit. A mood of rivalry and daring? Possessing almost no competitive spirit, Patrick could not grasp this, nor feel much sympathy for a deed which had cost them all such pain.

So improved did Hannah seem, that Patrick told himself he had been mistaken about her; he had seriously misjudged her and he felt ashamed. He recalled how splendid she had been from the time of the heavy snow, always with hot food waiting for them and a fire to dry their clothes. So strong and dependable. She seemed like her old self of years gone by. Surely, he had been all wrong about her. He prayed long and arduously about it. Of course, there had been the most dreadful muddles over money, but Hannah was a woman of good family, unused to handling finances, so the discrepancies could be largely discounted. As for the money she had supposedly inherited and taken away or had delivered to the farm (if the lawyer was speaking the truth) that was entirely his mother's own affair. If she had given it all away to some poor, distant relations, it was not his concern. He determined to put it all out of his mind, as belonging to the past.

He spoke to his mother, telling her of his various plans, trying to involve her, unable to see that her apparent improvement was but a surface showing, brought about through vast, abnormal activity in which she had been engaged. She had done instinctively what she had always done, efficiently and without question, but her mind was elsewhere.

But each time Patrick tried to seek his mother's support, she merely answered him,

"You know best, Patrick. You must please yourself."

He plunged then, awkwardly.

"Ma," he said gently, "I do want to save 'ee worry and all, but I reckon you're not the mere housekeeper, and it's all been a-troubling me a bit. If there's aught 'ee want or need special for you'self, any time, why there's a box under t'bed upstairs.... "

"I know," she said, sharply, unsmiling.

"Well, then, Ma. Take what 'ee likes. So long as 'ee says, so I know 'taint some.... "

She got up swiftly and left the room, going outside to the barton. When she came back in a few minutes, she looked calm enough and she changed the subject. Patrick's face was flushed. Where had he gone wrong this time? He had only wanted to be kind, to be scrupulously fair to her.

Hannah was thinking, how like Patrick this was! He and Luke had taken charge of all the farm's resources in the most high-handed manner! Now Patrick was having some serious scruples about this, was he? Couldn't he comprehend she did not need nor want his doubts? Even if he was wrong (and he had been very wrong) at least Thomas had stayed by his decision. So had her dearest Joseph - always. But not this one! He gave her no feeling whatsoever of security.... Well, thankfully, she did not need anything from Patrick's box. She had her own secret security and it was quite safe.... As though she would have taken anything from his stupid box, like some common thief! Even her temporary indignation aroused in Hannah feelings that almost approached her former warm, quick-tempered nature. But fleetingly. They could not stem the encroaching, irrevocable apathy. She shivered and once again her spirit was over-come. What did it matter, anyway? What did anything in the whole world matter?

In April Patrick came home with some news from The Bell, which he rarely had time to visit these days and which he thought might well interest his mother.

"'Ee'll never guess, Ma!" he burst out. "Friend o' yours got himself promised to wed, not till autumn, so's all seemly, but 'tis all fixed up, they do say. Young woman in Bristol."

"Oh, yes," said Hannah without interest, her voice neutral.

"Farmer Ridley, Ma! Now what d'ee think o' that, eh? He's not wasted too much time! Young woman, at that. Leastways, not young exactly, thirtyish. But too young for Farmer Ridley."

"He can marry who he likes," said Hannah. She added, indifferently, "Perhaps he wants an heir."

"Yes, well.... " He suddenly stared at his mother, pondering. Hadn't James Ridley been a regular caller at Redesdale for a time in the autumn, if he was not mistaken? Hadn't his mother mentioned his visits on several occasions? He had thought nothing of it, as they had been friends in their youth, but now he remembered the way Hannah had conducted herself on the night of the delayed sheep-shearing party at Farmer Ridley's, all those months back. She had truly embarrassed him with her coquettish ways. Was that how the wind had lain, then? Had she seriously imagined the farmer would be interested in her at her age? To young Patrick, it seemed little short of obscene, and widowed all these years! He glanced at her again, not knowing what to say. Then he brightened.

"One thing, Ma, 'ee'll be sure to be invited to t'wedding, so 'ee'll have to get something really special this time, won't 'ee?"

"I may or may not be invited to t'wedding," said Hannah carefully and coolly, "But I certainly won't go."

"Now then, Ma.... " He stopped, totally at a loss for words. And, for the first time, he was genuinely worried. His mother had not been out of the house, at least beyond the limits of the barton and the kitchen garden, the entire winter. She had not been to church. She had not been even to the village.

Each time he questioned her about this, or tried to suggest any outing that might take Hannah away from Redesdale for a few hours, she had made some excuses; the weather was still too cold, she was too busy, she was tired, or simply that she did not feel like going. He had accepted this, though the minister had begun pestering him about his mother's non-attendance at church, saying he would be calling upon her one of these days. Now Patrick became a little anxious. Was his mother ill, then? She seemed alright, but considering just how hard she had worked during the snows and the lambing, it was hardly to be expected if she was a bit 'run-down'.

"What 'ee needs is a good tonic," he said, suddenly, to assure himself as much as her. "I'll see what I can do for 'ee, Ma, when I get t'time."

That was another worrying thing. Most of the household needs, that the farm itself could not supply, such as soap, flour, rice, tea, sugar, dried pulses and so on, were delivered in bulk to Redesdale, but Hannah had always made at least one expedition a week, sometimes two, to purchase various small items from the general store or the haberdashery. She had taken the trap and these outings were as much social occasions (since she invariably called on some acquaintance for a short while) as for making purchases. Several times of late, she had asked her son to get various items, which was sometimes far from being convenient. Twice she had even sent young Jimmy, and Patrick had been annoyed, though he said nothing. Not only had she wasted the boy's time, when he could be better employed, perhaps in cleaning out the sty, another sow having been purchased, but Patrick was not at all sure the second trip, walking all the way to Whytbrook and back, thinly clad, had not been the start of Jimmy's illness. Then, again, the cripple was not to be trusted for long without supervision. He could as easily lose the slip of paper on which the required items had been written, as he could lose the change.

He supposed his mother might still be grieving about Thomas and even Luke, though she never mentioned either son's name these days. He did not understand. Not one little bit. He had felt so proud of her during all the crises, but now he was beginning to fear she was becoming most unreasonable. Most unreasonable, he repeated to himself.

In early May, Patrick attended Kimsley Mendip Fair, which was the first important fair of the year. He suggested his mother came with him, but she would not agree. Apart from acquiring some new small pieces of equipment for the farm - tools lasted long, but not for ever - he had it in mind to try to find some items for Cursons. The young man was hoping to marry at the end of the summer and, indeed, one of his reasons for leaving Canada, where he had worked for a year, was that he had a young lady in Whytbrook. The second reason was that he had found the winter too cold. Patrick was anxious to keep Cursons, if he could. The repairing of his cottage had meant leaving over the roof of the large barn, as Patrick would not borrow more than he could safely repay in a few weeks, hopefully. The roof was in a dreadful state, but Patrick thought they could patch it up themselves sufficiently and perhaps only use one half of the barn. Cursons had agreed with him. Patrick, a natural worrier, had known one awful tremor of anxiety in mid-winter when an over-heated boiler in a Kimsley chapel had started a fire, doing a great deal of damage. No-one had been hurt, and some members of the Church of England congregations had smirked not a little, since the chapel belonged to the hated dissenting Wesleyans.

There was no longer any maypole dancing in Kimsley, except at the schools. The pole that had formerly stood from year to year on the village green, had long since been removed as a nuisance and a danger; added to which the weather around the first of May could not be depended upon for young girls in flimsy attire. The Morris dancers, all male and more hearty and brawny, were in full evidence, however. By the time Patrick had made all his purchases and stored them in the cart and arranged for other things to be delivered, many of the dancers seemed to have imbibed a vast amount of cider. Morris dancing was notoriously thirsty work. A small number from the Kimsley Temperance League were also in evidence, as usual; mostly women, but there were also two or three elderly wrecks of males, who bore the looks of having very lately been redeemed and hopefully 'saved'.

Just about to leave the fair-ground, Patrick's eye was taken by a splendid-looking cart. It was already harnessed to a great black cart-horse, that could have been the brother of Sammy. But the cart, which was lightly loaded, far exceeded his own cart in grandeur. It reminded Patrick of one William had had made to his own drawings years ago and it was still about at Redesdale, somewhere or other, though now unused and badly in need of repair. Such a transporter was a work of great skill, a work of art even, for on the roughest journey the larger rind wheels could always be trusted to follow precisely in the ruts of the front wheels without the least slithering. The cart was beautifully painted. Patrick moved closer and saw the name 'Bailiff' in small gold letters at the back. Then he looked up and saw that a young girl was about to climb into the cart. For a moment he stayed still in surprise. She sat very upright, very quiet on one of the side benches. Maisie Bevan!

He greeted her and she turned her head to look at him.

"How are 'ee Maisie? A'right?"

"Yes, thank you," she answered, politely.

"Good - that's good. And -er you' family?"

"Yes, they're all right." Then she added, seeing he was too embarrassed to ask, "My baby's fine, too."

"Good", he said, grinning a little foolishly. "Already?"

"A little girl," said Maisie, quite naturally. "She arrived a bit soon, three weeks old now. I call her Lucy."

"Lucy," repeated Patrick. "That's a pretty name." He saw Mrs. Bailiff was climbing in to sit opposite Maisie and he nodded to her. She returned his nod, but he was unsure if she recognised him. Bailiff was now preparing to mount the driver's seat, fairly high up in front. He, too, nodded to Patrick, his face unsmiling.

"Maisie," said Patrick, all in a rush, "if there's aught we can do to help 'ee.... Any time 'ee need.... "

"I'm well looked after, thank you," the girl replied with quiet dignity.

Then Bailiff cracked his whip lightly, gave Patrick another curt nod and away they went.

Patrick was left standing, feeling a little dazed.

"So," said Hannah, when he told her, "a girl, is it, then?" She showed neither pleasure nor disappointment. "I'd not heard tell."

He stared at her. How could she possibly hear anything when she stayed all the time at Redesdale? He made up his mind. This was surely his chance, not only to do the right thing by Maisie, but to shift his mother from this dull mood into which she had allowed herself to fall.

"Ma," he said gravely, "it's more difficult for little girls, I do rightly believe, when they's born - born well - out of wedlock."

"A bastard, you mean," said Hannah, unflinching.

"Yes, well.... Ma, that little'un's our responsibility since Luke choose to run away and left her. Ma," he fiddled a little awkwardly, "don't 'ee think 'ee could take t'trap to Kimsley one day and go and see Maisie Bevan? 'Ee could ask then if there's aught she needs, any help with money, that is." He flushed. "It'd be much better coming from 'ee, I'm thinking."

She looked at him, surprised for a moment.

"I thought the Bevans refused help."

"Ma! The old man did, but Ma, she's born now, the little'un! She's alive! Now, wouldn't 'ee like to go and see your very own grandchild? Wouldn't 'ee, Ma?"

She was silent for quite a little while, then she said, slowly, "I must think about it."

"All right, then, Ma!" He turned away. He had the saddest impression that Hannah would not venture from the farm and certainly go nowhere near Maisie Bevan.

CHAPTER XI

Patrick had just left The Bell, where he had called in for a quick drink, feeling not only dry but a little unsettled in his mind. The wife of the landlord leaned across the bar counter, confidentially, and remarked,

"'E's lookin' right trim this eve'in'! Don' t see much o' 'e these'n days."

"Reckon as 'e's a lady friend," the little man, who never removed his cap, summer nor winter, remarked.

"Not roun' 'ere 'e h'aint," declared Sexton Barton, firmly.

For a minute the men fell silent, then the landlord's wife said she had heard tell that Mrs. Scott had not left Redesdale Farm all winter long, not even to go to church. There was desultory talk about this for a moment or two. Most of them knew women like this, though usually much older than Hannah Scott.

"They do say as 'ow her grieves after Thomas. 'E never writes no more. And her's shamed of young Luke goin' off as he did, leavin' young girl with a little'un."

No-one said a word, then Sexton Barton announced loudly, "Angry-phobie, Oi bin thinking". That's what's called. Angryphobie, when a woman won't leave 'er 'ome."

"Could't be a man?" someone dared to suggest, but Sexton Barton would have none of this. This was how women behaved when they came to their 'funny' time of life. Then, deliberately he changed the subject. Had any of them managed to get to the menagerie, which he heard had been in the area lately? He was referring to the famous Bostock and Wombwell menagerie, which had visited Wells on the twenty-first of the previous month. None of them had managed to spare either the time or money, but they tittered together and began digging up memories going back to their childhood, of acrobats and jugglers, lions and tight-rope walkers.

"Did 'ee go 'eesel'?" enquired the little man in the cap.

The sexton ignored this enquiry, but he told them decidedly the best circuses were 'the h'Amerycan Circuses'. Hassen 'ee 'eard o' they? T'were real vine show that'un, v'rom me own h'experience."

He was soon launched into his memories of old and no-one dared to interrupt, till the conversations gradually turned to this new fashion, growing fast, of keeping animals, only for show.

One man spoke up, "Oi'll not belief 'tis goo' sense to go an' breed h'animals jest to show 'er! 'Taint nat'ral. 'Er needs as much h'exercise an' change o' scene and field as all t'others, Oi reckon. Else 'er gets flabby-like."

The men fully agreed and soon they were launched on their favourite topic. One man had heard there had been another outbreak of swine fever at the Jackson's farm, the second this year and only May! Another voice chipped in that he was certain sure it all came down to the Jacksons not keeping their stys nice and dry and with plenty of good, clean straw. Heads nodded sagely in agreement as pipes were puffed, but the publican's wife sighed a little.

They were more interested in their animals, as was her own man, than in the doings of humans! Ah, well.... She wondered who might be the girl young Patrick Scott was courting, as he must surely be, all dressed up in his Sunday-best suit. She fell to wondering. She became almost convinced she must be one of the two daughters of the minister of Kimsley Mendip Parish church. Patrick Scott knew the minister well, she believed, and he deserved a really nice respectable and devout young lady.

By this time, Patrick was well on his way to Kimsley Mendip. But he was not going to visit the rector. He intended to call on the Bailiffs and on Maisie Bevan and this would be the fifth time in just over two weeks. When he had first called, a day or two after meeting the girl by chance at Kimsley

Mendip Fair, he had not the slightest intention of seeking to woo her. There was rather a kindly concern and curiosity about the child, who was his niece, together with a certain sense of shame. If he could see the baby and then manage to convey to his mother a picture that would interest her a little, might this not rouse her from her present gloomy state? He might even bridge the gap, he had told himself, so that the two women became good friends. Initially, his mother had seemed to like the girl and it was true that Hannah had not until now shown any jealousy towards younger women. (In fact, any threat seemed to Hannah to come from women of her own generation, women with husbands still alive and caring for them, supposedly, and a family staying close to home.)

Patrick had been greeted by all the family politely, but guardedly. It was some time before he had a chance to talk to Bailiff alone, indeed, just as he was about to mount his horse. If Maisie had any need of financial help, he tentatively asked, he would like to know. Bailiff had looked at him coolly. A prosperous, self-made man, who had worked hard, owned several shops and not a small amount of land, he was not likely to be accepted by the gentry, but he needed nothing from Patrick Scott. He had not himself married till middle-age, a much younger wife, the step-sister of Margaret Bevan. From the beginning he had been able to provide his wife with ample help in the home and any small luxury she might want.

"Maisie needs nothing," he said in his quiet almost educated voice, for he had worked hard to 'improve' himself also. "As far as we're concerned, the girl has a home here for the rest of her life, unless she marries, as no doubt she will in due course. We've grown very fond of young Maisie, my wife especially, as well as our children." He did not trouble to add that the young girl seemed to have a special gift with children and could make herself very useful at times. But he did add, to Patrick's enquiry, that he could call again by all means, if he so chose. Perhaps, little Lucy would be awake next time. Patrick nodded. The message was plain. They were proud people. None of them needed any favours.

Patrick had gone again and several times later to take small gifts to a child far too young to value them, as yet, but accepted kindly by her mother. He had been surprised by the baby. Small and dark, she seemed to Patrick, to bear more a resemblance to old man Bevan than either of her parents, though the clear grey eyes were those of Maisie. For the first time he realised that Bevan must have been quite a good-looking man in his youth. In fact, the dark fluff of wisps of hair, lightened in time and there was even a hint of dark red, but never the flaming glory that was so much a part of Maisie. The most astonishing thing about the child was her placidity. Never had he known a baby cry so little, appear so contented. How could this be with parents like Luke and Maisie? Then, he began to realise that the girl always seemed to anticipate the child's wants, which after all, were small, feeding, comfort and loving.

After his next visit, Patrick knew his interest was not confined to the baby. The atmosphere of the Bailiff home was peaceful, he told himself, with none of the awful hidden undercurrents he could sometimes feel at Redesdale. He had not known Maisie at all well, but he sensed she had changed a great deal since her sad experience. It had had a chastening effect. She smiled readily, especially at her child and the other children of the household and seemed content enough, but she had clearly lost much of her childish simplicity. She was a young woman.

Patrick watching her gentle ways with the children and learning about the various small domestic skills she practised, including making most of her own clothes, was impressed. It seemed to him she also had a natural grace and bearing, surprising considering her upbringing, which set her apart from other young girls. He became increasingly captivated. Yet, by what standards was he judging her? He knew almost nothing about women, except his mother whom, truth to tell, he hardly regarded as a woman, being too strong and both father and mother to them. Maisie seemed to him unique. And yet he hesitated. The idea of marrying the girl did not spring to mind. Even when Bailiff repeated his earlier words, saying his niece was very welcome to stay in his house till she married, Patrick did not see this as applying to himself. In fact, he was rather astonished that Bailiff should expect the girl to wed. The puritanical, conventional side of his nature was even a little shocked. He certainly did not expect her to continue the rest of her life in the penitence of sackcloth and ashes, but surely no young man would want such a maiden? Perhaps, he thought a moment later, a hard-pressed widower with several young children?

Yet, it was on the Sunday, a day or so after such thoughts, that the minister chose as his text for the sermon, Chapter Thirty-one of Proverbs, which begins with the words, "Who can find a virtuous woman? For her price is far above rubies.... "

Patrick heard not a further word of the very admirable sermon. For the amazing thing was that these words held for Patrick a totally different meaning to that intended by the minister! He was certain, absolutely certain, that God was speaking to him, Patrick, there in the church! And He was not thunderously exclaiming that virtue was a noble and rare attribute to be deeply treasured. Quite the reverse, in a way. This time (and very helpfully) it came to Patrick loud and clear that these old words were really the fore-runner of Christ's injunction that he who was 'without sin' should throw the first stone at the fallen woman. No-one had responded and neither, thought Patrick, spiritually exalted, would he do so. He had left the church knowing what he must do. He felt extraordinarily noble, more holy than he had done in a very long time. And there was no time to waste, if the child was to have the Scott name, for he would adopt it, of course.

He dressed himself neatly in his best suit and took the trap, rather than ride over as he had been doing, his intention being to ask if Maisie would like to come with him for a little drive, if she could spare the time. She hesitated, but her young aunt urged her, "Go for a drive, my dear. 'Tis a nice evening, and I don't suppose Mr. Scott can spare to be from the farm for long."

"All right, then. I'll get my shawl. I'll be back in plenty o' time for Lucy's feed." She was, of course, feeding the baby herself.

She was very quiet during the drive and he spoke of many things in half-sentences, that had nothing to do with themselves. It was not until an hour had gone by and they were almost back at the Bailiff home again, that he plucked up his courage and quietly asked her to share his life and fortunes. He was quite modest about what he had to offer, but he was also fairly certain, in his own mind, that all would go well.

Maisie turned him down, quietly, almost regretfully, but quite firmly, leaving no doubt about the matter.

Patrick came home utterly shaken, distressed as he had not been in a long time. How could this be? How could it happen like this? Naturally, he was disappointed, as he had grown quite fond of the girl in these two and more weeks, even if it was a bit soon, but he wanted the thing settled. She must see that, surely, for both their sakes; not only for the baby Lucy, but the demands of the farm would soon make it difficult for him to get away so often. He could not have placed his hand on his heart and sworn he was passionately in love with the wench and longing to get her into his bed. No man, in his view (and certainly not a farmer) ought to marry because he lusted over a pretty girl - not unless he was a total idiot. Marriage was a serious business.

No, his distress went far more deeply than his personal emotions. For hadn't God spoken to him, clearly? And how could God be so mistaken? As a tiny child he had beseeched the Lord for impossibilities and then been distressed when they did not duly arrive; until the time when his father had taken him upon his knee and pointed out that one could not expect everything one wanted, as the Lord knew best what each child needed. This explanation had hardly satisfied, but Patrick had tried to live his life by it as he grew older.

The Lord's Will.... or had Patrick merely deceived himself? He thought and prayed about it a good deal in the odd few minutes he could spare during his daily round of duties and he could not see where he had gone amiss. After all, the girl could hardly expect a long-drawn, leisurely courtship. That would be absurd and he had offered to see the child was not penalised in any way when they had other children later. It was all very puzzling. And worrying. He had more or less made up his mind not to go again, when it occurred to Patrick that a few words with Bailiff might help him to understand this mystery. Could it be young Maisie Bevan already had some other admirer?

So he went again, at a different time of day, though it was inconvenient; and it was Mrs. Bailiff who spoke to him that morning, when Maisie was out with the baby and the youngest child of the family. She deliberately came out to him, when she saw him approach the house and drew him aside.

"You did rather rush poor Maisie, the other evening," she remarked.

"She told you?"

"Of course."

"I thought she must understand how I expected things to go," he said, speaking very carefully, wondering why the girl should be 'poor Maisie' because he had asked her to share his life.

"Oh, it didn't upset her, really. But I can' t help feeling you aimed to get everything tidied up before the shearing started!"

Patrick flushed. This was so much an echo of his own thoughts about choosing a wife between the lambing and shearing.

"I don't rightly have a lot o' time," he said, more naturally, "not, that is, to go wooing a girl." He looked at his boots. "I thought she'd see that.... Not that I'd have rushed her to wed, though I can't see sense waiting if folks have made up their minds, but I'd have bided my time till she was good and ready, Mrs. Bailiff."

She smiled at him.

"Are you afraid she might find someone else? She's a very pretty girl."

"Yes, yes, I suppose she is pretty," admitted Patrick, reluctantly, as though that was the very last attribute he would expect in a wife. He chose not to reply to the first part of the question.

Mrs. Bailiff looked at him steadily.

"Maisie likes you, you know. She respects you and so does my husband. I think she could get fond of you in time, given a little more time."

Again Patrick flushed.

"I'd not have thought she'd be so silly as to go lookin' for romance, not now."

"No? Perhaps not." Mrs. Bailiff regarded him quietly. "On the other hand, the child's born now, bless her little heart, and there's nothing Maisie can do that'll alter that fact. So, it is my opinion she ought to look to her own happiness and not rush into marriage with another man unless she's sure. She's not had a lot of happiness, you know."

"I'd be good to her."

"I don't doubt it. And she likes you, as I said. Give it a few more weeks, a few more months, and you're quite willing to call when you wish to see the child."

"All right," said Patrick, very dubiously. "Perhaps I'll do that."

There was in Patrick no childish petulance. Any such tendency had been squashed out of him by the authority of an elder brother and the plaintiff demands of a nervous younger one, long before he reached maturity, but no man likes to be turned down, especially when he has been so profoundly certain he must be welcomed, as Patrick had been (in all humility, he told himself). He had simply suffered an all too human aberration. His own carnal desires he had masked to himself as God's Own Will. It was shattering, but it was better to face this. Clearly, he had been entirely wrong about the Lord's intentions for himself; it was not part of any plan, not at all. He had truly deceived himself here and he must not go to Kimsley Mendip to visit the Bailiffs and Maisie Bevan again. And just suppose Maisie turned him down a second time? No, he must not go back there!

For a whole week he kept to his decision. Then, when he thought he might just call for a brief visit out of friendliness and to let it be seen the reversal had not entirely flayed his spirit, he chose a Sunday afternoon. The family would most certainly be away from home visiting friends, or entertaining themselves, in which case he would go away immediately; in the event, Patrick would know very surely it was not meant to be.

The Bailiffs were from home, but Maisie was sitting in the garden, her own child and the youngest member of the Bailiff family near her. The conversation was fitful, a little strained. Patrick spoke not one word that was out of place. Maisie several times suggested he should wait a little till her relatives returned, pretending he had called to see them, saying they would be upset if he left before they returned. But the Bailiff family did not return. Maisie had tea brought out to them by a pert little maid. Even then, it did not occur to Patrick that he was attempting to persuade Maisie to give up a good deal of comfort. Presently, he took his leave. There was Evensong to attend and he had agreed to act as a Sidesman, temporarily, in the absence of the usual person.

The very next day, Bailiff came to call on him. He took the trouble to forego some of his duties and to ride out to the farm and seek out Patrick. They spoke of this and that for some little while, in the way of country people, the most important matters being left till later.

"It'll be isolated out here in winter, I'm thinking," said Bailiff, casually.

Patrick was startled. Never in his life had he thought of Redesdale Farm in such terms.

"Isolated," he repeated, as though he was unsure of the meaning of the word. "Why, 'tis only a couple o' miles from t'village, less'n that if one goes by t'fields!"

Bailiff looked at the other, pointedly.

"For me and you maybe. For a young girl with a baby.... ?" He left it in the air.

"She's turned me down," said Patrick, not without some stubbornness.

"She'd not be able to call on her family and friends, as she likes."

"Maisie could've taken the trap whenever she likes, but as she doesn't want to marry me.... "

"She could change her mind. You could change it for her."

Nothing was said for a full moment, then Patrick continued his protests, as though the other had not spoken.

"No-one could call Redesdale isolated! 'Sides she'd have had Ma to keep her company when I'm in the fields. My shepherd's getting married end of the summer and Maisie'd have had his wife for company. But I really can't see t'point."

"Can't you?"

Now came the hard part, the truly difficult bit, but Bailiff had not succeeded without using the brains he had been given.

"Maisie rubs along with most people well enough, but she might prefer her own friends. As for Mrs. Scott.... "

"What about her?" Patrick was alerted, as though he sensed a sudden attack.

"There's a lot of talk."

"What kind o' talk? There's always gossip about nothin', but my mother's alright, a bit depressed o' late, as is only nat'ral. A young woman in the house would've brightened her no end. However, as things are.... "

Bailiff came close and he suddenly put his hand on Patrick's arm.

"I admire you, Patrick," he said, gently, "and I think on the whole you're the best of your brothers, but I do think you should ask yourself honestly whether it would be in Maisie's best interests to come here. What have you really got to offer Patrick? Ponder that a little, my boy." With a quick, light tap to Patrick's arm, he turned away and was very soon mounting his horse.

The delicate flowers of spring, the primroses, violets and cowslips gave way to the summer growth, slovenly, lusty, fighting for a place in the sun against all the competition of sly weeds and insect life. Buttercups and clover and a multitude of many varieties of daisy abounded. The hedges near to Whytbrook really were white with the glory of several types of wild parsley, wild roses, convolvulus and, here and there, was a contrasting, heightening pink of the willow herbs. There were few fields where a group of poppies did not flaunt themselves, as though arrogantly amused in their striking brilliance by the efforts of the farmers to eradicate them. From the branches of the horse-chestnut trees hung chandeliers of pink and white blossom.

Patrick was altogether too busy to think much about the beauties of nature. Too busy even to think much about Maisie Bevan, though he did do so, from time to time, when he finally reached his bedroom, very wearily at night. Cursons was shaping very nicely as a shepherd, but he still needed a good deal of watching when it came to tackling jobs not confined to the sheep and other animals. He could be a bit slap-dash, as though resenting being asked to do such tasks.

The shearing went well, however, and Patrick was relieved that the price for the wool was rather better this year. Was this the turn of the tide? Would the prices now begin slowly to rise, after the long, worrying years of decline? He knew nothing of world politics, though he was well aware of the competition starting to come from New Zealand. But surely, he told himself, there could be nothing to touch good English wool and good English mutton, come to that?

Towards the end of July, he chanced upon Maisie Bevan in Whytbrook. She told him she was on a visit to Mrs. Squires (and her family, she added, though she was staying with Mrs. Squires). She was pushing one of these newfangled perambulators, which must have cost a great deal of money and she told him Mrs. Squires had bought it for her.

"You never call these days, Patrick."

"There's lots to do on t'farm in summer, Maisie, as 'ee must know, and I didn't think 'ee'd be wanting me to waste my time."

"Not wasted, Patrick. We did so enjoy your visits."

"Did you?" He looked at her, waiting for her to say more.

She said nothing of a direct nature, for that was not her way, but she told him she was staying for three weeks with her friend while her aunt went to the coast on holiday with her children. Her aunt had asked her to go with them, but she had thought she ought to go home for a while. She added, "Mrs. Squires knows you, though you mayn't know her. She goes out so seldom."

"Like Ma," he said and smiled at her.

He did call the very next evening, for he knew the house of the widow, as did most people in the village. He was shown into a smallish parlour by a neatly attired maid. There was a wrought iron guard before the fire, the brass top very well polished and gleaming, but a large plant, probably an aspidistra, hid the empty fireplace. An oil painting of dead birds and rabbits hung above the mantelpiece, which was cluttered, as was a good deal of the room, with treasures collected by the owner during her travels, most of them of little value, but with a few charming items, such as the Georgian snuff boxes. There were several small tables with cloths to the ground, two tapestry-covered foot-stools, faded photographs and a couple of domed glass cases containing stuffed birds. Patrick had always hated this particular fashion, though he had grown used to it; but despite the room, Mrs. Squires was not only a most amiable and cheerful old lady, she had a refreshing outlook, for the times. Patrick took to her immediately.

The coffee when it arrived was excellently made and served with chocolate biscuits. Then she offered Patrick, not some home-made wine, but a liqueur brandy, which he had never before in his life tasted, as a night-cap.

"That's a splendid carriage you bought Maisie," he remarked as he took his leave.

"Yes," she replied, not without some pride. "I ordered it from Bristol and it was sent down to me. Sometime ago I arranged it. I wrote to Maisie and told her she could not have it unless she came to see me with the baby!"

The girl flushed a little.

"I wanted to see you, but I didn't really want to come to Whytbrook - not yet."

"It was brave of 'ee," said Patrick.

"It had to be faced sooner or later," said Mrs. Squires, smoothly. "'Course the girl's mother had been over to Kimsley to see the child, but I said Maisie must come here! And I said - didn't I Maisie? - folks are going to stare, so let's give them something really grand to stare at. I meant the perambulator, of course!"

Patrick chuckled, feeling far more at ease with this woman than he had done with the Bailiffs, though he could well understand they thought they had Maisie's best interests at heart.

Just before the girl left to return to Kimsley Mendip, Patrick again asked her to marry him, rather more diffidently this time.

"You know I'm not in love with you, Patrick?"

"Yes, I do realise that, but 'ee cares a bit?"

"A good deal, more'n anyone I've known, men I mean." She flushed.

"I care for 'ee a lot, Maisie. I'd do aught to make 'ee happy, so if 'ee tells me to go away and not bother 'ee more, though 't'were hard, that I'll do."

"I trust you, Patrick, " she said and held out her hand to him. He bent and kissed her gently on the lips, holding very tightly to her hand, holding very tightly to his own, suddenly surging emotions.

By this time, Patrick's viewing of the situation had somewhat changed. No longer did he see himself as conferring upon a poor, unfortunate girl (whom his brother had wronged) the dignity of his name. He knew, and he knew it well, there was plenty of self-interest here. Why, he was getting a little treasure! But for her unfortunate experience he would never have thought of looking in her direction, so he owed much to his brother Luke. He hoped Maisie would come to see it in this light one day. Whatever her small failings might prove, he was sure he was to have a wife who would be loyal and devoted. Nothing and no-one would tempt her from him in the future. She was not a wanton; she had made a small error of judgement and learned immensely from it. Then again, hadn't she shown she was fully capable of bearing healthy, normal children and of caring for them? And Patrick wanted very much to have a good-sized family.

Before climbing into his high bed that night, after Maisie had agreed to put herself into his hands, he prayed long and earnestly (and, it is to be said, with total sincerity) desiring God to understand everything. He was not trying to set himself up as a man more saintly and forbearing than his fellows. He prayed with all his heart to be good to dear Maisie. On and on he went, the emotional prayers some small release for his pent-up feelings; on and on, telling the Good Lord all the things He already well knew and had no need whatsoever to be told.

One think shocked him a little, though. Maisie was adamant she would not marry in any church. It was not that she felt she was in any way unworthy, she simply did not want the fuss, with bans being called out. She had heard there was a way they could marry quickly - and she saw no need to wait now they had made up their minds - with some kind of licence you applied for, and in a registry office.

"But, Maisie, it won't seem like a wedding at all!"

"It will to me Patrick."

"You can have a little blessing ceremony, on your own in church later on," put in Mrs. Squires.

Reluctantly, Patrick agreed. He set about arranging matters. And in his heart he knew he was somewhat relieved. They would marry in Wells and this would help explain his mother's non-attendance at the wedding, for he knew, unhappily, that nothing would persuade Hannah to budge from Redesdale.

For the moment he felt a twinge of conscience. Was he being unfair to Maisie, as Bailiff had hinted he would be by taking the girl to the farm? His own hopes and love overruled such doubts. It would be alright. Maisie and the child would soon bring his mother out of her depressed condition. She was not making the effort. To his exasperation, he had come upon the bottle of tonic he had bought for her out of the vast array for horses and men always advertised in the spring months. He doubted if more than one spoonful had been taken; the medicine dribbled down the side of the bottle, a sticky mess. Wisely, however, he threw away the bottle and said not a word. In her own good time, no doubt. It was the old story of taking a horse to the water, but not always being able to make it drink when one chose.

Nevertheless, when Patrick told Hannah he was getting married, he still hoped she might show some reaction. She showed almost none.

"So that's why 'ee came home late o' nights," she remarked, but there was no humour nor interest in her voice.

"Did I disturb 'ee?" he asked surprised. He had been as quiet as he could during the time when he was going over to Kimsley Mendip.

"No," she said. "I don't sleep much these days."

"Ma, you've not asked me who I'm marrying, have 'ee?"

She sighed.

"All right," she said, "what's her name? I suppose you'll be bringing her here?"

"Of course!" he said astounded. "Where else, Ma? I was late 'cause I was going to Kimsley Mendip to see Maisie Bevan."

"Oh, yes," she said, flatly.

"And 'tis she I'm going to wed, Ma!" he burst out.

Hannah was silent so long he thought she could not have heard what he said.

"Ma!"

"Yes," she said, her voice neutral, "there's no need to shout. You're going to marry Maisie Bevan. That's all right, then." She was turning away, when he took her arm, "Ma," he asked patiently, "you'll come to t'wedding, won't 'ee? Maisie'll be upset, if 'ee don't. It'll be very quiet. In - in a registry office. In Wells."

She might not have heard.

"All right, then. I don' t mind."

"But will 'ee come? Will 'ee? Look, I'll hire a brougham for 'ee and get Rose to come along o' 'ee. She's back in the village now. You'd like that, wouldn't 'ee?"

Again she sighed.

"I'll think about it." Then, it was as though she had suddenly remembered something she ought to say. "I hope as you and Maisie'll be happy," she said, her voice still flat, almost bored.

She looked at him and he looked back at her almost despairingly for a moment. Then he brightened, patted her arm, failing to notice her slight shudder, and told her not to worry about it. He was trying, valiantly to reassure himself.

It was mid-September, not so warm as the previous year, but pleasant enough to have drawn out from their shells, a few old men, who were now settled comfortably in The Bell. It was nearing noon and most of the regulars were either in the fields working, or too hard-up to afford the luxury of a pint on a week day. The publican's wife bustled in to relieve Amy, the barmaid. She was fairly spilling over with her 'news', but she greatly feared there would be scant response from this little bunch. Not even Sexton Barton was present.

Bravely, she tried, however.

"What d'ee think on Pat'ick Scott goin' and marrying Maisie Bevan? Last week it were at Wells and not in church neither! And him so religious!"

"Who's Maisie Bevan?" someone dared to ask.

"'Tis Margaret Bevan," an old man with a white beard remarked, proud of his good memory.

"She's t'daughter of that old sod.... " began the publican's wife. Then she looked round the counter hastily. It was highly unlikely any of the Bevans would be in The Bell at this time of day; but, in fact, since the elder son, James had taken up work in a village some distance away, Matthew for reasons best known to himself had chosen to call in at The Woolpack (despite their truly shocking prices).

As for the old man, he had been advised severely by his doctor that if he did not cut down on the liquor he was as good as dead. This was after a most distressing illness in the winter. Telling Maisie's father to stop drinking would have been as useless as forbidding a bitch on heat not to copulate. But as a compromise, the old man had taken to walking across fields to join his elder son at a half-way hostelry, hopefully for a free drink or two. James might have a young lady and be hoping to marry, but he was not contributing to the household expenses overmuch, so old Bevan considered a little free refreshment his bounden right. Walking across fields on summer evenings may be good for the health and help to cut down on the amount of time available for drinking, but it became boring to a man (and there *are* such countrymen) who did not know the difference between a nut-cracker and a mistle thrush. So Bevan got himself a mongrel, a scruffy little dog, to keep him company. He had never cared much for dogs, but this little fellow, in the manner of his indiscriminate kind, loved his master with total loyalty and utter obedience. It would be pure sentimentality to suggest that even this wonderful little creature transformed old Bevan, so that he became abstemious and a kindly husband. He did not. But he did lavish upon his dog more devotion than he had upon any human for many a long year.

"H'aint nothin' wrong with bein' h'religious!" sternly remarked the little man, who always wore a cap, as though he had just realised what had been said by the publican's wife.

"Yes, but I mean - pickin' up his brother's leavings!"

There was a silence, a long considering silence.

"Well, oi don't know," said the old man with the white beard at length remarked, "Oi do reckon as Pat'ick Scott 'as some sense in 'is 'ead, at h'that. Young girl'll be so burstin' with thankfulness, 'er'll work all t'arder for 'e, never complain an' go astrayin'. An' when there do be two, vree more young'uns, who's to trouble 'is 'ead?"

There followed another silence. Then they were off about the things which really mattered to them, animals and the land. World events meant almost nothing to them. They had touched on the fighting that was going on in the Transvaal earlier in the year, as though it was a happening on Mars, but it did move them, one and all, to know their dear Queen Victoria had been in tears at the losses. She'd a good heart, the old queen.

"They do say now as white mustard ve' good vor young milch cows. Makes more milk, 'spec," said the old man with the beard, sagely.

"Well, oi'll be darl'd!"

"Hassen 'ee 'eard on it, then? Varmer Ridley's cousin 'as a gurt vield on it."

Someone then remarked that the strawberry-growing venture in Cheddar was going well, though he personally should never have thought it would take. Someone else added he'd heard they were actually sending over cheese to England from the U.S.A. and calling it 'Cheddar', which beat everything!

The man with the white beard shook his head. There was always someone trying to cheat the farmer. Land prices were down this year nearly twenty-five per cent! At this they all looked very solemn indeed, though none of them had owned so much as a square yard of land in his entire life. The little man with the cap looked at the beautiful day and asserted that a good drop of rain wouldn't harm to 'set the crops'. His tone had a note of angry, quivering peevishness, as though he suspected even the Lord was not quite playing honestly with the farming community.

How they enjoyed their grumbles! The barmaid had returned and the publican's wife, having given a swift, remonstrating mop to the counter, left them at it. What a sadly unromantic lot they were!

CHAPTER XII

Almost the very first thing Maisie did when she arrived at Redesdale Farm after the wedding, was to set about unpacking the trunk and box of personal effects, which had been sent up to the farm in advance. It might have seemed insensitive to be in such a hurry, but Maisie only knew, in that instant, after Patrick's departure from the kitchen, that she must do something on her own. Most of her young life she had created dreams about being at Redesdale, preferably with Thomas as her husband; well, Thomas was gone for good and, for her part, she did not care. But when she looked about her (*really* looked, as she had certainly not done that awful day last October) she was dismayed. How shabby everything seemed! Needlessly shabby, in the girl's view. After the immense comforts of living in the Bailiff home and even those of her dear friend, Auntie Squires, Redesdale was very depressing. She overlooked for the moment that her own mother was an indifferent housewife; at least, she told herself, there was some excuse at home, as her mother had never been strong and there had been scant money to spare on adornments. The house had been beautifully clean, though - well, she amended, *fairly* clean most of the time, as she and Matthew and James had ensured that much. Her father, paradoxically, was absurdly fastidious, as long as no-one ever expected him to contribute to the ease of the home.

Whatever had happened to Mrs. Scott? Maisie had heard a few rumours about her not going anywhere and it had not upset her in the least; after years of living with her own untidy, easy-going mother, she had been sure she would be capable of coping with Hannah Scott. She was simply being a bit difficult with the 'change' upon her. She could not conceive of such a strong-minded, determined woman like Mrs. Scott submitting to what was a natural, normal indisposition - not for long, that is. But now! It was all far, far worse that she had imagined it might be. Maisie could not help feeling upset. Why, she was as thin as the proverbial rake; those long, narrow wooden implements they used in the fields in summer! The picture did not bring any smile to her face. She was altogether too worried. It was almost *eerie*. There must be something very wrong with her. How could Patrick not have noticed his mother was ill? Perhaps, he'd got used to her appearance? She would have to have a quiet, tactful word with him. She felt quite shocked at this terrible change in her mother-in-law.

For a moment she paused in her unpacking to listen. Not a sound out of little Lucy. She was evidently still sleeping after her long day. She had left the baby in her bassinet in the kitchen, where Patrick had carried her. Hannah would keep an eye on her, wouldn't she?

Hannah had seemed almost pleased at the sight of the child and had even managed to let a faint smile soften her lips, though she had shrunk back, as though terrified, when Patrick had tried to place the little one in his mother's arms. She had made some excuse about fearing the child might be too heavy for her. Maisie, who could on occasion be very perceptive, had noticed this, but Patrick had apparently not done so.

Maisie shook herself impatiently. Well, she had made her bed now, so she must make the very best of it. It could have been far worse. She got on with her task.

On a large, mahogany chest she placed a travelling case, given to her by Mrs. Squires. It was not new, but was in excellent condition, (as though the proud owner had hardly cared to use it) from its red leather cover to its lining of red silk. Maisie thought it unlikely she would use it either, but it gave her a great satisfaction to look at the silver-topped cut-glass bottles and jars, the silver-backed brushes and silver-edged combs. Then there were various other little items, such as ivory-handled button hooks, a nail buffer, crotchet hooks, a paper-knife and some embroidery scissors. They all gleamed at her in their perfection and Maisie put her elbows on the chest for a moment to gaze at her small treasure. It was exquisite. She felt delight. It seemed to Maisie not only an example of beautiful workmanship, but also a symbol of real adventure and romance. To what strange places had not this case journeyed?

She sighed.

At that exact moment, Patrick burst into the bedroom. He looked for a moment almost surprised to see the girl there in his room. His eye immediately went to the travelling case.

"Pretty," he said, inadequately. Imposingly, the case seemed to loll there at the very centre of the functional, masculine chest-of-drawers. It seemed more than that; the case became a flag, courageously, but perhaps injudiciously staked in a strange, uncharted land. For the first time, it came to Patrick that he would be sharing his bedroom, not with his brother Luke, but with his wife.

They stared at each other, and for the first time were both embarrassed at being alone. After all, there was 'a time and place' for everything.

"Patrick," she said swiftly.

"Maisie," he said at exactly the same time. They laughed together and the moment of tension passed. He came to her and put his arm about her waist, but very cautiously, so as not to spoil her lovely gown.

Patrick suddenly remembered why he had come upstairs. He had briefly spoken to Cursons, but now he must see to the work of the farm. Half-difidently, he asked, would Maisie like to join him for a really good look at the farm before it got dark? Also, he'd have to introduce his wife to the Cursons and to little Jimmy, though she had already met him, he believed? And, he added, grinning, especially the dogs and his favourite, Jessie. She would like Jessie all right. Everyone did.

Maisie agreed at once. This would fill in the time very nicely till tea, which was really the main meal of the day, usually about six o'clock. She must change, though. This pearl grey would show every tiny mark. She had already removed her little flower-trimmed hat.

Patrick left her to change, as he believed that was considered the proper gentlemanly thing to do, after hesitating only a moment, uncertainly. He had, himself, managed already to find the time to change out of his new suit (which would have to serve for Sundays for many a long day) but he had not yet attired himself in his rough working clothes, the clothes his hard-working life demanded. Instead, he had chosen some of the clothes he wore casually in the evenings when he went to the village. It was a sub-conscious adjustment, a stepping-stone from reverie to reality. Oh, if only he could have been able to take her away on a honeymoon somewhere or other! He had no idea where he would take her and, in fact, had never really wanted to go far from his native soil, so this reckless notion did not remain long in his thoughts.

Meanwhile, Maisie who had observed Patrick's brief glance at the travelling case and felt, sadly, he could never appreciate it, had made up her mind. She would turn one of the rooms in this big house, so many of them empty, apparently, into a little sitting-room, a kind of sewing room, all for herself! She grew excited at the thought. It lifted her young heart, made her feel, momentarily like one of the grand ladies Mrs. Squires had often talked about. What was it called, now? A boudoir, that was it. A boudoir. Her own special room would have some pictures, too. Not gloomy, but like some she had seen somewhere or other, but could not recall where at present. There was one, she remembered, of lightly-clad Grecian maidens with urns on their shoulders, standing near a fountain, their long, long golden hair flowing down over their breasts. She hugged herself at the thought of such luxury, never having had a room of her own in her life. The room would be her own little refuge, which even Patrick would not be allowed to enter, unless he asked permission. (A strange thought for a bride, perhaps?)

Maisie did not at that moment also see that the proposed boudoir would be like a hedgerow, flourishing vigorously between herself and Hannah Scott.

Only someone as unworldly as Patrick could have innocently imagined Maisie Bevan (or Maisie Scott as she must now be termed) and Abigail Cursons could be 'friends'.

Maisie was vaguely acquainted with young Mrs. Cursons, but apart from the fact that the shepherd's wife was almost ten years older than herself, and had frequently been away from Whytbrook in service, there were more important differences. Abigail was attractive-looking, both in face and physique, but an essentially stupid girl, who masked from herself her crass stupidity, by loudly asserting that she was every bit 'as good as 'they' do be'. Her manner to her employers had often been barely short of impertinent and once she had been sent packing because of her rude tongue.

She did not really know Maisie, but she had already formed an unfavourable opinion of her. She thought Maisie gave herself airs, whatever that was supposed to mean. The daughter of a very unsuccessful farmer, a tenant farmer, she yet saw herself as far superior to a girl born into the Bevan household. Then, she had married in church, hadn't she, with a splendid wedding breakfast? (That would further impoverish her parents.) She had been able to bring as her dowry some splendid treasures, in the way of china and linen, hoarded for many a long year, since she had started her bottom-drawer well before she met her husband. (The linen and the china mattered more to her than the man.) Added to all these advantages, Abigail Cursons had most certainly not got herself in the family way before she was wed.

Maisie could almost guess the thoughts going through the other's head, but she was too young to know how to deal with veiled contempt. She would just keep well out of Mrs. Cursons' way, and she would certainly not be invited into her boudoir.

Patrick, of course, noticed nothing whatever amiss.

Jimmy Coxon who was there at the same time, gave his new mistress the most trusting of welcomes. He seemed to be saying that if this lady was the Master's wife, then she must be all right. Maisie was not repulsed by the appearance of young Jimmy, having grown used to seeing him round in the village at different times; and she immediately made up her mind to try to teach him a little, for she knew he was illiterate, or very nearly so. She spoke of this when the lamager had gone and Patrick looked pleased. Maisie wanted very much to please Patrick; there was also just a hint of shrewd remonstrance to Abigail Cursons, who clearly loathed the cripple.

Patrick did not go from the bedroom when he and his young wife got ready for bed, but he did turn his back towards her a bit awkwardly, talking most of the time of small matters, which had never been his habit when he shared his room with his brother.

Maisie undressed to her chemise, her 'shimmy', as she called it, and then she slipped over her head a large enveloping nightdress of white lawn trimmed with lace at neck and wrists, another gift from Mrs. Squires. Once in his plain, serviceable night-shirt, Patrick knelt by the bedside and very clearly he expected Maisie to do the same at the other side of the bed.

The prayer was very long-winded, touched with emotion; gratitude, hope and not a little apprehension. Maisie shivered. She had been used to saying very hasty prayers in bed. This was something she would have to change - by the winter, at any rate. The child, Lucy, became her ally. The baby put her fist into her tiny mouth for she was teething, looked about her at the strange room and began to whimper. She was the most patient of small babies and utterly trusting, but she needed reassuring and most of all, she needed feeding. Maisie said a hasty 'Amen' and arose to her feet. For the past minute or so, she had been aware of one of her breasts starting to leak. Prayers or no prayers, wedding-night or no wedding-night, Lucy must be fed. She came first.

"Put a shawl about'ee, me little love," said Patrick and he rose and unhooked a large, unused shepherd's shawl, which hung on a wall near the door, but Maisie did not seat herself in the only low and comfortable chair in the room (which Patrick had arranged should be brought in) but climbed back into the huge bed with the child.

"She's very good," she said, softly, half-apologetically, "she really is and usually goes right through the night without waking - she has done for a long time now. Soon, she'll be properly weaned, too, but she does like her last night drink of milk from the breast and a good cuddle, bless her."

In fact, the baby had not been breast-fed since early morning, as she had been left with the Bailiff's nursemaid till she and Patrick were ready to return to Redesdale.

"That's all right," said Patrick, calmly and he climbed in beside the girl, half-reclining on an arm, watching her. Ever since early childhood, he had watched a number of babies being nursed by different women, including his own mother and members of his family. It had embarrassed him not at all, and had no more interest for him than a ewe with her lamb, indeed a great deal less. Luke once remarked that a cat with her new-born kittens was far more enchanting to look at then any human mother, and Patrick had been inclined to agree; in any case, those woman had all been singularly discreet, never blatantly thrusting forth their large mammary glands. Feeding a child was a matter only concerning the baby and its mother.

But, somehow, it was different this time. It was not simply the rounded white breast fully displayed through the unbuttoned nightdress and being offered to the baby, which brought a sudden excitement to the watcher; Patrick was hardly conscious of any particular sexual arousal. He was aware, though, of a deeply intense emotional, even mystical, feeling, linked through his religion with The Child and with all children far into the past, far beyond anything he, himself, could recall. Then, again, forward into a future when his new wife would hold in her arms his own child, a child of his loins. Theirs. Even now, he felt towards the little child something he had not previously experienced, a tenderness, that was groping towards protectiveness. For the first time he loved this small creature, every bit as much as though she was his own flesh and blood.

He watched as Maisie gently returned the baby, already half-asleep, to her cradle near the big bed. He was transported. He gave himself a small mental shake, but he knew that love-making would not yet be possible.

He put his arms about his bride and talked to her very softly, and he stroked her as he talked as though she was some new-born lamb. Then gradually, without his being aware of, strokings and touchings became stronger, almost rough, as though Maisie had now become his beloved Jessie.

And Maisie lay, at first tense, alarmed, then slowly she began to respond a little, touching him in her turn. Despite her unfortunate experience, she had not been marred, but she did feel that this aspect of marriage should be got over as swiftly and comfortably as possible. Why was he taking so long about it? As the minutes slowly passed, a great sweetness began to steal over her and an unexpected happiness, that was almost, but not quite, contentment. There were other physical sensations, growing ever stronger, so that her whole body burned with a great yearning, mixed now with anxiety, with fear. What was wrong? Was he afraid? Were these pettings all he intended? She could not believe what some girl had once said and giggled about, that Patrick Scott was doubtless too holy to take any girl to his bed. Well, she was not *any* girl; she was his wife!

"Patrick," she whispered, turning towards him in the dark, "I do want to be your wife - properly, I mean. Really, I do, Patrick.... "

"Ah," he said, murmuring into her soft, braided hair, "then that's all we need then, isn't it, my little love?"

Maisie was very young, still only sixteen, and of a cheerful, hopeful disposition, so, despite a not too propitious beginning, she soon settled down at Redesdale, determined, she told herself, to make the very best of things. Two things, though, she must broach with Patrick. Firstly, Hannah.

"She's ill. Can't you see she's not well?"

"Ah, alas, she does worry me a bit, but she'll be better now she's some company. In a little while. See how she is with the baby. She loves Lucy."

"Yes," said Maisie, doubtfully. Her mother-in-law was willing enough to keep an eye on the child and to call Maisie when needed, or even, on occasion, to give the child a bottle in her basinette. She sometimes even managed a faint smile, but she had never taken the baby into her arms. From the beginning she had made the same little excuse that she was afraid she might drop the child, as she was quite heavy.

"She ought to see a doctor, Patrick. Really, she ought! I got a rare shock when I saw her again. She was not like Mrs. Scott, so decided a lady. When she sits she's not peaceful-like, but all twily."

"Yes, well," he answered and looked awkward. "'Ee can suggest calling a doctor, if 'ee like - I've done so myself - but I'm certain sure she won' t see none of them. And, after all, 'tis for her to decide." There was a long silence. "Now, don't 'ee go worrying your purty head, Maisie, my love." Maisie stared at him, with some exasperation. "'Tis but a phase she's a-going through, Maisie and it'll pass. She'd been doing a bit too much before 'ee came to Redesdale."

Maisie opened her mouth to protest. For this sounded almost like a rebuke, that Hannah Scott had busied herself excessively preparing for the new daughter-in-law and Lucy. If she had, the results appeared to Maisie scarcely worth the effort. Wisely, she brought up her second point.

"Then, if there's been too much for your mother to do, why isn't there any help in the house? I'm really surprised, Patrick, I really am, there's not even one maid."

Now he looked a bit embarrassed.

"It was different when all of us worked on the farm. We all helped Ma a bit.... "

"I wasn't expecting to be the grand lady," she said, though that was exactly what she had expected to be as a child when she had first started to day-dream about Thomas and Redesdale. "But even at home we'd a girl once or twice a week when Mother was poorly - and - and.... " She flushed. "When father was working regular, that is." This had been several years since. "'Tis a big house this, Patrick. The washerwoman isn't near enough, and if we're snowed out again like last winter, as you told me, then what?"

"Oh, it won't happen again like that! Not for several years, I don't reckon."

"But we don't know, do we?"

"Perhaps you can find yourself a girl to come up from the village now and then, do some sewing and mending for 'ee? I don't want 'ee doing too much, Maisie."

She looked at him, calmly.

"Sewing and mending I don't mind, you know that."

"I'll think on it. I'll let 'ee know in a little while if 'tis possible. Then you can find yourself someone, p'raps a girl from Kimsley Mendip Orphanage might suit."

He turned away. He had already thought of the matter, realising he was expecting too much of a young girl with a baby, realising, in his heart, that his mother had been doing as little as she could for some time, all effort seeming to exhaust her. Why did he even hesitate? He knew they could well afford the tiny wages and the keep a young housemaid would expect, even two such girls. Why did he consider the matter of any importance at all? If he was not watchful, he, too, might well turn into a - into a - what? A miser? Never, he thought! Hadn't he decided there had been terrible mismanagement? Well, then, here was another proof.

Secretly, of course, he was afraid to admit that here was further evidence pointing against Hannah Scott. He had to pretend to himself that various calculations would have to be made and adjustments allowed. He had to take his time. Anything less would have seemed like the most gross disloyalty to Hannah. She had battled alone all those years - he discounted for the present the considerable help she had had from her sons. But at the end, there was the persistent, unsought thought, 'What on earth did she do with the money?'

Annie had an adenoidal expression, was but thirteen years of age and had, indeed, come from the Kimsley Mendip Orphanage. She was clearly disturbed at eating her meals with the family, though her table manners were good - the orphanage had seen to that - and upset at poor Jimmy's appearance. But she worked hard and devotedly for Maisie and was soon very reliable with the baby. Maisie made the fullest use of the child.

She had expected to play the role of docile, accepting daughter-in-law, at least for a while. Hannah's indisposition and apathy made her realise she had more power than she had anticipated. At first, uncertainly, then with increasing authority, she took charge of the household arrangements. Tactfully, she deferred to Hannah, but it was always her mother-in-law who gave way, immediately.

"Please yourself, my dear. Do whatever you think best," Hannah would reply, dully. (Anything, just as long as Hannah herself was not troubled, nor expected to do anything.) So, presently Maisie had all the curtains that could be washed, taken down, room by room, and attended to while the weather was still fine. With satisfaction, she looked at the draped blackthorn hedges near the house. There seemed to be small danger here of some passing gypsy or even a neighbour with itching fingers, stealing the curtains! Furniture began to shine again, furniture which had not seen a good beeswax polishing for many a month, in Maisie's view. The meals also improved somewhat, whenever she took full charge, the same simple honest dishes; but cooked much better than Hannah had managed even at peak achievement. They were also laid out more attractively, for Maisie began to use some of the splendid dishes from the dresser.

Not that Patrick noticed much difference and certainly none whatsoever in his meals. Food was merely necessary sustenance for the body. He ate slowly, thoughtfully, as though his mind was on other matters, never gobbling down his meals as his young brother Luke had done and never over-eating; he neither complained nor praised.

"Didn't you like that, Patrick, then?" Maisie took to asking.

"Eh?" He looked astonished. No-one had ever asked him such a question in his life before.

"You did like the pudding, didn't you?" she might add, a bit shyly, as his mother was present.

"Yes, yes. Very good." Then he would smile at her. Women, it seemed needed humouring and Patrick had a lot to learn. Maisie never pursued the matter, but she doubted very much if he could recall anything he had eaten half-an-hour later. She supposed this was the way of it with saintly people. She did not mind too much at this stage. The satisfaction lay in being able to do all she did and in having a contented baby.

Patrick spent an hour of his precious time teaching Maisie how to handle the trap and horse and, with a little help from either Cursons or Jimmy, she was soon able to do much of the harnessing. Patrick had hoped that this would encourage Hannah to venture forth, but he was sadly disappointed. Every time she went to Whytbrook, Maisie always asked Hannah if she would like to come with her and always she was relieved when she refused, but often she brought her back little gifts. Ostensibly, she went to visit her parents and Mrs. Squires, or perhaps one of her friends. Sometimes she took young Annie along with her and the baby as well.

She went back to her Sunday School teaching, at Mrs. Squires' prompting. She had been very doubtful about this. How the children would stare! But, then they always stared at one thing or another. Mrs. Squires pointed out that as Maisie was not much older than her charges, she understood them better. Then, again, Mrs. Squires had added for good measure, smiling a little, "You've got to hold your head high, Maisie, let the children see you've not been wholly overlooked!" She was referring to the local expression meaning 'gone to the bad'.

The girls in the class wore spotless white pinafores, so as not to spoil dresses not easily cleaned. There were always more girls than boys, not only because even in Whytbrook on a Sunday the boys could find more interesting things to do; there were often small duties for the boys, especially in summer-time. They all sat solemn-faced, as they did at the village school (when they attended, for absenteeism was heavy in the summer months) and they listened intently, as Maisie told her favourite Bible story. There were no hymn books to spare for the children, but once the first line had been sung to them, they were expected to know the rest. Maisie did her best on a piano in the corner. (She had never had any lessons, except a little coaching from Mrs. Squires.)

Withall, the girl did not neglect herself. Every day, fullers' earth was gently smoothed into her hands, as the gentlewomen were advised they must do, if they were to keep them white; every day also her pretty teeth were cleaned with cotton, wrapped round a stick, and dipped in a soapy lather with a few drops of ammonia. Never, of course, were these things done before Patrick! In Mrs. Squires' ladies' magazines it was emphasised that beauty secrets must remain secret! It was perfectly in order to brush one's hair in front of a husband and Maisie wished her thick, curling red hair, which only reached to her shoulders, streamed down her back. Childish affectation, no doubt, but of immense importance to her at the time, a matter of small pride.

In November, there was word from Thomas at long last, in fact several post-cards arrived together, not intended for the coming Christmas, alas. They had been posted in Cape Town months before and at different times, no doubt, but had arrived in a bunch, like a delegation. It was as though the little scraps of card had been altogether too apprehensive and too shame-faced to travel all those thousands of miles alone and present themselves singly, a truly pitiful offering.

To Maisie, this small disturbing intrusion appeared unfortunate, but she did not pass any comment. Had Thomas himself forgotten to mail them? she wondered. To Hannah they were a short lifting from her gloom. She became quite animated, her face flushed and she talked about Thomas for an hour or two, as she had not talked about anything much for a long time. Then she grew silent. The cards were placed on the mantelpiece, after everyone had studied them.

"There you are, Ma!" said Patrick, brightly, making the very most of it, "I knew Thomas had not forgotten 'ee. He's in South Africa, I see. Well, he always wanted to go to sea, didn't he, Ma? You should be glad he got what he wanted."

Maisie, studying the cards on her own, noticed they were all of buildings, solidly Victorian, some of them quite splendid as good as Bristol, even. And so English-looking.

That night in their room, she spoke to Patrick.

"Have you never felt jealous of Thomas, when you were little, Patrick?"

"Jealous, what d'ee mean my little love? Why should I be jealous?"

"Your Ma always made so much of Thomas, didn't she?"

"Oh, he was her favourite all right, no hiding that fact!"

"Well, then.... ?"

"Oh, but one couldn't be jealous of Thomas! No-one was. He was special. He - he is special. He was special to me and Luke. Everyone he met.... " He was silent a moment. "Mind you," he added thoughtfully, "I was a good bit fed-up when he first left home, just up and goes, but I'm sure the choice was honest enough. Must have been."

"How did you decide.... ?"

"Well," he grinned in the darkness, remembering, "ee'll think it all a bit silly, but we just drew lots." He was telling her something he had not told a living soul till now. And as he told it, a thought came to him. Had it been so silly? Behind the nonsense of the straws had there not been some guidance? Some power? Was it all chance, or had God intended this from the beginning.

Maisie said little, but from that time there began to grow in her a new feeling for Patrick. In all the best loving between a man and a woman there must be something maternal and, without thinking it out in any clear manner, it seemed to Maisie that Patrick had sometimes been deprived. Her mother-in-law had never appreciated her middle son. So she grew protective towards Patrick, but careful not to fuss him.

In a day or two one of the cards fluttered down from the mantelpiece, blown by a small gust when a door was opened suddenly. It flew into the fire and was ashes in a few seconds. No-one knew whether Hannah had noticed or not, but presently the rest of the cards had been removed from the shelf.

Christmas drew near and on Christmas Eve Maisie went off with Mrs. Squires on her annual visit of good cheer. Mrs. Squires hired a brougham, as leaving her home so seldom, she did not keep any kind of trap. She saw that Maisie was collected first (Lucy being left in the care of young Annie) then, together, the two women piled up the small vehicle with gifts. First there were the housewives of the village and most of them had small gifts to offer in exchange, for they were proud and did not believe in accepting and not making tiny kind of return. There were many smiles of welcome and good wishes for Christmas and the coming New Year, and not a few women implored them to sip a little home-made wine. Politely, they had to refuse. Why, they would both be quite drunk if they stopped at every home to imbibe!

There was far more than the traditional exchanging of gifts involved. Dear Auntie Squires was letting everyone know that Maisie was still very much her devoted friend and this counted, as the old lady was both prosperous and respected. At one house a door was slammed in their faces. A man had come to the door and saw the gifts as some kind of charity and glimpsing Maisie, reacted rudely.

"A pity to deprive the girls," said Mrs. Squires, shrugging, "but I may be able to get them on their own, sometime."

"But, why.... "

"Who knows?" Mrs. Squires answered, calmly. "Does it matter?"

They called upon Maisie's own mother, who was all a-flutter, but glad to see them, if only for a few minutes.

After that there followed the real reason for the outing, a visit to Kimsley Mendip Workhouse and the Orphanage (from which young Annie had come) standing almost next-door to the Workhouse. Maisie had not cared to admit that she was visiting the Workhouse, for Hannah became unusually agitated that she might by chance be going into the place.

"I don't rightly know what makes her so frightened," said Maisie to Auntie Squires. "Is she scared I mightn't come out again?" she laughed. Some people had a dread of the Workhouse that was understandable, but not justified in Hannah's case, surely.

"I expect it's her health," said Mrs. Squires.

"Yes," said Maisie, soberly.

"Some people think it's nice and convenient having an orphanage and workhouse next to each other, as it were. It saved building expenses, of course. I heard a wit say once, if they could only put a good cemetery on the further side of the workhouse, then all one's needs would be supplied without having to move out of the road!"

Maisie looked at her in puzzlement.

The tots and small children at the orphanage were duly lined up, their faces expectant, though solemn. Any older child, who could earn a little towards its keep was elsewhere, or had been sent into an early apprenticeship or domestic service. They had already been given a letter, phrased in pompous terms, from the Chairman of the Committee, together with a cheap, brightly-coloured text and a not so brightly-coloured Christmas card. These they clasped to their little chests. Next day, after dinner, they would receive a few sweets, often home-made by one of the ladies of the committee. Now they were being given not only a package of sweets, but a small drawing-book from

Maisie and Mrs. Squires. Not one of the children attempted to open the small packages, but continued to gape with wide eyes.

"Now, children!" said the matron, firmly.

"Thank yew, very much, m'am," they all chorused carefully, having been well rehearsed. Then again, in case they had not quite got it right, "Thank yew, very much." This time the voices were not quite in unison.

The warden, who prided herself on her culture, had tried to impress on the children that to say, 'thee,' or as they said in Somerset 'ee' was not polite. It was much too familiar, like the French using the word 'tu'. None of them had understood, of course. She smiled now, however, well pleased with her efforts. They looked so neat and clean, a credit to her.

The Workhouse inmates, in complete contrast, to the small children, showed no restraint. They were nearly all elderly, forgotten souls and they were overwhelmingly grateful that they were remembered at all. Some even had tears in their eyes. Most of them were essentially decent people, who had met with misfortunes, apart from old age and poor health; a few were of very low intelligence and could not have been capable of earning a good living. Here, again, cards and sweets would be distributed and tobacco given to the men on the day itself, but Mrs. Squires (and here she was not alone, for there were others) handed out their own small contributions on Christmas Eve. There were some singularly inappropriate gifts, such as badly-made sunbonnets for the women and clumsy tobacco pouches (also home-made) for the men.

They returned to the orphanage, where they ate oxtail stew with a plentiful supply of boiled potatoes and cabbage, followed by rice pudding and custard. This was a tradition for helpers, committee members and those, including Mrs. Squires, who had given financial support during the year. But did the children always eat so well? Maisie wondered. The table manners of the children were excellent, the older children assisting the little ones. Maisie found herself wondering about this. Sometimes it did not seem quite natural, like a rehearsed scene, almost.

Before going back to Mrs. Squires' home, they made their last call of the day. This was upon the grandmother of three of the children in the orphanage. Seriously crippled with arthritis, the old lady was quite unable to cope with the children, or visit them easily, but she loved to hear how they all fared. After the exchanging of small gifts, they were compelled to sip watery tea, while the old lady dabbed at her eyes.

Maisie was unsure whether the woman was weeping, had some ailment, or was suffering from the smokey fire. The place was dismal in the extreme, for the floors were of blue lias, a soft porous stone, and were awash with condensation. The fire was quite inadequate to banish the dampness. It was of peat and every now and again, a gust of wind would send a vile cloud of smoke into the room. The rafters of the ceiling were blackened.

The old woman was but a step from the workhouse - and indeed, would have been far more comfortable and warm had she been there - but she clung fiercely to her independence, made possible by the Parish and the occasional gift of money from her nephew, living in America. Her own children were dead.

Maisie was by this time, so depressed that she began to weep a little on the way to her Auntie Squires' home.

"Why, Maisie, love, what's wrong? Has it all been too upsetting for you, my dear?"

The girl nodded, gulped, and knew this was not the cause, not entirely.

"Well, before I send you off home, let's have another cup of tea. A good cup, this time!"

"'Tis Mrs. Scott," said Maisie, dismally, lapsing into the local idiom, "she do funny things times, Auntie Squires. Really."

"What kind of funny things?"

"Well, she keeps going to the pantry, again and again, but then she comes out with nothing, more often than not; and if I go she's always waiting to see what I've taken, watching me. 'Tis awful! As though I might be a thief!"

"Hmm. Have you mentioned this to Patrick?"

"'Course I have!" Only a few nights since she had told him and he had got up, quietly, and gone downstairs to look for himself in the pantry.

"He was gone ages, an hour or more. I was almost asleep when he got back and I could see he was cross, though he said little. He said he had looked in every corner and there was nothing amiss. I said, 'I didn't make it up, Patrick! She does keep going in there!' But all he did was pat my arm and say she'd probably forgotten why she had gone into the pantry, just forgetfulness. And I mustn't worry!"

"Well, it could be like that, I suppose," said Mrs. Squires, doubtfully. "Sometimes even I forget why I've come upstairs, for instance. Old age, Maisie."

"Mrs. Scott isn't old and this happens many times a day, Auntie. It does! But I don't think Patrick believes me, that's what upsets me!"

Mrs. Squires was silent a moment, then she said, softly, "You must trust Patrick."

The young girl was still snivelling.

"What happens when the new baby come?"

"What?"

"Yes, already. It must've happened the first week we were wed. I'm three months gone!"

"Oh, Maisie. Well, I did think Patrick was a bit more considerate than that."

At once Maisie leapt to his defence.

"I don't see how it was any more his fault than mine!"

Mrs. Squires considered her, thoughtfully.

"Perhaps not, " she said, absently.

"But it's too soon, isn't it?" Maisie was wailing. I'm only sixteen now. Is this what my life is going to be, Auntie Squires, a baby every year?"

"Oh, I shouldn't think.... " she came towards Maisie and took both of her hands. "Does Patrick know - about the new baby, I mean?"

Maisie nodded.

"He's guessed. I'm sure he's guessed."

"You'll have to have more help than that Annie you've got now, won't you? Perhaps, I can have a quiet word with Patrick."

"Well, I don't know.... "

"I'll be tactful." She was grimly thinking, though she did not say it, that Patrick seemed to expect his wife to be the paragon of all domestic virtues Hannah Scott was supposed to have been - until she went all to pieces, that is.

"Listen Maisie, " she said, suddenly making up her mind, "I'm an old woman and I'm not going to live much longer."

"Oh, Auntie.... "

"No, one must face facts. You know, I married late and my lady was very good to me. I've no children, only the niece, whom you've met and she is well enough. She'll get some money, but I decided to leave this house to you, and the one next door." The two semi-detached cottages had been built for upper servants many years ago, and each house had a full half-an-acre of land, following the extravagant custom of the time. The estate to which they belonged had long since been sold off in varying lots, even before Mrs. Squires bought the cottages for her husband and herself.

"But.... "

"I decided this a long time ago, Maisie," her friend continued, "but the reason I'm telling you now is that you will know whatever happens, you'll have a roof over your head, Maisie."

"Oh, Auntie, I don't know what to say! You'll not go yet for years and years, surely? Promise me you won't? This house wouldn't be the same without you, not at all!"

Mrs. Squires managed to bring the girl to some degree of composure.

"It may be quite a while. It may not be, but this is your little secret, yours and mine. I don't want you even to tell Patrick. Promise?"

"Well, I don't understand, but.... "

Little more was said and presently Maisie was climbing into the brougham before returning to Redesdale Farm, trying not to be too fretful, as the driver was looking at her.

As for Mrs. Squires, she found herself thinking that if Hannah Scott had her secret treasure (according to local gossip, which was probably wildly exaggerated) then it was good to know her dear Maisie also had her safeguard against adversity. And, she thought, with deep satisfaction, these two cottages must be worth a good deal more than Hannah Scott's few hoarded sovereigns.

CHAPTER XIII

Katherine Elizabeth Scott, always to be known in the family as Kate, was born in early July. From one point of view, her entry was - and, indeed, always would be well-timed. The shearing was over as well as the early haymaking. The weather was warm but not hot, and by good fortune, Rose being back in Whytbrook again for a short spell, was able to spend a week at the farm, taking charge of the household and assisting the midwife.

It was not an easy birth, however, as Kate was a larger baby than Lucy had been, with a breadth of shoulder, reminiscent of her father. Indeed, but for the timely intervention of the doctor, frantically summoned by Patrick, it would have been an extremely difficult breech birth. As it was, Maisie soon recovered her strength, and the baby gave every appearance of going to be an exceptionally active, lively child.

"How odd," Maisie mused to herself, as she lay in that state of euphoria following a birth. How perverse nature could be! Her first, not-greatly desired baby had arrived with comparatively little pain or fuss, almost as though making her apologies for causing any kind of trouble at all. So Maisie had taken it for granted that a second child, especially one she clearly wanted, would also be an easy birth. She already sensed that Kate was going to be one of those children who demand attention, a restless child, sharply intelligent in many ways, but decidedly extrovert.

"But I love her," she thought, fiercely, "and she's going to be beautiful and make a success of her life, better than I've done."

Patrick unreservedly adored his tiny daughter from his very first glimpse of her.

Before she left, Rose sought out Patrick to tell him things she was sure 'he would not mind my saying' and swiftly began, whether he minded or not, to point out various matters that must be put right as soon as possible. Firstly, there were various things lying about the yard and the garden, which could be a source of danger to a young toddler. And he really must see about having a good strong gate fixed at the head of each flight of stairs, if he did not want an accident.

Patrick nodded. He knew she was right, but he wondered when he would find the time to attend to the gates. Lucy was a careful child and, perhaps, by the time his little Kate was walking, he could get someone in to see to this matter for them.

"And another thing, Patrick," said Rose, bringing out her most devilish card very firmly, "I'm sure you won't mind my saying this, but I do think as Mrs. Scott ought to be in t'infirm'ry!"

He stared back at her, red-faced with her vehement sense of propriety, with sudden dislike. He wondered how he could, even for an idle moment, have considered marryng Rose.

"Are 'ee saying Ma's mad? Are 'ee?" he demanded.

"Well, no, of course not," she said, her face growing even redder, "but are 'ee being fair to dear Maisie, Patrick? Mrs. Scott does almost no work when you're away from home, just sits and stares, often doesn't speak. Sits near the fire - in this weather! - all day long. Then she watches whatever goes on near her, the while, but says nothing."

"Maybe just this week, but I very much doubt she just sits when things be normal."

Rose pursed her lips.

"I'm not exaggerating! It's as I say. Maisie said as much."

"I'm sure she does her bit, but she's not been well o' late and she's worked hard in her time. Why, winter before last.... "

Rose put out her hand and touched Patrick's arm.

"Take heed, Patrick," she said, darkly. "To be honest, I've seen people like her in t'asylum afore now, all drawn into themselves, as she is. No different like. Not interested in nothing!"

"Well, I don't know what to say. P'raps I'd best speak to the doctor again," he said, heavily.

"You do that."

Without any prior warning to Hannah, Patrick managed to bring in a doctor from Kimsley Mendip one afternoon. The consultation took place in the parlour with Maisie sitting quietly on one side, not saying a word and not being asked anything, either. Patrick stayed in the kitchen, smoking a needed pipe. At the end of the visit, the doctor came out, smiling. There was nothing at all to worry about. Nothing at all! Maisie had listened to Hannah brightly answering all the questions put to her, without any hesitation. She was astounded. It was like a brilliant performance and it clearly had pulled the wool over the eyes of the doctor, in Maisie's opinion.

The doctor was speaking alone to Patrick when she returned with her mother-in-law and she heard him say, convincingly, that he had no fears for her at all. She would recover her cheerfulness in good time. It was simply her time of life.

"Just humour her, but not too much," he smiled. He almost made Hannah Scott seem like a perverse child. "You'll be all right, Mrs. Scott," he added, turning to his patient, briefly. "Wish I was as fit! You've worked hard, so enjoy your rest for the time being."

Not another tonic, thought Patrick wearily. But the doctor left without a further word. Maisie and he stared at each other, but not till much later was she able to tell him about the consultation.

"I couldn't believe my ears. She truly hood-winked the doctor, Patrick."

'Or us,' he thought; then wondered how she could keep it up so long, if that was the case? Did it all go back to Thomas? He did not understand.

"We must try to cheer her up all we can," he said. "No doubt the new baby'll help."

And he patted her arm in sympathy, without realising he had done so.

Meanwhile, there was suddenly news of Luke, not directly, but by means of the manager of the small Kimsley Mendip bank. It appeared that Luke Scott had decided at long last to repay the amount he had got from the sale of the mare and this small sum had been transferred from an Australian bank to England.

Patrick had long forgotten all about the stolen mare, and he even felt a little irritation towards Luke for reminding him of this incident. They certainly did not need the paltry amount, which was even less than he would have supposed the mare to have fetched. It was almost as though Luke was saying, in effect, he could well afford to pay the heavy charges involved in sending the money all this way. It was like a pointer, an indicator to the future.

"When I am rich - and I shall be one day - no-one will be able to say I got there by cheating."

Patrick told himself he must not think along such lines. So Luke was in Australia, was he? He said nothing to his mother at all, deeming this wisest, and for several days he kept it entirely to himself. Then the growing habit of confiding in his young wife, prompted him to speak to her.

"He always wanted to go and work in the sun somewhere, right from being a child. He used to talk of it, but it seemed unlikely, a hopeless dream. I'm glad he got what he wanted, but it would've been nice if there'd been a letter for Ma, telling her what he was actually doing and so on. Is he still working with sheep, I wonder?"

He sighed a little and felt Maisie tense in his arms.

"Now, now, my own little love, 'ee mustn't continue to resent. He did 'ee a great wrong, but 'tis all over, and but for this - I mean, it's all turned out for the best, hasn't it?.... And I don't think as 'ee'd have liked Australia, somehow. Too hot, and too far from your family."

Maisie said not a word.

He drew her closer and said, almost hesitantly, "Maisie, my own little love, I fear 'ee've married the duffer of the family."

"Oh, Patrick.... "

"'Tis true enough. They'll both fulfill their ambitions, Thomas and Luke. And me, I'll still be where I'm now in ten years time with no more ambition than an April shower.

"Oh, Patrick," she said again, "You mustn't talk like this."

"Do 'ee mind, that I'll never be rich?" He grinned in the darkness, enjoying the joke, that anyone could even expect more from him than what he well knew himself to be. "And I'll never travel to foreign places like Thomas."

"Whytbrook's good enough for me, Patrick," she said, loyally.

He was silent a moment longer, then he said, "I well know 'tis hard on 'ee, Maisie love, with - with Ma as she do seem to be these days. But she seems sensible enough and she'd never do any harm to 'ee nor the children."

"Of course not!"

"I'd have it on my conscience if - I mean, I don't think she's going to live that much longer, so we must just be patient with her and do our best, hard as it is on 'ee Maisie, my love."

"I can manage."

"Maisie love, you and me, we've got each other," he added, slowly, firmly, "each other and the children. But ask yourself, what has she got?"

Not saying a word, Maisie tightly wound her arms about him.

But it was only a week after this conversation, at the beginning of October, that Patrick came downstairs one dark dawn and dimly glimpsed a shape lying at the bottom. Trembling, he raced down the rest of the stairs, found and lit a lamp and held it high. Sprawled in an awkward position, legs apart and face downwards, lay a figure. He put down the lamp on one of the stair treads and gently tried to turn the body over. It was Hannah and he thought, at first, she was dead. But she moved a little and opened her eyes wide and as he studied her twisted face and tried to make her more comfortable, he realised she was trying desperately to speak to him. The words were clearly formed, but in such a whisper that he could scarcely make out what she said. He bent his ear. There was pain in her left leg and all down her side felt "funny".

Hannah Scott had, in fact, just had a stroke. And she had broken her leg in her fall. What she was doing on the stairs at all at this very early hour, and still in her nightdress, Patrick could not imagine. Having done his best for his mother, Patrick hastened back to Maisie, got her to go upstairs and call Annie, and then he hurried down the two fields to the Cursons' cottage to ask young Mr. Cursons to go and fetch a doctor. Even Mrs. Cursons was enlisted to help and she did so willingly enough, enjoying the sudden drama which had abruptly punctuated her monotonous existence.

When, some considerable time later, Hannah was carried out to a carefully padded trap, Patrick was given the shock of his life. Hannah, having feebly tried to resist being wrapped in blankets and conveyed from the farmhouse, suddenly shrieked aloud. It was a coarse voice Patrick had never heard her use and she poured forth an avalanche of abuse and of invective which, but for the occasion, would have greatly angered her son. Where had she learned such words? Where had she got it all from? He was not even sure he knew the meaning of some of it. He could only think it had been stored in her memory since childhood when she had chanced to overhear her people's employees quarrelling amongst themselves. Perhaps she had overheard, even without realising she had done so, on several occasions, and then secretly hoarded this unwholesome filth against a time of dire need and deep crisis. Patrick was appalled. Surely, his mother must be mad? This was the only explanation. The only possible explanation.

But Hannah was far from being mad and when, a short while later, Patrick was able to visit her with Maisie, she spoke, though slowly, quite rationally and calmly. She appeared to have completely forgotten her shameful outburst. She was trying hard to impress upon him now that all at Redesdale belonged to him and Maisie.

"Everything," she murmured. "The farm - everything. All yours, Patrick. It is as you deserve, Patrick. The money.... "

"Ma, ma," he said, a little wearily, but with kindness, "don't go bothering your head about such matters now. 'Ee're to get well and come back home to us. That's all Maisie and me want. Nothing else matters right now."

She gripped his hand with her right hand, showing remarkable strength and a strange look came into her eyes.

"Everything," she repeated.

It was a time of great strain and Patrick was compelled to rely upon Cursons a good deal. He even wished he had Jimmy around sometimes to help young Annie with the children, but Jimmy had gone back to the cooper in the spring, though he visited the Scotts frequently, especially on Sundays.

Then Hannah was back home again, her leg still in plaster. The doctor had been right. She had changed, though not as he foresaw. Extraordinarily, she seemed to have little recollection of what had taken place during the past many months, though she spoke vividly of the distant past. She even chatted about going to the christening - now when she could go nowhere at all! Another strange thing. She wept when Maisie did her any little kindness, and wept again when visitors from Whytbrook (mainly out of curiosity) came to call on her. She wept for no reason at all, distressing Patrick, who did not understand her condition. He was more frightened now, truth to tell, than he had been by her apathy and long silences. He could not get it out of his fancy that a devil of some kind must have got into his mother. It must be so, as they had long ago written about such things in the Bible. He tried hard to dismiss the notion as superstition. Yet, what else was he to think?

She had always been a settled factor in their lives, but ever since Thomas left home she had constantly shown a different, worrying side to her nature, that left him amazed. Were all women like this at heart? Could even his own precious little love turn out like this? Never, he thought, if he could help it; never if loving could keep her safe.

Once in a while a brief and puzzled look would come into Hannah's face, as though she struggled to recall something, and that it bothered her a little. She would pause as though listening for some prompting, then the look would pass and her face would again fall into its wistful expression. What no-one realised was that Hannah had completely forgotten about her secret hoarding, her treasure. It was all quite gone from her memory, as had the very place where it had been put for safety, and the perverted reason for its existence. All gone. So she wept and did not know why she wept, but looked so grateful to anyone who called upon her, or took any interest in her, that there was a good deal of whispering about her. No more understanding her health condition that did her family, the villagers hinted that a change of heart had come over Hannah. She must have committed some wrong and now when she drew close to her end, she was full of repentance.

But Hannah showed no sign of wishing to confess to any real or imagined wrong; and the days and the weeks passed.

It was on Boxing Day of that year, 1882, exactly two years to the day since Hannah had unwillingly left the farm, that the final change came. Little Annie went into the room which had been turned into a bedroom on the ground-floor, next to the parlour. She brought the usual tray with tea, which she placed by the sofa. Then she went to draw the curtains and looked to see how the fire had lasted during the night. It still gave out a gleam of light, but the candle had long since burnt away. There was no sound of movement from the large sofa, no murmured greeting.

"Mrs. Scott," she said, taking Hannah's pillows to plump them into greater comfort. The head sagged forward and Annie realised Mrs. Scott would not be needing tea, nor indeed anything else, not on this earth.

With great composure, for she had seen several deaths before, young though she was, she went off to advise Maisie, remembering to carry the tray back with her to the kitchen. Patrick was already out in the fields.

Patrick was deeply distressed. He had understood almost nothing of his mother's depression and the following stroke, but now he blamed himself needlessly, wearing for a short time the pietistic hair-shirt of penitence. Maisie, at this time, suddenly found herself in the position of being the stronger of the two, as she comforted him, assuring him over and over again he had done his very best for his mother.

"I should've gone after Thomas and made him come home! I did think on it once, even wrote to him, but I should've gone to him!"

"Dear Patrick, are you sure it would've helped? In the long run, I mean? Was it just Thomas's going made her so ill? The stroke.... "

But for a while longer he had to indulge his self-mortification, though he was basically too sensible a man to continue. Life went on. The farm, the animals made their demands on him. And his family. One must remember what Jesus had said about the dead, hard though that might seem. Maisie stroked his head and muttered the ever-lasting comfort,

"She's at peace, now, Patrick. No more suffering, Patrick, dear." (Though, in her secret core, she wondered whether Hannah Scott would ever be at peace, dead or alive. She was a strange spirit, that one.)

There was another surprise in store, a pleasant one this time. Against all expectations, it seemed Hannah had actually made a will, a fresh one, and it must have been made in those few weeks when Luke was supposedly planning to marry Maisie. It was plain she had resigned herself by then to losing her eldest son and she was determined that the farm should not be divided between Patrick and Luke in some way when she was gone. She had probably reasoned that Luke would take his bride abroad if he got the chance. Emigration would save a lot of speculation and gossip. So the farm and everything Redesdale contained belonged now to Patrick. It was a big relief to Maisie. There was a small gift of jewellery for the girl and some more items for the Jackson family, also a donation, quite a small one, to the church. There was no mention, however, of any large sum of money.

CHAPTER XIV

Again, for a second year running, the winter was comparatively mild and the land moved briskly and purposefully into spring.

Maisie was still coping with the work of the farmhouse, her two young children and the hens, with only young Annie to help her, apart from the weekly washerwoman. For a few weeks there had been a nursemaid, but as jealousy soon arose between her and Annie, she did not stay.

Patrick, as his farming duties allowed, did a great deal to help his young wife, more than might have seemed to be reasonable to the envious. Indeed, in The Bell, the landlord's wife said she had heard tell young Mrs. Scott could twist her husband right round her little finger! He not only dug the kitchen garden, but planted it out as well, which had always been the woman's task. And in the house he did more than might seem proper or even manly. He'd been seen on one occasion nursing the baby and changing its diaper, if you please!

In the spring, Cursons suddenly announced that he would not be remaining after the shearing was complete and the haymaking over. He had it in mind to go back to Canada and he felt he ought to be settled well before the winter came on. Patrick knew he would be sorry to see him go, as he had proved to be a good worker in most respects; but he strongly suspected his wife was the cause of his wishing to leave. Not infrequently, he had overheard the pair of them quarrelling loudly when he chanced to be in the vicinity of the cottage. So, perhaps the rigours of the Canadian winters were to be preferred. He also learned that Mrs. Cursons planned to remain in Whytbrook for the time being and follow her husband to Canada later on. (Or perhaps not?) Where would he get another man like Hawker? He prayed he would not have to waste time in the early summer trying to find someone suitable. The price of lamb had risen, in the strange, inexplicable manner of such happenings, and he hoped this would effect the prices he could get for his sheep. Patrick had no idea whether this rise had anything whatever to do with the fact that prices in the U.S.A. were said to have fallen rapidly of late (as some suggested) and he could not truly comprehend the half of it.

But later on, he had a piece of good luck. James Bevan, Maisie's elder brother came to see him. He had called several times during the past year, no doubt to see how his sister fared, and he had had many quiet chats with Patrick about the farming situation. This time, however, after a lengthy preamble, he came to the point. He was not content where he worked and would like to get back to Whytbrook, or rather nearer than where he was at present. He was having to pay a small rent for a cottage, which annoyed him; and the prospect of a free cottage appealed very much. Patrick was in a quandary. James was not a shepherd, but more of an all-rounder though, like all of them, he had some sound knowledge of sheep. He had many a time assisted with the shearing at different farms, and he was especially good with pigs. It would be nice, too, for his little love to have someone of her own near at hand.

So, in due course, towards the end of July, James and his wife moved into the cottage Cursons had vacated. Some time after this - though not for another eighteen months Matthew moved into the second cottage. He was still unmarried, but he brought his (by then) widowed mother to stay with him.

Inevitably, the customers in The Bell knew how to explain this situation. They referred, amongst themselves, to Redesdale, as Bevan Farm.

Meanwhile, life continued, quietly, peacefully enough, the daily dramas being small in their scale. There was another limited outbreak of swine-fever in the summer in their area, but it fortunately did not claim the Scott's animals, though it meant a return to the rigorous care and constant vigilance of former outbreaks. They had several healthy piglets at this time.

Having been duly served by one of Farmer Ridley's prize bulls, after nine long months of gestation a shorthorn had produced a healthy, lively calf. In early May, then, having more milk than usual, Maisie took it into her head to make a little cheese, assisted by Annie. The baby, Kate, now almost ten months old, had been laid on a thick blanket in the garden with her movements curtailed by several wooden chairs, laid on their sides. Her small sister, Lucy, was supposed to be keeping an eye on her and from time to time, she ran through the open doors from the front of the house to the kitchen to report any minor changes, for she took her duties as watcher seriously. It was as well the cheese-making was more in the nature of a game than a serious business. In a way, it was scarce worth all the trouble, but it would be nice to be able to tell Patrick later on that she had made the cheese herself!

Annie stared at the recipe they were using and wrinkled her brow in puzzlement.

"It do say here, it's got to be acid whether... "

"'Whether by design or chance.'" finished Maisie.

For a moment, the girls looked nonplussed.

"'But still sub - sub - 'What does this word mean, Mrs. Scott? I don't know this word."

"'Subordinate to the rennet,'" Maisie read aloud, wondering why on earth the recipe was so complicated and why it could not give you the exact amounts to use, though she supposed this would be a little difficult. "Ah, I see. This comes about, seeming, through the slip-scalding. Yes, of course, that's what make it acid."

Annie still looked perplexed.

"And the salt, Annie."

"Yes, we mustn't forget the salt. It'd taste somethin' awful without the salt!" She giggled.

Maisie bent her head to the recipe.

"And it say here, 'Salt is a good servant, but a bad master.'"

They both burst out laughing, more like two friends than mistress and maid.

Maisie had been vaguely aware, from time to time, of a distant bellowing cow through the open doors. It seemed no more than an appropriate background melody and, concentrated upon her work, she tried to ignore the noise. She entirely lacked Patrick's instinctive awareness of the needs of stock, but she did know by now that a cow, unlike human-beings, never bellows without due cause. Was something the matter with the cow? she wondered, absently.

Only a day or two past the calf had been moved to a neighbouring field, where it could no longer be unreasonably at the teats of its mother, but could still have a sight and sniff of her through the gate. If the cow, whose name she did not know, was still objecting to this arrangement then, thought Maisie, she must have some especially powerful maternal feelings

There was a cry from Jimmy, who was spending a few days at the farm as his chest had again been troublesome. He burst into the kitchen from the direction of the barton.

"Missus," he said, agitatedly, "Missus, where's Master? 'Ee've got to fetch Master!"

Maisie looked at the cripple, red-faced and tearful, in some surprise.

"Why he's gone to the fair with Mr. Cursons. You know that. He went this morning. What's wrong, Jimmy?" Cursons was, of course, still at Redesdale at this time.

"Gran'fer's gone and taken t'calf, Missus! He's a-taken 'er right away and 'im h'oughtn't to do that, ought't he?"

"Taken the calf? You must be mistaken, Jimmy. Why would he do that?"

"He's a-stolen 'er, Missus. Oi tried to stop 'e, but but.... " The poor fellow was now wringing his hands in deep distress, tears pouring down his ugly face. "'Ee've got to stop 'e, Missus, or Master'll be that cross!"

"Now, now, Jimmy, be calm. Master won't be cross with you. It's not your fault, is it? Now tell me quietly what's happened."

As the simple youth began to pour out his story, prompted from time to time by Maisie, she looked at him more closely. Gently, she took him by one of his long arms and drew him towards her. She saw then to her horror and indignation, that the lamager must have been shamefully beaten, then flung to the ground. His face was swollen, there was a cut above one eye-brow and he was covered with dust down one side of his clothes. The brute, thought Maisie, angrily, certain Patrick would be far more upset about this than the loss of even a valuable animal, which he would probably be able to retrieve. What a pity he was away at the fair! But, of course, this was why old man Coxon had chosen this particular time!

The cow still continued to bellow plaintively, like a bovine soul in torment.

Having tended to Jimmy as best she could, she ran out into the fields, where the calf had been only this morning. He was gone right enough, but there was absolutely nothing at all she could do till Patrick got back.

She got Annie to attend to the children and make some tea. The cheese-making was (for the time-being) completely forgotten.

When Patrick returned in the evening, tired but placidly satisfied with his day's business at the fair, Maisie proceeded to pour forth the whole story almost as soon as he had seated himself and removed his boots. The children were upstairs with Annie.

"Where's young Jimmy now?"

His young wife told him she had sent Jimmy to bed to rest. Without a word Patrick got up and padded into Jimmy's room in his slippers. He came back, in a moment, looking very angry indeed.

"But, Patrick," Maisie wailed, "there was nothing I could do! Nothing! I did go and look and the calf's certainly gone. I also threw out the swill for the sow," she added, with some pride.

He patted her arm. He was pulling on his boots again.

"Where're you going? Aren't you going to have your supper first?"

"It'll keep. This is more important, I reckon, while the light lasts."

"What about the horses?"

"They'll be all right. I'll get Cursons to do anything that's necessary. Don't worry, my little love. I'll be back as soon as I can."

"That dreadful man. Stealing a calf is terrible, like trying to steal your living! Not like taking a turnip or a young carrot," she added half-wistfully. She was musing on the times when, like most young children, she had also helped herself to a fresh vegetable to chew as she passed through a field. "But why, Patrick? Why would he do this?"

Said Patrick slowly, "He's always been peeved I didn't pay him ought for Jimmy's working for me, I reckon."

Perhaps he had taken other things, without his being aware of it, but this was going too far. He was, however, far more upset about the brutality shown to Jimmy, especially as he had been unwell of late.

By the time he reached the shack, his face was grim. He had called to his dog, though, as she had not been to the fair and had sadly missed him.

"Jessie'll look after me," said Patrick, grinning at his wife.

It was still light, but being in a slight hollow, one or two of the shacks showed the luxury of a gleaming candle; not so the hut occupied by Coxon and his woman. Patrick banged on the broken door and shouted out loud. A slatternly-looking woman with long, tangled hair, falling well below her shoulders and with a baby on one arm, came to the door. There was another vacant-eyed child of perhaps five years behind her, clutching her dirty skirts. She glowered with hostile eyes, though there was some fear in them.

"What d'ee want?" she eventually asked, belligerently.

"I want Mr. Coxon," said Patrick. "Who else?"

"Well 'e h'aint 'ere," the woman answered him sharply and made to slam the rickety door upon him.

Patrick was just pushing the door backwards when a voice from behind him said, slyly, "Well, if it h'aint Mister Scott!" Patrick swung round and in the fast-growing dusk, made out the figure of old Coxon.

"What've 'ee done with my calf, Mr. Coxon?"

"Calf? Oi knows nothin' 'bout no calf. But take a look round for yerself. Look h'any place yous a mind to. Oi don't mind."

"Jimmy saw 'ee taking the calf," said Patrick, angrily. "Have you sold it already? Have 'ee?"

The other said not a word for a moment, then he grinned.

"There h'aint no calf here Mister Scott." He suddenly kicked open the door and moved towards it. "Come on in, Mr. Scott, if 'ee can stummick the smell!" He guffawed and Patrick saw the man had been drinking, for the fumes on his breath were powerful. No doubt celebrating his victory over the calf. But he followed Coxon into his hovel, ashamed even in his anger that anyone could live in this state. There was a small fire burning, which gave out a certain amount of light.

The woman had gone back to stirring the pot at the fire, the baby still suckling at her breast and held, almost negligently, by one arm.

The altercation continued, prolonged and futile, for Patrick was now questioning the man about his grandson.

Then Coxon said the most terrible thing. Perhaps it was the drink loosening his tongue; or perhaps he was well past caring any longer about decencies.

"What gran'son? Oi've no gran'son! 'E's me son, h'aint 'e?"

"Dear Lord!" Patrick stared back and knew the man had spoken the truth, knew also that this was probably why he had so cruelly misused the lad after his wife died. 'He shames us all.' Hadn't he said something like that when he came to call on them all that long time ago? And this was the reason why his wretched daughter had fled, abandoning her baby.

Without premeditation, Patrick struck him as hard as he could in the chest. The other fell back but, old though he was, he was immensely tough and he came back with shuddering blows. It was a vicious fight for the time it lasted, outside of anything acceptable, for the old man kicked where he could, then began to reach for handy weapons; and Patrick well knew he was fighting a man years older than himself and, for all his seeming strength, nothing like so fit. Also very drunk. It was despicable. But during those long minutes which seemed like an eternity, the fight continued with fury.

Then the woman, without warning, dumped her howling baby on the floor in a corner, pushed aside the other child and came at Patrick in that cramped space with a heavy pan she had lifted down. From the corner of his eye, he saw her approach and knew he could do nothing. She would crack in his skull and that would be the end of him. He tried, in those few split seconds to avoid the blow. But something happened. There was a growl, a loud bark and there burst through the still open door Jessie, teeth bared. She went first for the woman, leaping high and toppling her, so that her pan fell from her hand and clattered to the mud floor, slightly grazing Jessie; but only slightly, for the next second, she was on to Coxon. Both small children were yelling, loudly.

The woman was suddenly terrified, cowering in the corner with her children. As for Patrick, as he panted and tried to regain his breath, he saw Jessie was at the man's throat.

"Pull 'im off!" cried the woman. And Patrick, not without some difficulty, at length succeeded.

"Come on, Jessie, time to go!"

"Oi'll see that h'animal's put down!" screamed the woman. Coxon was beyond saying anything, but he was at least alive and Patrick, as he walked back home in the dark, thanked God for that much.

Good old Jessie! Who would have thought such a gentle animal had it in her to fight like that? His anger was still high and he half-chuckled to himself as he felt the May breezes on his face. This would teach that brute to touch young Jimmy! This would teach him to come near Redesdale.

But the night wind had a cooling effect on his senses also. He no longer rejoiced. But for Jessie's intervention, murder must have been done by one of them; if not the Coxons, then he, himself. For, oh, yes, he had had murder in his heart all right. It was shattering to discover he was capable of this kind of rage. Did a man ever truly know his own nature? And why had he been so angry? Not just Jimmy's beating and the loss of his calf, surely? He must try not to think about it. He must forget it. He must remember, in future, that vengeance belonged solely to the Lord.

He had much for which to thank his bitch, Jessie. He felt humbled and disorientated, but he supposed this was due to the fight and his need of food.

Somehow, he managed to keep the nasty episode from Maisie; but for the first time since he was a tiny child, he did not kneel at the bedside to say his prayers that night.

The summer days continued to be very busy, but on the whole, also gratifying. Patrick had decided the episode concerning the calf was best forgotten, though he occasionally found himself wishing he had never had anything to do with the Coxons and had certainly had the good sense not to go near the old man on the night of the fight. There it was and the Good Book had plenty to say about this. No man could alter his past actions, merely try to make them comfortable with himself. On a couple of occasions the cooper had complained to him that Jimmy was no longer quite up to a full day's work, as he had been. He even hinted that the long spell he had taken from his routine work when he stayed with the Scotts had caused him to lose much of his skill as a cooper's assistant. This worried

Patrick. Had he, in the end, done the cripple any good at all? Certainly, he had never been of much use on the farm, as a large variety of different small tasks under different, changing circumstances had confused him, making him seem far denser than he was.

Cursons finally left and went to Canada and his wife also moved out of the cottage to Whytbrook; and within a week, hard-working, but taciturn James Bevan and his cheery wife moved into the small cottage near the road to Whytbrook.

Then, in early July there was the shocking discovery that was to cause gossip and speculation for years to come. A farm labourer had gone out with his dog one evening, taking his gun. Without warning, the gun-dog suddenly disappeared, following a scent. The man had some trouble locating the animal which, was not hidden in deep thickets, but burrowing deeply into the 'gruffy' land near the old lead mine. For one horrifying moment, the labourer thought his dog had vanished for ever, but when he dragged him forth he found the dog was holding on to a scrap of dirty cloth and what looked like the ulna of a human-being! It certainly did not belong to any animal he knew. The man peered and thought he could see what appeared to be the remains of a human skeleton.

Terrified, the man made the animal drop the bone and he took promptly to his heels. He reported it, though. He could not keep a happening like that to himself.

It transpired the remains had lain there many a year, perhaps twenty years or more, the police doctor surmised. They could tell they were of a young woman. That far, and not much further, had forensic science proceeded at the time.

Then the rumours began. There were those who speculated and came to the conclusion that the skeleton was that of poor Jimmy Coxon's mother, Hester, who had gone from the village twenty years or more ago, just after he was born. It must be her, since no-one else had gone missing from the village. They dismissed entirely the notion of others that the woman was some passing tinker's wife. It was said there were signs of an injury to the skull and whilst the cause was uncertain, immediately the customers in The Bell pronounced that this made it more certain than ever it was Jimmy's mother. She had been running away and had fallen. Fallen? More likely murdered! Hadn't there been stains on the bits of clothing, which proved to be blood?

And if murdered, then who else but that old man Coxon could have committed such a crime. He had plenty of cause, from all accounts, but the earth, like the sea, always gave up its secrets in the end. There was talk that Coxon had killed the girl out of shame, or in a temper when she resisted him. The stories became more and more blood-curdling. The Bell loved it. The Wool Pack, which normally kept itself aloof from petty tattle (as behoves a hostelry, charging a half-penny more for each cider pint) was, on this occasion, drawn into the local gossip. The rumours were quite wild. Coxon had been called in to 'question'! He had been arrested! He was coming up for trial!

In fact, this was not the case. In truth, nothing at all could be proven, nor ever would be. The remains of the body were to continue a mystery, a satisfying one, adding greatly to the gloom of the place, a warning to those who stayed too long at the fairs, coming home in the dark. A mystery, indeed. Yet, shortly afterwards, Coxon and his woman and children moved out of the area for good. This was no doubt pure coincidence, but it added fuel to the gossip. Patrick tried hard not to cogitate upon the matter himself, but he could not but feel very uneasy about young Jimmy, who had been left behind.

Almost as an anti-climax after all the excitement about the discovery of the dead woman's remains, there arrived at Redesdale a letter from Thomas. It was quite a lengthy letter this time and even contained a photograph of a plump, naked baby, lying on her stomach, which he said was his daughter, Miriam. Sadly, the letter was addressed to Hannah. Patrick read it aloud to Maisie, stunned at the bright, breezy tones, which seemed almost flippant. He was sure, he wrote, he would be forgiven for his long silence since his last letter (so there had been at least one earlier letter, then, which must have gone astray?) but he had, of course, been extremely busy, not only working, but studying. He was well on the way to being a qualified naval engineer now, for which he had to thank his skipper. He seemed to take it for granted that his marriage was known to them as he several times mentioned someone named Olivia. He enquired how they all were, especially herself, and assured Hannah he would surprise her one of these days. Who knows but what he would not suddenly turn up at Redesdale with his family? It was self-evident he was no longer in touch with the Jackson family in Glastonbury, nor his sister, Jane. He made a few jokes about his tough life, which he was clearly relishing, and signed himself, 'Ever your loving son.'

Patrick re-read the letter several times to himself, then he wrote to his brother, since there was a London address, and his own letter was crisp. Thomas's letter ought to have struck a note of deep poignancy, but somehow it had seemed shallow, almost false. This was grossly unfair, Patrick reminded himself, since Thomas was unaware of his mother's death. He wrote to Thomas that he was also married now and had two little girls, but he quite omitted to mention Maisie's name.

Swiftly back came a reply from Thomas, more sober now, deeply regretting his mother's passing. He sang her praises at some length. He hinted her life had been hard, perhaps too hard, and even had the gall to ponder if too much had not been expected of her. He wished Patrick himself every happiness in his married state.

That was all. After that, came total silence.

"Never mind," said Maisie, comfortingly, "he's changed and there it is. 'Tis all in the past, Patrick, dear. We must look to the future and I've good news. Have 'ee guessed, eh? (She sometimes adopted Patrick's way of speaking these days.) "I'm expecting again!"

"Oh, Maisie. I did so think I'd been that careful. However will 'ee cope?"

"I'll be fine, I'm sure. It's good news, Patrick. It's going to be a boy this time. You want a son, don't 'ee?"

"Oh, 'ee can't be sure!"

"I am sure. I feel it. It's going to be a boy!" She laughed out loud, happy for him and for herself. Then, in her roundabout way she said, "Annie's leaving, you know."

"No, I didn't. I'm sorry. That'll make things more difficult for 'ee, training in a new girl."

"I mean to get two girls this time, sisters if possible, from the orphanage. I'll persuade Annie to remain till the baby's come." She hoped to persuade her to change her mind completely. If Annie was in charge with the two girls under her, that would make a difference, wouldn't it? (In fact, Annie was not ambitious, but she did hope one day to meet some nice young man, not very likely at Redesdale.)

"And another thing, Patrick, dear, I want Jimmy to come back to us."

He sighed softly. "Not for good, d'ee mean? He'll not be much use to 'ee, Maisie, my little love. And all the time he's losing his skill with t'cooper, the skill he learnt so hard. I'm not sure I did rightly in taking him away."

"His cough's back, Patrick, you know that. He won't be able to work much longer, will he?"

"You think all the gossip might have upset Jimmy?"

"I doubt he even understands the half of it and he wasn't that fond of his family, but now we're his family, Patrick, and we've got to take care of him."

He saw it plainly. A man did a kindness, in a casual sort of way, then found that, for the rest of his life, he must carry a burden. And it would be a burden, having Jimmy. He felt it instinctively. Felt, also, in some way, it would prove a disaster. But he only said, "All right, then, my little love, if this is what your kind heart wants, and it won't be too much for 'ee."

A few weeks later, in early September, the second, to be precise and a date they were all to remember for ever, disaster struck. It came about through an action of Jimmy's though this was not appreciated till later.

Patrick had just made love to his wife, very gently, even more so than usual, so as not to disturb the baby in her womb; but also because having arrived at a reasonably accomplished routine, which appeared to bring satisfaction to them both, it would never, for a moment, have entered his head to alter it.

So, they lay, side by side in peace, content with their lot. Then Kate cried out loud. This was unusual as, by this time, she was well past her night-crying phase. Even more strange, was that little Lucy added her screams.

"Mammie, Mammie, there's a nasty smell! It's horrid, Mammie!"

Patrick gently pushed back his wife, who was about to rise, and went into the next room. He saw the window was open at the top and he did not entirely agree with these newfangled ideas of fresh-air at night. Then he smelt and, indeed, saw that smoke was coming into the bedroom.

He closed the window, pushing up the sash and then, pulling well back the heavy curtains, he stared out. Nothing appeared to be amiss, though the sky was brighter than it ought to be at this time of night with no moon.

"Maisie?" She had come to join him. "Where's this smell coming from?" He sniffed the unpleasant odour of smoke. "Can there be something burning?"

"My God." She shrieked and she rushed towards the cot and the still whimpering baby and scooped her into her own arms. "Take Lucy! We've got to get out of here fast!"

He still looked at her in some puzzlement.

"It's not the house. Can't be."

"Look out of the window in our room! The barn's all on fire! Listen! Can't you hear it? Oh, for God's sake, do something Patrick! Do something quickly, or we'll all be burnt alive in our beds!"

Jimmy Coxon had been back with the Scotts just two weeks when he awoke that warm, early September night feeling very unwell indeed. He retched a little into his chamber-pot, then feeling a little better, but still far from well and with his bowels churning heavily, he decided to make his way to the privy. Sickness was not something from which he often suffered and he was scared; far more scared, though, that he might prove a great nuisance to the Missus, then she would not want him in the house!

He dragged on his boots, put a jacket over his nightshirt (which had once belonged to Patrick) then, as the candle would not stay alight with the wind blowing, as he could hear, he struggled and managed to light the oil-lamp in his room. The privy was not at all conveniently placed for the family's use, being at the corner of the barton, crosswise from the kitchen; convenience, however, had not been the primary reason for placing it where it was. Jimmy crossed the yard. The night was dark, but pleasant, despite the breeze. He stayed in the privy sometime, and he was about to gather his strength for the return journey, feeling' still weak and not a little confused, when he was alerted by a sound.

Someone was whistling softly! Then he was sure, quite convinced, he could hear footsteps, walking near the wide entrance to the yard on the hard, packed earth. One of the Scott's dogs barked sharply, then was silent. Whoever was out there was being very quiet, but Jimmy was sure the man, for it must be a man, had gone into the yard! He listened intently, or so it seemed to him, and he soon began to confuse sounds of the night with dangers. A thief! Perhaps with a knife on him! He was not going back into that barton, not for nobody!

In fact, the prowler was no more than a poacher, who was taking a short cut back home, skirting several farms, so as to avoid going down the road into the village. He had his full bag, slung across his back and he was only interested in getting his spoil safely home. He went on his way, cheerfully. The cripple, however, still listening in terror, was positive that the 'vief' waited for him. What should he do? He knew he could not stay where he was all night. He must lie down somewhere. At length, after waiting for more than half-an-hour, he came outside, confused still, glancing nervously behind him as he made this way towards the barn, behind the main farm buildings. He would be safe there. There'd be plenty of straw he could lie down on, bury himself into, 'comferbul' so the 'diddikie' couldn't get him. For a moment, his conscience pricked him. He ought to warn Master, case anything happened! His terror, though, was far greater than these small goadings. Master'd understand.

Then he began to mount the few steps of the barn (for, the floor had been raised a little, hopefully, against rats), his long night-shirt began to trip him. He was in too great haste to bother about it and as he pushed open the heavy door, he stumbled to the floor. The lamp fled from his hand and went out, buried in the straw. Total darkness! Panic!

At length the familiar smell of the interior began to reassure him. It was as comforting a smell as he had ever known and young Jimmy curled up his body, hiding himself in the hay. Soon he was asleep.

But the lamp had not entirely gone out. It had merely died low down. And after a little while with the intense heat and the seeping oil, a small fire began. Really, quite small at first, gently smouldering. Such a little fire....

Patrick tried to calm his wife. There was no cause for any great alarm. The damage the fire must cause to the barn roof would be a nuisance, but no doubt it could be contained. If not, he thought ironically, then he would be compelled to have it fully repaired, as he ought to have done ages ago. It was the old story of the stitch in time. All the same, they mustn't waste time.

"Take it easy my little love," he advised, in his usual tones. "Naught awful'll happen if we keep our heads. Still, best to call young Annie, if she's still asleep and get her to keep an eye on the children. Get them warmly wrapped, just in case we've to go away suddenly."

Maisie shot him a look, almost of reproach. As if she needed to be told about the children! She was hastening with them, just as fast as she could and they were neither of them being co-operative, being much too tired and puzzled and frightened at this disturbance to their routine.

"Where're you goin'?" she said, sharply.

"See what I can do, o' course." He was fully dressed now. "I'll call young Jimmy." But Jimmy, of course, though his door was ajar, was not in his room on the ground-floor of the farmhouse.

Patrick crossed the yard, thinking to himself that it was lucky it was the time of the year when the animals were out in the fields. He guessed Jimmy might have gone to the privy, and as he neared the small building, he called out his name loudly. Then he saw the privy door was open and no-one appeared to be inside, but he still drew closer and again called aloud the boy's name. He had it in mind to send the cripple off to his brother-in-law, if he had not chanced to see the fire burning by now; and it was possible he had not, as the cottages were in a small dip. They must deal with the fire as quickly as possible, as the farm possessed no kind of fire-fighting equipment, other than a plentiful supply of buckets and the well, he thought grimly. Every hand would be needed, even young Annie and Jimmy.

Where was he, for goodness' sake?

"Jimmy!" he called out yet again.

He turned a corner of the farm buildings and stopped dead. For the first time he was truly alarmed. The whole of the barn roof was blazing and sparks were flying on the air. Buckets of water? It would be totally impossible to get anywhere near it! He stood for a moment, feeling utterly helpless; then he roused himself. His family must be ready to get away quickly, if need be, then James would have to go to Whytbrook and fetch the fire-fighting force, while he and Jimmy doused the yard buildings and did anything else they could think of. The fire service was, in fact, a wholly voluntary and erratic affair, but it did possess an engine of kinds, bought second-hand from Wells, and of which Whytbrook was duly proud. The service was on subscription. He was swiftly turning back to the house when a figure came towards him, blackened, clothes singed, like a bedraggled, long-forgotten scarecrow. Jimmy! Patrick ran towards the cripple, pulling off his coat as he came towards him and, flinging this about Jimmy, he rolled the poor wretch on the ground. He was screaming, but more from fright than with pain, as he had managed to squeeze through a narrow opening in the barn, high up and intended for ventilation, well before the flames reached him. He had hurt himself with his fall though, and for some little while he had lain on the ground, panting, moaning, unable to move. It was a miracle he had not broken a limb. Patrick gathered him up and carried him back to the farmhouse.

"Lamp," muttered Jimmy. "Jimmy's left' t'lamp!"

Patrick understood only too well, even if the cripple did not. He laid him on his bed, while he went back to Maisie and told her the situation.

"What're we to do?" Maisie cried.

"Stay in t'porch with t'door tight shut and under no circumstances go back inside the house!" Then, he told her, they must be ready to leave the instant he told them to. Then he turned to Annie. "Can you make your way to Mr. Bevan's?" The girl nodded. "You must tell him to fetch the fire people. Tell him it's urgent! Here, take this lamp! Hurry, but don't fall as you go in the dark."

"What can I do, Patrick?"

"Stay with the children. See they don't wander about."

"I'd best go'n fetch another light. They don't like being in the dark."

"No, Maisie! Listen, it's bad and t'wind's blowing in this direction. All I can do is try and stop it spreading. I'm off. Now mind what I say."

She waited till he was out of sight, then she fled back into the house, grabbed a lamp from the parlour and managed to light it with trembling hands. She was back in the porch in a flash, or so it seemed to her. Unfortunately, she had left the door into the passage wide open in her haste.

Patrick worked with fury, but all the time with a feeling of futility. Sweat poured down his face as he poured bucket after bucket onto the buildings in the barton. How thankful he was the farmhouse had such a good, solid roof of Welsh tiles. No harm would come to that, at any rate. But, if only he had someone to help him. He must just keep at it till help did arrive. He had a feeling there was a hose-pipe somewhere or other in one of the sheds, but he could not recall exactly where and he had no time to look now. He kept on doggedly.

For a moment, he stood upright to ease his back, then suddenly deliberately splashed some of the water over himself, and scooped some of the cooling liquid in his hands to drink it. He ran outside the barton to see how far the fire raged. The entire inside of the barn seemed to be alight. There had been weeks of warm weather and the contents.... Wood and straw.... Get up enough heat with those materials and even the old stones, and their dry cement, would soon begin to burn. He wished he could get near enough to deal with it.

Meanwhile, Annie had reached the Bevan cottage. She had quite a time arousing anyone, but presently young Mrs. Bevan came to a window and called out, then she hastened to the front door.

"I was that sound asleep.... " She listened to what Annie had to say. "But me husband's gone down to Whytbrook. Someone came for him early on this evenin' cause his father's took very ill!"

The two looked at each other in dismay. What could they do?

"I'd ride down, but he's taken the mare!" The mare was her own, her dowry and she was proud she could ride it so well, in spite of being heavily pregnant.

"I'd best walk," said Annie, reluctantly. She was very scared of the dark.

"I'd come with you, but.... "

She found Annie a more suitable lamp than the one brought from Redesdale farmhouse and the young girl set off, going down the rutted lane towards the road. It was further than going across the fields and more frightening with the high hedges each side; but Annie knew she dared not risk climbing over stiles in the dark and with so much rough ground. He heart thudding, she set off quickly as she could. In a way, though, it was exciting. There had not been much excitement at Redesdale.

Maisie was unwilling to wait until Annie returned from the Bevan cottage. She must do something to help! She severely bid her tiny half-asleep daughter, Lucy, to watch over Kate, then she ran round the farmhouse into the barton. At the far side she could hear Patrick at work, slushing water. She pushed open Jimmy's door and went inside. After a brief enquiry, she decided he was perfectly able to do something, if it was only staying with the young children till Annie returned, and having despatched him, she made her way to Patrick. The fire had now reached the byres. He glanced in her direction, but said nothing.

"I'll help fill the buckets!" She reached for the pump handle.

"All right, that'll be something, but be careful." He looked utterly drained. "I've done all I can in here. I'm going to fetch a ladder and climb on the byre roof. See if I can contain it." It was blazing on the far side.

"Perhaps, it'll burn itself out," she said, hopefully.

If only he had a hose-pipe! If only he had a few men from the village to help him! In fact, a lot of men, then they could make a chain, leading right from the pond to the barn. It was impossible and he knew it, but he was growing increasingly worried that the well was soon going to fail him. He continued to work, hastening back to collect large, filled buckets in each hand, splashing and wasting a good deal of precious water. He started to pray as he worked. Once, in a flash of light as the moon briefly appeared from behind clouds, he fancied he saw men coming towards the farm, silhouetted against the reddened sky. It was an illusion, like sighting an oasis in the desert. He gave his befuddled head a shake. Dear God, he mustn't collapse now! Where was James all this time? What was he doing? The passage of time seemed far longer than it had been.

He went on with his work. Then he grew anxious, for the fire did not seem to abate. He could not recall if he had sent the horses into a further field or not, or whether he had tethered them at all. He recalled nothing about the hens and the pigs, and it did not seem to matter much.

He continued with the pails. Slow work, but it was as though the mechanical operations could not now be stopped; even when he knew it to be utterly useless. He was drenched with sweat and his eyes smarted painfully so he could hardly see. He was vaguely aware of a smell of burning about his person; his clothes or hair must have caught flying sparks. That did not seem to matter either. There were little spurts of flames here and there on the ground where the fire had managed to take light. Then, from where he stood high up, he suddenly saw the barn roof come crashing down with a great roar. He was amazed it had lasted so long. Almost immediately, he noticed a broken and long discarded hand-cart had caught alight with a terrible blaze. It flared and hissed angrily. Even the useless metal parts seemed to Patrick to be red-hot, for now he could feel the searing heat reaching up to him.

Maisie! He was risking her life as well as his own! He called out to her, but she did not hear him for the noise of the fire. He scrambled down the ladder and raced to the girl. It was stifling hot, but the girl was still at her task, filling pails. The water level must be very low indeed by now.

He grabbed her arm.

"Leave it, leave it! There's nothing more we can do here! Let's get the children and wait by the road for the fire engine."

"But, Patrick," she began plaintively. it was as though she was unwilling to leave the buckets of water so laboriously collected.

"Come along, Maisie!" he pulled her now. "Let's got out of here! It's too dangerous.... "

Even as he half-dragged her through the opening, he saw evil small jets moving along the ground, like a plague of dragons, towards the yard's entrance. And they had barely reached the front of the farmhouse, when they heard another crash, much closer, the byre this time.

They collected the children and Jimmy, and made their way towards the Bevan cottage, Patrick carrying his daughter, Kate. Jimmy could not hurry and every now and again Maisie had to help him. They drew near the cottage and the lane up which the fire-engine must surely soon come. As they moved away from the wind's direction, the noise was slightly abated. Patrick tried to convince himself the fire was dying down. He thanked God for their escape. Surely, the worst was over now? But a short while later, while Maisie stood waiting to be admitted to the, cottage, he ran back to higher ground and he knew he was mistaken. The fire still raged. It had merely waited like a crafty, well-trained foe, gathering strength for a fresh onslaught, ready to pounce upon a different, unexpected course. Patrick could see smoke coming from every angle of the farm buildings and he suddenly knew, and his heart sank, that the farmhouse had also caught alight in places. He hastened back to Maisie, hoping she had not guessed this.

It appeared God did not want him to win this particular fight. It was to be a total incineration, he feared. He should be thankful they themselves were safe. He could hear faintly the sounds of animals, agitated and distressed, of horses whinneying. Maisie and Jimmy and the children had entered the Bevan cottage, but Patrick remained outside, listening.

He was approached by one of the men - there were even a few women - who questioned him.

Yes, they had come along to help. Some of them were squatters, like the Coxons, but humble, decent people. Some had come from the village, for the news had spread once Annie reached Whytbrook. Some had come because they had seen a brightness in the sky and were curious, but most were ill-prepared to help. None had realised how bad things were. So they stared, waiting for someone to direct them, staying a respectful distance from the fire. Some of the brave assured Patrick that once the fire-engine came, all would be well. Then they'd gladly lend a hand themselves.

So they continued to wait for the engine to arrive.

Inside the cottage, young Mrs. Bevan had put the two young Scotts down to sleep on a sofa, since they had but one bedroom. The two girls sipped tea and talked in whispers, frightened whispers. Maisie appreciated the calm presence of her sister-in-law, but she could not help being jittery. She had not seen the fire! Did not seem to be interested in seeing it! Maisie hated Patrick being away like this for so long. He was quite likely to do something rash, she thought, attaching to him her own emotional reaction.

"He'd do ought for those animals o' his, I'm sure - risk his own life, even! Oh, God, how I do wish it'd rain! A real good downpour!"

"Now, now, then, Maisie, I'm sure Patrick's sensible right 'nough. It doan't do to be so twily. Try an' not worry so much, Maisie, there's a dear."

"What's that?" Maisie suddenly put her hand to her mouth. "Can't 'ee hear it? The fire engine's come at last!"

The girls rushed to the front-door and, sure enough, the long-awaited engine was coming down the lane from the road, clanging loudly. It was all polished and gleaming with a pair of sleek black horses proudly swinging their tails and tossing their heads as though they were bound for a royal jubilee. If good appearances and even better intentions had been all that was required, the inferno would have been quelled in minutes.

As it was....

They soon found it was going to be a difficult and dangerous task to persuade the horses to drive into the yard. They backed away and who could blame them? One man ran inside, but came back a moment later to say it would be useless anyway as there was probably only a trickle of water. Patrick could have told them this, but no-one had thought to ask him.

Face and clothes blackened, the man who had entered the yard stood about, the hero of the moment; and Patrick swiftly suggested the watering pond. But naturally enough, the hose-pipe they carried could not hope to reach such a distance. More time was wasted over this. It was impossible to reach the fire. Several suggestions were made as to how to lengthen the hoses. Did any amongst them own such a thing as a hose-pipe of suitable size? The question was mere rhetoric, since by the time any such pipes had been located and attached - and by what means? - so as to ensure a truly lengthy pipe, the fire would have gone far beyond any restraint. Indeed, it had done so already, but none of them was willing to admit it.

Someone suggested what Patrick had long since had in mind, a human chain, passing the large pails of water from hand to hand. There were any number of would-be helpers now - when it was almost too late, but still they bravely made the effort, hating to admit defeat. Patrick joined them. Even so, no-one dared to go anywhere near the raging inferno around the barton and the great barn was a blackened shell, from which smoke poured filthily. Redesdale's farmhouse was clearly burning from within. Fire spurted from the front door and around several of the window frames. So they tried to save the house.

It seemed hopeless.

Soon, a few began to ease off their labours, only the stubborn ones remaining till Patrick himself quietly asked them to stop. He could see they were exhausted with sweat streaming down their bodies, several with clothes drenched and torn with their efforts. Then everyone was told rather officiously, by the leader of the fire-engine team, that they must move well back, as far as possible, please! A few did so, moving to higher ground for a better view of this ghastly scene, but they soon crept back when they saw the house had not collapsed. They looked dazed. Feelings were mixed, but mostly sad. If this had happened when William was alive, there might even have been some gloating. There was certainly no gloating now. Everyone liked Patrick and wished him well. After all, he was one of themselves and he deserved better than this. Patrick felt numb inside.

Then, miraculously, the prayers of Maisie - if they had indeed been prayers - were boisterously answered. Without the least warning, astonishing the crowd, the rain began to fall, heavily and with solid determination.

The crowd raised their heads and suddenly everyone burst out laughing.

CHAPTER XV

Patrick looked down, aware of a brushing against his legs and there was Jessie. Shivering violently, soaking wet, of course, but still with her cross-labrador tail vibrating hopefully. Dear old Jessie!

He bent to stroke her, and was afflicted with a sense of shame. He had not given any of the dogs a single thought. At the back of his mind had been the vague notion that, unchained, they must surely make their own ways to safety; perhaps even instinctively run into the fields where the sheep were to round them up and drive them to a place of greater protection. Whatever had happened to the collies, he should not have forgotten Jessie, who had saved his life!

Presently, James Bevan arrived, having ridden up from the village with young Annie nervously poised in front of him. She had had the good sense to go first to the home of the older Bevans.

"How's your father?" Patrick enquired, absently.

"False ala'm. 'Ee'll outlive all on us, I reckon!" He hesitated a moment. "I'm right sorry, Patrick. I mean - if I'd a'guessed something like this - how'd it happen do 'ee reckon?"

"I've a fancy young Jimmy Coxon dropped t'lamp."

James cursed softly.

"Anyway, you're all to come to us. Somehow, us'll fit 'ee in, if 'tis only on the floor."

Patrick nodded his gratitude. He would not sleep that night, nor even attempt to do so, but at least they could get dry and Jessie could have a rub-down. Then, as soon as it was light, he must see what he could possibly salvage.

His first thought in the dawn, though, was for the animals. The sheep, as he had hoped, were quite unharmed, for they were still well away from the farm buildings in their summer fields. He found one of the sheep-dogs there also, agitated, but unharmed. His second sheep-dog did not return for the best part of a week, very bedraggled and very hungry and he never found out where she had lain.

The sow and the piglets were well enough and James soon followed Patrick into their field with swill he had trundled up on a hand-cart. Though Patrick found that the pig-sty was untouched by the fire, he decided at once that he must sell the pigs and hens as soon as possible. They'd be too much of a nuisance at this time, else.

The cows were the biggest worry, though there were only four of them in lactation; but they urgently needed milking. For a brief moment, he thought ironically of the time when James Ridley had suggested he should concentrate on heifers. However, James Bevan solved this problem. He came out to Patrick a second time to advise him he'd arranged for the cows to stay for a while at another farm not too far away, where he had once worked. This belonged to an elderly man, who was slowly reducing his stock till the time when he was forced to move to live with his daughter. The farmer would not make any charge for the grazing nor the work of milking.

"Then, he must take all the milk."

"Only what 'ee can't use in t'circumstances. 'Tis a kindness, Patrick. 'Tis only natural everyone is wanting to help 'ee now."

The horses were well enough for the time being, and the sheds, which served as stables, being well away from the main buildings, were virtually undamaged. They went together to look at the barton, which apart from the barn, had suffered most. The byres were completely destroyed and most of the sheds, except for the one immediately next to the farmhouse, were in a wretched state. A great deal of equipment, as well as the two carts had been lost. Yet there was plenty of solid, blackened stone and it seemed to Patrick that new roofs and interiors and a good lick of white-wash might well perform miracles. He tried to feel more hopeful.

The barn was beyond reasonable repair. It was not only the roof. Most of the stones had somehow become dislodged and had fallen to one side into a jumbled pile. There had been little or no cement used. The steps were still intact, though cracked in places. Ah, well, Patrick told himself, it had been too large for their purpose and badly-made. He recalled the times when he had hesitated to spend good money on a new roof. The loss of the hay was annoying though.

Deliberately, he had left the house till last when he was alone again. The back door was burned down and some of the window-frames had a charred look, but he still convinced himself the house must have withstood the fire. The smell of smoke hung about inside. He opened windows. Everything was covered in a muffle of concealing black soot. He went upstairs and the stairs were burned in places and felt creaky. A window had been left open in one bedroom and sparks flying on the wind had done much damage. Various items of clothing were scorched and Maisie's beautiful curtains, newly made, were ruined. Poor dear Maisie, she had worked so hard, but no doubt she would soon make more. Most of the furniture seemed to have survived. Other rooms were not so bad, he thought. In the little room his wife had made her own, he suddenly noticed the small travelling case, she so prized, given to her by Mrs. Squires. The leather was discoloured, but he picked up the case and shoved it into his ample pocket.

Downstairs the situation was rather better, everything covered with its thick coating of soot, but mainly superficial damage, apart from the window frames. There were still large pools of water on the floor in the kitchen. The parlour had suffered least of all, for it had been at the front away from the main blast of the fire and its door and windows had been tightly closed. There was still a horrible stench, though, which Patrick could not identify. Ironically the cabinet and Hannah's collection of blue glass seemed to be unharmed. He felt the handle. It was securely locked and had been ever since the time, so long ago, when Coxon had stolen one of the pieces. A finger-bowl, if Patrick remembered rightly. How absurdly his mother had reacted! And how he had laughed.

He did not feel like laughing now. He was not at all sure he even knew where the key was kept. He jerked his shoulders in dismissal. It scarcely mattered anyhow.

Maisie was delighted with her travelling-case and opened it at once. The satin lining was damaged and stained, but the contents were intact, the silver only needing a thorough clean. She laughed out loud with pleasure, and it seemed to Patrick, her joy was out of all proportion.

Now, with hindsight, he could see what he ought to have done at the beginning. Get his family to safety, assure himself none of the animals was in any danger; then, having harnessed the large cart, piled it up with as much equipment as he could locate and which deserved saving. Instead of which, he had wasted valuable time and water, as well as energy. Still, it could have been much worse. As he told Maisie, the walls were still standing and the good Welsh tiled roof still held, though it might well need some repairing. But a few weeks of hard work and they'd soon get it into shape.

"Would 'ee like to come up and see, Maisie? There might be something 'ee need and can use right now?"

"No," she said, stubbornly.

"No?"

"I'm not feeling too well - and - and I don't want to go there. Not yet awhile."

In fact, she was feeling very out-of-sorts indeed, with a dull pain low down in her abdomen. At mid-afternoon, a message was sent from the Bailiff family by a driver with a small carriage. They had heard the news and they were now inviting Maisie and her children to go and stay with them for as long as possible.

Patrick was away again at the farm buildings, but Maisie did not hesitate. She collected her children, borrowed a few necessary items from her sister-in-law and, with her useless travelling case, she left. Patrick would understand that this was the best for them in the circumstances. Both Annie and Jimmy had found accommodation in the village and there had been a constant stream of people coming to the cottage, offering help. Some of the elderly, who had never gone further than The Bell, managed to make their creaking way, leaning heavily on sticks, though they could offer nothing but plentiful advice.

That night Maisie aborted and the doctor, hastily called, said there was every indication the child would have been a male.

In deep distress, Patrick rode over to Kimsley Mendip to see his wife. He was alarmed at her appearance. Her face showed not so much physical suffering - losing babies was commonplace enough - but a great spiritual misery. She was young and healthy. She would have other children. But something in the girl's expression prevented him from offering any easy comfort. Wisely, he did not pray over her. But he found it unbearable that she was so cold towards him, so distant. No doubt, this was natural enough, but recalling his mother's unhappy state of mind, he was desperate to do something to help her, but could think of nothing. She even turned her head away when he bent to kiss her, as though she blamed him! Was he, perhaps to blame?

If Maisie had told him frankly then she was not prepared to let him share the marital bed with her for the rest of their lives together, he knew he could have borne it somehow; sadly, but without bitterness, never reproaching her, never breathing a word to his cronies, whatever he endured. Maisie must know what was best for her. But this coldness! He simply could not bear it.... and at such a time when he most needed her support. He was almost glad to leave, but it came to him that he must somehow get Maisie and the children away from the influence of the Bailiffs, kind and well-meaning though they undoubtedly were, and as soon as possible. Otherwise, he might risk losing her for good.

A week after the fire he had an early morning visitor. He was now sleeping on the large sofa, his mother had used in the room next to the front parlour until the doors were repaired and the windows refitted. He also did not want to be too great a burden on the James Bevans', though he took his meals with them.

Farmer Ridley shook his head as he stepped into the farmhouse. He had been away, he said, at the time of the fire and had only just heard the sad news. Was there anything he or his men could do to help Patrick?

"We're managing, after a kind of fashion," said Patrick, grimly. "'Tis kind on 'ee though, Mr. Ridley. I've bought some second-hand stuff and I'm hoping to have the shorthorns back by next week."

Farmer Ridley pursed his lips. He had already been to take a look in the yard.

"We'll manage somehow," said Patrick, a trifle defensively.

"The house has suffered quite a bit." He followed Patrick into the kitchen.

"It'll clean. It's worse upstairs.... "

He had not intended his words as an invitation, but James Ridley took them as such and immediately turned round and made his way up the stairs. Patrick called after him to mind how he went as the stairs did not seem too safe in places. The other came down almost at once. He looked a bit shaken and moved to the outside of the farmhouse, staring upwards.

"It's going to cost a bit to put this to rights. And I don't suppose you're all that well insured." He was remembering Hannah Scott's parsimony.

"No," said Patrick, "not all that." In fact, the farmhouse itself was not insured at all. He was thinking, if only that window and the passage door had not been left open somehow or other.... "It'll all take a bit o' time, but the farm must come first."

"Of course. But is it worth it?"

The younger man looked at him, suddenly sensing what was coming. They talked for while longer, James Ridley asking several more questions and seeming to ponder their answer. Then he said, "Have you thought it might well pay you to sell these farm buildings for what you can get? With the insurance money you'd be in a better position all round, instead of being burdened for years."

"What use'd the buildings be without.... "

"Oh, with a bit of land, naturally."

"How much land?"

"Not a great deal. Say seventy acres, at most."

"Wasn't it 'ee said to Ma and to me also, I do well remember, 'Never sell your land?'"

"Yes, well - circumstances have greatly changed, haven't they?"

"What'd 'ee do with it? What use would it be, Mr. Ridley?" Or was he thinking, are you merely seeking a chance to buy land cheaply, for the sake of owning it?

"Oh, I'd use it right enough! I have it in mind to build up a small shoot, very small really. Remember that time - several times - we went shooting together?"

"Yes, I do remember."

"Well then. You'd carry on farming, of course, and I could doubtless let you have some land, if you needed more, nearer the village.

"To lease?"

"Most of the farmers here abouts are tenant farmers," said Ridley, sharply. "You'd not lose by it. In fact, it'd be more convenient all round, a house in the village. This place was never intended to be a farmhouse. Not originally, it wasn't."

"I well know that."

"I'd have thought, living nearer the village might suit your missus better." Belatedly, he had remembered Maisie's existence and he enquired after her. Patrick told him. Immediately, the face of the other changed. He was now remarried and had a healthy baby son, but he had never forgotten the long years of struggle and frustration. He gripped Patrick's shoulder hard for a moment, and in genuine concern, and he murmured his words of regret. "Rotten luck. Women take these things hard. And especially if it's a boy." He began to move away towards where he had tethered his horse. "Why don't you get your missus down to the coast for a spell? It's still nice enough and the change would do her good, brighten her up no end... " He mounted his horse with ease, despite his size.

"I'll think over what you've said," said Patrick. "About the farm... "

"And if you do decide to sell, I'll pay the full price for any land you've a mind to let go. Come to that, if it'd help you get started somewhere else, I'm willing to take the whole farm off your hands, Patrick, though it'd be a burden to me at present. But after this experience, your wife might well prefer a move. It's entirely up to you, though. I only want to help you, Patrick.... I'll be in touch."

"All right, I'll think about it," Patrick repeated, quietly.

Maisie had been at Weston-super-Mare three full days before a change began to come over her and her mood brightened. She had not wanted to go away at all, even though the thought of Weston, which she had visited only twice before in her life on day excursions (with the Bailiffs) was very exciting. She delayed, staying two days in Whytbrook with her mother, making the excuse that she was needed, as her father had not yet recovered. She also spent some time with Mrs. Squires, who was unwell. But, at length, she had allowed Patrick to take her, the children and young Annie to the coast. She had still protested that it was wrong for her to be going away at such a time. She ought to be helping....

Patrick had looked at her.

"Maisie, there's ought 'ee can do till t'place be more homelike." He did not mention the fact that she still refused to visit Redesdale Farm. He thought he comprehended. "'Ee've had a sad time 'o it, my little love. 'Ee need a change o' scene. Why not go to please me, eh?"

Put like that, she felt she must go and make the best of things. She had not wanted Annie with her, but as Patrick had insisted, she soon was very glad, for every day she went out alone, leaving the children in Annie's sensible care. Her lone walks seemed to her very daring.

The boarding-house, where they stayed, belonged to a woman who was a close relative of friends of Patrick. No-one in Whytbrook would have dreamed of staying in a place not thoroughly recommended, though there were, apparently, plenty of people who did just that; for next to the front-door was an enamelled, brass-framed sign, announcing, 'Apartments conducted by Mrs. Henry Coombes.'

Soon on her peaceful walks, Maisie began to day-dream and this was the start of her recovery. She became quite sure in a little while that this was what she wanted, her name on a similar house with the words spelled out, 'Apartments conducted by Mrs. Patrick Scott.' (Perhaps, she might leave it as 'Mrs. P. Scott' so as to save space.) It would be marvellous! The people she would meet! Hard work, of course, very hard work, but she was used to that. Besides, Maisie knew she could cook very well, a good deal better than Mrs. Henry Coombes. Little by little, she built up her visionary picture. Later on she would have the girls to help her, when they were older; and they would both have far better chances of a nice education and of being seen by pleasant young men, far better than in little Whytbrook.

Weston was clearly going to be a most enjoyable place in which to live before very long. Why, already they were seeing it as the future Brighton of the South West! Most of the summer crowds had left, but a few people still bathed though, quite properly, there was a separate beach for the ladies' use where their wheeled bathing machines could take them into the sea away from prying eyes. A few courageous souls still sat at the side of the beach, primly picnicking, often with a little primus stove in their midst, and well protected against any lingering sun. She watched a Punch and Judy show, which had a nigger baby, a crocodile and a policeman. Most unusual! Where did they get their ideas from? A few donkeys were still taking people sedately up and down the beach, not little children though. The donkeys were considered unsafe for tiny children and the rest were back at school. Maisie liked best of all the donkey-carts. Mrs. Coombes had one and she did all her marketing by this means. She had told Maisie there had been donkeys in service in the villages for many a long year.

Trams plied along the esplanade, as it was grandly named and, of course, as at Wells, there was gas lighting in the streets and most of the town houses were lit by gas. There was even talk of gas-cookers, which sounded highly alarming to Maisie, but inventive, she had to admit. It was certainly an up-and-coming little town, all bustle, but not *vulgar*, Maisie emphasised to herself. There were some quiet places and some quiet people. One day she watched some of the Quaker ladies go by in their dove-grey dresses, large white collars and wide-brimmed hats. She had to admit they looked most fetching. She was told they were not too orthodox as some of them even owned a piano, though it was kept apart in a separate room. She must tell Patrick this.

Every day, she added a fresh piece to her fantasies which, she told herself, were really quite practical, very different to those dreams of a few years ago. She would have her mother to visit for a long stay. Perhaps, later on, she could live with them. She would greatly benefit from the good sea air, as would the children and herself. She had even worked out a scheme for poor Jimmy Coxon. In Whytbrook, his barrels were merely used for cider-making and local storage, but in Weston there would be a wealth of uses, and she believed there were several breweries in the area. There would be plenty of scope for his skill, so they could continue to look after him.

And where, in all this, did Patrick figure?

She had puzzled greatly about Patrick. But at length, she had concluded (and the idea seemed to her brilliant) that naturally Patrick must be engaged in growing vegetables, fruit and even flowers for the increasing number of boarding-houses and hotels! It was perfect. She did not, however, ponder to think that suitable land, at an acceptable price, might not be available anywhere near her boarding-house.

After nearly two weeks of good sea air, and just prior to going home again, she added most of the final details. These included having either Jimmy or Patrick or someone they might chance to employ, make souvenirs for the visitors to take home with them. They could be in wood or pottery. This was the craze now and no-one went anywhere without buying a keepsake or a present for a friend. She even saw them making bottled drinks, cheap and colourful and not too harmful. Oh, the possibilities were endless!

Everything depended, of course, on Patrick's agreeing to sell the farm to Mr. Ridley. The whole farm, not just the acres he had at first suggested. He must know she had no intention of going back to Redesdale. She simply could not bear the thought of doing so. It frightened her. Redesdale Farm was bad luck for them all. It would make no difference how much work was done on the house. Patrick must know this. He must understand her feelings. But she was certain, as Patrick was so kind and good and loved her dearly, Maisie thought, smiling to herself, she would be able to win him round to her way of thinking. She really did not doubt she could persuade him towards the right decision for all of them. And it was the right decision to leave Redesdale. It really was. For all their sakes.

And, after all, Weston wasn't that far from Whytbrook and no doubt Mr. Ridley would find some suitable employment for James. She returned to her boarding-house, light of heart. Annie, who had decided to take the children out rather later than usual, had not yet returned, but waiting for her in the guest-room parlour was Patrick. His face was very solemn.

She smiled at him, forgetful of the fact that he was two days early. He saw a smiling face, which she had not been too careful about protecting from the sun. She ran to him, the freckles on her nose so plain to see, but she cheered his heart.

She looked a different person to the girl he had brought here two weeks ago. He was glad. She was going to need all her courage now.

"I wasn't coming till Saturday, Maisie, but.... "

"Never mind! Oh, 'tis good to see you! I've had enough of holidays and I'm happy to come home again. But, oh, Patrick, I've had the most splendid idea!"

And she poured it all out in a gabble of words, hardly pausing for breath.

He listened in total silence.

"But don't 'ee think it's a good idea, Patrick, dear?" she said coaxingly.

"Maisie," he began, "'ee've not asked me why I came today, ahead o' time."

She looked at him then, soberly.

"'Tis bad news, Patrick?"

He nodded. "Yes, my little love, I.... "

"Me father's dead?" she questioned, her voice harsh and sounding strongly of her birth-place. "Poor Mama. Well, 't'was to'bc 'spected, I daresay."

"Maisie, 'tis not your Pa, not yet. 'Tis your friend, Mrs. Squires."

"Oh, no!" She burst into tears immediately, sobbing violently, as she had not done when her baby was lost; all her pent-up feelings finding expression. "She was well 'nough when I saw her! Right as rain she was!"

He put his arms about her to try to comfort her.

It was some time later when Annie had returned with the children and been sent upstairs to pack and get the little ones ready for travelling back to Whytbrook, that Maisie lifted her tear-stained face to Patrick's and tentatively enquired,

"But - but we'll come back, won't we?"

"Of course. One day." She stood quite still, looking at him with fixed, doleful eyes.

"I mean - for good. To live. We will, won't we?"

To Patrick, she sounded like a child, seeking some fruitless consolation. And, after all, she was but a child, only eighteen years. He shifted uneasily.

"'Tis not the time to be discussing this, Maisie, my little love."

"But I must have your promise, Patrick! Not immediately, perhaps. Not for months, even a year, but we will come back? Promise!"

Now he was cornered. He drew her close into his arms, hating to hurt her.

"Maisie you must be sensible, my little love. What do I know 'bout except sheep? 'Sides, I'd feel badly if I sold the farm."

"The farm's all yours, isn't it? To do with as you like?"

"I don't feel it that way. I can't explain, but it just wouldn't be right somehow. I don't feel 'tis meant." He avoided any talk of God's Will. That self-satisfaction had gone; indeed, he hardly knew for sure what God intended for him these days. It was not as easy as he had once thought.

He blundered on.

"Suppose Thomas or Luke or even their children were in need?"

"They went away! The farm's yours!"

He sighed. "I know. I know. But I just can't let it go, Maisie. Ask anything of me you like, my little love, but somehow or other we must keep the farm. I'm sorry, I.... "

She fidgeted in his arms.

"Try not to worry your sweet little head at this time. There's enough to worry about, Maisie. We'll work something out, 'ee'll see."

"Yes," Maisie allowed, "yes, I suppose so." But in her heart she was thinking, that no matter what, she was never going back to Redesdale. Never!

Unbidden, there came into her mind the memory of the time when Mrs. Squires had told her that her house and the one next door would one day come to her, Maisie. 'Whatever happens, Maisie you'll always have a roof over your head.'

Deeply treacherous thoughts perhaps, at such a time.

CHAPTER XVI

The September days are again warm; in fact, an untimely drought stifles the land. But on this pleasant Sunday afternoon, Maisie is perfectly content to stay indoors near an open window, which gives the best light as she delicately sews at a piece of smocking.

She is quite elegantly attired in a green dress of a grenadine stuff, the colour purported to be 'like fresh spinach', and with a revealed bodice, cuffs and skirt frill of a softer green muslin. She has not made this gown herself, however. She is much too busy nowadays (as well as disdainful of her former home-made efforts).

Fastened above her left breast is a small gold watch, which now and again she glances at, turning its tiny face towards her own, assessing how much time she still has at her disposal before the others return. She is alone in the house, a luxury in itself these days, and the room she occupies was formerly the over-cluttered parlour of Mrs. Squires. It is still cluttered, but it is now used by Maisie as her personal room for her sewing and letter-writing.

The year is now 1899 and Maisie is a comely woman of thirty-four years; and though a little fuller in her figure, she is still shapely and keeps her corsets tightly laced about her slim waist. Her brilliant red hair is as startling as ever. Again she glances at her pretty watch. She has a little while yet. Kate, just seventeen, is taking a Sunday-school class, to be followed by a special practice of the Church Choir. Kate is not especially religious, but she will join anything that allows her to sing and use her admittedly charming, young soprano voice. Dear Lucy, always so helpful, has taken Jennifer, Maisie's youngest child, now three-and-a-half years old, for a walk and to call on friends. As for Patrick, though he really by rights ought to be resting after his busy week, he has taken the two boys with him to call on her brother, James, and to check how things are at the farm. Just as though he did not go there every single day! These two lads are Joseph (though more commonly called Joe, by his mother) aged thirteen, years and his younger brother, William Gladstone, aged ten (named partly after Patrick's grandfather and also in honour of Patrick's favourite statesman, William Ewart Gladstone), sometimes referred to as Will.

Maisie smiles to herself, contentedly. Five healthy children, even though one more baby was sadly lost after Will was born. But, most importantly, she has a husband who still adores her, even after all this long time and calls her his 'little love'. How many of the women she knew could say as much?

It had been a long struggle with many ups and downs, not always easy, but in the main things had vastly improved. A compromise, of course, but that is how life usually went.

They had made the right decision. Patrick had to keep the farm. Maisie had recognised that, at last. She could not part him from it, however resentful she might feel about it and she had been very resentful for a short time, for she was equally determined not to return to Redesdale, feeling it would be disastrous. For a few weeks she had stayed alone with Kate and Lucy in the house left to her by Mrs. Squires. Then it had come to her in a flash. Why couldn't they all of them live here? The house was small, but it so happened that the neighbouring tenant had decided to leave, perhaps not caring to remain after dear old Mrs. Squires had gone.

"If we pulled down the wall between the two houses and made it into one house, it might well serve us nicely," she had told Patrick on one of his frequent visits.

He had looked at her doubtfully, but for the first time with a gleam of hope in his eyes.

"I've got to be near the farm," he said, stubbornly. "'T'would be too much to be up and down all day long from the village and back again."

Maisie flushed. He was doing this at present, calling on her.

"No, you don't!" she said. "Not with James at t'cottage, keeping an eye on things. How many o' the farmers - I mean the bigger farmers - have all their land nicely tucked 'round their farms? Why, they have land all over, wherever they can get what's suitable. You know that, Patrick!"

"Yes," said Patrick, still doubtful. He knew only too well that in the past men had had to travel quite a distance to get to their grazing strips.

"'Tis up to you, Patrick, but if 'ee wants us to be together as a family this is the best way. Why, 'ee could build a small barn out at the back I don't doubt, and sheds and not bother 'bout Redesdale at all. 'Cept the land," she added, hastily, "for the sheep."

So it had come about, though not, of course, as easily as that. Everything with Patrick had to be done slowly, consideringly. He would not take risks and certainly not with borrowed money. That they had in some small measure prospered was in many ways due to Maisie. She it was who had urged him to buy land in Whytbrook when it came on the market, so they now grew many vegetables and always had a small herd of cattle. In effect, they had two farms, with James Bevan taking his turn in both places. He was assisted nowadays by Matthew Bevan. A year after the fire when Maisie's father finally died, her younger brother had left his job and gone to work for Patrick, taking up residence in the second restored cottage at Redesdale Farm. He had taken his mother to live with him and had continued unwed until some five years ago when Maisie's mother died, when Matthew had surprised them all by suddenly marrying a girl almost half his age.

Annie was back with them. After the Weston-super-Mare holiday, she had taken herself off to a large estate and the jollity of living and working with a big staff (who each knew his or her own place). Annie had even married, but as the marriage had turned out badly, Annie had requested she be allowed to come back to Whytbrook. She would never dream of seeking a divorce, of course, let alone of remarrying, but being needed and provided for by the Scotts kept her happy and saved her worrying about her old age. Indeed, Annie queened it not a little, as she invariably had two girls from Kimsley Mendip Orphanage under her charge. But they ate in the kitchen, the family nowadays eating in the dining-room. Annie thought this only right. She had always been embarrassed, having to eat with the family. It didn't show proper respect, somehow. Not that the Scotts were gentry. Goodness no! Not like the family she had worked for, but Annie did like everything and everyone in the proper place. The Scotts did quite a lot of socialising these days. At least, Mrs. Scott did.

As for young Jimmy, the poor young man had survived till ten years ago, quite happily, when he died suddenly during an influenza epidemic. To the last, he had regarded the Scotts as his real family.

Maisie, reminiscing, knew she would soon have to tuck away her sewing. Patrick did not care to see her busy with her needle on Sundays and Maisie was sensible enough to appear to agree with him.

There was the sound of soft footsteps. Kate had returned, sooner than expected and a moment later she burst into her mother's room without first knocking.

"How many times do I have to tell you.... ?" Maisie began when Kate interrupted her with a smiling, "Sorry!" She was sometimes faintly amused at her mother's valiant attempts to instill a little of the graciousness and expected good manners she had acquired long ago from an elderly friend. (It certainly could not have been from her grandmother, despite her supposed good education.)

"You're back very early, aren't you?"

Kate explained, and she pouted a little, that one of the choir members had a nasty throat, so the practice had been curtailed.

"So she made out, but you know she can't sing all that much even when her throat's perfect. It's my belief.... "

"Kate," said Maisie, warningly, "'Tis none of your business, now is it.... Anyhow, as you're so soon, you may as well set the table for tea." She was trying to forestall any ideas Kate might have about going off to play the harmonium. This instrument had been squeezed into what was now the parlour, but originally two small rooms in the second small house. It would be all right if Kate confined herself to hymns, but so often she forgot herself and sang quite naughty songs, of which Patrick disapproved, even on weekdays, let alone on Sunday. Annie and the other girls were all having an afternoon off duty. Maisie added for good measure, "I don't see why it should always have to be Lucy."

Kate gave an exaggerated shrug of her well-proportioned shoulders, as though the whole world were conspiring against her at that moment, but went quietly from the room. She was, in fact, a charming, lively girl, rather plumper and certainly much more assured than Maisie had been at seventeen years, but otherwise bearing a striking resemblance to her mother. Her hair was a glory.

Perhaps it was this echo of herself that caused Maisie to be strict, even severe, with the girl at times. Perhaps, also, it was a strained attempt not to show favouritism as against Lucy, a gentle easily mollified girl, looking at eighteen-and-a-half, actually younger than Kate especially so, as Patrick was clearly besotted with Kate as he had been at her birth. Though, to give him his full due, he was always fair-minded and genuinely loved Lucy as well. The two sisters were excellent friends, without a hint of rivalry. Kate, being self-confident, had found nothing in her sister of which to be jealous; and Lucy was quite devoid of this ugliness.

Maisie was thankful for this, but there were several things in Kate which irritated her increasingly during this past year or so.

Ever since Kate's choirmaster had told the girl her voice ought to be properly trained, well beyond his skill, it had seemed to Maisie there was no holding her younger daughter! Kate had been quite rebellious and arrogant when told this was nonsense. She made a scene when told quietly by Patrick that expensive professional training was out of the question. He had kindly suggested some woman living in Kimsley Mendip (who had been a concert singer in her youth) might be willing to give lessons to Kate. His daughter was outraged! She, it appeared, was set on being an opera singer, no less, however absurd that might seem to the rest of them.

"Kate," Maisie had said, firmly, "there's simply not the money for such. You've a pretty enough voice and it can be a - well an accomplishment for a young girl, but to waste money as you think we ought - why 't'would be a sin! It would, really a sin! Any road, you'll be marrying one of these fine days," she added, more gently. "You don't want to be an old maid, now do'ee?"

Kate had hotly declared she would not be marrying for ages and ages yet and if ever she did, it would certainly not be with anyone in Whytbrook.

(Not good enough for Kate, Maisie had supposed.)

"If there's any money to spare," continued Maisie, "it must go to the boys, that's only right and proper. They've got to make their ways and they'll have families to keep one day. Joe wants to go and learn about farm engines, I do believe, so he can help his father more, and I fancy Will might want to go to sea, like your uncle Thomas."

The boys had turned startled eyes in their mother's direction, wondering from where she had got hold of such ideas, since neither of them had breathed a word to her of their half-formed dreams.

Then there was the incident of the mistaken payment of a week ago. Farmer Ridley, as most people in the area still referred to him, though he did scant practical farming these days, had called upon Patrick to pay him for some tups his shepherd had bought a while back. He laid the money, in cash, in an envelope in front of Patrick; and it was only some little time later when Patrick took up the large envelope and counted the money, that he found there was five pounds too much. He ran to the door and called out, but he was too late. The farmer had disappeared down the road. Patrick came into the house at once and what would he have but that Kate, who chanced to be around, already attired in her hat and gloves and jacket, take herself down to Whytbrook House and return the excess note.

Kate had protested. This would make her late for her afternoon choir practice. Even Maisie had felt sympathy. She had suggested Patrick might like to wait till the boys returned from school, or Lucy, who was presently on an errand.

"No," said Patrick. "Mr. Ridley might go out. It's on your way to the church, Kate, so you'll not waste all your breath on the journey." And he had smiled.

"It seems a bit hard when it's his mistake," argued Kate.

"Could she not go first thing in t'morning, Father?" asked Maisie, in the tone of voice she always used when reminding her husband of his important role in the family as its head.

"No," said Patrick, again, quite firmly. "Tomorrow won't do. Someone's been a bit careless, no doubt, but 'tis no cause for us to be careless also, now is it?"

His tone was quite pleasant, almost conciliative. But Kate, though she adored her father, had suddenly been mutinous.

"The trouble with people like you, Papa," she retorted, "is you're so good yourself, you think everyone's the same. They're not! How d'you know that sly old man didn't put five pounds more in the envelope, just to try and catch you out?"

"Kate!" breathed Maisie, alarmed. Patrick looked suddenly stern.

"Come to that," Kate continued, recklessly, though she knew she was going too far, "I don't suppose Ridley'd even notice it if you didn't pay it back. Anyway, why should you? Its his mistake, not yours. Goodness knows, he's rich enough." She flushed.

"You'd best do as your father asks this very minute and not another word, my girl. Speaking to your father like that! I never heard the like!"

"Oh, all right," grumbled Kate.

"And mind your tones, my girl, or I'll take the strap to you, old as you are!"

Patrick said not a word. He had never laid a finger on any of his children, even the boys. It had seemed to Maisie at times, almost as though he was afraid to do so. Any chastisement had always been left to Maisie.

Next day, however, Kate was as bright and as cheerful as formerly and very willing to help Maisie, which was strange. Her mother strongly suspected it was not alone the resilience of youth. Patrick must have spoken to the girl. What he had said Maisie did not enquire into, but she hoped he had not raised false hopes in the girl. Kate undoubtedly had a very sweet voice, but to want to be an opera singer, indeed!

She heard voices and guessed Lucy and Jennifer had now returned. Reluctantly, she put aside her needlework and went into the dining-room. The large table almost filled the small room and, truth to tell, Patrick had never taken much to Maisie's idea of eating all his meals, except breakfast, in this 'silly, little room'. Even the kitchen, though much larger, was rather less than half the size of the Redesdale kitchen. Her two daughters were talking together, Lucy still in her out-door attire. She could not help but be pleased with their appearance. They both had good taste in clothes, guided firmly by herself. Both were in blue, Kate in a quite bright tone and Lucy in navy blue (now a very fashionable colour, especially when combined with white) with lots of braid about the hem.

From a small glass-fronted cupboard near the fire-place, Maisie removed one of her best plates and laid it on the table, ready for the small cakes. After all, it was Sunday and there might yet be a caller. Then from a drawer she took a frilled hostess apron of pale muslin, which exactly matched the frills of her dress and popped on this useless little frivolity. Then she paused to ask Lucy about her afternoon outing.

Kate burst in, "Oh, Lucy's been telling me she's just met the most frightfully attractive young man at the curate's, if you please!"

That was another thing of which Maisie did not approve, this tendency Kate had to use the new slang, such absurd expressions as, 'awfully nice', 'jolly good', and this one she had just used, 'frightfully attractive'. It was unladylike. Where had she heard such expressions in Whytbrook, for goodness' sake? She was glad Lucy did not emulate her sister.

She exchanged a few more words with the girls, then collected her youngest daughter, who was eyeing the table hopefully. The child was led away from temptation into the small, narrow passageway. She would take little Jennifer upstairs, remove her best dress and put a neat white, well-starched pinafore over her second-best frock.

The front-door knocker sounded. Maisie stood for a moment, uncertainly. Who could this be on a Sunday afternoon? Relations and intimate friends still made their appearance by means of the rear door and the kitchen; and others did not call uninvited, naturally. The knocker was again rapped. She called out to the girls that she would answer the door and sent little Jennifer into the kitchen.

Then she gave herself a swift look in a gilded mirror and opened the door.

A man in early middle life stood on the door-step and at first she did not recognise him, even when he removed his hat. He had a thick beard, darker than his light brown hair, which she saw was tinged with grey at both temples. But there was no mistaking those blue eyes. And there was no mistaking his voice, even though the Somerset accents had long since disappeared, as soon as he spoke.

"Does Mr. Scott live here? Mr. Patrick Scott? I was told I'd find him at this address."

"That's right," said Maisie and she flushed to the roots of her red hair in pleasure and embarrassment. She recovered swiftly, though. "I'm Mrs. Scott. You'd best come in. Patrick won't be long. Oh, he will be that delighted!"

"You know me.... ?"

"Of course! It's Thomas, isn't it? Of course, I know ee! Well, I never! After all this long time, just fancy!"

CHAPTER XVII

It was an exceedingly merry meal. Patrick could not recall when they had all laughed so much. Not that there were any brilliant jests, but they were all of them in high spirits, the boys especially, giggling about anything and everything. Young Jennifer had been placed on her high chair at one corner, as the table could not accommodate them all. She had most of Lucy's gentle attention. There was so much to talk about, bridging the long years; but never a word of recrimination did Patrick utter about Thomas's long silence. He was simply overjoyed to see his brother again, and before he asked one word about his elder brother's life, he was anxious to know if Thomas had managed to keep in touch with other members of the family, including his sister Jane in America. It seemed Thomas had not. There was a moment of silence.

"Oh, one means to write," said Thomas, easily, "but time passes." He shrugged. "You know how it is. I've been hellishly busy, you know." That was not an expression he would have once used. He had quite lost his lilting Somerset accent - it was sharper, louder - though now and again the odd Somerset-sounding word would come forth, as though he had not been quite sure what to put in its place, as though he was trying to please his hearers.

"But the Jacksons? You surely must've heard from them?" said Maisie, speaking the words Patrick had been about to speak.

"Yes, the Jacksons," Patrick echoed. His cousin's husband, David, still wrote fairly regularly. He was now retired, but he never failed to mention something about the railways. They were still his life.

"I must go and look them up. They were good to me." He could hardly remember what any of them looked like. He told Patrick and Maisie he was expecting to finalise arrangements for his next berth (as he called it) and he could call upon the Jacksons on the way down to London.

"'Ee do that," said Patrick. "Wish I'd the time to come along with 'ee, Thomas. 'Course Maisie's been down a few times with the children."

Only when every single relation, however distant, and every single former acquaintance had been mentioned, did Maisie dare to ask what had kept Thomas so long from Whytbrook.

Thomas did not answer directly. Then he laughed.

"Well, I'd the time to spare and I reckon I got sentimental!"

"Well, it's good to see 'ee, anyhow," said Patrick, quickly, "and looking so fit, too. But 'ee must remember Maisie, Thomas? She was quite a bit sweet on you as a young girl!" He grinned at Maisie and she flushed. Thomas thought, 'They're delightful people, but after a few days, what will they talk about?' He was glad he had booked himself into The Wool Pack. But he smiled at Maisie as though she had paid him a deep compliment by singling him out for her attention, though he could barely remember anything much about her. The red hair ought to have jogged his memory, he supposed, but there had been so many girls, so many women.... and life had been very crowded.

"Do 'ee ever hear from Luke?" Patrick asked later on after they had left the table and were sitting in the small parlour on their own. "He went out to Australia, 'ee know," he added, recalling the time the money for the mare had been sent with no message at all. "Sheep-farming, I believe," he added, not wanting to admit how little he knew.

Thomas showed some small interest. It just so happened the ship he was hoping to join as an engineer would be voyaging to Australia and New Zealand.

"Well, fancy," said Maisie, who had come into the room at that moment and added, in her innocence, "you might even meet up, Thomas!" She went from the room again.

"'Ee'll have heard about the terrible fire, of course?" asked Patrick suddenly, in a hushed, almost reverential tone, as though the fire had occurred only last month. "A bad business that."

"Yes," Thomas acknowledged and he did not look directly back at his brother. He had come down from Bristol and he had gone there in the first place because chance news had led him to his old friend Paddy O'Neil. He had heard the man was staying with one of his daughters and might well be dying. In fact, he was not, though certainly very ill and it had been Paddy himself, in a sentimental mood, who had strongly prompted Thomas to go down to Whytbrook and look up his family. He had arrived in the village the previous evening, but told himself it was too late for visiting and he must make enquiries. This morning he had walked across the fields to have a look for himself at the farmhouse. He wanted to be sure he could still recall the old rough road. There had been no intention to avoid being seen, but now he felt a curious reluctance to let Patrick know he had viewed Redesdale. It seemed as dreadful as unholy prying. The windows were boarded up, but he had managed to look into one downstairs room at the front, where slats had broken, and had seen the room was empty. Most of the debris had been removed, he could see, from the yard, but it was also plainly evident someone or some persons had been existing in the sheds and that recently. He ought to warn Patrick. They could cause another fire. He said nothing.

Patrick had stopped talking about the fire.

"There's still a bit o' time afore church," said Patrick, clearly assuming that Thomas would be accompanying them, and Thomas, who knew he would not do so, quickly prepared his excuses. There were people he ought to call upon while it was still light. Patrick smoked one of his rare pipes, since his wife did not care for the smell of tobacco in her parlour. As soon as she came back into the room, with the two girls following behind her, he put it out.

"Kate and me thought we might have a little concert," suggested Lucy, boldly. "I believe you have a fine voice, Uncle Thomas?"

Patrick frowned a little. He could well imagine the kind of songs his brother Thomas had been singing in past years. He also guessed Kate was seeking an occasion to show off her pretty voice, and not just hymns, which were all he usually allowed on Sunday evenings.

"Another time," he said, "we'll have to be getting ready for Evensong."

Thomas began to explain how he must hasten off to see some old people, but they must certainly have a little get-together another evening. The boys came into the room, their hair plastered down in Sunday tidiness. They sat on the window-seat and stared at this new uncle for a short while. Then Will said, his voice tinged with awe,

"Uncle Thomas, 'ave 'ee been right round t'world? Have 'ee?"

"Several times," said Thomas, amused. Patrick smiled indulgently at his sons.

"Lor'!" exclaimed Will, then put his hand to his mouth, not sure if this was something he ought to be saying on a Sunday. But it wasn't *swearing*, not really!

Thomas grinned at him. They were all innocents, he thought, as he stood up, preparing to leave. Patrick, obviously content with his very humble lot and his quiver of children, five so far. How had he come to marry a young woman like Maisie? She was pretty, charming in her way, but not at all the sort of girl he would have thought Patrick would settle for, remembering Hannah Scott's influence; yet they seemed perfectly happy together, exceptionally happy, in fact.

As for being an innocent, he continued his thoughts as he moved off down the village street, had he not been one himself? Oh, he owed a good deal to Captain Aldridge. Without his backing, he would never have achieved his qualifications, but he had done all the hard, grinding work himself. No-one could do that for him. He also owed him Olivia, whom Thomas had married as, from the beginning, he had sensed he might. What he had not for a moment realised, however, was that he had been selected, not merely out of whim, not even as a possible replacement for a lost and beloved nephew. No, he had been intended to provide Aldridge with healthy, ocean-loving heirs! Well, he was not the first man this had happened to and he had gone along comfortably enough with the idea, half-amused by it, half-relishing it. For by this time he was truly in love with Olivia. Captain Aldridge even hinted at a name change, if the first-born should be a son. But Olivia had disappointed her father. She had born only two daughters in rapid succession, then her health had made it plain she should not risk another pregnancy. Thomas had not minded. Olivia came first with him, but it had been the slow beginning of a rift between the captain and himself, the patron and his protégé. This childish, petulant resentment on the part of the Captain had helped to strengthen the bond between Olivia and Thomas. He loved her passionately. He would even have left the sea for her sake, had she asked him to do so. She never did. He was still very much in love with her when she died, so she had stayed enshrined in his deepest, most hidden feelings. And yet.... could it not be that his attachment gave him the excuse he needed never to marry again? The sea was his real mistress, he told himself.

When Captain Aldridge died suddenly, Thomas sold the shares he had in the company and looked once more for change. His two daughters had largely been brought up by the Aldridge family.

From one point of view, leaving the line was a bad move. By this time, with luck, he could have had the command of a vessel. He knew he had disappointed the Aldridge family, perhaps his own girls. There was even a terrible moment when he faced that he had disappointed a great many people in his lifetime. But hang it, they had all wanted to put chains on him! None of them had understood. He was feeling restless again.

So, for several exciting years he had gone back to 'sails', his great love, though his earnings had been slender and he well knew there was no future in it.

Once, he had almost made a fortune on a gun-running deal, but been cheated by his partners. He felt no bitterness. He spoke of most of his adventures with humour - those he could recount, that is, his more acceptable endeavours, such as being chased by pirates in the China Sea and later been boarded. He could imagine the typical boyish glee the sons of Patrick and Maisie would show when he told them some of his ventures. But the had met people none of them could begin to imagine, and done things even worldly-wise Paddy might not comprehend. Slave-dealing over? So his friend thought. It most assuredly was not. He had encountered plenty of slaves in his time, especially in the Persion Gulf, all of them born in Arabia and with black ancestry. He had met enough rascals in his time.

Now he was back with engines out of necessity and, even so, he had been compelled to step down for a while, despite his experience and qualifications. It was either that or engage in some tasteless, risky deal. He was expecting to be taken on as the Second Officer, not the Chief, as he had implied to Patrick. Never in the past had he lied about the facts, nor even embroidered them; now increasingly he found himself on the verge of dishonesty. So what did it matter? It would be back to sea again and all that this implied.

"D'ee never regret leaving here, Thomas?" Patrick had asked quietly, and Thomas had wondered if he could ever begin to explain how he felt about the sea. From the first time he had stood alone in the middle watch with the bright stars all about him and the heaving waters below, he had sensed a profound wisdom. Not for an instance had he felt lonely. Rather it was as though he had become aware for the first time of his essential part of the great whole of existence.

He was utterly enveloped in a stupendous peace and harmony. Such experiences were rare, but they were never forgotten. And what had he answered to his brother?

"Well, there's been' the challenge, y'know." He had shrugged. "Adventure, if you like."

"Adventure." Patrick had looked at his elder brother, wonderingly, as though this was a foolish child who spoke. "Adventure, is it?"

It was not really a question and he had not expected an answer. After a pause, he had said, half-diffidently, "'Ee know, Thomas, there's always a living on the land for 'ee, if 'ee wish. Hard work, as 'ee well know, but we make out. I'm employing both of Maisie's brothers nowadays and I daresay.... "

Thomas had merely smiled and shook his head. Then, feeling something was expected of him, he had added that he appreciated his brother's concern, but had made his choice. No more was said.

Patrick thought much about Thomas as he prepared to take his place in his usual pew in church. He would never leave the land, but it was far from easy. Aside from the vagaries of the weather and the diseases that could beset the animals (though they were getting more clever all the time at controlling these) there was the government to contend with nowadays. There seemed to be constant new acts being passed, fresh regulations to befuddle the farmer, more and more prying into this and that. In The Bell they were sure half of them were unnecessary and just dreamed up to give those folks in Whitehall something to do.

The following evening they were all back in the parlour, unusual for a Monday, but they had to make the most of Thomas's short stay in Whytbrook. He had spent much of the day with Patrick and now he listened to Kate's sweet voice, while Lucy accompanied her sister on the harmonica. His praise was genuine. He also noticed that this girl, whom he took to be the eldest daughter, was not in the very least shy, quite self-possessed, in fact. He sang a few ditties himself, careful to pick the less lusty of the ballads he knew.

"I always remember' your fine bass voice," breathed Maisie. Thomas did not contradict her. "But Kate's soprano voice is something else. A young girl's voice is a delicate instrument, I'm told."

"I want to be properly trained! I want to sing in opera!" Kate announced. She looked at her uncle. Maisie and Patrick also looked at him, as though this traveller must certainly know more about the world than themselves.

"It probably ought to be trained," said Thomas, casually, though he knew almost nothing about opera.

"There! I told you!" Kate was delighted.

Patrick and Maisie continued to look at Thomas, anxiously, Maisie wondering where on earth they would find the money for lessons, but, feeling she must not dash her daughter's hopes; Patrick suddenly solemn at the thought of losing his girl. He changed the subject.

"Things have altered some since your day, Thomas," he said with sudden cheerfulness. "As I showed you, much more mechanical all round. Don't know if it's better, though it'll suit the boys, I daresay, when their time comes to take over. Whytbrook's changing as well. Quite a busy place sometimes. I believe they're planning all manner of things for the new year. Pity 'ee couldn't be here then."

"Oh, you should've been here at the time of the good Queen's Golden Jubilee!" exclaimed Maisie. "In 1897 that were. Quite a lot of folks went up to London, y'know! I'd have gone myself, but with the baby it was a bit awkward." She chattered on happily and Thomas who had actually been in London at the time of the Golden Jubilee, said not a word.

Less than a week later, Thomas was back in London. His brother and his wife tried to persuade him to remain longer in Whytbrook, and indeed, they were clearly distressed that he seemed to prefer to stay at The Wool Pack, however inconvenient an additional person in the house might be for them. Despite all the people Thomas had been inveigled upon to visit, Patrick could still think of others his brother really ought to look up in Kimsley or even further afield.

Thomas had gone with his brother to take a look at Redesdale and he had spoken not a word about his earlier visit, which he was glad he had taken. The second viewing was less of a shock to him.

"I do know it'd upset 'ee Thomas. That's only nat'ral. But then again, it seems only right and proper, somehow."

Like visiting a grave, Thomas had thought. In the end, he had been drawn into making a half-promise to return at once to Whytbrook should he find his ship was to be delayed for any length of time. He had not thought this at all likely. He had grown fond of Patrick, perhaps more so than when he was a lad. He had mellowed a little and was not quite so painfully 'holy' as he had once been; perhaps this could be attributed to Maisie. In a way, he would almost like to return, even felt a little sad that he would not, for it was surely most unlikely. Not for some years, at any rate. He had called on the Jacksons, however, in company with Patrick and he had sensed at first their coldness. They were not as forgiving about his long silence as Patrick had been. He had visited his two daughters and made polite conversations with some of his late wife's relations. Now, he felt strongly the need for clean sea air.

To his dismay and surprise, he found there was likely to be a considerable delay before The New Westerner reached Tilbury. There had been an outbreak of infection, the ship had been compelled to make a diversion and she had not been able to find a berth quickly in Australia, all of which had delayed her sailing date back to England. To crown everything, the day she was due to leave, there had been trouble with an unpremeditated flare-up of the crew. Though the days of the dreadful malaise when strife could occur for the most trivial of petty reasons had yet to arrive with steam ships, it seemed to Thomas that these huge and sturdy vessels could no more guarantee their arrival times than had the sailing ships been able to do so. There were plenty of other factors besides the elements to upset schedules.

He was actually in the shipping office, pondering the fact that he could expect to kick his heels for another week at least, when he had an extraordinary encounter. At first when he noticed a slim man, slightly taller than himself, standing at a counter, he merely thought that he bore a resemblance to someone he must have met at one time. He had met so many people. He paused and looked more closely. At that moment, the man, who was talking to a clerk and elegantly attired in pale grey with a traditional pearl tie-pin, worn fashionably high, turned slightly. He had lain his hat and cane on the counter.

The two men looked at each other. That hair, bright brown, faintly ginger, worn very short (which was not especially fashionable) and splashed with careless bars of grey, seemed to convey something to Thomas. It could not be, surely? Again the two looked at each other, dumb-founded.

"I hope I'm not making a ghastly mistake, but you're uncommonly like someone I knew," said Thomas moving forward. Then he stopped, smiled broadly, and held out his hand. "By Jove, if you're not my brother Luke, you're his double! At least, what he must look like by now!"

"Good God!" said Luke, and he held out his own hand, sending his hat clumsily to the ground. He did not trouble himself about it, but left it to one of the clerks to retrieve it. He was grinning widely. After that moment of warm emotion, there had followed a pause of slight embarrassment, the recognition that they were strangers to each other now. How best to proceed?

Swiftly, Thomas solved the dilemma. He suggested that as soon as the other had completed his business, they make their way to his nearby hotel, so they could talk. Luke soon saw the hotel was cheap, though respectable, rather different to the hotel where he was himself staying. He wondered. In fact, Thomas would never waste money on what was, to him, unnecessary. It was not meanness; he cared almost nothing about his physical comforts.

Luke on the other hand, who had made a great deal of money in his long years away from England, equally liked to spend it, chiefly on himself and his family, for he had married a widow, only two or three years older than himself and who, conveniently, had owned a fair bit of land and the sheep to graze on it. Luke had worked relentlessly hard, taken risks and suffered several setbacks, but he had succeeded. He had two sons and there had been no other children at the time when he married his widow. He saw himself as a self-made success. It was the picture he wanted to convey.

Thomas smiled a little as he listened to Luke, so careful not to boast, but letting drop matters which were important to himself. He was over in England on business, he said.

"Now this darned ship, The New Westerner, I'm sailing on is delayed they tell me!"

"The New Westerner, eh?" Thomas hesitated a moment, then realised be could not keep the matter secret and why should he? "I'll be joining her myself as Chief Engineer."

Luke appeared impressed. "How did you manage.... ?"

Thomas explained briefly.

Luke nodded.

"I don't regret not having much education for myself. It's not necessary, but I'm determined to have it for my sons. I've two boys, y'know, ten and twelve years old now. And what about yourself? Did you marry?"

Thomas told him about his own life, but he saw that Luke was not greatly interested. Neither his manner, nor his way of speaking quite matched his elegant appearance and apparent financial standing. He had never quite known what role to adopt when he lived at Redesdale; he had often felt himself to be an outsider. He still felt himself to be so. He could not attract as the strong, natural leader, he suspected Thomas to be, so he had often been unnecessarily harsh and rigid, then fearing over-dislike, he had tried to balance this with occasional extravagance. He could never quite hit the happy medium, but his men stayed with him because he paid well and, despite his pose, they genuinely liked him; or, perhaps, they were sorry for him. He still aroused that mothering instinct in women.

Thomas paused and Luke, in almost boyish glee, told him of a new acquisition. He had just bought himself, his first motor-car, a two-cylinder four-seater Daimler, which it was opined had the power of no less than six horses. It was not quite brand new, but that was an advantage, in his view. Its owner had died suddenly. Luke had been arranging for the motor-car's transport from Coventry (where it was being put into perfect order at the works there) to the docks, ready for shipment to Australia.

"Won't be much use to you out there, will it?" asked Thomas dubiously.

"Not on the farm, perhaps. A horse is better. I'll probably keep it in the town. It'll be fine there, visiting friends and so on."

"Showing off?"

Luke was startled for a moment. No-one said things to him like that nowadays, but he grinned.

"What the hell and why not? We'd plenty of penny-pinching back at the farm, far too much of it." He firmed his lips to a hard line, wondering if they'd ever found where his mother hid her money.

"So you've grown rich?" asked Thomas, quite without envy.

"Well, not rich, exactly," Luke replied, cautiously, warily. "But we get by. We're comfortable."

"So it seems." There was a moment's pause. "I was up at Whytbrook recently. They'd a fire some years back, y'know, so they're living in a house in the village.

Luke had known two fairly disastrous fires in his time in Australia, so he tended to be a bit dismissive of the one Patrick and his family had experienced. He pursed his lips.

"It's insane to leave the farmhouse standing empty," he declared. "I don't like that at all. Patrick's married, I take it?"

Thomas told him, yes he was. Luke fell to musing. It was very evident that his brother Patrick had said not a word as to Luke's real reason for departing from Whytbrook. He decided to say nothing himself. It was all in the past. The girl herself - what was her name, now? - Maisie - no doubt she had married and left the village long ago. It was best forgotten. But at that moment, Thomas mentioned the name Bevan and Luke sat upright, for that name had certainly penetrated his subconscious.

"Bevan, did you say? Working at the farm? You're not referring to a couple of brothers I used to know with a drunken father? Used to come to The Bell, as I remember.

"That's right." Thomas went on to explain about the enlarging of the village house and the acquiring of more land. "He grows a lot more vegetables now and he's even gone in for small herds of heifers. He's doing all right. The Bevans have a sister called Maisie. Seems she had a fancy for me! Thomas laughed. "I've no clear recollection. "Anyhow, she's married to Patrick now. Oh, she must have been no more'n a child when we knew her."

"Maisie Bevan," breathed Luke. He had an almost irresistible desire to burst out laughing. His brother Patrick and Maisie! The idea of that sobersides married to little red-head Maisie was too incongruous! He got himself under control. "Any family?" he asked casually.

"Five to date." He spoke a little about them, though he had to think hard to recall little Jennifer's name.

Luke listened more carefully.

"And this girl Kate? You think she has some talent?"

"I can hardly judge, but she's plenty of vitality. She'd probably do well on the stage, but Patrick'd never hear of it, of course. Red hair, like her mother's. The other girl's too shy, though pretty in her way." He paused. "As a matter of fact they were keen to have me go back there for a day or two, if I found my ship was delayed."

"Well, why not?"

"I don't know. I'd almost like to. They made me very welcome.... but there doesn't seem much point, does there? I'd rather like to see an old friend of mine, whose been very ill. He's living in Bristol. I suppose I could fit him in as well. Be a good idea to get out of London. It's getting much too noisy. The traffic!"

Luke was hardly listening, but he was thinking hard. So he had a daughter.

Thomas was saying, "You'd probably have more in common with Patrick nowadays than me. At least you could jabber about sheep." He laughed. Suddenly an idea began to grow in Luke's imagination. If he was going back to Redesdale (and he'd always vowed he never would go back) then going back in the company of Thomas was obviously wisest. It would smooth over any lingering difficulties. He did not really foresee any after all this time and the girl had got Patrick to marry her, so what had she to complain about?

He heard himself saying, "Suppose we both go down to Whytbrook for a couple of days? How does that appeal?" He grew excited. "Tell you what we'll do, we'll go up to Coventry, collect my motor-car and then drive down to Somerset. We can spend one night in Coventry and make an early start, another on the way, if need be. They'll give us all the maps we need. How does that sound to you?"

"Sounds great, but suppose something did go wrong and I missed my sailing?"

"I'm on the same ship, don't forget. You won't miss it! We'll go on by train, after the visit and arrange for the Daimler to be sent on also."

"How soon?"

"What about first thing tomorrow morning? Let's go and have a decent meal somewhere and fix up the details. I'm famished. And I'll have to send off a few telegrams."

"Hope you can drive," smiled Thomas.

"There's nothing to it, old man! They showed me the mechanics when I bought it." He sounded excited, more like the Luke Thomas remembered in the past. "I might even let you take the steering wheel!"

One of the telegrams which was sent off came from Thomas. It was addressed to Patrick and it read:

'Hope arrive Whytbrook Thursday stop Travelling Daimler from Coventry stop Big surprise for you both stop Thomas.'

That sent the Patrick Scott family into a fury of speculation. What could Thomas mean? What was his big surprise?

"A Daimler's a motor-car, isn't it Dad?" Will asked.

"Yes, I believe so." Had Thomas bought this extravagant car, then?

Maisie, more romantic-minded, pondered the matter and came up with her suggestion.

"How many seats would this motor-car have?" She had been twice in cars which had only two seats and these had both been occasions when a couple had got married and all the invited guests had wanted to have a short run, in turns, from the church to the village hall.

"I've no idea," replied Patrick, wondering why on earth she asked such a question. "Why not wait and see?"

"It has four seats, said Joe, with patronising assurance.

"Four? Then I'm thinking Thomas is planning to surprise us by bringing his two young daughters to visit us. And his intended! That must be it!" She could not imagine anyone travelling in a car with empty seats. No, that must be it! He had got himself engaged to be married. She felt a glow of animation. There would be so much to do to prepare for them, in case they all wanted to sleep in the house. But even if they stayed at The Wool Pack, she must insist they take all their meals with the family.

Patrick seemed to read her thoughts.

"Even if 'tis a bit of a crush my little love, we'd best be ready for 'un. He's my own brother and his future wife that's coming." He was assuming that Maisie was right about this, as Maisie had proved so often to be right in the past. If a man had never married it was one thing, but a widow-man ought to have himself a wife, especially when there were young girls. But he could not get over the motor-car. Thomas must be better off than he believed. Unless the car had been hired.

Meanwhile, Luke and Thomas, having set off from Coventry on the long journey from Warwickshire to Somersetshire and finding they could not sensibly avoid the Cotswolds, had been grateful for the advice they had been given when they started. They spent some time in Bath, staying overnight, in fact, and Thomas made a quick visit to see his old friend Paddy while the motor-car was again attended to. Luke had done all the driving up till now and he had driven very carefully, anxious for the vehicle. But once on the troublesome roads to Whytbrook, either Luke became careless and overexcited or they were merely unfortunate, but they had more bother than during the entire previous journey. Once the engine became seriously over-heated. Luke had forgotten all about water, though thankfully this model did not require its dirty oil to be removed, as was customary. It merely ran out onto the floor, then more oil could be poured in. Each stop entailed the cranking up of the metal starting-handle, very hard work, then a swift dash back into the car in case it stalled. Luke was glad enough he had Thomas with him to keep the engine running, though he still stubbornly refused to let him drive. Thomas sat back with folded arms and occasionally made unhelpful remarks. The two brothers were no longer on the same friendly terms as when they set out. It was a relief to finally reach Whytbrook and Luke drove through the main street of the village with a flourish. Long before they reached Patrick's home, word had been spread and a surprising number of villagers were standing at their gates, pausing as they did their work, or hurrying towards the main street, mainly women and old men, but some children as well, though it was a good half-an-hour to dinner-time. As though they'd never seen a car before in their lives, Maisie had thought, though this, she soon saw was a particularly splendid vehicle. The leather seats were especially solid and comfortable-looking, more like a phaeton, in Joe's opinion, the lamps of solid brass, just like carriage lamps, gleaming brightly.

Maisie had flown back into the house at the first sight of the car and insisted the girls withdraw with her. They must wait till the motor-car arrived. She had not forgotten all the things she had learned from Mrs. Squires those long years ago. Gawping like peasants was not seemly. Neither Patrick nor the boys cared in the very least about such niceties, so coming down the path, he was the first to realise the motor-car only held two men. He was disappointed for Maisie's sake. For a moment he looked in puzzlement at the slim man, wearing a boater and a long dust coat, which he casually removed and tossed into the back seat on top of some luggage. He was clean-shaven, his face a deep pink and sun-cracked. But it was his hair, despite the sprinkling of grey, which caught his attention.

"Luke!" he exclaimed, genuinely delighted, recognising his younger brother. "Now where on earth did 'ee spring from?" He held out his hand and Luke took it, clasping it firmly. "This is a surprise!" He turned to Thomas. "Ah, this is what 'ee meant, I see in the telegram. Well, well, where did 'ee meet up, I'm wondering."

Thomas started to explain and the three men were talking loudly as they entered the house. Patrick turned towards Maisie, who had come to the door.

"What d'ee think about this, Maisie, my little love? Luke's turned up from Australia to see us all!"

His manner was perfectly natural, quite without any unease, but Maisie, as she shook hands and murmured a quiet welcome, was mortified. She noticed also, that while Luke's clasp was strong and his voice clear, he did not quite meet her eye.

Maisie swiftly retired to the kitchen to direct the meal. She had not given Luke a thought for years, yet now she found she was seething. How could he be so insensitive? How could Thomas? Then she realised Thomas probably knew nothing about the part Luke had played in her life. This still did not make her forgiving towards Thomas, even towards her dear Patrick. They ought to have warned her! They ought to have asked her if she minded. How like the Scotts!

Maisie spoke little during the meal, which was hardly noticed, as she was busy with the serving, keeping an eye on the younger children and helping Annie, who needed no eye to be kept on her by this time. She was superb, for which Maisie felt secret pride. The standards of cooking, too, were far superior to Hannah's day, at least when Luke had left home. Maisie doubted if Luke had anything to compare with the food and service where he lived. She held herself upright, proudly.

Then, the meal over, Luke suggested the young people might like a quick run in the motor-car around the village.

"Oh, we've all been in a motor-car before now," Maisie felt compelled to say, "but perhaps the boys.... "

"Only at weddings," said Kate, firmly, "and the motor-cars weren't like the one we saw from the window just now. I'd love to go for a little ride and I'm sure Lucy would also." She deliberately looked across at her middle-aged Uncle Luke, as though he was an eligible young man she had just met for the first time, and smiled at him. She did this with almost every man she met, unless she had taken some unexplained aversion to him and Luke smiled back at the girl. It was as though she shared some special secret with him. How delightful she was! How delightful they both were.

After this little adventure and it was clear the two boys had no intention of returning to school this day, they sat around talking, the three brothers and the young lads, that is, for Maisie hustled the others out of the way. Luke was wondering how to suggest visiting Redesdale, for he was curious to see it. Patrick made it easy for him.

"I'd like 'ee to come up and see James and Matthew Bevan, Luke. They'll remember 'ee all right. They remembered Thomas. They'll be disappointed if 'ee don't call on 'em. They do know that you're coming this day." He had had to let them know, so he would be free himself from duties. "I don't suppose you and Thomas's be staying that long?"

"Just the one night," said Thomas. "Daren't leave it longer."

Patrick gave a hint of a sigh and Luke was aware of a sudden childish churning in his bowels. Fear? After all this time?

"All right," said Luke, "if you want to, but while we're up there I want to take a good look at the old farmstead. P'raps we'd best go there first."

"You won't like it," said Patrick, shaking his head. "'Tis all boarded up, y'know." He glanced towards Thomas, as though seeking some assurance. Thomas merely said, "If we're going, we'd best go right away."

From a comparative short distance, the farmhouse did not look at all bad, for the stone was solid and some creepers had grown in places, hiding scars, blackened places. Close up, Luke soon saw it was a different story. He stood quite still and stared. He had already noticed a boarded entrance, where the kitchen door must have stood. Someone had clearly removed this he supposed and goodness only knows what else beside.

"What a shame! What a damned shame, to leave the place in this state! Couldn't something be done?"

There was a cynical look on Thomas's face and Patrick looked distressed. As far as Thomas was concerned the house had never possessed much in the way of beauty and he supposed Patrick had simply not had the money for the vast amount of repairs. He suggested this, quietly, adding that he thought they were better off where they were.

"We use most of the land, " said Patrick.

"And apparently, Maisie flatly refused to live in the place after the fire. Can't say I blame her."

This did not help matters.

"It's still a damned shame," said Luke, more quietly. "I wonder how much it would cost to put it right."

Thomas saw then, though Patrick did not, that Luke had it in mind to recreate a family home, something he could dream about, boast about, perhaps, while he took care himself not to live in it.

"Let's go," he said. "There's no point in mulling over the past." Most of the debris had been removed or stolen during the long years, but the boys ran about to and fro as though they still hoped to find something.

"That farm was our heritage," said Luke, coldly.

"Let's go," Thomas repeated. He was really angry now. "If we're going to see the Bevans we'd best not hang about any longer." He looked to Patrick, wanting him to say something that would put Luke in his place. His heritage, indeed! When he had run away, as he had done so himself.

Patrick said, "I'm afraid you don't understand. Farmer Ridley wanted to buy it for a shoot, but I wouldn't have that. We've kept most of the land, though." His voice was quiet, but without any hint of apology.

Luke had gone, without a word, still ferreting about, still trying to see what he could in the empty rooms. It was as though he was reluctant to leave the place, as though he felt it had some special hold on him, even though he knew he had never liked Redesdale all that much. It was his childhood and his youth, but he had never really liked it; yet, he could not bring himself to leave just at present. Something held him.

At that moment, the younger of the two boys, came whooping up, excitedly, the other following in his trail. Their small lives did not hold so much adventure that they could forego any chance of amusement. They had not been up to the farmhouse for years. Their mother had forbidden it, in case they met with an accident.

"Papa! Uncle Thomas! Uncle Luke!" they both screamed, and ten-year-old William had added, "I think I've found something!"

From their gabbling, it appeared they had gone into the open-fronted shed, immediately next to the former passageway. It smelled as though it might contain human excrement, but William poked about in the near dark, scrambling over debris and using a stick he supposed must have been left behind by a tramp. He saw the bricks were in poor shape with much of the cement missing. Excitedly, they had both pushed and shoved and managed to dislodge one of the old shed's stones, then peered inside. There was little to be seen, but their eyes were sharp. They flew back to the adults.

"Something like metal!" yelled Joe. "Shall I fetch a lamp from Uncle Matt's?"

"Just a minute," said Luke. "Not so fast. Let's take a look first. I've some matches on me." He lit one after another of the few remaining in the box and held them as far as he could reach into the gap. Then he called out to Patrick and Thomas.

Patrick's eyes were not as good as they had been. Something bright, but he thought they were wasting time. Bits of rubbish and mouse droppings, he thought. What else? What did they hope to find, for goodness' sake? Gently, he said, "There must be loose stone all over the property. Maisie won't like it if the boys hurt themselves."

Luke did not reply. He had already decided to send the older boy for a lamp. In any event, he thought, they must take a look.

"What you hoping to find, Luke?" Thomas asked, slightly amused. "You don't think Ma hid her spare cash in the shed, do you?"

Luke did not reply for a moment, then he turned from the wall and said, "There's something in there all right. Could have been there a very long time."

Said Patrick, "Have you forgotten this passage next to the shed was blocked up long ago, before any o' us can remember?

Ma and everyone used the shed to go through to her hens. The passage wasn't used at all. Why it was blocked off, I don't rightly recall now." But Luke was examining the stout wooden erection, still intact despite the fire. "Some people, not looking too careful, thought the farmhouse was joined to the little shed. I used to think so myself once when little." Patrick was worried. Nothing of any value had been kept in the shed, mainly firing, but he had suddenly remembered the night Maisie had made him get up and go downstairs to look about his mother's pantry and he had found nothing amiss. The pantry was next to the passageway.

Joe had returned with the lamp, which was soon re-lighted.

"Are we going to find out where Grandma hid all her gold?" he asked innocently.

"What 'ee on about, son?" asked Patrick, sharply. There's no gold." Joe flushed.

"Everyone says there is," chipped in William. "They say she hid it and forgot where she put it. But how could she get into the passage?"

They spent quite a time peering into the hole in turn.

"Well," said 'Luke at last, "I'm not ruining a good suit trying to get in there. There must be some other way. What's on the other side of the passage?" He had already looked at the heavy boarding over the former entrance.

"The pantry," answered Patrick, reluctantly. "'Ee remember that, surely?"

"Can we get into the house?"

"Not without you knocking down the boarding over one of these doors and a rare mess that'll make, putting it all to rights again so some sheep don't wander inside one of these days and get hurt." It was truly amazing where sheep could get, when they were in the mood. He did not wish to continue with this foolishness. He deliberately forgot that there was a key to the front-door, somewhere or other, back home. He was most reluctant to enter Redesdale farmhouse again. Thomas had said little, but now he said, "Best satisfy our curiosity. Let's see what we can find to smash down the back-door." He went off to look for something, a rusted crowbar, perhaps. Cynically, he was thinking, was money all Luke now wanted? And what about himself? He tried to tell himself money could make little difference in his life and a lot of money would be a renewal of chains. No thank you!

It took some time getting the boarding down and before they had done so, both Matthew and James Bevan had joined them, having been called by William. Then they all made their way into the old farm kitchen and so to the pantry, Luke still carrying the lamp. All of them, that is, except Patrick. He wished with all his heart, this had never happened, for he feared.... How he wished!...

It was several hours later. Patrick and Maisie were alone in the house, in the kitchen, the two brothers having left, presumably to go to The Wool Pack for the night. Thomas had promised to call upon the couple before their early departure next day. Luke had said nothing. There had been no time for visiting, no time for more entertaining. Every second had been taken up with the organising of their stupendous discovery. There was gold in the passage, all right, as well as paper-money, which had been gnawed by rodents over the years and some cloth-bags which had split. The hole in the pantry had seemed no bigger than a mouse-hole, hidden by a large, oblong butter-basket, which always stood on the floor in that place. They had been able to dislodge a couple of sovereigns easily but had had to return to the barton and spend a considerable amount of time and energy, with all the help they could muster, in removing the wooden barricade, so as to be able to get into the passage. It might have been far easier to have dislodged stones from the shed. Then the local bank manager had been sent for and they had had to sign papers, all of them, as witness to the removal of the money, though it seemed there would be several thousands of pounds. Hannah had clearly used the passage as a kind of piggy-bank, shoving in coins through the small hole near the ground in her pantry, knowing she would not be able to get them out again.

Patrick had felt wretched, realising at last just how ill Hannah must have been, and he had tried to deceive himself! What was appalling were the silver buttons, along with the money, which Patrick's mother must have put in there when Patrick began to control the household expenses. He felt sick. The dilapidated willow basket, intended for butter had remained in the pantry all those long years, not worth the trouble of removing, Patrick thought. He was deeply distressed. He blamed himself. He had turned a blind eye to all he did not wish to see.

"Oh, Patrick, it wasn't your fault!" Maisie tried to comfort him. "Who'd have dreamed.... ? I'm sure she just fancied she was a-hoarding for her old age."

Patrick looked at his wife.

"She wasn't mad," he said, stubbornly. He saw it all as a spiritual lack; an overwhelming fear, a total failure to trust in the Lord. Certainly, she had not trusted him. He sighed. "One thing's for certain, Maisie, you and me's not touching a penny o' that money! Not a penny! We don't want nor need it! I got the farm. I've already told Thomas as much."

"And Luke.... ?"

"And Thomas said he didn't want any money either, but he gave me the name and address o' a friend of his, who it seems has been on hard times. 'Tis up to him."

Suddenly, Maisie was quietly weeping.

"Now, now, then, my little love, what's all this about?" He put his arm about Maisie.

She gulped. She could not really explain how she felt, but she brought out, "It all sort of spoils things, doesn't it, Patrick?"

"How d'ee mean my little love?"

"All our work these long years. We needn't have troubled.... "

"But we did trouble," said Patrick, gravely. "We did and we got our reward, as was proper. It needed more than a bit a money, Maisie." But he could well appreciate her point of view. Years ago, even a tiny sum of money would have been a Godsend to them. "No, I've made up my mind, the money must be divided equally between Luke and Thomas, or else Luke and this friend of Thomas's. That's what we want, isn't it?"

Maisie nodded, but she suddenly felt a sudden flare of resentment. towards Luke. It didn't seem right somehow that he should run off as he had done and then prosper in the end. This was not what she had been taught as a small child at Sunday School, nor what she had taught others. 'Vengeance is Mine', they had been taught, but it did not appear the Lord had any intentions of taking his revenge. Quite the reverse. Oh, it didn't seem fair.

She said, "Even if we don't want anything for ourselves, Patrick, don't let pride make you forget the children's rights. Kate longs to be a singer one day. You mustn't spoil things for her." Then she said, musingly, "I wonder how much there will turn out to be? Perhaps not as much as it seems."

Patrick looked at his wife and sighed a little. Even his Maisie? He said, "I wish William and Joe hadn't gone to Redesdale today, nor started poking about in the shed. And I wish to God, with all my heart, Thomas hadn't brought Luke back with him. I shouldn't say it. He's my own brother, but I've a feeling if he hadn't come today, things could have stayed as they were!"

Maisie looked at him gently.

"Something would have changed sometime, Patrick, bound to. But, y'know, I wish neither of them had come back. We were all right as we were." Her face was flushed, not just from the fire.

"Oh, Thomas's all right," said Patrick, swiftly. "He's solid enough."

Maisie said nothing for a moment, then, "I don't suppose we'll see either of them after they leave here first thing tomorrow morning. Their lives are very different to our's now."

Patrick nodded.

"And frankly," Maisie added, her tear-stained face still flushed, "I don't care if we don't see them again. I really don't. I wouldn't care all that much if they didn't come back to see us, didn't take the trouble."

But this was by no means the last they were to hear of Luke and Thomas. In the small hours, Patrick was aroused from his bed by Annie, who had first been roused by a knocking at the door. From the gasped message, Patrick learned there was a policeman waiting downstairs to speak to him. It seemed there had been an accident. Patrick hastily dressed and hastened downstairs. He learned that the two brothers for some notion best known to themselves, had decided to set off back to Bath last night, with the intention of taking the first available train themselves to London and having the motor-car transported by rail. Recklesly, careering down a hill, they had all but collided with a late-travelling brougham, had swerved to avoid it, and met with disaster. The motor-car driver had been flung onto the road and had split his head. By the time his dazed companion had been helped and both had been got to the infirmary, he was dead. Patrick asked the bearer of this sad news to wait a short while till he flew back to their bedroom, to hurriedly throw on more clothes and tell Maisie the grim news.

She lay on her back after Patrick had departed, knowing full well she would not be able to sleep, yet too tired and upset to get up, since there was nothing she could do at this hour. Annie had been sent back to her bed and told to say nothing to the others. Once or twice, Maisie did doze off, dreaming distorted dreams, that were close to the terrible truth. There was a body lying in a ditch, soaked in blood, then the figure opened his eyes and stared, accusingly into her own. She gave a little cry of horror and came fully awake, her heart thudding wildly.

After a while when she had grown calmer, she told herself she would not have wished this to happen for all the world, not even to careless Luke. It was all very sad. She could feel a vague kind of pity for Luke's wife and his young sons, especially his sons. Yet, she was calm now, utterly calm, seeing everything as it was meant to be. Why, only a few short hours before, she had resented Luke's prosperity, his having gained so much more than her dear Patrick. It had not seemed fair, not at all. How foolish of her! What was it? The slow-grinding mills of God. The devil thrusting in his knife at the end – and the end, much too soon. She must not rejoice about this, but she must accept it, thankful Luke had not suffered for long months and years. Well, there would be money for the family, though that hardly compensated. It was hard on her dear Patrick, also. She said a little prayer, one she recalled from years back, for them all. She felt peaceful. It was the Lord's way of doing things.

In the early years after Luke had taken to his heels, she had sometimes fantasised, creating pictures of him returning penitent, while she, of course, looked at him either with scorn, or was nobly forgiving. She had even seen Luke as a version of the returning prodigal, down-at-heel, wretched, desperate for a crust of consideration. Which she, and dear Patrick, would graciously give. Nothing makes a person feel more noble than to forgive, but she had never wished Luke dead, she assured herself.

It came to her then, in the dark, that this accident could have happened earlier in the day and one of the children been killed! Or perhaps the children deprived of their father and bread-winner, had something happened to Patrick. Motor-cars were dangerous things, so people who rode in them ought to know what they were about. These thoughts made her feel a little better about Luke.

Then, in the dawn, after Patrick had returned home and she had restlessly tossed a while longer, she arose and insisted she come down and attend to Patrick's needs. He must have a bite before he go out again.

"Annie's a light sleeper. Let her rest a bit. There'll be plenty to do later."

Patrick was now changed into his working clothes. He must advise Maisie's brothers and do what he could himself, while he could spare the time. Belatedly, Maisie thought of Thomas. Had he been injured badly? If not, then Thomas could help Patrick with the funeral arrangements.

"What about Thomas?" she asked, hesitantly. "He was with him at the time, wasn't he?"

Patrick stood still and stared at Maisie as though unable to comprehend her meaning.

"Thomas," she repeated. "Is he all right?"

"Thomas," he said stupidly. He wiped his eyes with the back of one hand. "Didnt 'ee realise, Thomas's dead!"

"Oh, no!" she exclaimed. "Not both of them! I didn't know!"

He moistened his lips.

"No, not both. Just Thomas. Luke broke his wrist, but he's otherwise all right."

"I thought it was the driver!"

"Thomas was driving at the time. It - it was dark, 'ee see."

"But Thomas could drive anything, Patrick! He told Will so."

"P'rhaps they were in a hurry, trying to get to Bath – then this brougham – I don't know, I'm sure.... " He could not bring himself to say that Luke had told him they were arguing at the time. "Luke's very upset," he added.

"I don't believe it," said Maisie, dully. "Thomas. It - it's all wrong." It can't be Thomas, she thought to herself. Something must have gone wrong!

The funeral was a quiet affair, held a few days later in Whytbrook. Thomas's daughters had been located, as well as some few other members of his wife's family. All of them stayed overnight at The Wool Pack. A strange old man also made his appearance. This was Paddy O'Neil. How he had come to hear of his friend's death, and how he had managed to make his shakey way to Whytbrook (rising, it would seem, from his own death-bed) no-one knew. His daughter was with him, to keep an eye on him and he left immediately after the funeral, not talking to anyone.

Patrick had insisted Luke stay with them, as he felt they would be able to help him more, with his broken wrist, than would the inn. Maisie contrived to avoid him all she could. Not so Kate. The girl proved to be very helpful. Maisie glanced at her suspiciously once or twice. Was she trying to get round Luke for some reason of her own? *He* could not further her hopes to be a professional singer. And despite all the sad upheaval, Luke had arranged for his motor-car to have all the necessary repairs carried out and be sent to the docks. It was clear he going to have to miss the sailing of The New Westerner, and it was equally clear to all that he chafed at this delay. The car had suffered a good deal less than the occupants. Then he had had himself driven in another vehicle up to Bristol and had returned with the information that he would be sailing from there in a week's time. He got on everyone's nerves, except Kate's. Patrick was too busy making up for lost time to notice anything. He was perfectly content to let Luke attend to the matter of the discovered money. There were also a few pieces of jewellery, some of them of value, most of little worth. They had been 'missing' for many years. All in all, there was approaching nine thousand pounds, a small fortune, by the standards of the times, and given the circumstances under which the amount had been collected.

One evening at supper, Patrick found himself staring at his younger brother. He remembered him so well as a gangling, sometimes nervously giggling youngster. Far too easily excited, needing assurance, maddening at times and cocky, but intrinsically lovable. He recalled the times when Luke had greedily wolfed down his food, never putting on an ounce of extra weight. He ate quickly now, but politely and almost with indifference, as though his mind was occupied with other, more important matters than food. It appeared he did not consider Maisie's splendid dishes warranted greater attention. 'Where's he rushing to?' Patrick thought. 'What's driving him?'

Then Luke was gone. Slowly, the house began to slide back into its normal pace, to relax, to breathe steadily again.

Patrick could not find it in his heart to suffer the deep anguish over Thomas's passing he might once have felt, but there was a terrible desolation for a while, for all that. It seemed such a dreadful waste. He had been a man of such striking promise. Why, he had inspired confidence in all whom he met, men and women! Here was a man who seemed to have a mission in life, some deep sense of purpose - once he found it. He was beyond the commonplace. He was not content with compromise, as were most.

He supposed Thomas must have many a time risked his life and survived numerous potential dangers, real dangers, perhaps even worthwhile risks; so his death now seemed a terrible foolishness, that ought not to have happened, that God ought not to have allowed! For several days he could not pray, excusing this failure on tiredness and sadness of heart. When the habit of a lifetime was resumed, he was more tolerant towards the spiritual lapses of others and especially his own children, than he had ever been before. Maisie tried to help in her sweet way, but she failed. For the first time in his knowledge of her, Patrick did not find her lilting, creamy voice, as she chattered on, soothing to his humours, an unending delight, even when what she occasionally said was a trifle silly. He only wished dearest Maisie would keep quiet. But he said not a word.

The challenge of life. Hadn't Thomas once said that to him? An adventure?

It came to Patrick suddenly, revealingly, that his brother Thomas was now set upon the greatest adventure of them all, the procession into eternity.

CHAPTER XVIII

Autumn moved into early winter and work on the farms continued much as it had always done in the past, before the upheaval created by the brothers' visit. The entire village had been shaken and they spoke of the events for weeks on end in The Bell. The Sexton, Barton, was long dead, but there were plenty of other know-alls to take his place.

They had always felt sure there must be money hidden at Redesdale Farm. It stood to reason. Lucky they were they had not had it all taken long since by diddikies. They had speculated on the amount and even when it was generally known how much had been found, they exaggerated it to their own fancy. As for the return of Luke and Thomas Scott.... many had been sure of that also. Luke had come back to look for treasure. Thomas had returned because he was out-of-work. They wanted to believe this of Thomas. True, he had called in one evening and stood them all drinks, but Luke had not troubled to call at The Bell. So, they gossiped, but times were different. No longer could they be totally unaware of what was happening in the rest of the world. Letters arrived from the colonies from families who had emigrated and all the younger men could read the papers for themselves. So the events at Redesdale were a nine days' wonder. They began to talk again about the land and the animals, eternal, unchanging topics. Most of all they pondered what the new century would bring to Whytbrook. Various small activities were planned, mainly parties for the children and treats for the old folks. There was an excitement in the air, which even the sharp-witted could not entirely scorn.

Patrick learned that Paddy O'Neil had died only a week after his brother's funeral. Anxious to have the whole matter settled as soon as possible and forgotten, Patrick had suggested to the solicitor that when half the final sum was put at the disposal of Thomas's daughters, the solicitor should ask the girls if they would be willing to make a free gift to Paddy's family. It was not as simple as all that, apparently, since there had been no will. Nothing to do with the law ever was simple. But he received a few letters from the girls' guardians and at Christmas there was a lavish card. Patrick did not suppose there would be one another year.

There were many other cards, since more and more people were adopting this custom; from Jane in America, the Jacksons in Glastonbury and a variety of people Maisie and Patrick had to ponder to recall; also home-made Christmas cards from the children. There was nothing from Luke.

Then, on Christmas Eve, there arrived a long cable from Luke in Australia. Every one in Whytbrook must have been aware of its contents well before Patrick, but he still pretended that it was a secret. He found a chance to speak alone to Maisie, however.

Slowly, she read the cable and then looked at her husband.

"Well," she exclaimed, "what're we to make of this?" Fancy wasting money on a telegram, she was thinking. Why couldn't he have written a decent letter?

"'Spect he's wanting us to know his decision for Christmas. He wants to be fair, Maisie, since he's comfortably off himself, seemingly. It's very generous of him."

"Generous!" It was not going to cost him a penny of his own money, was it? She was contradicting her own earlier thoughts.

"Point is, what're we to do, Maisie?"

"Oh, you'll have to accept for the purposes he suggests." She looked at Patrick with gentle eyes. "Look at it this way, Patrick, we don't want nor need anything, but are we fair to the children if we refuse? To - to Kate, especially?"

He sighed.

"Oh, Maisie, it'll quite spoil Christmas, the thought of her going away!"

"It won't be for a while yet, but tell you what, leave it over till New Year. You'll have time to think about it a bit more. And I'll have a few words with James and Matthew. They've both good sound heads to them, and it's likely to - well, affect them one day, isn't it?"

"All right," said Patrick and he sighed a little.

Hard-working people did not normally stay up a minute longer than might be expected, year's end or no. It was true, this was a very special year's end, the ending of one century and the start of another; but it also happened to be a Sunday. So they went to church as usual and though Patrick allowed all of them (except young Jennifer) to stay up to drink a toast to the coming century, it was a fairly sedate occasion. There was no party, and while there were those who would be celebrating the arrival of the twentieth century with revels, most of the villagers had agreed that the entertainments must be reserved for the Monday evening. Both Lucy and Kate had new dresses for the ball they would be attending, and Maisie, who would be going along to watch and to chaperon the girls, had also had a dress made for this special occasion.

Patrick had his elder son read a few passages from the Bible, lines he had very carefully selected himself. He was fully aware that many superstitious people still opened the Good Book in haphazard fashion, reading whatever their eye chanced to fall upon, and regarding those lines as their settled fate for the coming year.

Not so Patrick. He had carefully chosen a few verses from his favourite prophet, Isaiah, to send his boys off to their beds, duly inspired. The giggles had been suppressed long enough for this, but when they reached upstairs there were sounds of noisy hilarity. For once, Patrick had too much on his mind to call up to the boys to be quiet. He asked Kate to stay downstairs a while as they wished to talk to her and Kate gripped her sister Lucy's arm very tightly and said that she wanted her to remain also. As though she was fully expecting some reprimand and wished to have Lucy's support.

Patrick said nothing, but he fussed about in his pockets for a while, seeking out the cable, then his reading glasses, and in the end asking Maisie to show Luke's cable to Kate, so she could read it for herself.

"She'd best see exactly what her uncle says."

Kate read quietly and swiftly to herself, Lucy leaning over her shoulder. Then she looked up.

"Is that all? Everyone in Whytbrook has some version. Uncle Luke wants you to use the money left by Grandma and start putting Redesdale in order. It'll cost a lot of money and take years, but yes, I think you should do something about it, Papa, I really do! Not for ourselves, but for one of the boys or maybe his children when he's older. If it's left much longer, it'll be too run-down and.... "

"Not Redesdale...." breathed Patrick.

"I think Kate's right," said Maisie, puzzled a little at this reaction. "The boys are growing up." She sighed herself. "Even if we sold the place in the end.... "

"But what about yourself, my girl?" Patrick demanded. That's the important thing. What about you, eh?"

"Oh, that, I'll have to think about it."

"Is that your only reaction?" asked her mother, amazed. "I thought you were dying to be a singer! Now, when you're offered the chance of some training, you sniff at it!"

"It's not much, is it! Just two years to see how I get on. It'll take a lot longer than that, I'm afraid. He's not risking much."

"It's a start.... " said Maisie, indignantly.

Suddenly, there was a loud gulp. Patrick stared with horror at his eldest girl. Her head was bent, her handkerchief was to her mouth. Was she weeping, then?

"Lucy, love, what is it?" He put her arm around her shoulder, comfortingly, and tried to look into her face. "'Ee mustn't worry yourself. Kate won't be going for a long while yet - if she goes away at all, that is." He looked anxiously at

Kate, who also had her head slightly bent and this was most unusual for Kate. Whatever was wrong?

"It's not that.... " There was another gulp, then a splutter and when Patrick tried to tilt Lucy's face towards his own, he saw she was not weeping at all. She was doing her best not to laugh! She glanced at Kate and it was like a signal passed between them. Soon they were both giggling loudly.

"What in heaven's name.... ?"

"Have you gone mad, the pair of you?" asked Maisie, sharply.

"It's not that - I'm sorry.... " Lucy tried hard to collect herself. Kate was still laughing, but quietly now.

"Seems everyone's gone a bit mad," said Patrick, smiling, but perplexed. "It must be the new year. Is that it?"

Lucy looked at him fondly.

"Papa," she said and she flushed. "You see, it should have been me."

"I don't understand," said her mother, her voice still sharp. "I don't know what you can mean," but her heart began to thud like a tolling bell, heavily, doomfully.

"She means," said Kate clearly, "all this wanting to have Redesdale restored and most of all, being prepared to help with my lessons, should have been for her, not me at all."

Still, there was a look of incomprehension on the older peoples' faces; and perhaps a hint of fear, of not wanting to understand.

"Oh, for goodness' sake! I can't make it plainer than that! Uncle Luke thinks I'm his daughter! He thought so all the time he was here. Lucy and I chuckled about it, didn't we, Lucy?"

The elder girl nodded, composed now. Maisie felt anything but composed. She flushed as she had not done for years. Then she looked at Patrick, seeking his help.

"How long have you guessed this, Lucy?" he asked, gently. There was no point denying it.

"You mean, about your not being my real father?" She was very quiet now. "Oh, years and years, really. We heard odd remarks sometimes, Kate and I and - and then we worked it out. I can't remember exactly. Does it matter?"

"Lucy always thought of you as her father, didn't you Lucy?" put in Kate.

Lucy nodded.

"As a matter of fact we used to romance about it. It did seem romantic, in a way. I hate to say this, Papa, but I almost envied Lucy with a mysterious father living on the other side of the world."

"But as soon as he appeared.... " said Lucy and she made a face.

"There's nothing wrong with him," said Patrick. "He was a nice-looking young man, a bit head-strong, maybe, but he's hard-working and honest and.... "

"Please!" said Lucy, laughing, "don't try to sell him to me! I know he doesn't need a job! All I meant was that I thought him a horrid let-down, a great disappointment. I'd much rather keep the Papa I've got!"

There were tears in Patrick's eyes.

"Bless you, Lucy." I'm a very lucky man, he thought.

"Just the same," said Maisie, suddenly, matter-of-factly, "I'd think carefully about your Uncle Luke's suggestion, Kate. It was *your* voice he was interested in." Pride could be the downfall of the Scotts, she thought, not for the first time.

"I doubt if I shall need his help Mama. You see, I'm going to try for a scholarship. Our choir-master seems to think I stand a fair chance."

"But Kate!"

"Oh, he doesn't give a fig about my voice," said Kate, smiling. "Uncle Thomas liked it, I think, but I fancy Luke's tone-deaf! All he wants is to pay off an old debt, you see!" She was laughing again.

He parents were not laughing and Maisie still felt very disturbed inwardly, despite her outward composure. But Patrick suddenly drew his wife towards him in one arm and stretched his other arm about the two girls.

"Bless 'ee all." He wished he could think of something splendid to say that expressed the feelings in his heart. After a moment, he said, "We'd best all be making for our beds, I'm thinking. 'Ee'll have a very late night tomorrow, so 'ee need your rest."

"Tonight!" chorused the girls. "Have you forgotten?" Kate continued, "It's already the twentieth century! You can forget about yesterday. That was the last century! But Nineteen Hundred is the start of all sorts of wonderful, wonderful new adventures, isn't it, Lucy?"